The Good Daughter

By the same author

Nobody But Us

The Good Daughter

LAURE VAN RENSBURG

MICHAEL JOSEPH

PENGUIN MICHAEL JOSEPH

UK | USA | Canada | Ireland | Australia
India | New Zealand | South Africa

Penguin Michael Joseph is part of the Penguin Random House group of companies
whose addresses can be found at global.penguinrandomhouse.com

First published 2023
001

Copyright © Laure van Rensburg, 2023

The moral right of the author has been asserted

Set in 13.5/16pt Garamond MT Std
Typeset by Jouve (UK), Milton Keynes
Printed and bound in Great Britain by Clays Ltd, Elcograf S.p.A.

The authorized representative in the EEA is Penguin Random House Ireland,
Morrison Chambers, 32 Nassau Street, Dublin D02 YH68

A CIP catalogue record for this book is available from the British Library

HARDBACK ISBN: 978–0–241–50821–3
TRADE PAPERBACK ISBN: 978–0–241–50822–0

www.greenpenguin.co.uk

To B.
Thank you for everything

PART ONE

Feel how your breathing makes more
space around you.
Let this darkness be a bell tower
and you the bell. As you ring,
what batters you becomes your strength.

Rainer Maria Rilke

MEMO

From: Leroy Trevorrow
To: Chief Deputy Larson
Re: Data from phone recovered at Newhaven Plantation

We have processed the phone recovered in the wreckage of Hunters Cottage, one of the properties at Newhaven Plantation, Jaspers Island. The phone has no contacts that could be recovered, nor calls or text log. We are still processing the photo app. However, we have recovered a certain number of audio files from the voice-recorder app, which I have attached here. Please note that in each recording, the same female is interviewing another person or persons. The recordings are not in chronological order and the quality varies from good to poor; in some recordings portions have not been recoverable.

Don't hesitate to contact me if you have any questions, and I will send you an update as soon as I have more information about any other recovered data from the phone or the other items still being processed. Please find below a key for the recording:

(...)	Unintelligible speech
LOUD	All caps indicates loud voices, shouting
Quiet	Italics indicates quieter voices, whispering
(Italics)	Non-verbal, background noises

AUDIO FILE #1

Audio Quality: Poor

[Voice A]:   Female
[Voice B]:   Female

[Voice A]:   (...) What does that mean? What if you want
              to leave?
[Voice B]:   People can leave if they want. It ain't no prison.
              God gave us free (...) have left before.
[Voice A]:   But can people still come and visit family and
              friends who are (...) church?
[Voice B]:   It ain't (...)
[Voice A]:   So it isn't an easy decision really. I mean, would
              you leave if you knew you could never return
              or see your mom or your siblings? That's a
              really fucked-up choice (...)
[Voice B]:   Why would I ever wanna leave? This is where
              I wanna (...) married and one day raise
              children. I love this place and I love my family.
              I never wanna be away from them. This place's
              perfect and nothin' can ever happen to me as
              long as I'm here. I wish (...)
[Voice A]:   (...) know what they say (...) careful what
              you wish (...)

4

1. Present day

Death has brought flies and strangers to our house. The former buzz around among the charred remains of the front room. The latter have dragged out chairs from the kitchen to the backyard, but I'm the only one sitting, surrounded by a wall of bodies clad in uniforms, five-pointed stars stitched on their breast pockets or upper sleeves as a means of protection. They said a local out in his boat by Hangman's Creek saw the smoke and called it in. Mr Abernathy is talking to more of them out in the front yard. Daddy would've refused to receive visitors out here. We've never had no visitors until now. But I suppose they're not really visitors anyway.

Daddy.   In the front room. With her. Red. Red and yellow flames. Skin tight from heat.   Twisted shapes on scorched floorboards. Two black bags that have been taken away. Turns out that is where you go after you die – a body bag.

So many people, and all we have to share is our silences until the roar of an approaching speedboat interrupts us. I look up at them feeling as though I'm the tide, rising and ebbing, in and out. Between the backyard and what's left of the front room, right now and a few hours ago, real and not real. I look at them and I wonder – can they spot the moments when I ain't really here?

A female officer sidles among the cluster of squared shoulders and stocky bodies, the ends of her hair licking the nape of her neck. She carries a cup-holder full of drinks from Joe's Café. A shiny badge above her left breast labels her as Deputy Pritchett. The rest of them – all men – are gathered around with their hands clasped behind their backs or with their arms crossed, their gaze shielded by wrap-around sunglasses. She shouldn't be with them, it's against her nature. Women are not meant for careers. They're meant to be mothers. Her ring finger's shamelessly naked. Daddy would call her another casualty. Steam rises from the cups, although the weather calls for a pitcher of sweet tea. I feel sorry for her.

Next to Deputy Pritchett, the figures of two officers frame one of the tupelo trees at the back. In front of it, an osprey hops on the grass, followed by another. Their beaks spear and shred something on the ground. I concentrate on them, on the tree, on the high fence in the distance, anything to stop my mind wandering back into the house, past the kitchen, past the closed door, past the hallway to the ashes of the front room.

Daddy   the black twisted shape of him, and her   I can't say the word. My chest burns just to think of it.   Of her.

Deputy Pritchett distributes drinks – including one she places in my bandaged hands – thanks are muttered, throats are cleared, before their study of me resumes. Darting glances land in my direction. Do they see a girl or just the ashes and soot she's caked in? Oh Lord, I've breathed the smoke in by the lungful. It's inside me. They're inside me, coating my throat and lungs. A dry heave rises, but nothing comes out.

These strangers never cared about us, so why pretend now? Maybe they're just curious about this place 'cause they know they ain't welcome. I wish they'd just leave. We don't need them. Their tacky police tape, loud crackling radios and flashing lights disrespect the grand, faded beauty that is Newhaven Plantation House. Their presence spells out what's happened here, the news sneaking through the front door, making its way down the corridors of Newhaven, the words carried by many different voices, whispered, and gasped, and stuttered – Fire. Tragedy. Pastor Heywood and his wife are gone. Dead.

The lid from my cup's off. I don't remember doing that. Milk has turned the dark brew into a soft beige. Daddy hated weak coffee. Or any other weaknesses. A weak nature is how sin gets in. My knees throb with that truth.

Suddenly, my name shrieks in the air, slicing through my thoughts. Mrs Calhoun wades through the mass of officers and firefighters like Moses parting the Red Sea, all elbows and determination.

'Thank the Lord you're safe. Don't drink that,' she adds, taking the cup away and setting it on the ground. She clasps her hands around mine while she looks at me, her eyes puffy and rimmed with pink. They widen as she takes in the blackened clothes, soot on my face, the roughness of bandaged hands and left forearm.

'Y'all right?' Her words are met by my prolonged silence; when it becomes too heavy she shatters it. 'Please, Abigail, say somethin'. Are you hurt? You got us so worried. You were missing; we'd been searching for you all of yesterday. And now this. Dear Lord.'

'Did you just say she was missin'?' one of the officers asks.

I open my mouth. Instead of words a cough spills out. Every breath revives the fire in my throat, bringing on more coughing. Mrs Calhoun's face dissolves behind a wall of tears. Someone thrusts a bottle against my lips, the rim digging into my flesh. Water soothes the rawness.

'She ain't hurt. Superficial burns and some smoke inhalation. We gave her oxygen for that,' says the paramedic who's taken care of me. 'She ain't said a word since we showed up, though. We're gonna take her –'

'Y'all ain't takin' her nowhere.' Mrs Calhoun shoots him down with a look, before turning to me. 'Your brothers and sister are safe. Abigail, do you understand? Elijah, Matthew and Sarah are safe at Newhaven. They spent the night there, thank the Lord.' With that, she turns on her heel, heading for what's left of the house.

'What are you doin'?' A large officer shifts his mass, blocking the sun and Mrs Calhoun's way. She squares her shoulders, the way she always does before slinging bales of laundry.

'I gotta go in. Matthew needs his inhaler. It's in the upstairs bathroom.' He still doesn't budge. 'He got asthma, are you tellin' me you're denyin' an orphan his medication? What kind of a Christian are you?'

'Don't you have spares at the main house?'

'No, we don't.'

'You can't go through this way, ma'am. The scene hasn't been cleared yet.'

'Which way do you expect me to go? Climb the drainpipe to the bathroom window?'

The officer throws a quick glance at whoever's in charge. There's always one. A head with a tuft of grey hair and a thick moustache nods.

'All right, follow me,' the officer sighs. The screen door whines open. An overpowering stench slithers out of the house and, as it hits her, Mrs Calhoun's face crumples. It's the kind of stench that sears a picture in your mind whether you want it or not. It clings to my clothes and hair too. She turns to me with horror etched on her face, before she adjusts it with a strained smile.

'I'll be right back, Abigail. Just gonna get your brother's medicine, and then we'll both go back to Newhaven. Don't you tell them nothin'.' She flashes the officer a don't-you-dare-stop-me look.

My gaze drifts to the floor, where steam still rises from my cup. If only I could touch it, press my fingertips against the heated cardboard until reality's impossible to ignore. But my hands are buried under layers of gauze.

They all keep staring at me, waiting for me to talk, but I ain't got no words for them. No answers to their questions. The fire's left me with nothing but charred memories with no shapes. It burned all my feelings and left me numb with questions of my own.

Is it me? Are they dead because of me? Because I don't remember. Not the fire, not them dying, not why I went missing the day before. I don't remember nothin' at all.

FIRE AT NEWHAVEN PLANTATION
CLAIMS TWO LIVES

By Marilynn Wasserman, Staff Reporter

A fire at Newhaven Plantation has claimed the lives of Pastor John Heywood (45 years old) and his wife, Genevieve (38 years old). Beau Travers was out on his boat by Hangman's Creek when he noticed the smoke and called 911. Parkerville Fire Brigade were called to the scene and quickly contained the fire. The Heywoods' elder daughter, Abigail Heywood (17 years old), was rescued from the blaze and suffered only minor injuries. The couple's other three children were at the main plantation house when the fire broke out. Firefighters arrived at the scene at about 6:45pm, according to reports, and alerted the sheriff's department on discovery of the bodies.

The official cause of the fire has not been released, but an investigation is under way. There is speculation that the family were using candles and kerosene lamps to light the house as the generator had malfunctioned during the storm. An autopsy will be carried out on both bodies to confirm the cause and manner of death, said Fire Marshal Wesley Dunlop. The fire was believed to have started in Hunters Cottage, one of several houses on the property. The blaze was quickly contained and did not spread to any other buildings.

Newhaven Plantation, which until thirty years ago was the

Newhaven Grand Hotel, is home to the South Carolina congregation of the New America Baptist Church (NABC). The church is known for its extreme conservative views, and for picketing local institutions such as Parkerville LGBTQ Community Center and the Planned Parenthood clinic on Mercer Street.

The tragedy comes only eight months after the accidental death of the NABC's previous pastor, from a fall down the stairs at the plantation house which broke his neck. Jeb Abernathy, who has now stepped up as the new pastor at Newhaven, and other NABC officials have declined to comment at this time.

COMMENTS:

Julie_Green1982
This is such a tragedy, and those poor children. What a horrible way to lose their parents.

ConfederateJoe
I'm sure libtards didn't like what they had to say and started that fire.

Anon_1978
They're not a church, they're a cult and kidnapping people all over the country. NABC is dangerous and should be investigated.

MissyCat
@ConfederateJoe Srsly that's the best you can come up with. Go drink some bleach, you MAGA moron.

Chad1287678
Seen them around town in their freaky uniforms and their hair all the same. All look like freaks if you ask me.

Anon_1978
They got what they deserved. They destroy lives.

JuicyJuice
Newhaven? Isn't that place haunted AF?

2. Early June

Mom wove tendrils of my hair between her fingers, binding them tight until the familiar tug at my scalp. *The obedient daughter keeps her hair in a demure fashion.* The strands, twisting around each other, were held in place perfectly – we Heywoods led by example. Everybody assumed I did it myself, being almost eighteen an'all, but it was our thing, and the braid was always so much nicer when Mom did it.

My hands spasmed around my notebook in rhythm with Mom weaving my hair – perfection demanded sacrifice. People expected things to be easy nowadays, handed to them on a plate. I silently mouthed the words on the notebook page. I knew the verses by heart, but still. Perfection. And I wanted to be as perfect as ever today – there was an outreach trip to one of the women's shelters in Charlotte being planned, and I was desperate to be part of the group that got to go.

'Done. Come on, hurry up.' Mom handed me a fresh scarf from the drawer, which I stuffed in my pocket.

Despite the early hour, the air outside was already thick with summer heat and the static of far-off conversations trapped within Newhaven, leaking through the open windows, hinting at the throng of people threatening to spill out through the main double doors. On the other side of the lawn, the Caines stepped out of Myrtle Cottage. Next to it, Pastor Favreau's old house tugged at my heart. Even after almost seven months, it still felt weird seeing the Garretts walk out of the door.

At the door of the church Daddy welcomed the congregation, nodding at every 'Mornin', Pastor Heywood'. Mom stood by him, her only welcome a smile on her face, Matthew and Elijah squirming at her feet, and baby Sarah sleeping in her arms. She kept shifting Sarah's weight. The urge to offer to take my sister tickled my throat, but now was not the time to speak. Thick, stifling heat leaked from inside the church, hinting at how uncomfortable the space would be. Being worthy of the Lord's love was not easy, otherwise anyone would be worthy. People wanted the faith without the inconvenience – delivered inside an air-conditioned auditorium, received on plump seats. Hypocrites.

We entered last. A smile split Mom's face as I relieved her of Sarah long enough for her to drape a scarf around her head. Up front, Mr Garrett clipped his phone to the tripod and aimed it towards the lectern. Every family settled on their bench. My spine straightened at the knowledge that the whole of Newhaven sat behind us. Mom sat to my right, and next to her stood the empty bench where Mrs Favreau, our former pastor's wife, used to sit – before she got too sick to leave her room. These days she relied on us to care for her and even take her meals to her.

Daddy stepped up and clipped his mic to the lapel of his jacket. With a motion of his hand he brought the congregation to its feet and led us into prayer, before we sat again, following the precise choreography we performed every Sunday. He slotted himself behind the lectern with a smile, pale blue eyes narrowing at the camera lens.

'Before I start with today's sermon, I wanted to remind y'all of the fundraising for Janet Munro and her children up in Wellmont. We're coming to the six-month anniversary of the tragedy that took the lives of our dear brother from the Florida congregation of our church: Pastor Munro and his eldest daughter, Fleur. It's up to us to rally around Janet. Among the cruelties of this world, it is up to us to make sure she and her own are cared for. Pastor Munro would've done the same for any of our families. For people watchin' at home, you can donate to the GoFundMe page we've set up. Link in the video comments. In a world brimming with self-ishness, be an instrument of His love. God has placed people in our lives to help us better see His goodness . . .'

On the podium a blown-up picture of Fleur and her daddy had been propped on an easel. Her arms wrapped around his neck, their faces squashed together, her locket dangling from her neck. From the day her daddy gave it to her she was never seen without it. She used to slide it up and down on its chain whenever she thought real hard about something. It'd become an extension of her. A toothy grin stretched her mouth into a smile, the gap between her teeth on display. Tears pricked at the back of my eyes. Even after half a year, I still couldn't believe she was gone. Her absence swelled in my chest. We'd spent most of our summers together, this was the first one without her. My tongue rubbed against my front teeth. We had the same gap when we were little, back when Mom called me 'Honey-bunny'. Mine closed over the years, hers didn't. We looked similar too – wheat-colour hair, blue eyes and the same bow-shaped mouth – and shared secrets, swapped clothes. She'd been like the sister I never had. Until baby Sarah.

Despite Daddy's magnetism, my attention drifted, slipped into the spaces between his words, and then on outside the church, down to the water. Fleur and her daddy had visited every few months, he on church business, and she to come and play with me. We had run around on that shore for hours.

As we got older, we stopped playing games but were closer than ever, staying with one another on visits. They were supposed to drive here the day after the senseless crime that took them away from us. A tragedy heightened by the fact Daddy had been away on church business, unable to console me when the news first broke. Did Fleur realise she was about to die when she heard that first shot? In my mind she hid from death, cowering in her closet or at other times lying flat under her bed, a hand clasped over her mouth. Daddy said God wielded death blindly, it didn't matter to Him who you were, just that your actions would dictate where you ended up. I wished He'd let her stay on earth longer. I squashed a tear at the corner of my eye.

Mom elbowed a warning into my ribs. I jerked, and my gaze latched on Daddy's – stern eyes above a beard stretched with a benevolent smile. Behind him, the heavy curtain twitched from a breeze. A shudder slithered down my spine. Death was a part of life, Daddy said. Death didn't need to be so close, I thought.

After handing back baby Sarah, I joined the rest of the choir on the podium, second from the right in a front row of girls, the boys standing in the second row on the step. Always in the same order. A breath fell on my neck, teasing the small hairs that had escaped their braided prison.

Anita Jones slotted behind the little keyboard. After a collective whispered inhale, our voices soared with the first notes of 'All Hail the Power of Our Lord'. The melody lifted my spirits, pulled at the corners of my mouth, and the hold of the braid on my scalp slackened. I silently dedicated my singing to Fleur. From his seat, Matthew smiled at me, swinging his little legs in rhythm with the music. I loved choir, the feeling of dizziness when I stepped on the podium the first few times, light-headed, followed by the rush rising from the centre of my body, but today's singing was tainted with sadness.

We launched into our second hymn, 'Come, Let Us Lift Our Joyful Eyes'. My attention skipped over the strata of congregation spread across the room. In the third row, his unruly blond curls slicked back for church, Tom sat a head above the rest, giving him a clear line of sight. His gaze sliced through me like the blade of a knife, stripping clothes from the flesh, and flesh from the bones. He'd joined the congregation less than a year ago, and a sense of unease had slithered in with him. He tried to fit in with us, but his former life clung to him in the jagged lines of his body from living a life without purpose, playing video games in between dead-end jobs, and it clung in his Yankee accent too. He tried once to say 'y'all' – Birdie and I laughed so hard, we cried. His face twisted with such quiet fury it scared the laugh right out of our chests. Now, he stared as if I was the last pitcher of sweet tea in a heatwave.

Outside, the tide of the congregation flowed towards the dark entrance of the main community building. Time had stamped a film of dust onto the once white façade of Newhaven, while the heat and humidity had licked the plaster a dirty yellow. Nature had asserted its dominance on the former grand hotel, but still Newhaven's pride shone through, with its colonnades and second-floor balcony.

Soon, inside the old ballroom, everybody would be finding their place for our weekly meal together – sitting on chairs that had been carved and polished by the hands that had harvested and prepared, and now served the food. Here on Jaspers Island, 'I' gave way to 'we'; it was both comforting

17

and unavoidable, that togetherness. Sometimes it hugged and yet smothered you in the same embrace.

The basic furniture in the ballroom, which the founders of our congregation had claimed as the community hall, was at odds with the grandeur of the space. Heavy-legged tables cohabited with the delicate and elaborate cornices that adorned the ceiling. Not even the peeling wallpaper or damp patches could stop the nobility of the room from shining through. Especially when looking up at the impressive chandelier hanging from the centre of the ceiling. It had stopped working decades ago, and the brass had tarnished in places, but I didn't care. The dangling crystals always reminded me of morning dew caught in a giant spider's web.

Amidst this antebellum beauty, we would all stand holding hands, a human chain binding us together, while Daddy said grace. As always the simple food would taste delicious: steaming piles of scrambled eggs, grits with honey, and the smell of freshly baked cornbread still holding the warmth of the oven. As I walked towards the main entrance, my mouth flooded with saliva – until my right knee unexpectedly buckled, almost sending me to the ground.

I spun around to find Daddy laughing at his favourite trick. Even after all these years he always caught me when I least expected it – a subtle kick to the back of my knee.

'Daddy.' I smiled.

'Gotta stay sharp, darlin'.' He hooked his arm around my shoulders and pulled me forward, into the building.

3.

The twins looked so small in their big boy beds – the last remnants of babyhood still clinging to their frames in little clumps of pudginess. They are growing up so fast, I thought as I closed the door. I loved them just for the fact that they were born – little full stops swaddled in cotton at the end of Mom's ordeal. With each failed pregnancy God had tested her, asked her to prove her resolve. I stopped counting after five. Despite her increasingly fragile state, she hadn't stopped trying, determined. I'd prayed, even bargained with God, until the twins screamed their way into the world, followed a few months ago by baby Sarah.

After the yammer at Newhaven, Hunters Cottage sagged with a heavy silence. Most of the congregation lived in Newhaven itself; only a few families like ours chose to inhabit the scatter of smaller houses. In the kitchen, Mom garnished the bread basket while I washed my hands at the sink. With a simple nod from her, I strode down the hallway to the only closed door.

A quiet knock. 'Dinner's ready.'

I didn't wait for an answer. In the dining room, Mom fussed over the different dishes, straightening a glass, realigning a wayward fork, smoothing an invisible crease on the tablecloth – her hands never stopped. She was so devoted to our family. Daddy's cough echoing close stopped Mom's fidgeting. He slotted into his seat, and we arranged ourselves on either side before he said grace.

'Did the twins give you much trouble?' he asked me as Mom filled his plate.

'One reading of *Blessing from Above*, and they were out.'

'"Children are a heritage from the Lord. Blessed is the man whose quiver is full of them,"' he said, before spearing a piece of meatloaf.

My slice drowned under tomato sauce. The edge crumbled under my fork before it melted in my mouth. Soon I'd have a husband and kids of my own, follow the path God had laid down for me. Cook them healthy food, not processed junk like deep-dish pizza, cardboard translucent with oil. Gross. A memory floated of the tang of tomato sauce, sharing a slice for breakfast, the dough stiff with age. We had so little back then, sharing everything out of necessity. Until Daddy brought us to Newhaven for a better, safer life. Nothing bad could happen here.

'Daddy, could I go with the others to the Shermont DV Shelter in Charlotte next week?'

'Why do you wanna go?'

I delivered the words that until now had only been rehearsed to my reflection in the mirror. 'I feel it's my calling to spread the Lord's words and help rescue others from sins and a life of hardship. Mark 16:15, "And he said to them, go into all the world and proclaim the gospel to the whole creation. Whoever believes and is baptized will be saved, but whoever does not believe will be condemned."'

'That's very commendable, darlin'.'

'I don't know, John,' Mom said. 'Shermont's really far, and she's never stayed away anywhere overnight.'

I wasn't surprised. She hated me leaving Newhaven. But why did Mom have to get into the middle of it? Just 'cause she never ventured past Newhaven's high wire fence didn't mean she should stifle my calling for outreach work. I wasn't a kid no more. I'd stayed with Fleur and her family at their home in Florida before. I was fine.

'I don't know, Genevieve. Maybe I should decide what's best for my family, and you should concentrate on making a decent meatloaf.'

Mom's fork stopped mashing her food. Silence fell across the dining room, uncomfortable like the summer heat outside. The light flickered with unease, casting dancing shadows on the dining-room walls – the generator close to packing it in again. Daddy liked to joke it was the thing in here with the biggest temper.

'It's the same recipe as usual . . .' Mom's fork eroded her slice as if looking for the answer among the flecks of meat. She dragged her gaze down to her plate. I could read the thoughts racing through her head. Her main job was to take care of her family and hard-working husband. At the corner of my eye, Daddy threw a conspiratorial wink at me. My lips thinned out, pressed hard against my teeth so as not to give the game away.

'John, I'm . . . I'm sorry . . .'

His stern face split into a wide grin. 'I'm just joking. Where's your sense of humour?'

The bubble building inside of my chest snagged on the corner of his smirk and fits of giggles rung out of me. Mom joined in too, but her laughter somehow drowned under ours. Daddy was right, Mom might be a devoted wife and mother, but she had a lousy sense of humour.

Daddy sat at his desk, poring over books and pages darkened by his scrunched handwriting, likely for his next sermon.

'I brought you some sweet tea.'

'Thank you, Abigail.'

My name elongated under his Southern drawl.

'I wanted to ask . . .'

'Yes?'

'Did you make a decision about the trip to Charlotte?'

The pen stopped scratching paper. The only sound now came from the clock on the mantelpiece, counting the beats of the silence. I waited, the tumbler slippery in my hand from condensation. For some reason, I felt I couldn't even move until he spoke. He slowly twisted the cap in place before he set the pen down on his desk. He smiled, cracking his neck. My fingertips had gone numb from the chill of the drink. The glass slid a little in my hand.

'Just put it down, before I have to lick my sweet tea off the floor.'

I set the tumbler on the designated coaster – a necessity in a place where the furniture was made of wood and the weather sweated all drinks.

'Let's see how the trip to Parkerville goes on Thursday first. Mrs Calhoun says you're still shaky with some of your arguments. The NABC has never been under more scrutiny – Wade Pruitt was accosted by some girl claiming to be researching for a documentary about us when he was in Parkerville last week. Imagine if she'd spoken to you, and you'd faltered.'

My shoulders dropped. 'I can do it. I've been practising.'

'It ain't that I don't trust you, darlin', but the world outside of Newhaven and Parkerville's a scary and dangerous place. I'd never forgive myself if anything ever happened to you.'

I nodded in response. *The obedient daughter respects her Father's command.*

AUDIO FILE #2

Audio Quality: Good

[Voice A]:   Female

[Voice A]:   *(Heavy breathing)* Shit. It just happened again.
Woke up to total darkness, absolutely no clue
where I was. *(Heavy breathing.)* The old man
said it's good to talk about these things. Helps
process all that shit. He called it trauma
instead of shit, though.

Those nights of confusion, I always think I'm
back. I'm in the dark apart from the light from
my phone. I can see the door and I'm fucking
terrified. I'm convinced that if I try the handle,
it will be locked from the outside. Fuck, on
those nights I'm back there. Back with The
Fear. They called me an animal, had names for
me that live under my skin. They remained
long after the bruises faded.

(Clicking noise.) Green carpet, pine dresser,
TV chained to the wall, flowery bedspread on
the floor ... I'm in a cheap-ass motel room. I'm
here. I'm free. I've left, but the cage still exists
in my mind; I carry it everywhere I go.

I hate her for this. She fucking did this to me.

4. Present day

They sit in a row on the other side of a table that's been dragged out under the hanging tree. Same uniforms, different faces, I think. Deputy Pritchett isn't here this time. Perhaps she's back at the station making more cups of coffee. Perhaps she's come to her senses and quit. My chair wobbles on the uneven ground. Pastor Abernathy won't have them set foot inside Newhaven. Weird to think of him as pastor now. No time wasted.

'Can't we do this inside?' The question comes from the uniform in the middle, probably the one in charge. Was he in the backyard three days ago? I stop the thought before my mind ventures too far. I don't want to go back there. They can't make me go back there, with those charred remains.

'Do you have a warrant?' Mrs Calhoun asks them, chin slightly tilted up. She's here for support, even though I didn't ask for it.

The uniform-in-chief sighs. Above us, the hanging tree stretches wide, branches unfurled as if in a forlorn invitation for a hug. A trail of Spanish moss brushes the back of my neck like phantom swaying toes.

'We don't want to search the place. Might just be more comfortable inside,' the chief says, eyeing Newhaven.

'Let's just get on with this.' Pastor Abernathy drags a chair and takes his place at the table. The legs leave a furrow in the grass. He takes up the width of two of the officers sitting opposite him.

Nobody speaks for a while. Eventually the chief says, 'How are you feelin', Abigail?'

My mouth opens, but the words come out of Mrs Calhoun's. 'How do you think she feels? She has been deeply traumatised. Do you have any news? If you do, just come out with it and let us be. She needs peace in order to heal.'

Her palm is clammy against my skin as she squeezes my wrist just above the bandages. I don't know how to ask for my hand back. She's been holding it since fetching me from the room they've put me in on the second floor. Perhaps she's worried that if she lets go the uniforms will take me away. They've agreed to question me here rather than the sheriff's office – for now. Not that Pastor Abernathy and Mrs Calhoun left them much of a choice. But instead of my body, they took my clothes back to Parkerville, to be examined.

I want to speak to them. I want to ask if they know the things I don't. If they've found any of my memories in the front room or in the folds of my clothes. So much from that day and the weeks before are missing, and they have thoroughly searched the whole house. Do they know where I went when I was missing the day before the fire? Mrs Calhoun keeps asking me, and I keep failing to answer. Maybe the blaze destroyed my memories like it did everything else. Please, Lord, bring them back to me. Give me the answers I seek. Please.

'The Fire Marshal is working on his report, and we should have autopsy results from the coroner within the next few days.'

'And?' Pastor Abernathy asks.

'And we aren't ruling anything out at this stage but it does seem pretty straightforward,' uniform-in-chief replies. 'Anyway, the sooner we finish here, the sooner we'll leave y'all alone.' Before Pastor Abernathy or Mrs Calhoun can reply, his gaze shifts to me. 'Do you remember anythin' from that day? Even the smallest of details can help. Did you see anyone?'

I shake my head.

'I understand you went missing the day before the fire. Where were you?'

I shake my head.

'No, you don't want to tell us, or no, you don't know.'

'Stop badgering her,' Mrs Calhoun says.

'I don't remember.' The words breathe out of me.

They all stare at me bug-eyed and speechless like the devil got their tongue, until the one in charge regains his composure.

'Do you mean you don't remember how the fire started, or where you went when you were missin'?'

'Nothin'. I don't remember nothin'. It's all dark.' My voice thickens with frustration.

'What's the last thing you remember?' asks uniform-in-chief.

Their gazes and expectations pile up on me.

'The service for the six-month anniversary for Pastor Munro and Fleur.'

My answer draws a gasp from Mrs Calhoun. 'But Abigail, that was weeks ago.'

'Nothing after that?'

I shake my head again. It's useless. The musky smell of burnt wood drifts on a warm breeze. The charred façade of Hunters Cottage looms in the background like a gate to hell, taunting me. The conversation around dulls to static. The house stares at me, down to my core. I follow its gaze inward. My mind is just a shattered mirror, details glimpsed in shards of glass, too small and moving too rapidly to make sense. My hand's burning.

Like it was that night. Something crawls inside my veins.

5. June

Land chewed on by rivers and creeks unfurled around our boat as Newhaven receded and we approached the chaotic world of the mainland. Spray whipped at my face as we heaved over the waves, slicing through the foam. Finally, the outline of Parkerville and its waterfront gained focus, getting more defined as the boat got closer: the shore decorated with a garland of flat-fronted stores, restaurants with colonnades and wrap-around balconies, tables spilling onto terraces.

The nausea had finally subsided, but the queasiness had nothing to do with the waves. I'd run down the stairs that morning, dizzy with the knowledge that my behaviour on today's trip to Parkerville would determine if Daddy would let me go further afield, to Charlotte. At the breakfast table the twins screeched, and my arms opened into an invitation for a hug. They almost knocked me down as they landed against my chest. I let them go after a good smothering. Daddy's fingers picked at the shell of a boiled egg, removing the pieces slowly to expose the white flesh inside. Once it lay completely naked between his fingers he sank his teeth in; crumbs of yolk trapped in the bristles of his moustache. He chewed, a smile on his face, before rubbing his hands together.

'Morning, Dad—'

Everything stopped. A blue envelope crowned the pile of mail. He followed my gaze — cornflower blue had become an ominous colour around here.

'Is that —?'

'I'm afraid so, darlin'.'

'What does it say?'

He handed me the envelope as his only response. My finger ran along the torn edge where he'd opened it. A single piece of paper was folded inside, the same blue colour. No need to open it to know that the words would be carved in capital letters, dripping in red ink. The letters had been showing up at irregular intervals for a few months, always catching us by surprise, the only constant apart from the choice of stationery colour being the hatred they were loaded with. This one was no different.

YOU SHOULDN'T BE ALLOWED INTO THE WORLD. YOU'RE A SICKNESS. YOU SHOULD BE BURNING IN HELL AND SOON YOU WILL BE.

'Why are people so hateful? They don't even know us.'

'People often fear what they don't understand, darlin'. It's easier to hate than do the work. That's why your mama and I worry every time you're out in the world like today. You can't trust those people, they're hateful and mean, and those letters prove it. You be careful, all right? You just keep away from them.'

He trapped me into one of his bear hugs, and I burrowed deeper into his chest. A part of me wanted to cling and never let go, live in the safety of his arms and Newhaven, but another part resolved not to let fear win. If people outside of Newhaven were scared of what they didn't understand, then I'd explain it to them.

I put the envelope out of my mind as we disembarked our boat and stepped into the brutality of town. Parkerville heaved like a great beast, roaring with the whirr of cars, the shrieks from seagulls competing with smatters of conversation. The boardwalk was an explosion of colours, bloated with out-of-towners in their 'I ♥ South Carolina' shirts, the air loaded with so many smells pulling at us – pungent tar heated under the sun, the greasy smell of fried seafood, perfumes barely concealing the ripeness of sweating bodies, sweet and rotting. The onslaught left me dizzy. Parkerville's chaotic life pulsed through my body, and my lungs cowered in my chest at its craziness, making it hard to breathe. For a second I yearned for the peace of Newhaven. On Jaspers Island, noises flowed in harmony with the place and the people, never intruding. It wasn't really an island, sitting along the coast from Parkerville, but the land was so chewed up with water it felt disconnected from the rest. Still, as much as I loved home, excitement ran through me. We were here to do God's work. It was needed everywhere.

Despite my excitement, it was impossible to ignore the lingering looks being shot at our group: pinched lips, whispers exchanged behind cupped hands, smirks of disdain. The scrutiny weighed heavy at the corner of my lips until the smile crumbled. I knew we stood out. The uniformity of our clothes was unavoidable amidst the scream of colours all around. Rebellion itched in my throat, screamed vanity was something to be ashamed of, not celebrated. But now was not the time – God's work awaited. Daddy's warning about the danger of the wider world, and the hateful words of that morning's blue letter, still dominated my thoughts and pushed my gaze to the ground.

'What time is it?' Mr Garrett asked. He always led our trips to Parkerville, a role he held proudly.

'11:35,' his wife answered.

'Good, our newcomers should be arriving right about now. Remember, y'all, they're gonna be tired and disoriented.'

Parkerville Greyhound Station squatted at the corner of Liberty and Dunbar, all red bricks and swathes of glass. Inside, the chill from the A/C drew goosebumps over my arms. A trickle of people filtered through the door. I drifted away from the group. People wearing barely anything whirled around me in what seemed to be a well-choreographed routine.

My eyes caught on the sign pointing to the slick metallic counter where uniformed people sat in windowed booths, the top covered with little displays filled with leaflets. Jackson Caine fidgeted next to a pile of train and bus schedules. He was such a gangly kid, his brown floppy hair brushing his ears adding to the lankiness. He needed a cut or he'd get into trouble. His dad liked a neat haircut. Hands shoved deep in his pockets, he studied the schedules, hundreds of destinations, departures and arrivals. As I watched, he stuffed his pockets with a handful of those leaflets and darted off.

A bus screeched to a halt before spilling its load of passengers onto the sidewalk. A flock of people squeezed through the doors, their features obscured by the white of surgical masks, the dangers of the outside world stretched over their faces. People who obviously lacked faith. The sludge of people swallowed me, sending my heart thundering in my chest.

I scanned the crowd for Mr Garrett. His head appeared on the far side of the passenger hall, bobbing over the flow of people swirling around. Something wasn't right. His eyes had retreated into slits, and his arms were firmly crossed over his chest as he spoke to someone. His lips moved quickly, tensed with frustration, and even from my spot on the other side, the flying flecks of saliva were unmissable. God was testing him. As the crowd thinned out, I got a better look at who he was speaking to.

It was a girl, or woman – her body seemed to dither at the threshold. Maybe a couple of years older than me. Long limbs that glowed under a sheen of perspiration, and long wavy dark hair a shade lighter than her skin, held back by a slash of red bandana. A muscle tightened deep in the pit of my stomach as she argued with Mr Garrett before stalking away. The way she sliced through the crowd, she looked madder than a wet hen.

My lips parted ready to ask about her, but Mr Garrett quickly said, 'Looks like the bus from Raleigh is thirty minutes late.'

Clearly he wasn't inclined to discuss what had just happened, so instead of probing I decided to make good use of our spare time. 'Do you mind if I go to the craft store to pick up some supplies for the twins while we wait?'

The craft store greeted me with every surface decked in an array of colours – palettes of paints like rainbows in boxes, baskets overflowing with glittering necklaces and bracelets, rails packed with swimsuits and shirts like fireworks. Those were an easy path to vanity and temptation. This need to adorn yourself with the latest fashion, bright colours to parade in. *Likewise also that women should adorn themselves in respectable apparel, with modesty and self-control.* Beige, brown and khaki, or white, grey and black for special occasions, those were earnest colours for earnest hearts, as Daddy would say.

At the checkout the middle-aged woman in front of me stank of an overpowering, flowery smell. She dropped a couple of magazines and crumpled bills on the counter.

31

'Do you know where the Newhaven cult is?' she asked the clerk.

My shoulders slumped, and I wrapped my arms around myself, hiding behind my purchase.

'You one of them?' the clerk asked.

'No, just have business with them.'

'Jaspers Island. Best way to get there's by boat.'

The woman grabbed her change and whooshed past me.

I left the store with a bag full of colouring books and crayons for the twins, a novel for myself. At the end of the street the 'Let's Go Burn Them' Center, as Daddy called it, taunted me. My skin crawled at the idea of walking past its walls, breathing the same air as 'those people'. Men kissing men, women kissing women. My stomach tightened. Rather than walk past, I took the side alley back to the Greyhound Station, ignoring the rainbow flag flapping about.

The woman from the store occupied my thoughts. The forceful swish of her ponytail as she stalked out the door. What business did she have with us? She couldn't mean official business, but what other kind could there be?

I was wrapped up in speculating when a stranger's voice startled me.

'Hey. Nice dress.'

6.

The boy leaned against the side of a parked car, hands tucked in the front pockets of stained jeans, thumbs hooked over the edge. On either side of him a couple more boys waited to take their cue from whatever his next action would be. Strangely, so did I. They all looked about twenty.

'What you got in there?'

In the absence of an answer, he peeled himself off the car door. He walked slowly, his face frozen in a smirk I couldn't look away from. Up close he smelled of strong aftershave, barely concealing an undertow of sweat, smoke, and bad ideas. I breathed in a little deeper. He hooked a finger over the top of the bag and pulled at the stiff paper until it sagged enough to reveal its contents squashed against my chest.

'What you gonna do with all this junk? You're a shy one,' he added with another smirk when I didn't respond.

So many words jammed into my throat, I couldn't even swallow let alone talk. Daddy's warning flashed in my mind. This was a test God had poured into the shape of this boy, and I had to pass in order to earn my place on the next trip to Charlotte.

'None of your business.' I jerked the bag away from him.

'Yeah?' The word came out from him like a yawn. Unabashed gaping mouth, where some chewing gum rolled around, coated in saliva and deformed by teeth marks. My own mouth flooded with saliva. I wondered how the gum tasted, if the consistency would be soft or stiff from being overworked. Processed sugar rotted brain and teeth, Mrs Calhoun admonished us.

'What's that?' He manhandled the novel I had bought, his fingers leaving stains on the pristine pages, cracking the spine with disregard. '*The Homestead Girl.*' He laughed.

'That ain't yours. Give it back.' I straightened up and channelled my inner Mrs Calhoun. 'Or you're a thief?'

'No, ma'am,' he answered, hands up in a mock sign of surrender, laughter still rattling in his throat. Tension built inside my arm, my fist stabbing my thigh.

'Hey, Zach, maybe she can read you something,' one of the other boys said, followed by a chorus of laughter. Their eyes were trained on him, their bodies tensed behind their crossed arms.

'What's your name?' Zach asked, closing the gap between us. 'Give me back my book.'

I snatched my property back. His hands now free, he played with my braid, rolling the end between his fingers, the crescents of his nails black from oil and dirt trapped underneath. He just wouldn't relent. I froze like a raccoon caught stealing. His hot breath, seasoned with something sour, fell heavy on my ear, and a shiver slithered down my neck. These boys weren't nothing like the boys at Newhaven – same physiology, but somehow a completely different species. Most boys like Zach had sex with girls outside of marriage, expecting everything to come to them easy.

The sun glared down on us, and I felt its bite on the back of my neck. Out of the corner of my eye, the others moved closer. Behind Zach, the main road taunted me, close yet out of reach.

'C'mon, let's go. Austin's got a table and a pitcher waiting for us at Sal's.' The reminder came from the tallest one of the group, his stubble speckled with acne. The promise of alcohol split Zach's face into a wide grin, exposing gleaming canines and reddish gums.

'Why don't you come along?' He hooked his arm around my neck, his skin warm and clammy. As his armpit raised, the sharp tang of his sweat hit me.

No, that was all I needed to say – just two letters to let them know I wouldn't come. I wasn't that kind of girl. But the word stuck to the roof of my mouth as he started pulling me away from the main road, back the way I had come.

A rivulet of sweat poured down my spine. He was taking me away. He held me so close that I couldn't squirm – his fingers dangling, threatening my breast. Smiling, he pulled me again; turning back, the alleyway lay empty, the main road shrinking behind us. Warm air pressed in around me. Another bead of sweat rolled down my spine. Daddy was right – I wasn't ready.

The click of a car being unlocked sent a chill through my bones. Zach ushered me towards the door of the pick-up, held open by one of his friends. Panic rose in my chest.

'Let me go.'

I wriggled but the move only tightened his grip, its clamminess now unbearable, his sweat overpowering.

'C'mon. The guys and I are going to a little party in the swamp. Why don't you join us? You can be our guest of honour.'

He pushed me towards the open door. A wave of heat leaked out of the car, heavy with the smell of leather. Fast-food wrappers littered the floor. My mind travelled back to that first Easter feast at Newhaven and the lamb's high-pitch bleating, struggling against the rope pulling it forward, instinctively sensing its fate. That same fear kicked under my skin now, and I bucked against Zach's hold at the back of my head, pushing me inside the car.

'Please let me go.'

'Hey, dickhead. She told you to stop,' a voice said.

'What?'

'You deaf or dumb? She told you to let her go.'

The jab seemed to nip at Zach's pride, and he flinched, his hand spasming at the back of my neck, still half in and half out of the truck. The accent didn't belong to anyone from Newhaven or the NABC, but I still wasn't sure if that was a good or a bad thing. Zach turned around to face whoever had challenged his intelligence. The girl I'd seen arguing with Mr Garrett at the Greyhound Station stood shrouded in shadows at the mouth of the alley.

'And who's gonna make me . . . You?'

'If I have to.' A flash of silver in her hand loosened his resolve, and his grip on me. His Adam's apple bobbed from fear. It was enough for me to bolt out of the snare of his embrace. Still his smell clung to me.

'Now, get the fuck outta here before I call the cops on your ass for kidnapping.'

'Bitch,' Zach spat at her. 'C'mon, guys, she ain't worth it,' he added, before stalking off with his pack.

My chest heaved with relief. The young woman and I stared at each other. The shirt she had been wearing inside the station was now firmly knotted around her waist. Every inch of her indecently clad body celebrated what was wrong with society: her low-slung tank top in a screaming yellow barely concealing the lines of her bra, and her uncovered legs. Ribbons of bare skin on display. A true city slut, Mrs Calhoun would've labelled her after one look-over, before lecturing me on the different ways women defiled their bodies, and finally reminding me *the obedient daughter dresses modestly*. Still, despite all that was wrong with her, it was undeniable she'd just saved me. God's help took many different forms.

'You good?' the girl said.

I felt too weird thinking of her as a woman. A woman in my mind involved a husband, and often a child hitched on the hip. I nodded, still light-headed from the shock of it all. We stood on the edge of light and shadows, the sun still beating on my neck, but that wasn't all; something else kicked under my skin like the pulse of a new organ I didn't know I had. She stared too but wore on her face a fierceness which I knew was missing from mine – the bravery to stand up for myself. To think what might have happened if they'd bundled me into that pick-up. Where I'd have ended up. A vivid horror weakened my legs and I staggered.

'Shit, you OK?' Her hand slipped under my elbow. A rasp rumbled in my throat, but shock still stopped words from forming.

'What's that?'

She snatched the book where it had fallen on the ground. She read the blurb, a smile growing with each word.

'Wow, that story is quite something. Is this for real?'

'Give it back. Please.'

'She speaks. I thought maybe you were mute or something,' she said, handing it back. I closed my arms around the book, tethering myself to it. It felt safe and familiar. 'Listen, you better be careful about the company you keep. I'm Summer, by the way.'

Her familiarity unnerved me. I couldn't help but think how her name fitted perfectly – this girl was the stifling heat: blinding, uncomfortable and unavoidable. One of the straps of her tank top dangled at the cliff of her shoulder, threatening to fall and expose her at any time, and yet she didn't seem to care enough to hike it back into place. My hands itched with the want to fix it for her.

'I'm in town for a podcast. Podcast research, actually.'

'I know who you are,' I said, remembering what Daddy had said about the person who'd questioned Wade Pruitt.

'Oh yeah?'

'Documentary girl.'

'Podcast, actually. And you are . . . ?'

I hesitated. 'Abigail. Pleased to meet you.' My hand shot out in front of me, fingers still shaking with a small tremor. I shouldn't forget my Southern manners. Her handshake was firm. My fingers brushed against her wrist, the kick of blood under my fingertips. Her skin felt warm and slippery, a waft of something sugary drifting from her. An undertow of stale tobacco lingered below the sickly sweet. That sweetness smelled familiar, it skirted around the edges of the word I needed to name it, but the more I reached for it, the further it slipped away.

'I know who you are too,' she said, sizing me up from my braid to my dress. 'You're part of the NABC – New America Baptist Church.'

The words rung without the usual disdain or distrust of locals around here. Once Summer retracted her hand, she crossed her arms under her breasts, and again I couldn't help but stare. She didn't seem to care.

'You know for a church so big on gratitude, you could say thanks. I mean, without me, God knows what those guys would have done. Although it's not hard to guess.'

Despite the heat, a shudder rippled down my back. I didn't allow my mind to stray past the pick-up, to imagine the future it would've led me to.

'Sorry. Thank you. Thank you very much.'

'Maybe you could let me interview you for my podcast? As a thank you.'

Me, being interviewed for a documentary? Daddy would never give his permission for that. Anyway, I didn't have nothing important or relevant to say.

'Come on, that's the least you could do. I won't use your name or anything. You can tell me more about your church and the work you do, answer some questions. C'mon, help a girlfriend out here.'

'I don't know . . .'

'Seriously, no funny business. I might even let you try to convert me.'

She laughed, but there was no mockery weighing it down. She looked at me straight on, and her openness threw me. Suddenly, Summer looked like God's way of offering me a chance to prove my dedication. Do the outreach work and spread our important message through Summer's documentary, or podcast, or whatever it was. She could have walked past instead of rescuing me, but she had a good heart buried under the indecent clothing, foul language, and rebellious demeanour. Now it was my turn to fish out her soul from the deepest recesses of corruption and rescue her.

From: Jeb Abernathy
Date: Sunday, August 21, 2022 at 9:27 AM
To: Cameron McPherson
Subject: Heywood Tragedy

Dear Pastor McPherson,

I pray this email finds you well.

As agreed, I am keeping you informed on the tragedy which
has claimed the lives of Pastor Heywood and his wife, Genevieve.
We have managed to keep the sheriff's department away from
Newhaven and poor Abigail. Of course, they are all too keen to
interrogate her on her own; any excuse to put their noses in our
business. Our Lord only knows what they would try to get her to
admit. Most likely they would ask about the church and matters
that don't concern them. You can rest assured that we are
looking after her and sheltering her from their damaging
influence.

The poor girl has been deeply shocked, as you can imagine. Not
only did she lose her parents, but in such a tragic way. Thank
the Lord for showing mercy and sparing her. He means to test
us and doesn't give us more than we can handle. *That He might
humble you, testing you to know what was in your heart,
whether you would keep His commandments or not.* He is
testing our Abigail, and we will stand next to her and help her
under His guidance.

She still has no memories of the night in question, but more
worryingly she cannot remember the weeks leading to the fire.
And she says she doesn't know where she was when she went
missing the day before. She has also been suffering from the most

violent nightmares and often wakes up screaming. We are praying for her memories to come back so we can make sense of this tragic accident.

I was wondering whether you could organise a prayer session with the different congregations to help our Abigail remember so we can give the sheriff's department some answers that will keep them out of Newhaven and our business.

Under His guidance. Have a blessed day.

Pastor Jeb Abernathy

7. Present day

It comes to me at night.

The Fire.   So much of it.

The heat on my hands. They don't look like mine.

My head is full of screams, deafening echoes hitting the walls of a cave; they mingle with roars from the fire, but there's something else underneath them, scratching to get out.

But I can never see past that shattered mirror, the pieces only allowing me to catch a glimpse of a detail, never enough for a full picture, for anything to make sense.

Always a red fire.   So much red.   A red that burns.

My screams bring Mrs Calhoun rushing in, and an explosion of light above the bed bleaches the room, dissolving shadows. Outside the window, I think I see a spark flickering into the night, but when I look again I only see darkness.

The world comes back in snapshots with every blink until it's all-encompassing again – the room, my body, who I am. The brutality of loss chokes me. Mrs Calhoun pulls me to her, head against her chest, rocking me as if I was a toddler. But I crave other arms.

'You're safe. He's with us, His love is with us.' She repeats the words over and over, and I wonder if they are for me or if she's talking to herself. My damp cheek sticks to her night-dress; the ridges of her breastbone sharp under my skin. The swampy sheets stick to my legs, my own nightdress sticks to my chest – the air around us damp with heat. The urge to push her away sweeps through me, to spring out of bed, run into the night and jump in the water. Let it swallow me whole. Before the words 'I'm fine' can leave my mouth, her hands clasp my wrists.

'Our Lord, bless this child with your light, protect her from the all-consuming darkness. Show her the way, oh Lord, under Your guidance.'

A reflex 'amen' from me unlocks her. She lets go of my wrists, where her fervour has left crescent-shaped marks.

'Did you remember somethin'?'

A scraping sound distracts me. On the other side of the room, Tom loiters in the doorway, moonlight catching his blond curls. Now I'm sleeping at Newhaven, his room's only three doors down. I don't know if I like it. The way he looks at me with shiny eyes, with the same intensity that he used to look at me in church, the mole under the left eye sharper than usual under the bright light. His pyjama shirt is buttoned unevenly – a ribbon of skin visible above the waist of his pyjama bottom, paler than his tanned neck. The sight of him pulses under my skin. He looks concerned.

'Is everything all right, Mrs Calhoun?'

'I'm fine,' I answer before she can.

'Are you sure, sweetheart? Do you want some water? I could stay if you want. We can pray,' she says, her hands cradling my face. Her fingers are cold on my cheeks, or my skin is on fire.

'Really.'

'Come.' She nudges Tom, whose eyes haven't left me for a second, and they both walk out, taking the light with them as they close the door.

Once silence has been reinstated I slip out of bed, the

floorboards rough under my feet. The woods sprawl on the other side of the window. Amid the darkness stitching the trees together, a flicker of light pulses like a heartbeat. It sends out a code, telling me to remember, but I can't — whatever it is, it's slid too far inside to grasp.

8. June

I stepped out of Hunters Cottage and began walking up the lawn to Newhaven, on my way to take Mrs Favreau her lunch. The humidity instantly dampened the back of my dress and my upper lip. The heatwave tasted salty. This time of year the sun was an unavoidable presence that burned clouds off the sky. The huge building waited at the end of the lawn, an imposing presence I never got tired of. Moss crept on the colonnades in patches of faded green, and rust bloomed on the black wrought-iron balcony. There's beauty in everything—even decay.

I stepped into the foyer, my eyes adjusting to the shadows. The grand staircase creaked, littering my arms with goosebumps. The white balusters had creeped me out as a kid – they looked like carved bones stuck to a mahogany spine.

A noise from above made me jump. Tom loitered halfway up the stairs, leaning back against the faded striped wallpaper, his face pinched into a sneer. I knew I was supposed to welcome new arrivals, but he made me feel wary. I wondered how he had space in him for the word of God when he seemed so full of himself already.

His lips parted, but before a word got out I turned on my heels and headed in the opposite direction. I held my breath, waiting, but no noise followed. Then the groan of a floorboard sent me running towards the back staircase and the comfort of the basement kitchen.

The downstairs hallway was bathed in darkness apart from a slice of light coming from the main office.

Hushed voices filtered through the open door. Something in the tone slowed my steps; I spied glimpses of the room through the hinges. A man's profile, a pair of legs from someone sitting on one of the chairs. Only Daddy usually used that office, and now I could see him talking with Corey Palicki. He leaned, lips moving quickly, whispered words falling out of them too fast to catch. The atmosphere leaking from the room felt like the charge before a storm. He hunched over, forehead pressed against Corey's forehead, noses nestled against one another. Daddy mentioned Corey had needed a lot of guidance lately. My breathing changed, heavier. I'd never seen such an intimate gesture, especially between two men. Instinct told me I'd stumbled onto something private, something I didn't understand or wasn't meant to see. Still touching foreheads, he cupped Corey's face. I slowly backed away from what might happen next. I had a lunch to deliver.

The landing unfurled under the eaves where the light seldom ventured. I didn't blame it, I'd rather not linger here either. Darkness mingled with silence, dust motes and a faint scent of mildew to create an unsettling atmosphere. If Newhaven was haunted, this was where the ghosts congregated. As much as I loved the place, the top floor creeped me out. Each door stood guard to an empty room filled with forgotten memories. Lengths of creaky pipes hid behind plasterboard, or under floorboards; gurgling water ran inside their copper casing; wind whistled in through crumbling window joints; wood whined with age; mice rattled behind the baseboards, filling Newhaven's top floor with a thousand ghosts. And rising above it all, from Mrs Favreau's room, the haunting clatter of metal keys under bony fingers. She never stopped writing these days. Each clang compressed the nobs of my spine like teeth dragging on a fork. By the time I reached the door, the ruckus of metal hitting metal had worked its way under my skin. It stopped abruptly before I knocked, as if she knew someone stood on the other side. I'd better just get on with it. I unlocked the door, my load precariously balanced on my arm. The air on the other side smothered me with its thickness and musty smell. I braced myself.

AUDIO FILE #3

Audio Quality: Moderate

[Voice A]:   Female
[Voice B]:   Female

[Voice A]:   OK, let's get started. We haven't got much time.
[Voice B]:   Sorry I'm late. I was on Mrs Favreau duties.
[Voice A]:   You were on what?
[Voice B]:   (...) duties. Mom couldn't get her lunch so I had to do it. Daddy's very protective of her. Only Mom and I look after her.
[Voice A]:   What does he do for her, if she's that important to him?
[Voice B]:   Visitin' her every other day, readin' the Bible to her, he prays with her too.
[Voice A]:   Is she his mom?
[Voice B]:   She's Pastor Favreau's wife. I mean widow. When Daddy came to Newhaven they kinda took him under their wing, her and her husband. I reckon he kinda reminded them of the son they lost years ago. I guess Daddy was like ... How do you call it ...?
[Voice A]:   Surrogate son?
[Voice B]:   Yes, like a surrogate son. He felt the same for her. Like she was the mother he never had. So

48

after Pastor Favreau passed away, he felt it was his duty to care for her.

[Voice A]: Care how?

[Voice B]: She ain't well; she can't look after herself.

(Heavy breathing and crackling sound, likely from a lit cigarette.)

[Voice A]: Is she sick or something?

[Voice B]: She gets confused and most of the time she didn't make a lot of sense. Said some horrible things, like the devil has taken hold of her. She forgets who people are or what year it is, but she hasn't really talked since her husband died. He had an ... an accident. (...) really angry too (...) lashes out (...) restrained (...) She even harmed herself. (...) scratched my mom's face real bad.

[Voice A]: (...) messed up. Why don't you put her in a care facility where she (...) looked after by professionals?

[Voice B]: That costs a lot of money, it ain't like we got private insurance an'all. Anyway, Daddy wouldn't allow (...)

[Voice A]: (...) medication? (...)

[Voice B]: (...) not that kind of sick (...) love and prayer (...)

[Voice A]: Aren't you worried (...) calling social services?

[Voice B]: (...) none of their business (...)

[Rest of recording too damaged to recover.]

9.

I locked Mrs Favreau's door behind me. Back in the hallway, fresh air climbed into my lungs. I would never get used to it, those eyes, those scars. My heart had finally stopped hammering in my chest when I heard a noise, faint at first, then the rising sound slowed down my footsteps – it sounded like the thuds of a heartbeat, coming from somewhere within the walls. The eaves were unoccupied apart from Mrs Favreau's. I crept towards the noise until something zoomed by on the floor, startling me. A blue rubber ball rested against the side of my canvas shoe.

Setting the lunch tray down, I bent, hand extended, before the ball was snatched by another set of fingers. I jolted back again.

'Abigail, it's me.'

'Damn, you scared me to death.' I swatted Jackson's arm. Stupid kid. What on earth was he doin' up here? Last I saw him he was snatching those schedules at Parkerville Greyhound Station.

He laughed in response, but it sounded hollow. Trailing back inside one of the bedrooms, he slumped on the cot bed, his body laden with the surliness normally seen in the Parkerville teenage-boy population. I settled next to him, shoulders rubbing. That close he smelled like hard labour. The rubber ball hit the wall, leaving a shadow of dust before bouncing back into his hand in an endless cycle. My eyes followed the ball as it hit the plaster pockmarked with dusty imprints.

'Shouldn't you be with the other men, working in the computer room?'

He threw the ball again in response.

'You must be the only kid I know who doesn't like goin' online and chatting.'

'I ain't no kid. I'm fourteen.'

'Sorry.' I suppressed a smile.

'I hate them forums. There're some real weirdos on there. Some of the stuff they say . . .'

'That's the point. It's our mission to rescue them. Show them there's another path. A righteous path. There are lost souls among those weirdos.'

The ball picked up speed, chipping flecks of plaster as it hit the wall.

'Do you ever think maybe we are?'

'What?'

'The weirdos.'

'Jackson . . .'

'I mean, do you ever think about Mrs Favreau?'

Sometimes hard choices had to be made for the greater good. Daddy loved her like a mother, and he agonised over what had to be done with her after Pastor Favreau's death and her reaction to it. Jackson didn't see that, but I did.

'We didn't have no choice.'

'Sometimes I just hate it here.'

'You don't mean it.'

'I do.'

I covered his hand with mine. Sadness pinched my heart. He would never admit it, but he missed his mom. She hadn't been seen for years, not since she abandoned him out of selfishness. What kind of woman walked away from her children?

'I saw you taking those leaflets at the station the other day.'

The ball stopped the same way someone held their breath. The air in the room shifted with Jackson's energy – anger tainted with fear.

'Please don't tell nobody.'

'I won't.'

'Especially not your dad. I know you think he's great an'all, that he can save everyone. But the last thing I need is for him to tell my dad.'

'I said I won't. I promise.' My answer propelled the ball out of his hand and on a collision course with the wall.

'You ever think about leaving Newhaven?'

The question surprised me. Jackson was born at Newhaven, slipped out his mom like a wet eel in one of the second-floor rooms. His first screams still lived in the walls of this place. It was tangled in his DNA like the vines tangled around the outside columns. We belonged to a safe community where we all knew and trusted each other, where kids could play outside without being prey to sexual deviants or drugs.

Without warning, the ball smacked the wall so hard, a big chunk of plaster crumbled to the floor.

Back home, shrieks and laughter invaded the hallway; I followed them to the front room. Daddy crawled on the rug on all fours while Matthew and Elijah climbed the jungle gym of his body, Matthew sitting astride his back.

'Faster, Dada. Faster.'

He laughed. 'Oh yes?' He swooped Matthew in his arms before tickling him while Elijah now jumped on Daddy's back, throwing his little arms around his neck.

Their game creased the lines around Daddy's eyes, softened the lines of his body. He had never played with me like that. He'd never got down on the floor, he'd stayed a figure of straight lines and sharp angles. It ain't for fathers to know their daughters' games. Instead he sat by my bed every night, reading to me, or gushed over my drawings, but the closeness wasn't the same. The memories knotted at the back of my throat with a tinge of envy, and I swallowed the lump. Leaning against the doorframe, I watched them until Daddy rolled onto his side and propped himself on his elbow.

'Hey, darlin'.'

His greeting unleashed the little monsters on me.

'Come, Abbay. Dada taking us to see the chickens.' Grabbing my hands, they pulled me to the centre of the room.

'All right, all right.' I laughed.

Daddy, up on his feet, lifted Elijah in his arms while Matthew nipped at him on the other side, demanding to be carried too.

'How did it go today?'

'It all went well. Got Mrs Favreau her lunch.'

'How did she behave?' His eyes studied my face as if the answer was written there instead of in my words.

'She was fine. Pretty much acted like I wasn't there anyway. Her attention was on her typewriter. I didn't look, as usual.'

'Let's go, Dada. Let's go,' the twins chanted.

'How's Corey doing?' The question slipped out of me, taking on a life of its own.

'What was that?' The words were for me, but his attention was firmly focused on the twins, especially Matthew, who swung from his other arm.

'Earlier on, I walked past your office. You were in there with Corey Palicki.' Slivers of images flitted through my mind – eyes trained on Corey's face as if it held the secret to eternal salvation. Hands heavy on Corey's shoulders, foreheads connected, how my heart had crept in my chest, trying to hide from the scene. I shook my head to dispel the silly unease.

'I have no idea what you're talking about, darlin'.'

'I saw you. The door was opened a bit,' I said, my voice shaky with doubt.

A smile etched on his face, his eyes steadfast. 'You saw wrong, darlin'. I was at the church all morning.'

'Oh . . .'

'It's all right, can happen to anyone. Last week, I was sure I saw your mother in the vegetable patch and it turned out to be Anita Jones.'

The memory drew a chuckle out of him. My eyes narrowed as I replayed the moment in my mind. The door barely open, glimpses out of focus filtering through a sliver of space. I saw Daddy because his face was always at the forefront of my mind.

He scooped Matthew in his free arm. 'Come on, boys, let's go see the chickens.'

The images softened in my mind. The more I scrutinised them the blurrier they became until the faces had dissolved into anonymous outlines. I had been distracted by Tom's presence on the stairs, and fear had distorted things. My heart beat with the conviction Daddy would never lie to me. That was impossible.

10. Present day

A nightmare jolts me awake. At least now I wake up without screaming. No one bursts through my door; there's no violent explosion of blinding light; no one invades my space, there are no clammy, uninvited hands on my skin. Still, everyone looks at me funny, but it's not from resentment because I woke them up during the night – it's because they can't wrap their minds around the fact I got no memories of the last few weeks. How can someone forget so much?

The nightmare clings to me. It's left me breathless and drenched in sweat. The smell of smoke is stuffed in my nose. The sheet is tangled around my ankles. I fight with it until I'm free.

My mind's like an empty truck battery. Maybe all it needs is a jump start. Newhaven is still lost to sleep, which makes it easy to scurry barefoot down the corridors. My hand glides down the banister of the grand staircase. One thing I know is that I like this building. We're the same. It used to be something else too. It has lived other lives, traces of those other existences still trapped within its walls, displayed in the faded rectangles stamped on peeling wallpapers where memories used to hang. I've got those same stamps somewhere beneath my skin. Across the foyer my feet smack against the floorboards. The antique mirror catches a glimpse of someone, a slash of red amid dark curls, but when I look again it's gone, or it was never there.

I slip through the front door and into the stuffy night air.

The sun's long gone but its warmth still presses on me. Like moving through molasses. The grass tickles the soles of my feet. Light from the full moon has stained everything from the lawn to the leaves silver, turning this place into a ghost world. Hunters Cottage stands impenetrable, empty black windows staring at me like gouged-out eyes, but it looks untouched. The darkness conceals most of the damage. I feel my feet move towards my old home.

The back-door screen whines open, but there's nobody to hear it. Inside smells of charred flesh, like spoiled meat and cooked fat. I shouldn't be here. The fire chief said something about the structural integrity of the building being compromised. Dust and ash tickles my nose. The urge to grab a broom and sweep the place spotless itches in my arms, but now is not the time. I creep deeper into the house, an invisible line pulling my body forward. My skin bristles with apprehension, until it warms under the flames of a ghost fire. Another step. The air thickens with heat. The blaze from that day materialises in my mind.

The heat of flames pulling at the skin over my cheeks. A woman screaming. But are the screams mine?   Another step.   It's there underneath the screams. There is something under the surface, under the fire.   Something warm and slippery. It's under my nails too. It comes in flashes like light caught in the blade of a knife.   Someone else was here. The words hum with absolute certainty. Two body bags left the cottage. But someone else was here with me. I'm sure of it.

I stand at the entrance of the front room. The burns on my hands throb, remembering a scream that ripped through my flesh. The memories spark a new fire, it reignites flames over the front room. They lick scorched walls and furniture.

The screams continue, the blaze stings my eyes, pushing me back, banishing me out of the house. A warning not to come back. Panic whips me around.

A man's silhouette blocks the end of the hallway, cutting off the way out through the kitchen. His hand rises, ready to snatch me. I bolt through the front door, damaged floorboards protesting under my weight.

I run across the lawn, faster – until nature trips me and I tumble to the ground. Dust fills my mouth.

'Abigail. Abigail. Calm down.'

Hands grip my arms and I thrash against a chest.

'Abigail. It's me. It's Tom.'

The name pushes through the screaming in my head. Tom's face glows under the moonlight, one eye covered by a curl of blond hair.

'You scared me to death.'

'*I* scared *you* to death.' He chuckles as he sinks onto the grass next to me, raking his fingers through his hair.

'What were you doing inside the house?'

'I saw you running out of Newhaven and I followed you. What were you doing?'

'Tryin' to remember.'

'And . . . did it work?'

I shook my head, failure swelling up in my throat.

'It'll come back to you.'

I envy his certainty. 'Why are you up?'

'Couldn't sleep, this damn heat. Still not used to it. Then I saw you crossing the lawn from my window.'

I pull at the blades of grass at my feet, the soles black with soot.

His fingers graze next to mine, our knees almost touching. A silence nestles between us as we pluck bits of grass, uprooting some, others buried in so deep that they break clean off. He ain't like the Tom I remember. In my last images of him he sits in church, staring at me with eyes that send a shiver tumbling down my spine. But my mind ain't so reliable these days. What's in front of me, that's real.

'I know we weren't really friends before. Quite the opposite.' I open my mouth to protest, but he continues. 'No, it's OK. I know I can be a jerk sometimes. You really don't remember those last weeks, do you?'

'Nope.' The word is wet with tears I'm trying real hard to wrangle in. I keep my eyes on the grass. When I dare a glance up, he is rubbing the back of his neck.

'We'd been getting closer in the last few weeks before the fire. After the time we ran into each other in the kitchen.' He smiles. 'Don't worry, it'll come back to you.'

11. Early July

She was late. She'd forgotten our deal – my chance to prove my devotion.

That morning, Daddy's office had been slashed with streaks of light and shadow from the shutters when I'd walked in, a glass of sweet tea in my hand and a whole bunch of words rehearsed in my head: a request to go to Parkerville again, so soon after my last trip. The smell of his cologne had seasoned the air. He'd been hunched over his pad, not even looking up when I put the glass down on the desk. I'd got the words out, and they hadn't made a dent in his attention. I'd cleared my throat and tried again. His pen had slowed down. That time Daddy's gaze had flicked to me. A 'fine' had tumbled from his lips.

I had been dishonest, for the first time I could remember, sneaking off under the pretence of buying supplies for the twins. I'd put my soul on the line, and now she wasn't coming.

The fake leather of the seat stuck to the back of my calves, squeaking with my every move. My alibi was propped next to me. I sat in hell, or more precisely Allie's Diner, surrounded by people shaped by sins – flesh flabby with sloth or gluttony, breasts inflated by vanity.

Four tables down, the woman I'd seen asking about us in the craft store ordered coffee. I was surprised to see her – it had sounded that day like she wasn't from round here. Her tone had hinted at unpleasant business. I slunk down in my seat – no way I wanted her to notice me and my uniform standing out in this place. The clock on the wall showed 2:10pm.

The bell dinged above the door. My heart jumped in my throat, but a couple of teenagers sauntered in, firing peals of laughter. Come on, hurry up. Five more minutes and then I'm going. Hopefully I should be able to sneak past that woman undetected.

I sunk a little lower. Even though I'd chosen the booth furthest away from the windows, each passing silhouette could be someone from Newhaven, someone who could recognise me, someone who would ask questions. Daddy couldn't know I was here, trying to convince Summer ours was the right path, until I had some results to show him. My fingers played with the corners of one of the little flags on the tables – one of the many decorations in town for Fourth of July celebrations.

Summer suddenly crashed into the seat opposite, jolting me. The paper flag ripped. She screamed to the world in a technicoloured shirt thrown over a red bikini top. A burning embarrassment crept up my cheeks, and I kept my eyes on the cutlery.

'Sorry I'm late. Life got in the way.'

'I don't have long,' I replied, addressing my fork.

'Let's get on with it then.' Summer dropped her phone on the table. Her fingers darted over the screen.

'What you doin' that for?'

'Recording, so it's all legit.' I frowned in response. 'So I can't twist or change your words. Plus it beats taking notes. You cool with that?'

One of her hands had disappeared and was rummaging inside the bowels of her bag. I watched like a child would watch the hand of a magician plunged into a top hat, but instead of a rabbit she pulled out a pack of cigarettes which she tossed on the table, taking one out and holding a flame to it with a brightly coloured lighter she pulled from her pocket.

'I fucking love this state for its smoking regulations. Or lack of.' The words escaped with a plume of smoke.

'What can I get you?'

I wondered how we must have looked to the waitress – the girl in the beige dress, and the other, barely covered by an explosion of colours, sitting at the same table. Two girls together, with nothing in common.

'Can I get some fries and a Diet Coke?'

'What about you, sweetheart?'

'Just some water, please.'

After the waitress left, we sat in silence. The world whirled around us. A world where I didn't fit in. My leg shook under the table. The idea of walking out of the air-conditioned unease of the diner and straight back into the familiar heat of Newhaven was enticing. The clang from the bell warned me of another arrival and I sank again in my seat – but it was just an old man in a baseball cap and sunglasses.

'Shit, you ashamed of being seen with me or something?'

'Can we start?'

'Relax. So, Abigail, have you always lived in . . . what's the name of that place? Newhaven Plantation?'

'Yes.' Technically that wasn't true, but we never talked of our lives before Newhaven. That was the rule, one I wasn't prepared to break. 'We just call it Newhaven. No Plantation.'

'Are most people in your congregation from here?'

'Some, but we welcome a lot of folks. People come from all over to find salvation and redemption at Newhaven.'

'What kind of salvation is that?'

Her questions rose one after the other over the peals of lively conversation and the clang of cutlery. I leaned my elbows on the table, ready. All those rehearsals in front of my mirror finally had a purpose.

'Livin' life according to the teachin' of the scriptures, and the roles our Lord created for men and women. "But only the one who does the will of my Father who is in heaven, will enter His kingdom."'

The waitress brought our order. The smell of fried potatoes filled the air. My mouth flooded with saliva, and I anchored myself to my glass of water. *Be honest and open, show them the way, but only they can walk through the door*, as Daddy would say. Summer squirted ketchup, drowning her fries in red. A burst of voices on the other side of the window jolted me, but it was just a random group of strangers.

'Is that what you believe, or are you just repeating what you've been told?' Summer traded the words for a mouthful of fries, which she reduced to a pink sludge.

'It's what I believe. We're helpin' people. Look at the world around, the unemployment, the birth rate falling, abandon-ment of family values, kids being groomed in state schools, women forgetting their true nature. We want to provide an escape from all that.'

Summer shoved another handful of fries in her mouth. Ketchup stained her fingers. She licked the red off. She could be so much more, and I was the door to her salvation.

'How is hating and oppressing women helping them?'

Her accusation tickled the back of my throat. The words tasted foul. Newhaven was a place where women were cele-brated for what they were: mothers and wives. They played a central and nurturing role; they raised the future generations.

Daddy doted on Mom; with a smile of love and thanks after every meal she cooked, the bouquet of wild flowers he still brought to her every month, even after all those years. He created an aura of safety so strong Mom didn't ever want to leave.

'Newhaven doesn't hate women. We celebrate women for what they are.'

'What are they?'

'Wives and mothers.'

'You mean a housekeeper and human incubator. People who do as they're told, and blindly follow orders.'

Her tone, sodden with contempt, straightened my spine. 'I can't wait to be a mother.'

'How old are you? Like, fifteen?'

'I'll be eighteen in a few months.'

'Jeez . . .'

'You're gettin' it wrong. If you just listened . . .'

'Have you ever heard of Stockholm Syndrome? It's quite common in cults like yours.'

This was a disaster. Why couldn't she just listen? I took long gulps of my drink, drowning the frustration. The door burst open, the bell screaming as a family poured into the diner, two little boys running ahead. For a moment I half expected them to jump on my lap, screaming 'Abbay, we found you,' but it wasn't my family. Still my heart didn't stop throwing itself against my ribs. I scooped up the paper bag next to me.

'I gotta go. This was a bad idea.'

'Listen, we can meet somewhere else. Somewhere more private. I'm sorry. No filter, that's my big problem.' She grabbed my wrist as I scrambled to get out. 'Wait. I got something for you.' She thrust a book into my hands. The title said

Little Women. 'I think you might like it. Much better story than that novel of yours. All you need is inside. OK? Just look inside.'

I ran outside and into a wall of blistering air. My forehead immediately dampened with sweat. My heart hammered in anticipation of being reunited with the others and on the boat back to Newhaven. A blur of rainbow colours unspooled next to me. I had reached the temple of depravity, each sin stamped with a different letter to make a ridiculous acronym.

'Abigail.'

The call sliced through me before I rounded the corner. The voice that had thundered my name didn't belong here, and stopped me in my tracks. He wasn't supposed to come on this trip. I'd left him at his desk, writing a sermon, before putting an expanse of water between him and my meeting with Summer. The sun in front of me, I shielded my eyes with a hand. This wasn't a mirage. Daddy's silhouette cut against the blue sky, a couple of shrieking seagulls hovering above him.

AUDIO FILE #4

Audio Quality: Moderate

[Voice A]: Female
[Voice B]: Female

[First section of recording too damaged to recover.]

[Voice A]: Isn't that a bit of a sweeping generalisation?
            Surely not everybody over there is a bad
            person or has bad intentions.
[Voice B]: Lemme tell you, the old pastor, he was a nice
            man. Always polite, never met a stranger in his
            life. He used to come in here and buy pralines
            for his wife. That new one though. He's walkin'
            around like he's God's chosen one. Thinks
            himself so much better than everybody else.
            But the look in his eyes ... I don't trust the
            man. He's a gator paradin' as a sheep. Lemme
            tell you, I wouldn't want him as my pastor,
            even less as my husband. I feel sorry for that
            man's family.

[Rest of recording too damaged to recover.]

By the time Daddy reached me, all that was left of me was a heart no longer beating but merely bracing for impact. Something terrible must have happened for him to come to find me here. Please let Mom, Sarah and the twins be OK. My bulging pocket felt heavy with Summer's gift.

'What's wrong? What's happened?'

'What's wrong? What's wrong is that you've scared us to death, Abigail.' The tension rolling off his words scattered passers-by, leaving me on my own in the middle of the sidewalk. Anger pulsed beneath his skin, tensing his jaw. His reaction didn't make sense. Then in a blink the storm of his emotions passed, and molten anger curdled into a look of concern that drew lines between his brows.

'We didn't know where you were. Your mama's been goin' out of her mind.'

'I told the rest of the group where I was goin'. Did they call you? I was just . . . I bought some stuff . . . for the twins. Sorry . . . if I was longer than expected.' I kept tripping on his frustration. I held out the proof in my arms – the few things I'd bought before meeting Summer. His fingers dug into the flesh above my elbow.

'Your mama's been frantic with worry. You know how she gets. How could you do this to her?'

'Are you all right, sweetheart? Is that man botherin' you?' A woman with short hair and big red-rimmed glasses had appeared next to us, brows pulled together by concern, but my attention snagged on the metal bar piercing the left one.

'She's fine,' Daddy answered.

'I ain't askin' you. I'm askin' her.' She scowled at him. 'Are you all right, sweetheart?'

I nodded in response. Light flared on the woman's rainbow pin; my pulse quickened. I prayed for her to just go away.

'It's a family matter. Leave me and my daughter alone.'

'Way to treat your family. Listen, sweetheart, if you ever need a safe place or just to talk, you're always welcome here. The Center is open to anyone.'

'So you can corrupt her mind? My daughter will never set foot in your grooming centre to be brainwashed. "For this is the will of God, your sanctification: that you abstain from sexual immorality; that –"'

'Please spare me your religious BS. Does it make you feel like a man to scare a little girl?'

The woman wedged herself deeper between us. She'd got it wrong – Daddy didn't scare me, he was concerned, although the why still confounded me.

The air around us shifted. 'Get away from us,' he growled. 'You ain't foolin' me. I know about your kind and I won't let you groom my daughter to be as depraved as y'all.'

A blob of saliva landed on his face and congealed in the bristle of his beard. A darkness veiled his eyes and tensed the sinew in his neck. The tension tightened his fingers on my arm until they dimpled my skin.

'Babe, Tania, come on. He isn't worth it.' A woman in a flowery dress, her cornrows twisted into a low bun, pulled the woman back by the shoulders before steering her away.

Daddy wiped the spit off with his handkerchief. I wanted

to comfort him, but I didn't know how. Others had confronted him in front of me before. His passion and faith had riled sinners and the weak-minded, but this felt different; a more intimate affront. His hand loosened around my arm and settled on my shoulder instead, the heaviness telling me it was time to go. We walked back accompanied by an uncomfortable silence.

'Pastor Heywood, we didn't reckon you were here today,' Wade Pruitt said, breaking from the group when he spotted us.

'I had to come over when I found out Abigail had snuck here without tellin' us. Her mother's sick with worry.'

My mouth slackened with confusion.

'I apologise; she said she'd told you.' The words stuttered out of Wade Pruitt's mouth. I had never seen him so unnerved, but Daddy's disapproval could have that effect on people.

'Abigail?'

'I did. I have. I came to your office to ask you. I brought you a glass of sweet tea and asked if I could go. I even asked you twice. Don't you remember?'

'You came to my office and you brought me sweet tea, that's right.'

My tongue stopped pushing against my teeth, and my mouth twitched with a smile.

'But you never told me nothin' about comin' here, and I would certainly remember if I'd given my permission. Do you think I would put your mama through that?'

Shame burned my cheeks. I had left with the conviction I had his approval to come. He'd grunted, I remembered, but maybe his attention had been focused on a more important task. He liked writing his sermon long-hand, made him feel closer to God's words. A seed of doubt bloomed in my mind.

What if he hadn't heard me? I had taken a grunt of dismissal for a grunt of approval, reshaped it into a 'fine'.

'I'm so sorry. I thought you heard me and you were all right with it. I didn't wanna scare you or Mom. I'm so sorry.'

The group blurred behind a wall of tears. The humiliation felt intimate, as if Daddy had stripped me naked in the street in front of everyone, people I saw every day. People who would remember and remind me. The possibility that my misunderstanding might not have been genuine had already darkened their eyes. The situation would be gossiped about behind closed doors – that I thought I could get away with it. This was beyond humiliating. Nobody liked a liar. Even worse than disappointing them, I had let him down.

13.

We waited by the marina entrance, the others absorbed in their own thoughts or pockets of conversation, all united in their effort to look everywhere except at me. I scanned the intersection ahead. Still no sign of Daddy since he had stalked off ten minutes ago. I wasn't sure where he'd gone, just that we couldn't leave without him.

A face emerged from the crowd, but not the one I expected. One with oversized red glasses and a pierced eyebrow. The woman who'd intervened earlier, Tania. She walked down the street, holding hands with the woman in the flowery dress and beautiful hairstyle. Their intertwined fingers spoke a secret language that intrigued and unnerved me. Somehow, Summer floated into my mind, fingers disappearing into her mouth, pushing fries. The women slowed down at the pedestrian crossing as the countdown edged closer to red, before stopping at the kerb. Waiting, they leaned in, lips connecting. Something tightened inside my stomach. Their kiss grew unbashful, mouths and cheeks moving like cows grazing on hay. My throat constricted with an invisible lump. God should strike them right now for their defiance. Still I couldn't look away. A small crowd congealed around them — oblivious to the spectacle they put on — waiting for the light to change.

The chatter around me dulled into a low static, blending with the droning rhythm of traffic. What was Summer doing right now? My mind sat her at the same booth I'd left her in, head tilted back as she downed her Diet Coke before wiping her mouth with the back of her hand. Summer wouldn't bother herself with napkins or proper manners. Every gesture and word coming out of her mouth was evidence she needed to be saved, like those two women. With my help she could avoid eternal damnation. The book pulled at my skirt pocket. *Little Women* – what kind of a title was that, some feminist manifesto? My hand brushed against the shape under the fabric as a blurred silhouette brushed past Tania and her friend.

A scream yanked me out of my daydreaming, before splintering into several others, ripping through the crowd at the intersection. In the seconds it took to reach the source of the noise, panic had morphed into hysteria. The crowd had soaked up more passers-by, the sidewalk now bloated with them. I slid through a breach between two bodies. Moving through them felt like wading through the swamp on Jaspers Island, limbs brushing past, sweaty skin sticking to mine, the smell of perspiration in the heat, hair drifting like Spanish moss.

On the other side of the crush of people, a delivery truck had stopped in the middle of the road, its yellow hood splattered with what looked like red paint. On the opposite sidewalk, the woman from the diner and the craft store was staring at me with dark eyes, while everyone else stared at the road or looked away altogether.

Voices thickened like people were talking underwater. My brain couldn't process what was happening until I saw it: a pair of broken red-rimmed glasses on the road, lenses cracked. Tania lay on her back, unfocused eyes staring at the sky, her arms and legs following unnatural jagged lines. Her friend kneeled next to her body, her face darkened with screams and slick with tears. Her mouth didn't seem human, her screams heart-rending. I didn't know how to react to her pain.

Despite the heat, I shivered. The air, already heavy, sagged with a metallic smell that pushed bile into my throat. Blood crept from under Tania's head, pooling over the asphalt. I looked down, almost expecting blood on my hands, but they were clean and shaking. Slowly, a chaos of sentences emerged from the general confusion.

'Someone call 911.'

'She just tripped and fell.'

'It's like her legs gave way.'

'I couldn't stop her. I just couldn't stop her.'

'I can't believe that just happened.'

'Is she breathing?'

Less than an hour ago that body had been wedged between me and Daddy, bristling with life and indignation. A split second, and her skin already had a sallow undertone. The thought chilled my bones. My attention focused on her chest, searching for the slightest rise, like when I watched baby Sarah or the twins sleeping. It sometimes took a second to detect the subtle rise, the right angle, but there was nothing there. Tania's chest was still with death. I wrapped her soul with a silent prayer before it would be delivered for the final judgement.

I felt his presence, even before the comfort of his hands weighted on my shoulders.

'Daddy, it's so horrible. That poor woman.' I buried my face in his chest.

His arm wrapped around tight, cradling me into a cocoon of safety I never wanted to leave. He kissed the top of my head. His heart beat against my ear, the steadfast rhythm a comfort. I tethered my breathing to it, following its cadence.

'It's all right, darlin'. I'm here. Daddy's here.'

He looked down on me, and with his thumb brushed away a tear I didn't know I was shedding.

'It's such a tragedy. We spoke to her just an hour ago, and now . . .' I retreated into his embrace once again, mayhem still unfolding around us.

'I know, darlin'. It's a tragedy, but our Lord always finds a way to punish the wicked.' He delivered the words so softly. My body tensed, before softening again. He was right. The devil often hid behind an angelic face. Tania being nice to me earlier didn't change what she was.

'You! It's you.'

Her shouts turned us around. Tania's friend stared at Daddy with a look of pain and pure hatred that jammed a breath in my throat. Her flowery dress was matted with blood. He remained silent next to me, but his body stiffened as she continued.

'I know it was you. It's your fault. It's your damn fault.'

Her words disintegrated into a howl. I looked up to face him.

'Daddy, what does she mean?'

'You know how those people are, darlin', they like to blame their problems and misfortunes on everybody but themselves.'

Without another word, Daddy steered us away, until he'd completely extricated us from the crowd, and the commotion dulled to incoherent whispers.

Briar County, Office of the Coroner
Case Number: 234
Preliminary Autopsy Report (Extract)

Sex: Female
Age: 20–40 years
Race: Caucasian
Weight: 115 lbs
Height: 5'6"

RECORDED NOTES

The body is female, consistent with a woman between the ages
of twenty and forty years. The victim sustained third-degree
burns over 95% of her body, and all clothing has been burnt or
melted with the flesh. Identification via fingerprints is not
possible. Briar County Sheriff's Department is trying to locate
dental records for a formal identification. Uterus and pelvic
area are too damaged to confirm if the victim has ever given
birth. Pastor Jeb Abernathy has confirmed to the Sheriff's
Department that, to the best of his knowledge, the only females
present in the house at the time of the fire were Abigail
Heywood, 17, who survived, and Genevieve Heywood, 38. He
further confirmed that no other woman is unaccounted for at
Newhaven Plantation. A wedding ring has been removed from
the body's left ring finger and identified as belonging to
Genevieve Heywood. All of the physiological findings, including

estimated height and weight, suggest that the body is that of Genevieve Heywood.

The pattern of burns shows accelerant was present on the victim's clothing and this accounts for the severity of the burns. Samples have been sent to the county lab for analysis.

Presence of smoke in the lungs and throat indicate that the decedent was alive at the start of the fire. However the body wasn't found in a foetal position which seems to indicate that the victim was unconscious when she burned. Unfortunately the body has suffered extensive damage due to the fire. After close examination the body doesn't exhibit any clear injuries besides the extensive burns.

At this stage of the autopsy the cause of death is asphyxiation due to smoke inhalation, and extensive burns; however the manner of death (accident/suicide/homicide) is currently undetermined pending the result of the county sheriff investigation.

14. Present day

Today's the day. I try to smile, and Mom smiles back at me. I can't remember when the picture was taken. Her face is younger, before the twins, but the hair and the hint of pale blue in her clothing, the rounded collar, mean it's from here.

The nights I don't have nightmares, she haunts my dreams. We do stupid stuff like cooking or playing with the twins, dancing to the radio. And then I wake up. And it's like being ripped apart while staying whole. Sometimes I wish she would just leave. Leave me alone.

My upper lip is damp with sweat. The heat so heavy the flower arrangements wilt by the minute. A gust of warm air swirls in through the open doors and along with it the tangy smell of water, rushing down the aisle like latecomers looking for a seat. The wind ain't the only intruder. Nobody acknowledges the two deputies leaving the church, but everybody witnessed the words exchanged between the representatives of the law and those of our community. How Pastor Abernathy's shoulders tensed up at uniforms which aren't ours, at the deputies' crossed arms, at their refusal to leave until they'd spoken with me.

'You should come with us down to Parkerville. Could make for a nice day trip. What do you say, Abigail?'

Can't they all stop using my name? Somehow I can't stand it no more. It sounds like teeth scraping a fork.

'This child ain't goin' nowhere with you. Not as long as she's in our care,' Mrs Calhoun says.

I'm no child. I'm almost eighteen.

'We'd like for Abigail to see a specialist about her memory loss.'

'You got a warrant?'

'There ain't no need for that. Sometimes intense emotional trauma can cause amnesia, but some forms of therapy can help recover memories.'

'Therapy?' Mrs Calhoun sneers. 'That's modern society snake oil; only our Lord can provide guidance. Is she under arrest?'

'Of course she ain't –'

'In that case, I'd like you to leave. This is private property,' Pastor Abernathy tells them, a hand resting on the grip of his holstered gun.

Amid all the arguing both sides have forgotten to ask me what I want. My fingers play with the end of my braid; the familiar brittleness soothes me. The memory of Mom braiding my hair before Sunday service swells in my throat and glazes my eyes with tears that don't come.

'This is a private event, and I'd like you to leave right now. Or do y'all have no respect? You've upset an orphaned child. Y'all have no shame.' Pastor Abernathy gestures towards me.

The deputies stomp out, their words drifting in from the outside.

'I wonder why we bother helpin' those people. It's like they don't even wanna know what happened here.'

Next to me the twins wiggle on the bench, arms outstretched towards her face, her smile. 'Momma, Momma,' they call, not understanding why she's not coming, not picking them up in her arms like she always did back when their voices were enough to summon her. Their little eyes are wet with tears. They got Daddy's eyes, the same icy blue, but Mom's auburn hair. I wonder who they will resemble most when they grow up.

'Momma, Momma.' Their voices rise with frustration, a shrill sound that drills into my bones, compresses the nobs of my spine. An excruciating reminder that she isn't coming back. Ever.

'Shush.' The warning bounces off the high ceiling.

Their cries crumble into quiet whimpers. The congregation's attention narrows down on us. The air bristles with the apprehension of what I will do next. My hands hover inches from the boys, but I ain't sure how to comfort them. Whatever I do I ain't what they need. I ain't her, even if I carry traces in my blood and in my marrow.

'You're all right, boys. All right.' Rushing over, Mrs Calhoun soothes them, a growing presence like ivy over a scarred wall. Trusted, unavoidable Mrs Calhoun. She can have the twins if she wants. Baby Sarah too. I'm no good for them, she'll make a far better family. She had to wrench baby Sarah from my arms yesterday, after I failed to notice that the bottle I was feeding my sister was empty and her face was red with cries. My attention had drifted back to the black holes of my memory, desperately grabbing at their edges for a glimpse, an image. I'm no good for them. Growing up I would only remind them of what they've lost, always making them wish she was there instead of me. How can I be their mother when I can't even remember how to be their sister?

Two pictures, propped on easels among flower arrangements. That's all we have. The curtain twitches. My mind skirts around it, not thinking about the room behind. About her body trapped with his in the metal canister of the incinerator. About the column of flames from the burner. About the fire finishing what it started. About a heat so intense all that's left is smoke and ashes. Ashes. The thought of her ashes mixed up with his soothes me. Until death do us part, but not even then.

'Abigail, how you doin'?' Mrs Calhoun asks.

My mouth tenses. *Why aren't you crying*, that's what she means. Can they see it? The emptiness which fills me? The shock's scooped everything out of me, even the tears. The expressions on their faces flitter and never settle, their inner conflict pulling at the muscles – pity, suspicion, sympathy, wariness, comfort, distance.

They can't help but wonder, like me. What happened that night? Where did I go missing for that entire day and night, when they searched for me? I've been catching the tail of conversations in the kitchen, questions with no definite answers, the erosion of their faith – not in our Lord, but in me: do you think she's faking? I'm sure she was in Parkerville, up to no good. I wouldn't be surprised if there was a guy . . .

If I could remember. Maybe if I *can* remember, in here. After all, my memories end within these walls – on a similar day, commemorating the lives of Pastor Munro and Fleur, different happy faces propped on the same easels. The last day of my old life that I can recall.

Eyes closed, I search the darkness inside my head. The heat ignites a spark. Cries rise – mine, his, hers, the flames. They mingle, bleed into one another. Which came first – their screams or the fire? A silhouette slumped against the living-room wall.

Eyes open, my hands rest on my lap, dressed in soot. So much black it almost glistens. They look so small and childish under all that dripping black.   Concentrate. The beats of a heart, the rise and fall of a chest under my fingers. They slow down.   A life under my hands, unable to catch it before it slips away.   Something else underneath. If I get past the fire, maybe I can see what's behind, its origins.   Under the unshaped pandemonium of screams, Daddy's voice rises, sharp like the fingernail crowning the end of an accusing finger.

Pastor Abernathy is delivering his eulogy, and I ain't caught a word of it. Her picture is the centre of my focus, her soft features, lips that kissed my cheeks, my lids, the tip of my nose, my every finger and toe, that kissed me even when I didn't deserve it. *Just us girls, Honey-bunny*, she used to say, back when we were each other's world.

I see her face in a different moment, eyes rolling back inside her head, lips mouthing invisible words, life dissolving from her cheeks. A frantic panic squeezes my chest. The images bring along with them an echo of a voice. Daddy's shouts rise from the depths of a black hole in my mind. Words from before the fire, finding their way back to me.

What have you done, Abigail? What have you done?

From: Cameron McPherson
Date: Tuesday, August 30, 2022 at 11:34 AM
To: Jeb Abernathy
Subject: RE: Concerns – guidance needed

My dear Pastor Abernathy,

Thank you for your latest update.

I am disturbed to hear that the police interrupted the memorial for Pastor Heywood and his wife. The last thing we want is for them to interfere in our affairs. We take care of our own. People resent us for the work we do, and for living our lives according to God, both law enforcement and the general public. We cannot exclude that the fire was started as an act of violence against our church and one of its leaders, especially after losing Pastor Munro in a senseless act of violence. Who are we to say Pastor Heywood didn't suffer a similar fate? I agree that patrols need to be increased for safety reasons, and law enforcement shouldn't be allowed on Newhaven ground. For all we know, they could be responsible for the fire. This is an opportunity to remind our people of the dangers that lurk outside of the church. Now is the time to close ranks.

Please send me a copy of your latest weapon inventory and I can arrange for an order of additional handguns or semi-automatic rifles and ammunition if needed.

I leave it in your good hands, but if you want my opinion I believe travel to Parkerville should be kept to a very strict minimum, and Abigail should stay at Newhaven.

Under His guidance. Have a blessed day.

Pastor Cameron McPherson

15. July

After the Parkerville trip, the eyes on me changed. They flickered with a mix of sadness and something else, undefined – as if I was sick, and they searched for visible symptoms. *The obedient daughter doesn't lie.* To them, I wasn't an obedient daughter no more. The group in Parkerville had witnessed it, and the news spread through Newhaven like dandelion seeds caught in a hurricane. *She lied to her own father. She should have been back at home.* Shame tightened my lungs every time I saw their disapproval, but it was mixed with something else: an ember of resentment for not believing my genuine mistake. I tried to snuff that ember every time, before anger and arrogance would consume my soul.

'Feminism.'

The word swelled under the rafters of the church, hovered like dark clouds before a storm. Daddy stood at the lectern, every face turned towards him. Heat sat among the congregation – an omnipotent presence, even the paper fans out in droves that morning couldn't swat away. A rivulet of sweat crawled down my spine; I squirmed, the swirling fans above doing nothing more than rearranging the warm air. The scarf wrapped around my head didn't help.

'Feminism's the devil that poisons the mainland by pretending to liberate women. Liberate a woman from what? From a lovin' family, from a husband who will look after her, provide for her, from livin' a fulfilling life as a mother and bringin' up children? "Women will be saved through childbearing – if they continue in faith, love and holiness with propriety." Feminism's the pretext for women to turn away from the Lord and the role he created for them, choosin' instead to be sexually promiscuous, selfish. We left all this behind when we moved here. But don't be complacent.'

He paused for effect, staring down the lens of the phone on its stand. The only sound the drone from the congregation's paper-fan wings. I imagined faces watching at home, inching towards their screen, pulled forward by Daddy's charisma.

'Don't be complacent y'all, for I tell you this: corruption can be found on our island too, in our very hearts. We must be vigilant. Under His guidance we can live within His truth. We know what happens to the wicked. We witnessed it a few days ago in Parkerville when God struck one down.'

Silence engulfed the church again, allowing his words to soak into people's brains. I replayed a different scene in my head for the millionth time, watching my mouth and the words that fell out, the response that came from him. Hating myself for making such a stupid mistake. He'd never been that disappointed in me before. Losing his trust had wrung me so tight I could hardly breathe. I hated how he looked at me, how his lips pursed with discontent, but at least he hadn't shunned me like others had.

I could almost hear the thoughts buzzing around. The weight of the congregation's gaze piled on my back. Daddy's eyes swept through the congregation before he brought his hands up towards the ceiling.

'For those of you watchin' online, who have been supportin' us with your donations. You are in our prayers. Under His guidance. Have a blessed day.'

'Amen.'

The velvet curtain behind him glowed redder than usual. Tania's face blazed through my mind, her lifeless body splayed on the asphalt. *God always finds a way to punish the wicked.* Knowing the truth was one thing, seeing it in blood was another. Her image hadn't left me since Parkerville. She deserved God's punishment for what she was, but I couldn't reconcile the brutality of her reckoning with the woman who had worried about my welfare on that street in Parkerville. Tania haunted me, but I kept that to myself.

AUDIO FILE #5

Audio Quality: Poor

[Voice A]: Female
[Voice B]: Male

[First minute too damaged to recover.]

[Voice A]: As a man of faith, how do you feel about the
            NABC?
[Voice B]: Those people take the word of God and twist
            it to justify their narrow-minded hatred. (…)
            passage in the Bible: 'And what I am doing I
            will continue to do, in order to undermine the
            claim of those who would like to claim that in
            their boasted mission they work on the same
            terms as we do. For such men are false apos-
            tles, deceitful workmen, disguising themselves
            as apostles of Christ. And no wonder, for even
            Satan disguises himself as an angel of light.'
[Voice A]: Have (…) to confront them?
[Voice B]: (…) crazy? (…) my life (…) too much.

[Rest of recording too damaged to recover.]

16.

Egg yolk broke under my knife. The slimy yellow spilled over and slowly swallowed the white expanse of porcelain before I wiped it with a piece of cornbread. The sludge of food hurt when I swallowed and sat heavy in the pit of my stomach. Breakfast was no better than Sunday service. Silence ruled our table. Daddy, in his concern, had confronted me in front of everyone, singling me out as being defective. Might as well have just called me a feminist in front of everyone. Their judgement was inescapable. It was in every fork scrape, every cough, every click of a tongue, every inhale of breath, every throat cleared, in every word they held back from me. All magnified ten-, a hundredfold.

'Can I be excused?' The chair legs whined against the old floorboards.

'Abigail, I don't think –'

'Let her be,' Daddy said as he covered Mom's hand with his.

Outside, the heat smothered me like the devil's embrace, the sun chasing away the shadows and leaving me no place to hide. Jackson sat on the edge of the old fountain, facing the woods that hemmed the north side of the fence, his hair now cut to a more respectable length above his ears. My attention snagged on a rustle in the undergrowth, but there was nothing there. I joined him; we sat in silence, surrounded by the garden's many statues. Time and the elements had eroded their features, turning them into ideas of what people looked like. They freaked him out as much they did me. He stared at the woods, I stared at my hands, both united in our discontent.

'I thought you'd run away or somethin'.'

'I didn't.' At least he still spoke to me. I doubted his father would like that.

'You were my hero for however long you were gone.' He punctuated his comment with a deflated laugh.

The news of my going missing had festered in Newhaven while Daddy was in Parkerville to fetch me. As we'd approached the shore, a lone figure had lingered at the edge of the water, growing into the shape of Mom. As soon as my foot touched the ground, she had smothered me in a fierce embrace while I bided my time, my skin against her wet cheek. She babbled words between sobs – *I thought I'd lost you, I thought they'd got to you and taken you away* – desperation robbing her of the ability to make sense, and fuelling my shame. The whole of Newhaven had gathered around to witness how I had dishonoured my father and upset my mother. She hadn't forgiven me for scaring her like that. Her words to me still carried an edge of frost.

'It was just a misunderstandin',' I told Jackson.

'I believe you. This place twists everything.' His heel kicked the base of the fountain. It was weird seeing him like this. Jackson never got angry. That was one of the things I liked about him. 'Your dad included.'

'Is this about what happened the other day?'

I had come home to change my dress after it had got stained cleaning one of the upstairs rooms for a new arrival. Voices had strained against the closed door of Daddy's office.

87

'How can you say you'll do nothin'?' Jackson's voice was unmistakeable. Daddy's response rang too low to hear anything past a few muffled words. Unease pushed me forward, hoping to avoid whatever confrontation was taking place, when the door flew open.

'You're such a fraud. God will judge you for turnin' a blind eye on this.'

Jackson blew past me. I wasn't even sure if he'd seen me. The door yawned open, and Daddy leaned over his desk, his hands flat on the top, face pinched in disapproval, some unknown emotion twitching at the corner of his mouth. He held his breath as if trying to contain something that was threatening to spill. I poked my head through the doorway.

'Is everythin' OK?'

He looked up at me, suddenly calm.

'Fine, darlin'. Jackson is having a crisis of faith and is actin' out.'

After that Jackson had been even more withdrawn, to his father's despair. Mr Caine was not the kind of man you wanted to let down, and he had high expectations of Jackson. I felt sorry for him, he was just a kid who really missed his mom.

'People refuse to see it,' he said, kicking the base of the fountain. 'But I see it, and your mama too –'

'What are you moping about?' From behind us, the contempt in Tom's words pricked the skin between my shoulders. The way he always seemed to just appear reminded me of snakes in the tall grass. Jackson's body stiffened next to me.

'I say this with all due respect, but you really need to start acting like a man, Jackson, not some kind of pussy. I mean, grow a pair. Maybe your old man will respect you after that, and stop using you for target practice.'

'Don't be rude.' I frowned at Tom. 'What does he mean?'
I asked Jackson.

'I mean he needs to stand up for himself,' Tom said. 'How
will he ever get a girl if he keeps acting like one himself?'

Jackson's eyes glistened with frustration and his hands
curled into fists so hard his body vibrated. I wrapped my
arm around his shoulders. As a twenty-three-year-old, Tom
should know better. Jackson was still a kid in comparison.

'He'll make a better man than you are.'

'Don't knock it till you try it,' Tom said, winking.

My tongue rubbed against my front teeth, and a shiver ran
across my shoulders. Every look from him felt like phantom
fingers crawling around my waist.

Jackson sprung to his feet. 'Don't disrespect her.'

Tom cocked his head, smirking at Jackson's clenched fists,
his face maroon with anger.

'What are you going to do, fight me?' Tom snorted.
'Haven't you been beaten enough already?'

A guttural howl escaped Jackson as he launched himself at
Tom, the violence between them exploding bright and hot
like the fireworks that had been scarring the sky for the
Fourth of July celebrations. Tom pushed Jackson back, but
Jackson kept coming at him until he landed a punch. Tom's
fist caught him in the ribs in response, folding him.

'Stop it,' I shouted, but my plea got lost in their anger.

From his bent position, Jackson ploughed into Tom head
first, and both of them tumbled to the ground, where they
wrestled in a tangle of limbs, raising dust from the parched
ground. Tom got the advantage. He sat astride, laughing at
every punch Jackson landed. Finally one caught the corner
of Tom's chin. The blow narrowed his eyes and unleashed a
shower of punches on Jackson's ribs.

My attention flicked from the boys to Newhaven, its stern windows glaring down on us. Making up my mind, I fled, but couldn't outrun my own cowardliness. Too scared to be judged again, even by association.

AUDIO FILE #6

Audio Quality: Good

[Voice A]:   Female
[Voice B]:   Female

[Voice A]:   What's that for?
[Voice B]:   My podcast. Are you OK for me to record you?
[Voice A]:   Yeah, all right.
[Voice B]:   Cool. Have you lived in Parkerville all your life?
[Voice A]:   I grew up in Charleston. I came here after I got married. My husband's from round here, though.
[Voice B]:   What do you make of the people at Newhaven Plantation and the New American Baptist Church?
[Voice A]:   You gonna use my name?
[Voice B]:   Not if you don't want me to.
[Voice A]:   All right then. Those folks ain't true Christians. They take the word of the Lord and they twist it to suit them. God's about love. He gave us free will. They preach hate. We see them in town all dressed up the same, the girls with those dresses like that old TV show with that family, the Ingalls.
[Voice B]:   *Little House on the Prairie.*

[Voice A]: That's the one.

[Voice B]: Do you think they would let an outsider inside Newhaven?

[Voice A]: Is that what you wanna do? Lemme tell you, you shouldn't go there. That's why they live there 'cause they don't want no strangers up there. They say they worship the Lord, but God ain't in that swamp. It's a place for devils and plat-eyes.

[Voice B]: Sorry, plat-what?

[Voice A]: Plat-eyes. Evil spirits. Them people at Newhaven, they ain't right. Nothing better than swamp rats, if you ask me. You hear about all them people they lure there, young women. Once they get you in, you ain't ever leaving. *(Rustling noises.)* Is that all?

[Voice B]: Yeah.

[Voice A]: That's thirty-two dollars and fifty-five cents. Cash or card?

[Voice B]: Cash.

[Voice A]: Trust me, you don't wanna go there. Swamp on Jaspers Island's a dangerous place, especially for an outsider. That's why them people live out in the boonies, so people keep their noses out their business.

17.

The woods waited for me on the other side of the fence. Daddy said the fence was to keep people out, not the other way around. The empty basket swung in my hand. I didn't really lie when I said I was off to pick some wild blackberries for a pie. But needs must. On the other side, the thick canopy of trees provided shade but didn't stop the heat from spreading, the air still heavy with the insufferable summer. I trudged deeper into the undergrowth, making my own path, until the trees thinned out and the first shimmers of the swamp peeked through the foliage.

Sunlight broke on the surface in shimmering shards. The beauty of the swamp shone with summer light bouncing off vivid green. So different from the eeriness of winter when a breath of fog licked the surface of the water. Today the light framed the old boardwalk splitting the water, the planks dark with age, moss covering them in places. The path was almost impossible to find unless you knew where to look – or you stumbled upon it like we had. Fleur and I'd been off picking wild blackberries one summer, outside the fence. Jaspers Island was our domain. We didn't get no strangers around these parts. Of course, her fearlessness meant she stepped on the rotten old planks first.

The wood sagged under my feet, the smell of decay rising, but I knew it would support my weight. Cypress trees sprouted from the water, branches dripping with webs of Spanish moss, trunks twisted with sinew. The sight slowed my heartbeat. Green lived everywhere; it clung to the branches of trees, slicked the surface of the water, decorated the bullfrogs that crouched like ornaments. This place belonged to nature alone; I was merely allowed here. How could people renounce a God who created such beauty?

A chorus of croaks accompanied me down the path, under the watchful eyes of a couple of herons and unseen animals. Soon the cypress trees thinned out. The sun glared down on me, momentarily bleaching the shape of the landscape. I continued past Marshall Point until the water ended and ground rose from the swamp.

The old shack stood back against the woods, abandoned like an old witch cast out by a village to live on the outskirts so people could pretend she didn't exist. Clutching her locket, Fleur had shrieked with excitement when we'd first seen the house. Her face had split with a grin, tooth-gap on display. My heart tightened at the memory. As the distance dwindled and the building grew larger, apprehension mixed with anticipation tingled between my shoulders.

One side of the shack was engulfed by ivy, grown like scar tissue over the charred façade, hiding the black lick of fire on wood; the other was flanked with the rotting carcass of an old pick-up, kudzu vines picking their way through holes in the rusty body. On the right, a myrtle tree rebelled against the sea of green and brown with an explosion of fuchsia. The shack's roof sagged, as if exhausted from standing in this heat. I hacked my way to a front porch half swallowed by trailing ivy. As usual the door moaned open – the house greeting me with the whining of rusty hinges. Inside, the mix of damp and burnt wood tickled the back of my throat. The place had lain abandoned for a while. You might have thought human scavengers would have picked the house clean, leaving only the bones of the building, but the old tattered sofa still squatted in the living room, along with most of the furniture. The kitchen had also been left intact, derelict cabinets still full of dusty tableware, even the old refrigerator and stove still standing. I guessed even in these parts, where most lived on the wrong side of the poverty line, people were afraid to steal from the dead.

Nature had sidled through the gaps and reclaimed its territory, veins of ivy snaking through the broken windows and sprawling on the ceiling. The earth had wrangled its way back in great clumps of soil, and a family of ferns had rooted themselves in the far corner of the living room. I had no idea what the second floor looked like, too scared to be confronted with the relics of the tragedy that had made this place what it was.

Suddenly, a floorboard groaned behind me, and a voice cried out: 'This place's a bitch to find, you need to work on your directions. Seriously, we couldn't have met somewhere easier? I mean, I had to abandon my car at a parking spot about half a mile away and walk the rest.'

Summer took a drag from her cigarette. 'But still. Looks like I was right to leave my number and email address in that copy of *Little Women*.'

18.

Summer hovered at the threshold of the living room in cut-off denim and workman's boots, a cigarette dangling dangerously from the corner of her mouth, her hair scraped back into a messy knot crowning her head. Her upper lip and hairline shone under a film of perspiration. Ignoring the old sofa, she dropped cross-legged onto the floor before pulling out a Coke from her bag, the bottle slick with condensation. She swallowed long gulps which pulsed down her neck.

'Want some?' She wiped her mouth with the back of her hand. 'Nobody here to judge you,' she added when I didn't respond.

The bottle weighed heavy and slippery in my hands. My lips cupped the neck where Summer's mouth had been. I took a long swallow as a show of good faith. Fizziness hit my tongue; a hint of coldness still clung to the soda as it sloshed around in my mouth. It tasted of another life, one when I'd use two hands to hold the bottle, the thrill that it could spill out, and the satisfaction when it didn't. A life where I waited at a counter taller than I was while a storm of cents rained down on it, the agonising minutes while the clerk counted the money. The small sips to make the drink last longer. Mom only a dark silhouette against the summer sun who made a show of drinking but really would let me have most of it.

'Sorry for acting like a bitch at the diner. I had a shitty night, followed by a shittier day.'

I flinched at the b-word as I handed the bottle back.

'Shouldn't have gone at you that way.'

'Why d'you hate us so much? You don't even know us. Aren't you supposed to be impartial if you're makin' a documentary?'

'Podcast, but touché. It's hard sometimes.'

'Why d'you do it then?'

'I'm trying to understand how people whose faith is supposed to be all about forgiveness and compassion can be so hateful. That's why it's called "A Question of Faith", among other things. I mean, if it's legal and between consenting adults why do you care about who people love or what they do with their lives?'

Tania's face flashed inside my head, how she'd wedged her body between me and Daddy, that same body I saw broken on the asphalt. The screams from her friend in the flowery dress, how they felt driven from a place of love and not lust. Lost lust didn't ravage you that way. Grief is the continuation of love. Pastor Favreau had said it more than once at funerals.

'Women should be and do anything they like, yet they come to this place that gives them no freedom.'

'But women can do what they like. If they want to live a life of sin, then it's their choice.'

'Sins according to whom? God? And based on what? Some texts and customs that date back to before proper science and shit. I mean, people back then thought it was cool to have slaves or stone people to death.'

Summer spoke how she sat, unrestrained, slouching elbows resting on her knees, the smoke of a cigarette unfurling from her mouth. She tossed the stub in the fireplace.

'Shit, it reeks in here. Come on.'

Without waiting for a response, she pulled us both up standing. Outside the brutal heat greeted us. Toe to heel, Summer slipped off her boots and stalked towards the derelict pier that once housed a row boat which had long sunk into the swamp, hands pulling her shirt over her head, the expanse of her back divided by the line of a bra. A 'Fuck, this heat' got tangled in the fabric of her top. By the time she was halfway down the pier, her shorts had been abandoned on the dusty planks next to her bra, leaving only a triangle of cotton to cover her buttocks. She launched herself at the water before I could warn her. The smash of her body hitting the water jolted me. She punched through the surface with a gasp, wiping the excess water from her face. The sun stood guard behind her, threatening me with burns if I got too close.

'Fuck, this feels good.'

'Get out of there. The water ain't safe.'

'What?'

'A whole lotta critters swim in there.'

'Lot of what?'

'Alligators and snakes!'

'Shit.'

Summer splashed about towards the bank. She waded out of the water, tangled weed and tall grass brushing her legs, feet covered in muck. I sat on the pier, toes dangling over the edge, the water shimmering below. Gators didn't normally venture that far inland but you never knew with critters. I grabbed my braid from behind my back as my tongue pushed against my front teeth, looking for the familiar gap puberty had closed. Fleur had loved the water too. She kept yammering about the swimming hole next to her house, going there with her brothers. Her absence pinched my heart. The water grew darker.

Summer dropped next to me, hair dripping onto the pier. Her eyes shone a dark honey. That close she smelled of coconut and swampy water. Blood rushed to the surface, kicking under my skin. After wiping her hands with her shirt, she took her phone out of her shorts pocket and placed it on the plank between us.

'You wanna record me?'

'If you don't mind.'

She took my shrug as agreement.

'Why'd you call us a cult the other day at the diner?' I asked.

'That's what you are, isn't it?'

'No, we ain't. We're a church, a place of worship.' Daddy always spoke about Newhaven being the light in the darkness. I breathed in deep, channelling his wisdom. 'We're a haven for those seeking to live the way God intended. Corruption lives inside the internet, movies, in the education system, in women's selfishness, wanting a career and gratification instead of caring for a family. Ignorant people call us a religious cult, when colleges, sororities, and feminist organisations are the real cults. They brainwash women into forgetting their place in society. People come to Newhaven to rediscover that truth and their place.'

Her legs swung next to mine but her toes managed to break the surface. Mine fell short and didn't dent the water.

'Is that what you believe?'

'Sure is.'

'Or are you just repeating what your pastor tells you?'

I felt my cheeks burn a bright red; still I continued. 'Wouldn't it be a more fulfilling life for you to care for a husband and children as part of a community than wander aimlessly for some documentary?'

'Podcast. And no. I don't like being tied down. Or told what to do. Anyway, so you got all this water and you never swim?'

I shook my head.

'Seriously, like never? C'mon, there aren't predators everywhere.'

'I can't swim.' A flush of embarrassment burned my cheeks more than the sun ever could.

'Shit, here I go acting like a bitch again. Sorry.'

A memory of Fleur floated to the surface of my mind. When we were kids and I used to stay with her in Florida, she would launch herself using a rope at the swimming hole near her house, driven by absolute fearlessness. As the swing reached its peak she would just let go and let gravity claim her. She always punctuated her fall with the highest shriek as her body slammed into the turquoise water. I would watch her sitting on one of the flat rocks, body safely tucked inside the towel's colourful lines. Those days tasted like heaven, and corn on the cob. A lump swelled in my throat. I swiped the sweat off my brow.

'Let's just wet our legs a little.' Summer stood, holding out her hand. 'I won't let anything happen to you. Promise.'

I hesitated for a moment. She was still only a stranger.

'C'mon. You gotta have faith.'

Her words shimmied at the back of my arms, and pulled me off the pier. I tied the skirt of my dress around my waist before making my way to the water with Summer. This one's for you, Fleur, I thought. Mud squelched between my toes, the ooze making me queasy, but still they curled into the ground, as if some unknown undertow might sweep me under. My hand rested on Summer's arm for support. I threw a quick glance towards the comfort of the sun-baked, steady ground. With every step, another piece of me disappeared under the water. Something brushed against my skin. There wasn't nothing lurking in the murky water, I told myself. My attention flitted between Summer and the end of the board-walk. No one was there. Suddenly, my foot skidded and I faltered, but Summer stopped my fall. My heart drummed in my chest, for sure, but from what kind of fear, I didn't know.

19.

Despite my warning Summer dunked herself again in the water to cool off. Something told me gators wouldn't dare go after her. She gripped the pier's edge and pulled herself out. Her underwear stuck to her skin. I tried not to look, but she was like bait at the end of an invisible fishing line. She dropped on the ground, arms raised above her head, offering her body to the sun. In the ribbon of skin above the elastic of her underwear sprawled a line of inked letters – the language unknown to me. The stern font looked intimidating, like a warning. I fixed my attention to a nearby tree as if my salvation depended on it.

'What's the deal with this shack, anyway? Who used to live here?'

'It's such a tragic story. It happened a while ago. The man who lived here tried to burn down the house before shooting himself in the head. Did it right up there in the bedroom.' I motioned with my head.

'Why did he do it?'

'They reckon his wife left, and it just broke him. Can you imagine somethin' so horrible?'

'I've heard worse. Way worse.'

Sitting down, I drew my legs close to my chest. The swamp clung to my skin with a muddy smell. It had claimed me as one of its own, erasing the soapy scent of Newhaven living. A rustle coming from the trees perked me up, but there was nothing to see. I was listening to Summer, but my attention stayed on the boardwalk cutting through the clusters of cypress and tupelo trees.

'There was this guy in Idaho,' Summer went on, 'who had four women chained in the basement of his house right in the middle of the suburbs. They were there for like a decade, and no one noticed. One of them even had his kid. Or this woman, Tiffany Bryce, she left her husband and next thing she knows he tries to burn the house with her in it.'

Her voice rang high with annoyance, but I couldn't figure out why. Didn't that man deserve to be pitied for what he lost?

'Or there was this guy in Alabama, can't remember the town's name, it was something ending with "-ston". Anyway, young guy with a pretty wife, a little girl and a baby boy. Perfect family by your standards. He works at the local factory, she's a stay-at-home mom. It's a nice life, until the factory runs into financial problems, and he's laid off. Can't find another job, then failure makes him mean. Neighbours said they heard those fights, which normally ended with her threatening to leave him with the kids, and him storming out of the house and into the nearest bar.'

Summer interrupted her tale to light a roll-up cigarette, her damp fingers turning the paper translucent. She pulled hard, the tobacco hissed, and the ember glowed a bright orange. Her mouth released a cloud of smoke, tainting the air with an acrid smell a lot more potent than normal tobacco. It tickled the back of my throat.

'Anyway, one day the little girl doesn't make it to kindergarten. School calls the house but no one answers. The wife, her name was Karen, Karen Elsher, she never shows up to lunch with her girlfriends. She isn't answering her cell, so they decide to swing by her place after they eat their devilled

103

eggs and barbecued ribs. Man, they shouldn't have eaten before going to that house, I'm telling you.'

The story worked its way under my skin. I wasn't sure I wanted to know how it ended but felt compelled to listen to the end of Karen's tale. Like I somehow owed it to her. Summer propped herself on an elbow. That close, her chest – dappled with sweat – glistened in the sunlight. She took a long drag from her cigarette and stared at me from behind the ribbon of smoke escaping from her mouth. I swallowed hard.

'They found Karen in bed. Her throat was slit from ear to ear, that's why nobody heard her scream. Do you know what arterial spray does to a room? Fucking Jackson Pollock, man.'

Her eyes turned hard, their honey darkened with anger. I didn't dare ask, my mind still desperately clinging to a foolish hope, praying for God's mercy.

'The cops found the kids in their respective beds, bullets in their heads. I mean, what kind of fucked-up person shoots a one-year-old? Of course, that piece of shit was long gone. They never found him.'

'You reckon the killer hid his body?'

'You really that naïve? *He* killed them. He killed his whole family.'

'Why?'

'Dude decided he needed a do-over but couldn't have it with an ex-wife and kids weighing him down. That was his fucked-up idea of a clean slate. How does your God let something like that happen?'

I opened my mouth, but she got there first.

'And please spare me the "God works in mysterious ways" BS.'

My mind darkened with gruesome images – the twins in

their beds, red streaking the white sheets, their little mouths slack with death, Sarah's cot a mess of blood, a dark silhouette with a deformed rictus slashing their face, looming over, eyes shining with insanity.

'Are you crying?'

I quickly wiped away the incriminating evidence.

'I better split. Got an interview in town.'

The idea I wasn't the only one she was speaking to tightened my stomach. She swept her clothes up and stared at the house for a moment. I followed her gaze, but there was nothing to see apart from an ugly old shack.

'Anyway, you have my number and email. Otherwise, I'll be back here tomorrow at two if you really wanna talk and not just sprout church propaganda.'

She waved, a hand high in the air as if she had always belonged in this territory. The tangle of her dark curls swished down her back before the darkness stitched between the trees swallowed her body.

As I walked back, my basket full of blackberries and my head full of Summer, I stumbled into Jackson and Tom and a cluster of other boys at the edge of the woods and Newhaven's fence, their backs to me. Whatever held their attention meant my arrival went unnoticed. They shoved and shifted about, until I saw what enthralled them – a possum, caught in a snare. Jackson hovered at the fringes of the violence whipped up by Tom. Of course, he had to be the instigator, even though he was too old for this kind of behaviour. Jackson's reactions unfolded out of sync with the rest of the group. Like reciting a prayer you didn't really know the words of. The possum thrashed about, terror kicking under its soft fur. The boys were feeding off each other's energy and off the animal's visceral fear. Fingers that would lace into prayer during Sunday service now poked and prodded the terrified animal until one hand wrapped around its furry neck. Fear kicked under my own skin. I should rescue the poor animal, but I didn't want the boys' attention turned on me. I didn't linger to witness the end of their violence. It was like Daddy always said – boys will be boys.

AUDIO FILE #7

Audio Quality: Moderate

[Voice A]:   Female
[Voice B]:   Female

[Start of recording too damaged to recover.]

[Voice A]:   (...) Original Sin?
[Voice B]:   It means we are all born sinful. We believe that
             we gotta live a righteous life to atone for that
             first sin.
[Voice A]:   (*Long exhale.*) I actually kinda like that idea.
[Voice B]:   To atone?
[Voice A]:   No. That no matter who we are, we are all
             born essentially fucked. We are all born from
             fire. Let me guess, it has to do with Eve and
             that apple.
[Voice B]:   You should come to Sunday service. You'd
             learn so much more. I reckon you could stay
             for Sunday lunch too.
[Voice A]:   Yeah, as tempting as it is I don't think your folks
             would be happy to entertain me for lunch.
             Don't have the right outfit for church anyway.
[Voice B]:   I could lend you a dress.
             (*One person laughing.*)

[Voice B]: What?
[Voice A]: Can you imagine me in one of your dresses?
(Two people laughing.)
[Voice A]: (...) sure I'm not quite right for (...) Can I
have (...) think about (...)

[Rest of recording too damaged to recover.]

20. Present day

I ain't told nobody about Daddy's words. The ones I remembered during the memorial. *What have you done, Abigail?* I'm worried what people might make of them, when I ain't sure myself. I haunt Newhaven and the garden, drifting about in crinkled clothes. Mrs Calhoun has given up fixing my braid. She can't do it like Mom. The only things I haven't given up are my siblings and caring for Mrs Favreau. I like being around her. Her room's peaceful. I got a feeling nobody wants me around, anyway.

Except for the twins. Fearless, they run around me and the statues in Newhaven's garden, enjoying the sunshine. Baby Sarah sleeps somewhere inside Mrs Calhoun's room. She reckons sharing the load and letting her look after my baby sister will do me good. That being outside will do me good too. I fail to see how, but I comply. Brittle grass sucked dry by the ferocious heat tickles my palms. The twins brim with life. They dash back and forth, dropping little tokens in the sag of my dress: stones, flowers, a twig, white and smooth as bone.

'Watch me, Abbay, watch me,' Matthew says before he rolls around in the grass. My eyes drift to him, but my gaze snags on the birch trees hemming the border of the woods. The air carries a whiff from the swamp. There's a hint of something sweet, reeling me in. Wade Pruitt and Mr Garrett walk the perimeter fence, their rifles slung low in front of them. The second time they've been around in an hour.

'Abbay, you ain't watchin'!'

'Sorry.'

Matthew rolls and rolls while Elijah climbs over my body.

'I miss Momma,' Elijah says.

'I wanna see Momma and Daddy,' Matthew adds, stopping in his tracks.

'I miss them too.'

I pull them both into my arms. Breathing in their familiar scent I smother them into a hug, until their little bodies wiggle out of my grasp. If they came to Hunters Cottage they could see them. The colour of their skin still etched on what's left of the front room's floorboards and walls. The twins could press their hands against the wood and plaster and touch them. Our parents still exist there, but the place's unsafe, and I don't want them getting hurt, especially not because of me.

Newhaven presses on my back. All three floors, with its arteries of hallways, all connecting back to a spinal staircase, and a flow of people bleeding through Newhaven's innards from the top to the bowels of the kitchen. It swallows me every evening to spit me out in the morning after the night's chewed on my mind. Last night, sleep dropped me inside another nightmare, with a red door that sagged open like lips. There was a girl there too, just the outline of a silhouette with long hair, who radiated with importance. Looking at her was like looking straight at the sun, but her face was all shadow. Fire surrounded her. And the walls spoke to me in Mom and Daddy's voices, saying *She's here, she's here.*

'Abbay, you ain't watchin'.'

'Abbay?'

What have you done, Abigail?

'Abbay, watch!'

Abigail, how could you? Your own mother . . .

'Stop, please stop!'

The words bellow out of me, my fist hammering against my thigh. The twins' eyes well up with tears. I reach out to them, but my hand hovers halfway, my heart tight with shame.

'Boys, there's sweet tea and molasses cookies in the kitchen,' a man's voice behind me says.

In a blink they zip out of view, racing after the promise of melting crumbs and a sugar rush.

'I thought you could do with a break,' Tom adds, pulling me up to a stand.

We walk side by side towards the hanging tree, hands dangling next to each other, knuckles almost grazing. He looks like the idea of him, a memory from long ago, an overlay that doesn't really match the picture underneath. He talks, and my gaze hovers above his shoulder, probing the space between the trees. The wind picks up and the forest whispers. Wade Pruitt and Mr Garrett disappear around the corner, checking the opposite perimeter.

'Have there always been this many patrols?'

'No, they've been on the up since . . . You know. Not everyone believes this was an accident.'

I ain't sure how to answer. Daddy used to say people hated us, but still, to think someone would go that far.

'What do you reckon?' I ask.

'It's possible. A lot of people don't like the work we do or the way we live. They'll do anything to stop us. I'm just glad that they didn't get to you, and you made it through.'

We lean against the tree. His hand reaches out for mine and squeezes it. The bandages have been gone for a couple of days now. His palm is slick with sweat and leaves a sheen on my skin. The fire has left it lighter in places, branding me. He smiles, and his face lights up with Daddy's ghost. A younger, beardless version of him with lighter hair. Maybe it's just wishful thinking. The nose and mouth are all wrong. The corner of my mouth curls. I wonder what happened – in the kitchen, he said – to change our relationship. I ain't ready to ask him yet.

'We have to be careful. Whoever did this, they're still out there.'

His fingers pluck bits of Spanish moss, before discarding them on the ground. They remind me of when we pulled wings off flies when we were little. The small acts of every-day violence that passed as play. He looks at me with an unwavering gaze.

'They could still come after you. You could have seen them and not remember.'

My eyes widen at the possibility. I've never considered it. My fingers tighten around a branch until the bark cuts into my skin like fingernails. What if they come after the twins, or baby Sarah?

'Don't worry. I'll keep you safe.'

He slides closer to me. He keeps talking but I ain't listening. Behind him, the woods stare with the eyes of a dozen birch trees. *Summer is here, summer is here*, nature whispers with every shard of sunlight pinning me to the grass. But maybe summer is gone and all we're left with is the ghost of heat, stifling the air.

A woman stares at me on the other side of the fence, still and stiff like one of the trees. The alarm catches in my throat. Even from this distance, she has eyes like she wants to hurt something or someone. The fence doesn't look strong enough to hold her back. It feels like if she wanted to she could march right over to us. She puts a finger to her lips, before the same finger draws a line across her throat. *She's here*, Daddy whispers in my ear.

'Abigail, did you hear what I said?'

Tom's face eclipses the woman for a second. A smile and a nod is all it takes. When he retreats, the woman's gone.

21. Present day

Later that day, grief eats me raw. It devours everything inside, like the fire consumed the inside of our house. Even an afternoon with Tom and the twins hasn't dampened its flames. Mrs Calhoun and Birdie escort me down the stairs, down to the old ballroom, their pleas still rattling inside my head — *It ain't healthy for you to stay in your or Mrs Favreau's room all day. Getting back to normal will help.* Apparently normal is having dinner with the rest of Newhaven, watching families eating together.

The old ballroom never fails to impress me. Garlands of fairy lights, nailed to the once delicate plaster cornice of flowers, twinkle like tangled stars. I remember stepping into this room for the very first time. Head tilted up at the chandelier, sprawling like a spider web frozen with mildew, thinking it was the biggest, most beautiful thing I had ever seen.

Eyes flicker to me with every step I take, all those unanswered questions and lost memories kindling for the flames of their suspicion. They look at me. They think I don't notice. Here I stand, a thing to be observed, every gesture, facial expression, word or silence to be dissected for a clue as to whether I'm faking it. Once the last latecomer sits down Pastor Abernathy starts to say grace, but his words are interrupted by my ragged cough, gathering strength as it unspools and billows. I double over in my chair. The air in the room is loaded with the smell of barbecued meat. The emptiness inside fills with images of charred remains on the living-room floor. The cough intensifies, pulls at the skin of my cheeks, liquefies my eyes. People around me blur but not enough to miss the scared looks, mothers' hands pulling their children closer to them. My body fights for a normal breath, but the air in my throat roars as if something is clawing its way out. Panic rises in my chest. A hand rubs my back. Mom used to do that. The memory pinches my heart. Her touch has been burned and sealed inside an urn. The next inhale bends me backwards. Someone screams.

The room belongs to darkness and a sleeping silhouette. After locking the door, I crawl under the table where the chair hides me. Only me, Mrs Favreau and the silence. In the moonlight the scarred skin around her eyes and mouth faintly glows. I swear sometimes you can still smell the bleach on her skin. I can't fathom how corrupted your mind must be to harm yourself that way. The cough's gone, along with the stench of cooked meat, outrun somewhere between the ballroom and the eaves. Nobody's come after me. Deep breaths in and out lull my heart, guide it back to its normal rhythm. Mrs Favreau sleeps in her single bed, oblivious to my presence.

I still don't have any answers for them – Newhaven, the cops, Tom. Their patience is thinning out, I can see it. Today's sermon still resonates in my head. Pastor Abernathy paced the platform, the air in the church fizzing with devotion and the need for answers.

'Outsiders hate the work we do. We show them there's a better way to live, remind them of the sins they garnish their purposeless existence with. They know we're right and they'll do anything in their power to sabotage and discourage us. Do anything to hurt us.'

He abruptly stopped pacing, and his gaze dragged over the whole congregation. From the newly created silence rose the frantic whirr of handheld paper fans like fretting heartbeats.

'Anything like starting a fire in the home of our beloved Pastor Heywood. We can't rule out that the fire isn't a result of that hatred. We need to be vigilant. We know where the police stand. They can't be trusted. We need to turn inwards and depend on each other. Increase patrols – and men, be sure to carry wherever you go.'

Daddy had warned me about the hatred the outside had for us. He'd sat at the kitchen table reminding me every time those damn blue letters showed up – proof that someone outside wished us harm. I crawl out of my hiding place, before dusting myself off. As I walk back to my room, thoughts gather into a plan. If these hate-filled letters could have found their way into our home, the hands that wrote them could have lit the match. A shiver tumbles down my spine at the idea anybody could hate us enough to want to burn us down.

From: Jeb Abernathy
Date: Sunday, September 4, 2022 at 3:50 PM
To: Cameron McPherson
Subject: Re: Concerns – guidance needed

Dear Pastor McPherson,

I pray that this email finds you well.

I am reaching out to you again for guidance. I am afraid that Abigail isn't improving; on the contrary, I feel that her faith is deteriorating. She hasn't recovered any of her memories, but even worse, the other night at dinner she became violently ill with a coughing fit as we said grace, as if the words of our Lord were making her physically sick. She's causing more and more disruption.

A lot of the congregation are becoming suspicious, and several husbands have instructed their wives to keep their children away from her. She still says that she cannot remember that day she went missing before the fire. I'm afraid something has happened and some evil has taken root inside her. We are praying for her salvation, but I worry we're losing the battle.

Under His guidance. Have a blessed day.

Pastor Jeb Abernathy

22. July

I rummaged through the deserted kitchen. Faint sounds of clattering keys and light coughs drifted through the open door. The men were busy preaching online, saving souls on forums. I smiled at the idea of Mr Garrett hunched over the keyboard, two fingers jabbing the keys, brow creased in concentration.

The bottle of sweet tea joined the cornbread on the counter. No one would miss it, one among so many. Sharing food was a Christian thing to do. I reckoned Summer needed some proper food, not the over-processed junk that rotted your brain and flooded stores like the Piggly Wiggly or the vending machine at the motel she stayed at. After seeing her at the diner, she hadn't struck me as a healthy eater. This package would show her how we take care of our own, not just spiritually. She had to see the positives.

Body half-wedged in one of the pantries, I scanned the shelves for the jars of honey – the finishing touch. It wasn't often I had the Newhaven kitchen to myself. A big group had gone to Charlotte to preach outside the women's shelter. The fact I wasn't among them stuck in my throat. Mom moved somewhere upstairs. Nothing could dislodge her from Newhaven, her outreach work mainly being confined to helping newcomers settle and learn to navigate their new environment. She had a knack for putting single mothers at ease.

My fingers grazed a jar of honey, still slightly out of reach.

Someone had stashed them way down the back. Likely away from the little ones' hands, especially after little Michael Pruitt demolished three jars and got sick all over the fresh laundry. My lips twitched at the memory.

'Feeling a bit peckish?'

The question sent a jolt down my spine; my head banged against the top shelf.

'What you doin' here?' Men didn't belong in the kitchen unless they were boys under ten, or they'd got lost.

Tom leaned against the doorframe, hands tucked under his armpits, his gaze on the supplies on the counter, my crimes on display. I jumped in front of them, fingers twisting the end of my braid.

'Need help?'

His damp blond curls were plastered to his cheeks and the back of his neck, and his face glistened under a sheen of perspiration. The mole under his eye seemed darker than usual. He must have been working on the new animal enclosure. His sodden t-shirt stuck in patches to his torso, the outline of his chest visible. His musky smell reached me across the room. My mouth dried up. Chewing on my bottom lip I simply shook my head like some kind of mute.

'Don't worry, I won't tell. It can be our little secret.' He winked, raking his fingers through his hair.

'There ain't nothin' to tell. I was just feelin' hungry, that's all.' I put the cornbread back into the pantry. 'I'd better go.'

'Don't leave on my account.'

His body filled the doorway, leaving no space for me. The musky smell radiated from him, the same odour that followed Daddy home after he spent a day labouring outside. He called it the smell of hard work and providing for your family. I waited, my tongue rubbing against my front teeth, for the joke to be over and Tom to move out of my way. My silence pushed one corner of his mouth into a lopsided smile. His cheek dimpled. I never noticed that before. His gaze latched on mine and wouldn't let go.

'Why don't you like me?'

'I don't. Not like you. I mean, I don't hate you, but I don't like you either. I don't really feel anythin' about you. I mean . . . You know what I mean.'

My word salad extended the smile on his face. A warm flush of embarrassment crept up my neck. If I could just get past him.

'Why are you here, anyway?' I asked.

'I'm hankering for something. Something sweet like a peach.'

I shook my head. 'Not sure we got any.'

He picked up my braid and rolled the end between his fingers like Zach had that day in the alley when Summer rescued me. My body went very still, apart from the skin at the back of my neck, bristling.

'You know you remind me of someone. She was sweet too.'

My braid fell back on my chest. My body sprang into action and I ducked under his arm, but he grabbed my wrist and pulled me against him. My heart thumped in my chest. His arm clamped high around my waist, his hand resting dangerously close to my breast. A scream jammed in my throat, suffocating me. Pinned against him, he swayed us to the tune of an invisible melody. I should've pushed him away, I should've screamed, I should've done something, anything. But I froze, staying in his embrace while his thumb stroked the curve of my breast, and a terrifying hardness pressed on my hip. My fear reflected in his face, it dislocated his mouth into another lopsided smile, creeping up on the left side towards the mole under his eye. His whole face twisted in a malevolent smirk, eyes shining with intent.

I didn't want to be there for what would happen next. I swallowed hard. 'Please let me go.' My voice sounded thick.

'You're going to need a husband soon.'

'C'mon, Tom.'

'How does it go? Oh, yes, "Wives, submit to your husbands as to the Lord. For the husband is the head of the wife as Christ is the head of the church." See? I know my scriptures. What do you say?'

He leaned, his face so close he was only eyes, a giant mole, just a detail, cruel, obliterating the world of the kitchen. Something yeasty lingered on his breath. It blew against my lips. My mouth dried up.

'Want to be my wife, Abigail?'

'Please . . .'

The rest of the words dissolved inside his mouth as his tongue slithered between my lips, pushing past the barrage of my teeth, invading my mouth. I tasted his stale breath along with the salt of tears pooling at the corners of my lips. The warmth of his saliva mingled with mine. His hand crept up and cupped my breast. Bile and a sudden urge to fight burned my throat. My fists pummelled his shoulders, but the vice of his embrace just tightened around me and his hardness dug into my hip. His hand molested my breast, pinching the nipple so hard I whimpered. He ate that scream too. The fatality of the situation sunk into my flesh, and my body slackened in his arms, waiting for the moment it would all be over. His arms finally fell to his sides, and his mouth released mine. I glimpsed a moment when he was distracted by his own victory. Abandoning everything, I bolted out of the pantry, out of Newhaven, crashing into Mrs Calhoun in the entrance hall.

'Watch out,' she said, the warning unable to catch up to me as I leapt over the porch steps.

Mom sat on the sofa repairing a pair of Daddy's pants, a basketful of more work at her feet. In another life she couldn't even fix a loose button. We wore clothes until they fell apart and then we got new ones at the thrift store. Finding new clothes felt like a scavenger hunt back then.

The memory pinched my already battered heart. Mom barely had the time to put her work down before I flung myself at her.

'What is it, sweetheart?'

The words poured out of me, sentences chopped by sobs and sniffles. I wiped my nose with the back of my hand, trying to clear the way for all I had to say.

'Careful, needles,' Mom said, holding me away from the pants still on her lap. After what Tom had just done needles couldn't hurt me. My heart had been ripped apart while still staying in the same place. 'Just slow down —'

'He kissed me. And . . . and he touched me.' I sunk to my knees, laying my head on her lap as an offering to be comforted. She stroked my cheek, and it eased the knot in my chest.

'You're not making sense. Who kissed you?'

'Tom. Tom did.'

Her legs tensed beneath my cheek, and silence fell on us, heavy like a coffin's lid. I translated her silence as her processing the horror of what I had just been through. Someone hurt her baby, someone molested her own flesh, the one she took nine months to shape into her daughter. The outrage could be enough to wake up the spirit of my old mom. *Thou shalt*

122

not covet thy neighbour's wife, but what about your pastor's daughter? Maybe my ordeal was what would get Tom kicked out.

'And what did you do?'

'I left as soon as I could. Ran straight here. I even bumped into Mrs Calhoun on my way back. I reckon I should apologise to her.'

My head flopped on the sofa as she sprang off it without warning, the soft velvet against my cheek of no comfort.

'I have to tell your dad.'

'What? No, Mom, please.' Daddy would be crushed, and I felt so ashamed. I should've screamed, scratched him. I was so stupid. Daddy was already disappointed in me. This would forever change how he saw me.

'Stay here.'

'Please, don't leave me.'

But she had already turned into footsteps in the hallway.

'Please, I need you now.'

The thump of the front door punctuated my plea.

'Mom!' The word burned, the rawness of it scraping the back of my throat. She was merely on the other side of the lawn but she'd never felt so far away.

23. Present day

Last evening's idea has solidified overnight into a certainty – the answer's in the blue letters. Back at Hunters Cottage, the smell of death forces me to breathe through my mouth. The kitchen stands almost intact. The blaze didn't unleash its carnage here. If you didn't know what happened outside these walls you couldn't guess from looking. Still, my eyes pick out the differences. My hands ache to grab a broom and start sweeping. Mom kept her kitchen spotless, but the floor's been trampled by a dozen feet in boots that have left their marks and smudges behind. Mom. The memory of her sparks a different kind of blaze in my chest.

I hover at the office threshold. It feels wrong to be in here without Daddy. Like trespassing. The desk looms in the middle of the room; somehow it looks smaller without his imposing presence behind it. The room has been stripped of its previous aura. He's really gone. The reality punches me in the throat and my heart hammers in my chest.

Out of nowhere a familiar voice lets me know I'm not alone.

'I thought maybe you wanted some company.'

'Yes, that'd be good. Thanks, Tom,' I say with a shaky voice.

Without another word he takes my hand, and we step into the room like you'd jump off a cliff into a swimming hole. Once inside, the desk draws me. I run a finger along the top, the grain soft and smooth under my skin. My finger follows the faint half-moon of a scar in the wood from when I had brought Daddy a glass of sweet tea and forgotten to put it on the coaster. I must have been seven. It wasn't long after we moved into the house, after Pastor Favreau had insisted we take it over from him. I had cried so hard when I realised my mistake. Daddy had sat on the sofa, pulling me on his lap, promising that no, I wouldn't go to hell just because I forgot the coaster.

'So, what are we doing here?'

'I'm lookin' for somethin'. We got these letters . . . I reckon they might be important and I'm hopin' Daddy kept them.'

He smiles, and for a second his eyes shine like Daddy's used to. He squeezes my hand, and I feel like maybe I ain't alone in this. The idea of tethering myself to his hand, to him, flits in my mind – a way to stop that endless feeling of slipping under.

'Should we start with the desk?'

I nod, and offer him a wry smile. We divide the work, each taking a side and a row of drawers. Tom gets to work straight away, belongings rattling under his hands as he explores the contents of the first drawer. Mine hesitate. Deep breath in and I open the top drawer, which ends up being a shallow tray filled with pens, paper clips and other stationery supplies. The next one yields more promise, filled with stacks of papers and a few notebooks. My fingers flick through the pages before upending the books, but nothing falls out of them.

'Is this what you're looking for?'

My heart skips a beat at his question. Tom holds a plain window envelope with a printed address visible through it. My heart resumes a regular rhythm with a tinge of disappointment.

'No. It should be a blue envelope.'

'On it, ma'am.' He adds a mock military salute that curls the corners of my mouth.

We resume our search. The next drawer houses a suspended file system, the first one labelled 'Sermons'. My throat constricts at the legal pad in my hands, its pages darkened with Daddy's slanted writing. His written words were made of sharp, jagged lines, whereas his speech was all about elongated consonants and rounded vowels. I kneel down and flick through until the last half-written sermon. The reality that it will never be finished mists my eyes. A corner of blue swims behind the wall of tears and I drop the pad. I reach out for the last file at the very back of the drawer.

The letter weighs heavily in the centre of my hand, block caps screaming our address, the sender's anger visible in the furrows the pen has scratched into the paper. The stamp – a US flag flapping in an invisible wind – is slightly askew. It had met with someone's tongue, soaked up their saliva along with their hatred for us. Tom has abandoned his side of the desk and is now kneeling beside me, chin lightly resting on my shoulder.

'Is that one of them?'

I nod as my finger runs along the pristine top edge of the envelope. Daddy never had the chance to check its contents.

'Should we open it?'

'All right.'

In the absence of a letter opener, my finger slips under one of the corners. The envelope comes apart in ragged edges. The single piece of folded paper inside is the same cornflower blue. It trembles in my hands as we both absorb the horror of the short message. So much hatred concentrated within such a small piece of paper.

ONE NIGHT I'M GONNA COME INSIDE YOUR HOUSE WHEN YOU'RE SLEEPING . . . YOU'LL NEVER KNOW WHICH DAY WILL BE YOUR FAMILY'S LAST.

'That's quite something,' Tom says, his breath warm on my ear.

'I know.'

The letter was proof – that much hatred could certainly fuel the desire to burn us in a fire. I stuff the letter back in the envelope and then into my pocket. We stand, and the room swims in front of me. Tom's hand finds its way under my elbow for support.

'You need some fresh air.'

In the hallway, the staircase and the second floor beckon me.

'There's a thing I gotta do,' I say.

My head tilts towards the ceiling, my mind already filled with what's waiting upstairs. That's not why I came, but now I'm here I've got to do it. Tom takes a few steps towards the stairs, but I don't follow. When he doesn't feel my presence behind him, he turns. My tongue runs against the back of my front teeth. He's been so nice, I feel terrible for not wanting him around for this next part.

'Do you mind?'

'I'll wait for you outside.'

I shouldn't be here. The firefighters said the floor could collapse and send the main bedroom crashing into the front room. Their clothes hang side by side in the wardrobe like outlines of people waiting to be filled and given life. The laundry hamper waits next to it. I pull one of Mom's dresses to me and press the fabric to my face. The smell brings tears to my eyes. I search for memories in the folds of fabric. She's everywhere and nowhere at once. Grief pushes my body to the ground and reshapes it into a ball. In the privacy of their bedroom the tears finally come in heaves and sobs, and still that terrifying worry squirms in the pit of my stomach that I might be responsible for some of it or worse. *What have you done, Abigail?* Mom's scent wraps itself around me – fresh soap and lavender – until another replaces it, an acrid, rusty smell. A memory hitches a ride on that smell and rises from the swamp of my mind, the image sharp – flames licking the fabric of Mom's dress, feeding on the blood drenching it . . . blood.

Oh Lord, there was so much blood.

AUDIO FILE #8

Audio Quality: Poor

[Voice A]:   Female
[Voice B]:   Female

[Voice A]:   Is it OK (...) you?
[Voice B]:   (...) course.

[Next section too damaged to recover.]

[Voice A]:   What's your dad like? (...)
[Voice B]:   What do you mean? My daddy's great.
              I love him.
[Voice A]:   But how is it being raised by a man who
              believes that you're inferior, or less than
              because of your gender.
[Voice B]:   It ain't like that. Dad thinks men and women
              are equals, it's just their duties and responsi-
              bilities that are different. I agree with him.
              Mama agrees with him too. It's her choice to
              stay at home and raise her children.
[Voice A]:   Is that a widespread (*long exhale*) belief?
[Voice B]:   Some say Daddy and other men like him are
              soft, I think they're a minority, but ...

[Voice A]:   But what?

[Voice B]:   I heard him talk the other day with my best friend's dad. Her daddy said to mine that he was too soft with me, and he was letting me run wild and it didn't reflect well on him. It showed weakness. I never liked him, but now I feel even more sorry for my friend Abigail.

24. July

Daddy announced his arrival with heavy footsteps. I'd parked my body on the sofa, face washed and rubbed clean, but my mind was all over the place, fretting like a possum in a cage.

The cushions slanted under his weight, my body sliding towards his. The tip of my tongue rubbed against my front teeth. Shame coated the back of my throat and my eyes focused on the ground. A film of dust covered his shoes. He would buff them out later on. He liked shiny shoes, a job he didn't trust anybody but himself to do. His own father taught him. It might have been one of the only times he spoke of his dad. He mentioned him one other time to say he was a small man, but I wasn't sure he meant his height.

I peeked through my lashes. Mom's willowy silhouette stood behind him. Even after all those years her drastic weight-loss always surprised me. Faith and an earnest life had sharpened her features, burned away the laziness and lust that had congealed within her flesh, honed her muscles with purpose, unearthed furrows between her ribs, skin tight over the architecture of bones that held her together along with her new-found faith.

'Your mama told me what happened.' The flat tone of his voice didn't offer any clues to his feelings. 'She said it was Tom.'

His sentence didn't curve into a question but still I nodded, my throat too constricted for even a simple yes. After that, he made me retell him everything that happened in

Newhaven's kitchen. A hand on my knee, eyes locked on mine, he listened, nodding or frowning in all the right places. My voice grew more confident, but when I tripped over the memory of Tom's hardness, or the bruise of his kiss, Daddy squeezed my hand. The end of the story took everything out of me and left me hollow.

Thin-lipped, he wore a solemn expression so different from Mom's wild-eyed reaction to the same story. I wondered how much trouble Tom would be in and how much of a public display would be made. His guilt perhaps paraded as a cautionary tale. The whole of Newhaven would know – all the excruciating details offered up to be dissected, weighed, discussed. What happened would live behind everybody's gaze, tainting the way they looked at me evermore, turning the future into a mirror reflecting the incident over and over again. It would become inescapable. It would've been easier to just keep quiet and forget about the whole thing.

He palmed his beard; behind him Mom shifted her weight from one foot to the other.

'What did you do, Abigail?'

'Like I told Mom, I ran straight home –'

'No. What did you do?'

The words dragged out of him, this time laden with implication. The drawl in his tone elongated my name as if trying to eviscerate it with disappointment. Each word nailed me to the spot. He was supposed to leap off that sofa with indignation and bring fire and brimstone raining down onto Tom. He was supposed to sweep me into his arms and make everything all right again. I wasn't some kind of feminist flaunting myself to men. A flush of embarrassment burned my cheeks. Before my mind could form a response he continued.

'A man doesn't act this way unless provoked.'

His accusation bolted through me like lightning. My hands jerked back but they were trapped by the firm pressure of fingers much stronger than mine. His unbridled love and care had been an unwavering constant in my life, the knowledge he would always be on my side. I was his little girl. Even at almost eighteen I was still his little girl, as he liked to tease me. Now the security of his love had been stripped away. He hadn't looked at me the same way since the Parkerville incident. And now his assumption of my guilt sent the room spinning.

'I didn't do nothin'.'

'Why were you in the kitchen?'

'I . . . I wanted to bring some sweet tea and molasses cookies home. For the twins. But I didn't do nothin'.'

'No? Like you didn't do nothin' when you sneaked off to Parkerville? Think.' His dig stung. His voice stayed smooth, the same familiar tone he used during Sunday service to welcome and guide the congregation inside the church.

I journeyed back to the kitchen. Standing in a corner of my mind I watched myself, body half-buried in the pantry, rummaging for food to bring Summer – not the twins. So Daddy was right. I already wasn't being entirely honest. Under his palms, my hands felt clammy. Back inside my mind, Tom walked into the room to the sight of my body burrowed deep in the cupboard. *Feeling a bit peckish?* he had said. Men could be tempted, which is why women had to stay modest – not to become an instrument for the devil and devilish thoughts. Flesh was weak.

'He surprised me. I didn't hear him coming in.'

'I see. Did you fiddle with your braid like you usually do, grabbing it from the back, arching yourself?' The question

133

got dragged by his Southern drawl, making it sound heavy with implication.

There was no need to respond; the answer somehow smeared itself all over my face as it reflected in his eyes.

'There you have it, flaunting yourself, chest on display. What did you expect? *A man cannot walk on hot coals, without his feet being scorched.*'

'I didn't do it on purpose.'

'You gotta learn to restrain yourself, be aware of what you are. Otherwise, you're askin' for it, and you can't blame a man like Tom for actin' out. Spirit is willin', but the flesh is weak. Don't lead him into temptation. You've changed, Abigail. Where's my little girl gone? This kind of behaviour reflects badly on you and this whole family.'

His hands squeezed mine too tight. I wanted to run to my room, but he wouldn't let me leave.

'You ain't a child no more. You're soon eighteen. You can't walk around flaunting yourself like one of those Parkerville whores.'

I flinched at the slur. He'd never used such a horrible word to describe me before, but it was nothing compared to his next words which liquefied my insides.

'I'm ashamed to call you my daughter.'

25. Present day

After discovering the new letter at Hunters Cottage, Tom heads to the computer room for an afternoon of online outreach, while I haunt my room in the attic. He's promised to come fetch me later. The sweltering heat keeps me company while I bide my time. They moved me up to an empty room under the eaves after the coughing incident. The only other occupant of this floor is Mrs Favreau, and the clattering of keys from her typewriter going off at all hours. I really wish Pastor Favreau hadn't given it to her fifty years ago.

From the window I see them – men like dark ants against the yellow grass, searching for something. I can just make out the patches on their uniforms and their wrap-around sunglasses. In between us is the ghost of me in the glass. More stray hairs have escaped my braid. It hangs loose, fraying edges that used to keep me together. My fingers tighten on the fork in my hand. A prong eats into the soft wood of the windowsill. Scratching words which make no sense – *Solve, Et* – but it keeps me busy and distracted. I understand now why Mrs Favreau uses the typewriter so much. From the grooves in the wood the smell of reeds and muddy water rises, the heat of the sun baking my skin, someone else's laughter in my head.

They walk past the hanging tree. Something catches my eye, a body in a nightdress and braid, swinging from a low branch. Before I can make sense of it, the image disappears behind the fog of my breath hitting the glass. I quickly wipe it with my arm, but instead of a body it's just a lanky piece of Spanish moss rocked by the wind. The blue letter weighs heavy in my pocket. I planned to give it to Pastor Abernathy tonight. Now I have a shot at giving it to *them*, all of them. But a kernel of doubt still lodges at the back of my throat. They wait for my memories, but I still don't have any full ones to give them, just flashes of images that don't make no sense and I'm scared what they would think. At least the letter proves that Pastor Abernathy might be correct about a threat from the outside.

Out on the lawn, Mrs Calhoun comes to greet them, no longer ants but tiny deputies. Even from this height her red hair is unmissable. Wade Pruitt accompanies her, his rifle slung low in front. An officer's hand rests lightly on his own holstered gun. She motions at them, arms milling the air, barring the way. My fingers play with the torn edges of the envelope as I rehearse the words for the deputies about the origin of the letters.

A click interrupts my thoughts. The noise jolts me to my feet. The door knob rattles but the door doesn't budge.

'Hey? Is someone out there?'

I try the handle. The door rattles furiously under my growing annoyance. The brass knob slides in my sweaty palm.

'Hey! I'm locked in.'

Muffled words and raised voices travel up to my window. If I don't hurry they'll be gone, and they won't know. Of all the days, it has to happen today. This is the worst timing ever. The door shakes violently against my growing exasperation. I'm going to miss them. Frustration is gathering in my throat as a low rumble, when the door gives way and my body flies backward. Jackson stands in the doorframe in all his lankiness, hand clenched around his rubber ball.

136

'Jackson? Why'd you lock me in for?'

His fingers strangle the ball before he takes a step towards me. 'I didn't. I'm the one who let you out.'

I race past him and down the stairs. Voices rise from the entrance, amplified by the high ceilings.

'Look . . .' The word is whipped with exasperation. My mind shapes a body for that disembodied voice – plump face and a pop of grey hair. I fashioned him in the image of the officer in the backyard that first day.

'We need to speak to her. You can make it easy or we can make things complicated for you. When was the last time DSS came for a visit –?'

'I reckon y'all should go.' Pastor Abernathy's voice cleaves through the officer's sentence. 'Now.'

I'd never heard Pastor Abernathy raise his voice that way before, asserting his authority. In that moment, Daddy's ghost haunts him. Silence follows as I glimpse from the mezzanine the legs of a cop uniform disappear through the double doors and into the blinding whiteness of the outside. My mouth opens, but Mrs Calhoun's voice fills the space.

'They ain't leavin' us alone as long as she's here.'

Her comment stops me cold, and I drop to my knees. Pastor Abernathy sighs heavily. They stand slightly out of sight.

'That worries me too, but would it be fair to hand over responsibility to another congregation?'

The idea of being separated from Sarah and the twins works its way under my skin, more uncomfortable than the sweat drenching my back. I might not be fit to look after them, but I can still watch them grow up. They can't just send me away.

'I've been asking Pastor McPherson for guidance about

what to do with her. After what happened with Elizabeth Favreau, Abigail's behaviour worries me.'

The mention of my name has birthed a silence between them. My mind places them on Newhaven's front steps, Pastor Abernathy palming his beard as he always does before starting a sermon, and Mrs Calhoun looking at him expectantly. Even when standing she always seems to be looking up to him.

'I worry about her. The nightmares, her apathy. It's like she doesn't care about nothin'. The girl has lost her parents and she doesn't even cry. And where did she go missin' that day? Something ain't right there. Even before, the lies, the outbursts . . . Things haven't been right with her for a while. If you ask me, the devil's got into that girl.'

'I agree, the amnesia feels . . . convenient, and the previous issues with her behaviour, like you say . . . Anyway, not here. Let's go to the office.' Their footsteps echo inside the foyer. 'I don't know, maybe a change of scenery would help.'

Fear blazes through my body at the idea of being cast away even for a short period. I shove the letter deep in my pocket as I tiptoe back from my hiding place on the mezzanine to the second floor and Mrs Calhoun's room. The pink wallpaper gives it a peaceful feel and contrasts with the mahogany floor. Baby Sarah barely stirs when I lift her out of her bassinet. She kicks her little legs, and her smile coaxes mine out of hiding. My face buries in the soft down of her hair, surrounding myself with her baby smell like warm biscuits. I whisper the lullaby Mom sang to her. She coos in recognition and her fingers bury themselves in the loops of my braid.

Pastor Abernathy's comments have followed me here. The answer waits for me in Sarah's blue eyes, in the weight of her body in my arms, the weight of my responsibilities. I won't give them no more reasons to send me away.

Back under the eaves, Jackson slumps against a cot frame, his ball bouncing back and forth. On the mattress, a small pile of blueberries is nestled on his handkerchief. I grab a couple before settling next to him. I pop one in my mouth; it bursts under my teeth, the sweetness hitting my tongue before the sourness screws up my face. My hands still smell like baby Sarah, her warmth still nestled in the crook of my arm.

'I'm gonna go down and help Calhoun with dinner.'

'Why're you helping them? Don't you see how they're treatin' you?' The ball smacks the wall before flying back into his hand. 'Half of them think you did it, that you've been acting out for weeks before the fire and you've been unreliable. The other half believe the conspiracy theories Pastor Abernathy feeds them at Sunday service, that the rest of the world hates us so much that they've tried to burn us to the ground.'

I flinch at the idea half of Newhaven blames me for the fire. But how can I blame them when those same doubts sometimes cross my mind late at night. Actions speak louder than words. I need to show them my value as a member of this community, that my place is at Newhaven with the twins and Sarah.

'They're the only family I've got left.'

'Does that include Tom?'

His question is met by my silence. Tom. Tom who checked up on me that night I snuck into Hunters Cottage, who helped me search the office. I remember the slight pressure of his chin on my shoulder, the shiver down my back. We might not have got on in the past, but my short-term memory loss has given us a clean slate. I'd like to think God sent him

139

to Newhaven as He knew I'd need support after Mom and Daddy were gone. I pop another blueberry in my mouth. It rolls around on my tongue.

The ball stops. Jackson's hand rakes through the mass of his dark hair, revealing the red beginnings of a bruise, buried at the hairline. Boys and their bruises; the twins always harvest a collection from playing. You'd think Jackson would've grown out of them by now.

'You know Tom's the one who locked you in, right?'

The blueberry lodges in the back of my throat. It hurts to swallow it. Jackson searches my face for the aftermath to his comment, but he's just a kid, surely he saw wrong. Why would Tom do that when we've been getting on so well? That makes no sense at all.

AUDIO FILE #9

Audio Quality: Poor

[Voice A]:   Female
[Voice B]:   Male

[First minute too damaged to recover.]

[Voice A]:   Thank (...) talking to me.
[Voice B]:   (...) problem.
[Voice A]:   Why do you think people join the NABC? It's not like just going to church, you're leaving everything behind to move into a new community. What makes people do that?
[Voice B]:   People (...) searching (...) answers and guidance on how to live, (...) Lord has plenty of both for those who listen. (...) are looking for connection, they are searching for family. (...) congregation and compound is a family on its own.
[Voice A]:   Family? What (...) allegation (...) breaks family. What about people who said their loved one joined the church (...) cut all contacts soon after? Is it really that safe a place? What kind of family acts like that?

[Rest of recording too damaged to recover.]

26. Three weeks before the fire

The air inside the barn stank with trampled hay and animal sweat. Still, it was better than Newhaven when I could run into Tom. I breathed through my mouth as I patted Bessie's damp neck. At the top of the ladder, the privacy of the loft called to me.

I collapsed into a mattress of straw. Sleep had exhausted me the night before. My dreams had plucked me out of my bedroom and dropped me back in Newhaven's kitchen, fear freezing me to the spot as Tom peeled the clothes off my body like Daddy would peel a hard-boiled egg. Behind him, Tania's disarticulated body bled over the chequered floor. Her fingers curled with life, her mouth curved around phantom words. I wanted to help her, but Daddy had appeared between us, staring at me with dead eyes. *The Lord always finds a way to punish the wicked*, he said. The bruise of Tom's kiss throbbed on my lips. I bolted upright in my bed, fear dampening my back and the fold between my breasts, my breath shallow.

Straw tickled the backs of my arms. An aching tiredness weighted my lids, eye-blinks slurred until my lids were more closed than open. But before I drifted off, raised voices inched towards the entrance.

'Don't you walk away from me, son!'

The words rumbled like thunder during a summer storm, and my body flattened against the floor of the hayloft.

Through a gap between floorboards I glimpsed Jackson scurrying inside. His father charged through the entrance, shoulders rising with tension. Jackson backed against Bessie's stall. Mr Caine grabbed Jackson by the jaw, almost lifting him off the ground. My breathing slowed at the sudden display of violence.

'You've been running your mouth to Pastor Heywood, you little shit.'

'No, sir, I didn't.'

'Don't you lie to me, son. Pastor Heywood talked to me about the "concerns" you have.'

A darkness veiled Jackson's eyes before they clouded with tears.

'As your father and the head of the family, I'll discipline you any damn way I please. Maybe, if you just stop acting like a pussy and behaved like a man, I wouldn't have to work you so hard.' Mr Caine jammed his face close to Jackson's. 'Is that understood?'

'Yes. Sir.' The words barely escaped through Jackson's clenched jaw.

Mr Caine ended the conversation by tossing Jackson back into one of the supporting posts. The back of his head connected hard with the wood. I winced in sympathy and clamped my hand over my mouth, smothering a whimper.

Mr Caine stormed out. Jackson kneeled on the floor, his tears creating a little puddle of mud on the ground. I remained in the hayloft. I didn't know what to say. I couldn't reconcile Mr Caine's violent outburst with Newhaven's values. I watched as his hurt curdled into anger; his fist pummelled the earth over and over, each blow punctuated by a 'Fuck you, Pastor Heywood!' Nobody at Newhaven had ever shown anger or even resentment towards Daddy. I stayed up there, feeling complicit in my silence. It took an eternity before Jackson dragged himself out of the barn. Outside, pot-bellied clouds the colour of old bruises had hijacked the sky, the air heavy with the day's violence.

27.

The hallway at Hunters Cottage was crowded with shadows. I walked down towards the kitchen, distracted by the images of what had just happened to Jackson. My thoughts knotted every which way. I'd stumbled into some alternate reality where the outside darkness had infiltrated Newhaven. A couple of feet away from the kitchen, words escaped through a sliver of open door.

'I don't want Abigail to ever go back to Parkerville or anywhere else.' Mom's voice fretted with anxiety.

The response was too quiet to make sense of.

'But what if they spot her?'

Spot me? I didn't understand what she was talking about. Fresh from the barn, I'd stumbled onto more secrets. I held my breath.

'. . . worryin'. Haven't I kept y'all safe all these years?' Daddy's voice said.

'But . . . what would they do . . . find us . . . ?'

'Have faith in your husband.'

The need for understanding pulled me forward. A floorboard creaked under my foot, and the kitchen fell silent. I hurried and pushed the door open. Mom busied herself around the kitchen while Daddy washed his hands, but their enactment of domestic life was tainted with an undertow of unease. They avoided each other's gaze, but focused on me at the same time. I pinned a smile on my face. The grime of the day clung to my parents in the sweat that dappled their skin, in their furrowed brows. Even the twins were slumped in a corner of the kitchen with no energy to push around their toy cars or jump on me. Today's heat had been brutal, and we all waited for the weather to turn violent.

'I worked in the barn,' I lied. 'I'll go wash.'

'Dinner's in ten minutes.'

Upstairs, I splashed water on my face, but still the day refused to let go, gathering in black crescents under my fingernails, in the recesses of my mind. Dizzy, I sat on the edge of the bath. I tried to banish the images of the attack in the barn, but they throbbed behind my eyes like a headache – Jackson's body slamming into the post, the thud when his skull connected with the wood. Parents must discipline their children, but Jackson didn't deserve this violence. He was such a quiet, sweet kid who loved to pick blueberries and always offered some to anybody he crossed paths with.

I needed to trust in the Lord. He had a reason for everything. But the words lacked conviction. I rubbed my eyes with the heel of my hands.

Daddy sat alone at the table. My heart felt so conflicted, pulling me apart. The urge to please him and regain his trust still dominated, but his reaction to what had happened to me in the kitchen with Tom had birthed a resentment. I could taste it, sour in the back of my mouth. The smell of so much food unsettled my stomach. Mom slipped into her seat, and the two of them at the family table brought back the hushed conversation I'd overheard earlier. Them keeping things away from me.

The room bathed in a heavy silence.

'Where are the twins?'

'Bed. It's only us tonight, darlin',' Daddy said.

I flinched inside at the word. How could he keep calling me that when his other words and actions told me he didn't believe me worthy enough to be a daughter?

The candles and two kerosene lamps cast a dim glow over the room and made long shadows of our faces, turning dinner into some kind of gloomy live tableau. The generator didn't survive the heat either. We ate in silence, our mouths too tired for juggling chewing and words. My fork mainly bullied my food around the plate.

Finally Daddy spoke. 'Owen Nolan stopped by today.'

'Is he all right?' Mom asked.

'He wanted to set a date for his wedding to Melanie Le Roux.'

'Isn't that a little soon? Melanie's still so . . . young.'

'Our Lord brought them together. Who are we to stand in their way? His wisdom will keep her safe and in her right place.' He patted Mom's hand and offered one of his benevolent smiles, which coaxed hers out too.

Melanie getting married? She was two years younger than me, and she stood closer to having her own husband and family than I was. Owen Nolan wouldn't be my choice though, his hair was a lanky grey and his face more wrinkled than a prune. His less-than-favourable aesthetics didn't stop a wave of confusion rising in my chest. Every girl wanted to get married and become a wife. It was what God intended. Was I falling behind? I stuffed a piece of chicken and some carrots in my mouth and chewed down on them.

'I also counselled Tom Vermont this afternoon.'

My fingers strangled the cutlery, knuckles white. The candles flickered in the middle of the table. The next thirty seconds unfolded amid a tense silence only nicked by the

147

screeches of knives on porcelain. I pushed a piece of chicken around my plate.

'The incident in the kitchen shook his faith and I've been helpin' him. Flesh is weak, but can be controlled with a mind strengthened by God.'

My stomach clenched in response to the mention of Tom's distress, and how the event affected him. I felt Daddy's words feed the resentment growing inside me.

'May I be excused?'

'Why should we excuse you?' Daddy asked.

'I ain't feeling well.' The phantom headache from earlier now pressed behind my eyes. Outside the window, a flash of blue light illuminated the room. Dark clouds had snuffed out the day and night had moved in early.

'I don't reckon that's it,' he said, his eyes and smile unwavering.

'It is. I got a headache. I just wanna get an early night.' I spoke slowly to keep at bay the crackling energy building inside. It gathered in the pit of my belly, in the tips of my fingers, creeping up the ladder of my ribs, vibrating in my bones. My fingers curled into a fist ready to strike my thigh.

'I wanna help you, Abigail, but how can I do that when you ain't being honest with me?'

Honest? The word waved behind my eyes like a red rag to a bull. Hypocrisy rearing its ugly head again. It wasn't just the word, but the disappointment it was laden with that did it. The storm gathering inside became too big for my small frame and something snapped.

'That's a lie.'

'Abigail!'

He held out his hand to Mom. 'Let her speak. How's that a lie?'

'You say you wanna help me. But the way you made me feel after what Tom did ... You made me feel so small and ... alone. How's that supposed to help me?'

'What did I –?'

'You ... you abandoned me.' My voice thickened with tears. 'You should've been on my side.' I didn't blink. I refused to cry in front of him. I wouldn't give him that power. Not tonight.

'That ain't what I did.'

'Course you did. And you called me a liar in front of everyone in Parkerville when you said I snuck out of Newhaven without your permission. I didn't lie. I forgot or misunderstood, but I didn't lie. I shouldn't be punished for that.'

'Remember Proverbs 19:18, "Discipline your children, for in that there is hope." Maybe you shouldn't be goin' to Parkerville for a while. It's for your own good.'

'Is that the only reason?'

'Of course. How you're acting right now speaks for itself. Look at you. I'm doin' this out of love.'

'How's this love when you blame me for what Tom did? That ain't fair. I ain't no feminist.'

Mom opened her mouth, but he held out his hand, smothering the words before they got out.

'Everything I do is because I love you, Abigail.' The word fed the fire inside me. Love. Abandoning me when I needed him the most, not believing me, hiding things from me ... You didn't do that to someone you loved.

'Goddammit, it ain't fair. *You* ain't fair –'

'Enough.' The word rolled out of him like thunder. 'I won't have you disrespect me or the Lord in my house. There're limits, especially after all I've done for you.'

'Mom, how can you let him –?'

149

'It's for your own good.' She stood between us, slumped shoulders, her eyes fixed on some imaginary point on the white tablecloth. 'Your father is right to keep you away from Parkerville.'

'No he ain't!'

'You don't understand. He keeps us safe.'

Keeps us safe from what? I wondered if it had anything to do with the blue letters. She avoided my eyes. Daddy walked around the table and slipped his arm around her shoulders; she moved into him.

'What about us, Mom? Just us girls?'

Something in the words ignited a flash in her eyes. The past flared in the room, bright like the storm outside. Daddy tensed next to her, fingers clenched around her arm.

'Please. Listen to your father.'

'He ain't . . . I can't. I'm sleepin' at Newhaven tonight.'

I ran out of the dining room and out of the house as a streak of lightning tore across the sky. I ran before I said something I would truly regret.

28.

The outline of the shack cut against a sky scarred with purple lightning, the carcass of the old truck beside it like a dog, faithful even in death. The next flash revealed a silhouette behind the wheel. My breath hitched in my throat. I stopped, my whole attention focused on the truck, wondering if I could make it to the shack before they got out – until the silhouette morphed back into what it really was, just the driver's seat. I slowly released the breath I'd been holding.

I hadn't stopped after I bolted towards Newhaven, turning towards the shack only once I was sure Mom and Daddy hadn't followed. The run through the woods and the swamp had tested my resolve, roots like unseen hands tripping me along the way, sending me tumbling to the ground a couple of times, soil filling my mouth and nostrils. A warped plank almost sent me over the edge of the boardwalk. Gusts of wind lashed at my body, but I pushed against them. I didn't bother brushing myself off every time I got up, dashing again through the darkness, not once looking back.

The front door whined open onto a dark and silent hallway. I wanted to be truly alone and the old shack felt like the right place. Another flash of lightning greeted me. The absence of thunder somehow made the storm scarier, like a scream without a voice. I tiptoed in, the place devoid of a presence, like a body which had lost its internal organs – the opposite of Newhaven. I shuddered. Being alone here still beat being trapped at a home festering with resentment. I turned into the living room at the same time as a round of lightning flashed inside. A snapshot of a sleeping bag stopped me in my track. Panic bolted through me. The air inside the room wrapped around me with a smoky taste to it, remnants of the tragedy still clinging to the atmosphere. I slowly back-tracked towards the entrance until a floorboard groaned under my weight. A draught teased the hair at the back of my neck.

'Fuck, you scared me.'

The voice ripped a scream out of me. Another flash illu-minated Summer, flat against the wall, box-cutter in hand. Determination had darkened her eyes and set her mouth into a thin line. A shudder ran down my spine. Another flash of lightning rearranged the lines of her face, her mouth slackened.

'What are you doin' here?' I asked.

'Me? What are *you* doing here? Are you allowed out this late?' She strode across the room against another curtain of lightning. The knife retreated into the back pocket of her denim cut-offs. Her t-shirt was knotted under her breasts, showing off her stomach.

'I needed . . . space to think.'

Before I could add anything else, a beam of light swung onto my face, blinding me.

'Shit. What happened to you?'

The flashlight highlighted the dirt on my sleeves, the front of my dress, my shins, and the scrapes on my hands. Several parts of my body hummed with pain. I must have looked an absolute mess, the sweat rolling off me. I felt so small, suddenly so tired. I should go back to Newhaven, like I said. Find an empty room to sleep in.

'Sit down.' She threw one of the sofa cushions on the

floor before disappearing into the kitchen. Its dust-crusted fabric felt rough under my hand.

A water bottle flew through the air and landed on my lap, startling me. A rag was wrapped around it. Summer swapped the handheld flashlight for a freestanding one she propped in the space between us. I stared at the bottle, unsure about her expectations, but my raw throat told me I could do with a drink after that run. I waited, stretching my indecisiveness to the edge of Summer's patience. She sighed, pinching the bridge of her nose, and that puff of air made me feel real small. Kneeling, she snatched the rag and bottle from the ground. She cleaned the grime off my skin, dabbed the grazes on my hands and legs. My eyes drifted towards the entrance. I expected Daddy's shape to fill the doorway in a flash of lightning, but it stood empty.

My skin tingled wherever Summer touched it. She held my wrist, wiping my grazed palm, my blood kicking under her fingertips. The gentleness with which she tended to my injuries surprised me. I expected her to look down on my clumsiness, but she didn't. Concentration drew little parentheses that framed her mouth. Her gestures reminded me of Mom, back when a grazed knee or hand were a part of our everyday life. She would alternate between dabbing antiseptic and blowing on the cut, her face close to my skin. Back when it was just us girls. The memory and her absence swelled in my chest.

Once she finished, Summer handed me the bottle. I gulped it down, rivulets running down the corners of my mouth, dampening the collar of my dress. I didn't realise how thirsty I was. A sound whipped my head around, water spilling down my chin. My heartbeat rose with apprehension. Seconds ticked down along with the beads of sweat running down my spine, but nobody rounded the corner.

A sense of safety washed over me, and I attacked the bottle again with greed. *The obedient daughter watches her manners.* To hell with the obedient daughter, Daddy and his holy judgement, Mom and her allegiance. I should feel ashamed, but the discovery that they were keeping something from me eased the guilt. *What if they find her*, they'd said. The door hadn't stopped those words from slipping out.

'The water's so cold.'

'Brought in some gas and got the generator working.' Summer slumped next to me, a cigarette in the corner of her mouth.

'How?'

'I'm good at figuring out stuff by myself. That and YouTube. Anyway, what happened?' The question rose on a plume of smoke. The earlier gentleness had retreated behind her usual cool exterior and pungent tobacco smell.

'Something happened.'

'Just spit it out.'

The sharpness of her tone nipped at me, and it all came pouring out – Newhaven's kitchen, Tom, his words, the humiliation, first by his hand, then Mom's, who told Daddy, and his questions, which robbed me of feeling attacked, of being a victim, how I would've been better off not saying anything. Summer listened, never interrupting, never asking questions. When I paused, unsure how to pin words to the chaos of emotions inside, she waited, burning time to ashes one cigarette after another. Each drag hollowed her cheeks, lips pinched tight against the filter. The lightning danced on her face, framed by hair wild with the humidity saturating the air. Finally came the fight at the dinner table that led me to run here. I had no more words. Still she didn't speak, her mouth pinched despite no cigarette, eyes narrowed into slits.

'What did you expect?'

The words pulled my brow into a frown.

'I mean, I hate to be a bitch, but you live with men who view women as possessions: something to be passed from father to husband.'

Her lack of sympathy stunned me. The sky unleashed its anger and a flash of lightning jolted through me.

'I ain't no possession. I ain't –'

She grabbed me by the shoulders. 'Of course you're not. *They're* in the wrong, not you.'

She was the last person I expected to be on my side – a stranger. She dropped her head until her gaze latched on mine. Once she got me in her sights she didn't let go. 'Listen to me, that guy, Tom, is an asshole and a predator. One of those guys who came here because he couldn't find what he was looking for in the real world. Forget what your dad said. It's not your fault.' I shook my head. She shook me. 'Look at me. You did nothing wrong. You're the victim here. It shouldn't have happened to you.'

Her gaze didn't waver. She believed every word she said. I collapsed against her chest. The gesture startled her, but with my head nestled in the hollow of her shoulder, I felt safe. My arms pushed through the gap between her arms and body and I hugged her waist, sobbing against her chest. Slowly her arms found their way around me and rested against my shoulders.

'I'm sorry. I'm sorry. You don't deserve shit like this. I'm so sorry. It's always the same. Different places, same old shit.'

I sniffed and nodded, unsure what she meant. The storm outside intensified, lightning thrashing across the sky. My emotions threw themselves against my ribs, crashing like waves splitting on rocks. Faces flashed in my mind – Tania's, Fleur's, Tom's, Daddy's.

'I can't breathe. I can't.'

'You need to let it all out. Don't let them smother you and how you feel.'

A small spark tingled at my fingertips, rippling outwards until the electricity from the storm raging outside coursed through my veins. It connected with a rage buried in my core where it had been festering, so deep it turned blood-dark. Now it flowed through me. In that moment, I hated my father. In that moment, bones felt like beautiful things to break.

'I hate him. I hate him. I hate him. So much.' I felt the anger foaming at my mouth with saliva.

'Good. Hold on to that feeling. Let it all out.'

Rage burned through me. I fed my memories of Daddy to imaginary flames, tossed in all of his words, his disappointment. I threw in the pages from 'The Obedient Daughter' manifesto. It escaped out of me in bursts of screams, it leapt out with all the tension in my muscles as I jumped around. I danced like I was possessed. The desire to burn it all down ignited every cell in my body. My fist stamped bruises into my thigh until Summer held a pillow in front of me. I pounded my anger into the soft filling. My shoulder burned, but I didn't stop. A scream ripped out of me, Summer joined in. We screamed until tears pricked our eyes and our throats burned.

The flashes outside lit us up intermittently. I caught jagged snapshots of Summer – our bond flicking between sheer darkness to pure moments of light. I barely knew her. Still I craved her, and not just because she was an outsider, something else pulled me towards her. It hit me: I trusted her. Exhaustion finally claimed me and I collapsed to the ground.

Tentacles of ivy flashed on the ceiling in rhythm with the storm outside and my jagged breath. Rage tasted smoky at the back of my throat. It tickled a peal of laughter out of me until it ran unchecked around the room.

'Abigail?'

'Please, don't say that name. That's not who I am.'

From: Jeb Abernathy
Date: Thursday, September 8, 2022 at 7:14 AM
To: Cameron McPherson
Subject: Re: Concerns – guidance needed

Dear Lord, I still can't believe what has happened!!

I've tried to call, but your assistant mentioned that you were in a meeting and couldn't be disturbed. Something deeply unsettling has happened. Please call me as soon as you read this email.

I fear the situation is getting out of hand. Pray for us, oh Lord!!

29. Present day

My fingers work quickly, but they keep slipping. The stench is overpowering and I breathe through my mouth. My nails scratch at the knot, but the string won't budge. If only I could loosen it just a little. My fingers slide along the slimy string and its rubbery consistency. Then it hits me. My stomach clenches in horror – that's no string between my fingers, but a tiny ribbon of intestine, sleek with blood.

A rabbit has been gutted and strung up on the fence with its own entrails. It's not alone. This section of the fence is littered with strung-up animal carcasses – mainly possums and rabbits – still warm with life.

My eyes go back to the task at hand. Don't look at them, just concentrate on that one knot. Sweat drips into my eyes and I wipe it away with the back of my hand. I wonder if they have babies, waiting for them in a hole in the ground, unaware that they ain't never coming back. I say a silent prayer for them.

'Abigail? What's in the Lord's name . . . ?'

The words whip me around just as the end of that sentence dies in Wade Pruitt's mouth. His fingers tense around the handguard of his rifle. His eyes widen as he takes in the state of me. I open my mouth, but he speaks first.

'Corey, go fetch Pastor Abernathy. Quick.'

Corey bolts towards Newhaven like one of the strung-up rabbits. Panic tingles under my skin – this is real bad. Pastor Abernathy's threat to send me away plays in a loop in my head. Wade Pruitt gawks at the fence. I have never seen a man's face drain of all colour before, not even when Mr Garrett fell, hand first, on a rusty nail. We stand in silence as I swat flies that have answered the call of blood. They can sense death from a mile away. The buzzing sets my teeth on edge. One hovers around my face and ears. I bat my hand around, jumping back to escape it. My reaction startles Wade and the rifle's barrel jerks up in my direction. Fear leaps in my throat.

We stare at each other through the eyes of strangers until a rustle drifts from the switchgrass. Corey shows the way to Pastor Abernathy, followed by Mrs Calhoun. Her hands clutch her skirt as she waddles through the tall grass, red hair falling out of her tight bun. She stops panting, and her hand flies to her throat.

'Dear Lord, what's this abomination?'

Their faces slacken in shock. A storm brews in Pastor Abernathy's eyes at the sight of the gutted animals on the fence, their entrails glistening in the early morning sun. A slight breeze carries the stench of death, coppery and not unlike rotting onion. Pastor Abernathy takes a step forward. Anger has added length and bulk to his body.

'What's this, Abigail?' His grumbling voice sends me hiding deeper into myself. 'Answer me.'

I want to explain, but words have scattered under his anger. I want to tell him, a nightmare woke me up as the day stood on the edge of sunrise. My mind kept circling back to the silhouette I'd glimpsed by the fence that day with Tom. I slipped out of bed and out of Newhaven with an urge to find her. I trekked barefoot in my nightdress towards the spot where she'd appeared. If she loiters around here, maybe she saw something the day of the fire.

'Abigail? Abigail, look at me.' Fingers click in front of my face; behind them Pastor Abernathy's face tenses, nostrils flaring. 'What did you do?'

'Me? I . . .' I look back at the garland of carcasses, fur matted with blood. 'No. I didn't do this. Found them that way. That's all, I swear.'

'You found them?' he says, giving me a look over.

Blood is smeared all over the front of my nightdress, all over my face, my hands. They look at me with disgust and disappointment. I want to tell them they're wrong, that the blood is from my attempts to get the dead animals down, that I couldn't look at one more death even if it was just an animal. All I wanted was to get them down and give them a proper burial. I open my mouth.

'Rebecca, please take her back to Newhaven,' Pastor Abernathy says. 'Make sure nobody sees her on the way.'

'Of course.'

Mrs Calhoun's hand hovers behind my shoulder, making sure not to touch me. I follow, head down in resignation. My hands glisten with a red sheen of blood. Every organ in me tightens at the sight. A forgotten memory shimmers in the blood. It takes my breath away. I rub my hands over my nightdress but it won't go away. It's not animal blood, it's her blood. Guilt hitches in my throat. My hands are covered in slick warm red as I kneel in the living room at Hunters Cottage on the day of the fire. Mom's blood. All over my hands. The image overwhelms me, and then the screaming starts.

30. Three weeks before the fire

My skin, clammy from exertion and excitement, stuck to Summer's under the sleeping bag, but I didn't move. She lit one of the roll-up cigarettes she'd smoked that day she jumped in the swamp and told me those gruesome stories; its acrid smell mingled with the tanginess of our sweat. She handed it to me.

'I don't smoke.'

'It's not really a cigarette. This is what freedom tastes like.'

The cigarette twirled at the end of her fingers, the tip smouldering with possibilities. How could something so small hide something so big? My pulse quickened at the transgression. I turned towards the door. Still no one was there. But shame tugged at my ribs. I had strayed so far already, howling like an animal, punching a pillow with all the rage I had. I shook my head, but I didn't move, my shoulder and bare arm rubbing with hers. Shimmies spread across my back. A part of me clung to the comfort of her skin even if it was wrong.

'Suit yourself.'

A strange emotion flitted across her face. I watched her take a deep inhale, the ember's orange glow blazing like a dying sun. She smirked before blowing the smoke into my face. It entered my nose, riding Summer's breath. Her lips hovered dangerously close to mine, and warmth spread through my stomach. The smoke slithered down my lungs with an acrid taste, the tail snagging on the back of my throat.

The cough came thick and fast, any attempt to smother it only made it worse. Summer's face dissolved behind a glaze of tears.

'Sorry, I can be such a bitch sometimes. Everybody coughs the first time.'

Something told me it didn't happen to her the first time; somehow she was the exception to all the rules. As if reading my mind, she inhaled deeply, locked her breath for a couple of seconds, showing off, before expelling the smoke towards the ceiling. A dark blue cloud suspended above us before it dissipated.

The tendrils of smoke disintegrated inside my chest and loosened the ties of my ribcage, my lungs inflating like balloons held by strings of veins. I sank under the sleeping bag. The material clung to my arms in a synthetic embrace. On the ceiling vine tentacles slithered across the plaster. My heart floated in my chest along with a memory of Fleur. We were sitting cross-legged on her bed, kissing the backs of our hands, practising for when we would have husbands. Until she suggested a more straightforward way to practise which had sounded innocent at the time, just a desire to be ready for the right boy. The memory tasted of Fleur's minty toothpaste. I wondered what she would think of me being here with Summer.

'You're sure you don't wanna try?'

Her question punched through my thoughts, scattering Fleur's face like smoke.

'You didn't tell me. What you doin' here?'

'Been squatting here. My motel's costing me a bomb and cash's running low.'

'Don't you get paid lots to make a documentary?'

'Podcast, and I wish. My sponsors mainly cover equipment

and travel costs, and my sub-let barely covers the rent for my tiny walk-up in East Brunswick. This place is free and low-key. Just a shame I have to park my car half a mile away. Damn, I'd kill for a Sloppy Joe right now.'

I listened to Summer and the mysterious words she used, reminding me how big the world outside our patch of land was, and how little I knew of it. Walk-up, sub-let, Sloppy Joe – each felt like the key to a door I hadn't discovered yet.

'Anyway, shouldn't you be going back?'

The obedient daughter in me ached to go back and ask for forgiveness, but another me – a new one – was still riled by Daddy drawing a line on the ground and standing on Tom's side. The idea of going back to Hunters Cottage, Mom sitting at the kitchen table, Daddy standing vigil behind, his hands firmly resting on her shoulders . . . I shook my head against the images.

'I can't, not tonight. Don't make me leave.' My voice rasped from the air overloaded with acrid smoke, and I stifled a cough.

'Not my style.' Her shoulder bumped mine. 'Won't you get into trouble though?'

'I don't care. They think I'm sleepin' at Newhaven. I've done it before.'

If I went home now, he'd smell the sin on my skin, he'd see it in the flush burning my cheeks. There'd be no hiding the shameful behaviour I indulged in. The flesh was weak, and I couldn't care less in that moment what the man had to say. A new thought bloomed in the darkness and rose like the smoke unfurling from Summer's mouth – maybe he didn't know everything. He might have drawn a line dividing us, but Summer had just drawn a circle and stepped inside it with me.

'I don't blame you. Your dad's a hypocrite. I understand your religion is supposed to be based on forgiveness and shit, but giving a free pass to the guy who assaulted his daughter? Welcome to the patriarchy. That's real dickhead behaviour.'

'He ain't, though.'

'How can you still defend him?'

'No. I mean, he ain't my daddy. He ain't my dad. Not really.'

31.

Summer propped herself on an elbow, her silhouette barely cutting against the darkness.

'What did you say?'

'He ain't my daddy.' The truth just slipped out, and it felt weird saying it out loud. That truth had stayed buried in the back of my mind for years. I flipped onto my stomach, chin resting on my folded arms. 'We're not from around here. Me and Mom. We're from Chicago. Daddy brought us here when I was a kid. He's the only father I've ever known, though. I've always called him Daddy. Don't think that'll ever change.'

Summer mirrored my stance. Not looking at each other but towards the same darkness. 'Where in Chicago?'

'I ain't sure, I was too young when we left. I just remember big towers, endless staircases because the elevator was always out of service. They stank of urine.'

'How young?'

'I reckon I was about six.'

'So your . . . stepdad isn't from Chicago?'

I shook my head.

'Do you know where he's from?'

'We don't talk about those things.'

'What do you mean?'

'We don't talk about our lives before coming to Newhaven. Before stepping into His light there's only darkness.'

'What was he doing in Chicago?'

'He did a lot of outreach work in the city back then. He was part of the church delegation out there.'

'Was it just the two of you? You and your mom?' In the darkness, Summer's voice shifted, breathless, the smoking and too much screaming catching up with her.

'Never knew my real daddy. Mom had boyfriends, but they never stuck around. She was livin' in sin until he came about.'

'No one else?'

'Just us girls. That's what she used to say.'

'How did he "come about"?'

'Just showed up one day. He hung around where we lived. It was one of them huge high-rise blocks. I remember 'cause I had to tilt my head so far back to look at it all. He talked to people about getting a better life, the evil of the city. People didn't talk back, they laughed at him mostly. He didn't care. One day he spoke to Mom outside. I think she asked him for ten bucks to get milk from the bodega or somethin'. He talked his way up to our apartment, carryin' her bags. After that first time he was there every day, long conversations at the kitchen table, on the sofa. He took us to a church support meeting downtown, showed her she didn't have to do it alone. He was different from the others. He wore a suit, smelled nice. He used to bring me those pralines. I sucked on them, watchin' TV. Then . . .'

After we arrived at Newhaven, memories from Chicago followed me everywhere; I stamped them down like a game of Whac-A-Mole. Daddy had explained – we need to be looking forward, darlin', not back. Over the years, Chicago dulled into some intangible feelings and smells that sometimes brought along a flurry of images, pieces of conversation.

'Then?'

I fingered a loose thread sticking out of the sleeping bag

lining. 'Then we were in Newhaven. Livin' a life in a safer place.'

'That's wild, Abs.'

'That ain't my real name.'

'Sorry. Abigail.'

'No, Abigail ain't my name,' I said, facing her. She wore a deep frown on her face. 'He gave it to me after we got here.'

One night after dinner he sat me down on the sofa in his office. My feet didn't touch the ground. The tattered velvet felt soft under my fingertips. I have a gift for you, he'd said – a name. I already had one, one I had wanted to keep, but it was the custom at Newhaven. And I liked it here. Mom didn't scream or cry here. There was food on the table, the weather was nicer. People talked funny compared to Chicago, but they didn't shout. A gift wasn't such a bad thing. He explained its meaning – 'Father's joy'. I learned my new name like you did a prayer or a new rule, by listening and repeating over and over until it embedded itself into every fibre that made me. Every day since then I'd worked hard to live up to this new name – to be my daddy's joy – and until recently I succeeded.

'My real name's Faith.'

The silence grew between us like mould on the living-room walls. A new storm was brewing. I felt Summer's disapproval gathering in her body, tensing her muscles. It was one thing to be born into Newhaven and the New America Baptist Church, but coming here willingly . . . Her body vibrated next to me.

'Damn, this fucking heat.' The words escaped through her gritted teeth as she leapt to her feet and escaped the shack. She became a whisper of grass in the night, until she turned into a splash of water.

In the silence that followed, doubts crept out of the

shadows like critters, and up my spine. I tried to shake them off, but it didn't work. I'd disappointed everybody, Summer included. My mouth felt dry. I patted around for the bottle of water. My hand scurried over Summer's bag, and I felt the outline of something hard. Instead of a bottle, my fingers ran over the slick surface of a book. It weighed heavy in my hand. The bright orange and pink cover simply read *On the Road*. I wondered if the paper would smell like her, faint tobacco and coconut left behind from turning pages. I used to watch a movie about a yellow-brick road back in Chicago, perhaps this was a similar kind of story. An old paperback, its spine so cracked it had turned into a permanent crescent, ear-marked pages, stained with life – smudges, spilled drinks, words or sentences underlined in pencil, and an odd bulge in the middle, paper curving under a foreign shape. The book fell open to reveal its secret.

A little plastic bag lay tucked between pages 124 and 125. One look at its contents, and my blood slowed down to a chill. Even though the plastic was cloudy with the smear of fingerprints there was no denying what was inside. I swallowed, but my mouth had dried up and my tongue stuck to its roof. I last saw this in a blown-up picture propped on an easel in church for the six-month anniversary of their death, dangling from her neck. I didn't need to open the locket to know the inside housed the portrait of a smiling girl with buck teeth and, on the other side, a man with crinkled eyes and a sandy moustache. The fancy 'F' etched onto the gold surface screamed a name, the rusted blood coating it screamed about the violence of what happened. I threw the plastic bag onto the floor and scrambled away in a panic, hand clasped over my mouth.

Outside, a night without stars had overtaken the sky now

the storm was over. Summer existed in splashes of water, sharp noises slicing through the night. Sitting on the floor, I corralled my body in my arms, slowly rocking myself, but it did nothing to soothe the confusion scrambling my thoughts. Summer had Fleur's necklace. The locket she used to slide on the chain whenever she listened real hard to something. I saw it happen a hundred times. How did Summer have Fleur's necklace? A necklace she never took off?

AUDIO FILE #10

Audio Quality: Poor

[Voice A]:   Female
[Voice B]:   Female

[First minute too damaged to recover.]

[Voice A]:   Why do you always have so many questions about my family, 'specially my parents?

[Voice B]:   I'm trying to understand the dynamics of the congregation, and your dad being the pastor, the head of that hierarchy, is an important figure to understand.

[Voice A]:   But it ain't just my daddy, you're askin' all this stuff about my mama too, and she ain't nobody in that hierarchy you talk about. There ain't no need. I don't feel comfortable talkin' about my daddy anymore, all right?

[Voice B]:   It's cool, we can talk about anything you like.

[Next part too damaged to recover.]

[Voice A]:   You never quit, do you? I told you to leave it alone. Dammit, Summer, don't you just quit, like ever?
             (Muffled noises.)

[Voice B]:   Come back! Look, I'm sorry, I didn't mean to.
             (More muffled noises.)
[Voice B]:   Fuck, I'm so sorry. Shit, I'm sorry. Just come
             back. I didn't mean it, Fleur. Sorry. FLEUR!

PART TWO

Before you become forest again, and water,
and widening wilderness,
in that hour of inconceivable terror
when you take back your name from all things.

Rainer Maria Rilke

32. Present day

Mrs Favreau nods along to her audiobook, her black head-phones a stark contrast against the shock of white hair. Her gaze sets on the window, looking at a sky she can barely see. The scars are etched deep around her milky eyes and mouth and still a raw pink after all this time. She chased the evil clouding her eyes and twisting her words with a bottle of bleach, the ordeal a testament to her dedication to her faith. If Daddy hadn't found her in time she would've surely downed the whole thing. His shouts still haunt the hallway, along with his unwavering faith she should be cared for by her own. No matter how busy he got he always found time to visit her. All she needs is love and for us to remember to keep her locked in at all times. Mrs Finch said it was unlikely her vocal cords were completely destroyed, yet she hasn't said a word since.

I shift my weight about, back sore from hours of bending over the table, folding and refolding her clothes to perfection. The monotony of the task dulls the images that haven't left me since the fence – Mom's blood dripping from my hands, the same blood soaking her dress. The more I remember the less I want to know.

Mrs Favreau doesn't acknowledge my presence, but she knows I'm here. Like every day. Apart from the muffled narration, it's quiet up here, so quiet you could forget about the floors below filled with people who don't want me around. This morning, Melissa Pruitt pulled her daughter close when I walked past them to get to Young Women class. I live in fear every time Pastor Abernathy opens his mouth it's to tell me I'm going.

A coloured square cuts against the white of the bedsheets. The photograph feels brittle between my fingers as if it has been carved from Mrs Favreau's skin. Daddy stands next to Pastor Favreau, who has his arm wrapped around his wife. My fingertip runs along Daddy's face. My heart tightens, and I sink to the floor. All of them are smiling, her whole unscarred face on display. The only one still here, the other two gone.

The image is imbued with a not-so-distant past, before the devil controlled her tongue and forced her to yammer on against our faith, before she was discovered at the bottom of the stairs standing over her husband's lifeless body, screaming that the devil got him. Two days after his death, she burst into the old ballroom, dishevelled and wild-eyed, shouting she couldn't find her husband. She stood pointing a finger at Daddy. A couple of women and several children burst into tears, the twins included. He had been devastated; Pastor Floyd Favreau had been his mentor ever since he arrived in Newhaven, and it was only a few weeks before we lost Pastor Munro and Fleur. The angel of death kept circling our church. Daddy rose up to the challenge and accepted the burden of leadership.

The sharp clang of a keystroke scatters my thoughts like dust from a whipped sheet. Audiobook discarded, Mrs Favreau slumps over that awful machine, bones rounded by grief and madness piling up on them, her spindly fingers poised on the keys. She's aged ten years in less than twelve months. The photo has fallen on the floor. I pick it up and drop it next to her on the desk where her fingers will find it later.

She waits. My back straightens, attention piqued. I'm

waiting too. I shouldn't look, but her stillness draws me in. A plank groans as my weight shifts to the ball of my foot. The tendons in her neck twist until her white eyes lock on me. The move sends a chill tumbling down my back.

'You want somethin'?'

The last word hasn't fully curved into a question when sharp keystrokes slice through it with an answer, the letters stamping onto the page with what feels like violence.

WHERE'S FLOYD?

I guess she has even fewer memories than me. Is that how it all starts? The devil eating at your memory to make space for the darkness to take root?

'He's gone, Mrs Favreau. Don't you remember?'

The next sentence stamped onto the paper chills my bones.

ABIGAIL DANGER ABIGAIL DANGER ABIGAIL DANGER.

'I don't understand. I'm Abigail.' I try to swallow but my tongue feels like sand. The lack of connective confuses me, making me in equal part the danger or in danger – victim or perpetrator.

Keys pummel a new piece of paper – she just slid it around the barrel – in a rising pandemonium that sets me on edge. The ruckus causes tingles under my skin, and my fingers creep closer to Mrs Favreau's shoulders. The urge to shut her up burns through me, until I can't bear it anymore. My hand shoots out. I snatch the new sheet without looking at the words, before running off, Mrs Favreau's message a crumpled ball nestled inside my skirt.

I jolt awake at the threshold of sleep. Stupid mind of mine, with more holes than a feminist's morals. I forgot to collect Mrs Favreau's tray after dinner. I ease her door open and tiptoe in, willing her not to wake up. At this hour the rest of

Newhaven is fast asleep. I can sneak the tray to the kitchen and clean its contents without Mrs Calhoun noticing. No need to give her more reason to be disappointed or an excuse to send me away.

The carpet itches under my bare feet and sweat has stuck my nightdress to my back. The dusty air is stuffy, almost foreboding. I breathe through my mouth. Halfway back down the hallway with the tray and the light flickers, giving the darkness a heartbeat. A floorboard groans somewhere behind me. It's an old house. Only it groans again with the regularity of a presence. The hair on my neck bristles with the possibility of all that could be looming at my back. I spin around. The light flutters, and someone is there, amid light and darkness fighting for the space – a woman shaped by shadows. My heart leaps. The only other person on this floor is Mrs Favreau, and I just locked her in her room. The woman steps forward. Cutlery rattles on the tray. She slowly raises her arm, finger pressed against her lips. I retreat until the floor seems to vanish under my left heel, gravity tugging me backwards. Ice runs through my veins. The light gathers into a storm around her, fragmenting reality. A scream cowers in my throat, too terrified to come out. She motions for me to come to her. Two words burn in my mind – *She's here.*

The tray crashes onto the floor, and the shock finally rips a scream from my throat.

'Help! Please. Someone help.'

I drop to the ground, my fingers manhandling the contents of the tray, padding around until my fingers curl around the handle of the knife. The light settles. I thrust the blade forward, only to be confronted by an empty hallway. She's vanished.

'Abigail?' A hand crashes on my shoulder and rips another scream out of me.

Pastor Abernathy peels my fingers from the knife before guiding me to a standing position.

'There was a woman. At the end of the hallway. She tried to take me. Pastor, I swear she did.'

'What woman?' His breath smells like sour cheese.

'I don't know. I looked up and she was gone. Vanished or somethin'. I swear, I ain't crazy.'

'It's all right. It's all right. You've been through a lot. Your mind's just confused. Rebecca, would you take Abigail back to her room?'

'I ain't lyin', she was right there.' I point an accusing finger towards the end of the hallway.

'Wade, Ezra, would you check all the rooms on this floor.'

Without a word, they slip past us and start checking doors. Jagged breaths jam in my throat along with too many words. I inhale furiously but I feel like I'm drowning in oxygen. My fingers spasm around Mrs Calhoun's arm.

'Can't. Breathe.'

She smiles, but it doesn't reach her eyes. 'It's all right. Just your body tryin' to repel the evil. Closin' itself to it. Let's go back to your room and pray.'

Hand under my elbow she guides me back to my room.

Back in bed and I'm chasing sleep. I toss and turn, terrified at the idea that if I open my eyes, the woman will be standing at the foot of my bed, finger slicing through her lips, that my hands will be covered in blood. The heat accentuates the smell of damp in the room, pushing it down my throat until I gag on it. Mrs Favreau's note I snatched earlier replaces the blood and the woman in my head. Faded letters branded so forcefully I can still see the depression in the paper – THE DEVILS HERE. THE DEVILS HERE. THE DEVILS HERE.

Exhaustion sits heavy on my lids. The woman from the hallway infiltrates my mind. She sits cross-legged at the end of my bed, staring at me with eyes the colour of honey, smoke unfurling from her parted mouth. She's brought smells and images like small offerings — the pungency of burnt things, shards of light on the water, the groan of floor-boards, all coated with a familiarity I can't remember. The smell of smoke surrounds me as if she's really been here. It's like someone has mixed the pieces from a dozen puzzles together.

The devil's here.

She's here. She's here.

Who's here?

'Summer.' The name slides past my lips with a whisper without even thinking. 'Summer's here.'

From: Cameron McPherson
Date: Friday, September 9, 2022 at 4:35 PM
To: Jeb Abernathy
Subject: Re: Concerns – guidance needed

My dear Pastor Abernathy,

Thank you for your message and for keeping me updated on the situation at Newhaven.

I agree, something is not right, and the situation needs to be monitored closely, especially with the police still lurking around.

We cannot allow evil to spread through Newhaven and make people question their faith and safety. Especially after what happened with Pastor Favreau, and dear Elizabeth Favreau. That incident at the fence with the dead animals is most disturbing.

I might have a solution that could help solve all of your issues with Abigail, but I will need to speak with the Elders Council first to seek their approval. I will get back to you as soon as I have solid information.

Under His guidance. Have a blessed day.

Pastor Cameron McPherson

PS You will be glad to know that the GoFundMe page for Abigail and the children has reached $58,000 and the fund will be transferred to the Newhaven account minus the donation to the NABC global fund.

33. Three weeks before the fire

The sun singed the horizon with blood-orange. Finally, morning was here. I'd had to stay last night, the swamp impossible to cross in pitch darkness, but I hadn't slept after the discovery of the locket. Now the porch steps from the old shack grated the soles of my feet. The storm had swept through the island, taking with it the tension that had bent the air for weeks. Apart from the burning line of the horizon, most of the sky still belonged to the night. Against the indigo sky and the darkness of a copse of trees something pulsed red.

Summer was still asleep. Since my discovery, thoughts of the locket hadn't left me, even now as flaxen grass tickled the soles of my feet. Now was the time. I should hurry, but the strange phenomenon at the edge of the woods pulled me forward. I hadn't asked Summer about the locket. I wasn't sure I wanted to know, and I didn't wanna admit I'd been snooping. I'd lain next to her, stiff as a picket fence while she curled on her side. Even without the locket, the stench of cold tobacco was enough to keep me awake.

A brazen tongue ran up the length of a tree, splitting the grey bark like cracked earth. The amber glowed like a breath, its heat tight on my face. I wondered if that's what a doorway to hell looked like.

'That's what happens when lightning hits a tree.' Her voice jolted me. Summer appeared by my side, cigarette in hand. She edged close to the scarred trunk. The slow flames licking the soft inside of the wood reflected in strands of her hair, igniting her honey-colour eyes to amber and tinting her skin with an incandescent glow. It looked like the tree and she were struck from the same molten wound.

The last remnants of sleep swam in her eyes along with something else I couldn't identify. I'd seen that kind of look before but I couldn't remember where. I pursed my lips at the crumpled vest Summer wore, striped with a clash of yellow, turquoise, purple, blue and orange and paired with neon-yellow running shorts. She looked like a demented rainbow.

'What? I spent a long time in a place where colours weren't an option.' She drew on her cigarette harder.

The personal detail startled me. I didn't say nothing, worried I would scare off what she might say next. I wanted to hear it as much as I wanted to scamper out of there.

'That's why I don't like rules, or sleeping for too long in the same place. There's a big sky above us, and I intend to see every part of it.'

'What about your family?'

'I haven't got any.'

That was ridiculous, everybody had a family, we all came from somewhere. Her revelation rooted between us, growing into an uncomfortable silence. She dragged again on her cigarette.

'Faith.' She said my old name like you hold someone's picture next to their face.

'I better go.'

'Maybe it's time to leave this place altogether.'

The elusive meaning of her words unsettled me. In the silence that followed, she smiled as she tucked a strand of hair behind my ear. I froze. The intimacy of the gesture

183

slowed my breathing. Her fingertips glided on my cheek with a waft of nicotine. A softness I had never witnessed before slackened her face. I rolled the end of my braid between my fingers, shifting my weight from one leg to the other, biding my time. She had to let me go. She might've protected me in that alley, cleaned my scrapes, but she was still a stranger. A stranger asking questions. A lot of questions. And around here, we weren't usually trusting of that.

'Yeah, you should go.' The softness which had taken over her face fled like a scared bird. 'Don't want your mom to worry.'

The long drag she took from her cigarette hollowed her cheeks, and the ember screamed with a glowing orange before she flicked the stub in the water. I frowned.

'What? Don't wanna start a fire.'

I was running along the boardwalk when the day taking over stopped me in my tracks. Shards of orange light stabbed the spaces between dark tupelo trees. They hit the water and set the swamp on fire. At least that was how it seemed. Nature's fiery beauty reminded me of Summer. A part of me wanted to linger here indefinitely, bathed in that fire, but I carried on.

I picked my way through the undergrowth accompanied by thoughts of the locket. Last night's certainty that it had been Fleur's had faded under the morning light. It wasn't a bespoke piece of jewellery. Fleur's daddy bought hers at a store, and she wasn't the only girl with a name starting with an F.

Under my feet, the stiffness of planks morphed into the softness of soil.

The locket could belong to a Fiona or a Felicity. It could even be hers – Summer could be her middle name, or a nickname. After all, I hadn't been honest with her about mine. I kicked the tall grass in the way, I should've taken it out of the plastic bag, checked the inside. Be certain. Any chance to dispel suspicions were gone now. I snapped a dry twig. It was ridiculous, Summer being in possession of Fleur's necklace didn't make no sense. I'd rushed to conclusions. *Slow down and read the question to the end*, Mrs Calhoun would caution me during Young Women classes whenever my hand shot up before she'd finished. I'd been too quick to judge, like the people in Parkerville who judged us all the time. God put Summer on my path for a reason, and to give up on her for what could be a simple misunderstanding wasn't a good enough reason to abandon a lost soul.

Frustration groaned in my throat when a crunch of footsteps disturbed the silence. I froze. A rustle of leaves ahead sent me ducking into the tall grass. A silhouette loitered in the undergrowth. I crouched lower. Ahead, a ponytail swished among the leaves, counting the beats until I might be discovered. A baseball cap pushed down low concealed her face. Whoever it was, she didn't wear a Newhaven uniform. She waded through the undergrowth at the edge of the woods. So close you could see parts of Newhaven's fence. A flash of recognition zapped through my mind – the woman from the store and the diner, who'd been asking where we lived. The woman who glared at us the day of Tania's accident.

Phone in hand, she snapped pictures of the fence and what I assumed was Newhaven in the distance. She leaned in closer, her shirt riding up her back revealing a ribbon of skin and a familiar black shape that chilled my bones.

What kind of business did this stranger have with us, that involved spying and a gun tucked in the waistband of her jeans?

185

AUDIO FILE #11

Audio Quality: Good

[Voice A]:   Female
[Voice B]:   Female

[Voice A]:   I don't have to give you my name.
[Voice B]:   That's fine. You can stay anonymous if you
             want to.
[Voice A]:   So nobody'll know it's comin' from me?
[Voice B]:   I won't use your name at all or anything that
             can identify you.
[Voice A]:   All right. A woman, Samantha, she visited the
             station where I work. I'm the receptionist
             there. She got there real mad, demanded to
             see a detective to report a kidnappin' – sister,
             and her nephew. She insisted her sister left
             their home in Virginia to follow members
             of the New America Baptist Church to
             Newhaven Plantation. She was all fidgety or
             somethin'. I reckon maybe she was on some-
             thin' but no way I was askin' her.
                I called one of the detectives and he took
             her to the conference room. He basically
             explained to her that there wasn't nothin' that
             could be done. Her sister's a grown woman,

186

and there ain't no evidence she got taken against her will. Lemme tell you, she couldn't provide no evidence of 'foul play'.

[Voice B]: Foul play?

[Voice A]: Work with cops long enough, I guess. *(Laughter.)* Anyway, she stormed out of the conference room screamin', and refused to leave until a report got filed and an investigation opened. Detective Parker told her to leave the premises otherwise she'd be arrested for disorderly conduct.

[Voice B]: What happened?

[Voice A]: She finally left of her own accord but she threatened to take matters into her own hands and break into Newhaven to rescue her sister and make those people pay. The look in her eyes gave me the heebie-jeebies.

34.

Mom kneaded fresh dough at the kitchen table. She pushed the blob around, its shape changing under the pressure of hands caked in flour. In the corner of the room, baby Sarah slept in the bassinet.

'Finally.'

Mom's gaze scrutinised me as if to check the whole of me had made it back to the house.

'Mom . . .' The word stretched like dough under the weight of unease. I opened my mouth ready to tell her about the woman and the gun, spying on us, but another answer slipped through. 'I went straight to Young Women class this morning.'

'I know, but you could have come home first.'

'Sorry.'

The patrol could deal with the intruder. I didn't want to explain how I'd seen her anyway. I looked at Mom, but she was still the woman who stood silently next to Daddy the other night.

Mom's hands returned to their work. They sunk deeper into the dough. One side stuck to the table as if wanting to escape, but she just threw some more flour at it and worked it back into the shape she wanted. Under the heat of the oven it would crackle into a hard crust.

In the aftermath of Summer's presence, my mind drifted back to Chicago. I suddenly missed the soft bread from the convenience store, square and squishy. The best bread for mayo sandwiches, or PB&J. The sugar would help with Mom's sore head back when she suffered from headaches. The jelly would ooze from the sides with every bite, I'd lick it from my fingers or the edges of the bread. Sometimes my tongue wouldn't be quick enough and a blob would fall on my shirt or the sofa cushion. Mom would just laugh it off, her own mouth full of bread sludge. Not anymore. Not since Daddy. He expected a spotless house.

'I didn't get the chance to shower. I better go clean up.' I stalked out of the room before she could pick on any incriminating smells. Along with all the sweat and dust that had congealed into an itchy grime, a waft of Summer's cigarette smoke had nested in my hair and clothes.

Upstairs belonged to silence, the twins still fast asleep in their beds. I lingered at their open door. At some point during the night Matthew had crawled into Elijah's bed. They lay facing each other, their hands balled into fists, lips puckered with sleep. Their closeness tightened a string inside me. Whatever happened they would always have each other, a link so powerful I envied them, but without any jealousy. Eyes closed, I realised that the smell of stale cigarettes and mildew in the old shack had taken me back to Chicago and snuggling up to Mom.

In the shower, lukewarm water pelted my body. I lathered the soap until every inch of my skin smelled of milk, washing last night off, but no amount of water or scrubbing would erase the memories of my behaviour. Newhaven had felt a million miles away last night. The flesh was weak, Daddy said. Maybe Newhaven's perfection had been slipping, but I would still rather live here than in an outside world that allowed horrible tragedies like what'd happened to that woman Karen Elsher. I scrubbed harder. If the incident with Tom could happen here, just imagine what might happen to me outside the community.

Propped up by the stiffness of a clean dress, I headed back downstairs. In the kitchen, the dough had disappeared into the oven and was being baked into shape, a crust slowing forming. Mom followed me into the hallway.

'You should apologise to your dad tonight.'

'I know, but . . . it ain't all my fault. Tom was wrong too.'

'It's not that simple, sweetheart. It's easy for men to be tempted. We have to be careful. Be grateful it was only a kiss.'

'You should've stuck up for me. Ain't that a simple truth? How about just us girls, Mom?' I said, my voice thick with hurt.

She reached out, pulling me into a hug. The weight of her arms around me lifted a weight from my chest. 'I'm sorry, sweetheart.'

'You chose Daddy over me.'

'He's my husband. I had to. What he's done for us. The sacrifices, the risks he's taken . . .'

'What do you mean?'

'We need to keep a low profile.'

Their earlier conversation, overheard from this very hallway, crept into my head. 'You ain't making no sense,' I said, disentangling myself from her embrace.

'All you need to know is he provides a good life for us. We have food on the table, we're safe. We should be grateful to him. We lived in a filthy place before, not an environment fit to raise a child.'

The apartment might have been small, and we might not have had much money, but that doesn't make a place unfit.

The small space had been littered with motherly touches like the glow-in-the-dark stars she had stuck to the closet ceiling for when I went 'camping'. Hearing Mom talk about Chicago – something she never did – woke up more memories. I landed in the childhood of another life. A life where Mom wore her hair an unnatural blond, a cigarette dangling from a red mouth as if held by some magic trick, and she swayed along to music. The memory smelled of mildew like the old shack, the cold had worked its way under my skin, but my fingers had been warm inside Mom's hands, and her smile had lit up the room. We sang along to the radio, sang loudly until our throats hurt and our laughter ate the words, until the room wasn't cold no more and the carpet didn't itch, until we collapsed on the tattered couch in a heap of limbs.

'It wasn't all bad.'

She didn't hear me. 'You'll learn that we all have to compromise and adapt if we want to make it. The outside's not safe. We need to stick with people we know and trust. After all the sacrifices I've made to keep you safe.'

'I know about them evils out there.'

'No you don't.' She sighed. 'You're just a child.'

The tree glowed in the darkness of my mind, the slither of fire inside the bark hot on my skin, a gateway to something old and something new which had found its way onto Jaspers Island. Her sigh blew on those embers, flames springing from them.

'I ain't no goddamn child. I'm almost eighteen.'

Her hand hovered in the air, her anger suspended above me. I flinched, and her hand dropped, heavy with regret, before clutching mine.

'Never take the name of the Lord in vain. Especially not

in front of your father. Everything is already strained enough as it is. Please.'

Mom hadn't almost lost it like that in a very long time, but something else quivered amidst the anger, a tremor in that 'Please'. The hint of a truth that she wasn't telling me, something important.

35.

In spite of what I'd told myself, thoughts of the locket followed me everywhere. As much as I tried to make excuses for it being in Summer's bag, it dominated my thoughts. As I stripped off the sheets from Mrs Favreau's bed, as I cleaned the bathroom, as my hands scrubbed and washed, swept the floor, used muscle memory on tasks carried out hundreds of times – still, the locket. The hard bristle of the brush rasped against the floorboards, I pushed hard against it until my hand cramped and arm burned. Sweat dripped from my nose. Still locket, locket, locket. When the floor had nothing more to give, my attention turned to the windows. I dragged the rag over the glass as the woods sprawled on the other side, and all I saw was the locket, nestled in Summer's book. It was like Summer had left it for me to find to bewitch me with it or somethin'. Cleaning usually soothed me. Not today.

The thoughts followed me outside for lunch duties. Despite the heat, Birdie sauntered as we both lugged baskets across the lawn. The sun had burned all the clouds that had crowded the sky only the day before. If I hadn't witnessed the smouldering tree outside the old shack it would've been as if the storm never existed.

Shouts and bursts of laughter reached us long before the barn came into view. Men worked dismantling the animal enclosure, upper lips and foreheads glistening, t-shirts sticking to their backs. Under calloused hands, old planks were ripped off and thrown into a pile before being stored and recycled into fuel for the winter – the generator never seemed to be enough. I didn't mind. A cold day or night meant a roaring fire in the old ballroom's fireplace. I loved how the smoke smelled, how the heat tightened the skin on my cheeks and the wood crackled. 'Fire music' I used to call it when I was little.

Men stretched their backs at the sight of our arrival. A few wiped their foreheads with the hem of their t-shirts. An array of smiles greeted me and Birdie. None of them belonged to Daddy.

'Lunch,' Wade Pruitt said, clapping his hands before rubbing them together.

A flurry of 'Blessed it be' echoed in the group. I spotted Jackson amongst the men, busy prying a plank away. He was the only one wearing gloves. His back strained against the soaked fabric of his t-shirt, tensing the muscles in his arms. I wondered how much his head and back hurt. The incident in the barn added a new dimension to the fight Jackson had had with Tom, when Tom asked if he'd had enough of getting kicked around. As the group gathered around us, Jackson loitered at the back.

'Jackson, come on, boy. We ain't got all day, boy.' Jackson flinched at his father's order, each 'boy' a nail pinning him to a never-ending childhood, never to be a man. Mr Caine's tone tensed my shoulders, too. He wasn't a tall man but his body was taut, muscles coiled tight around his bones, and his skin too short to wrap it all. There was nothing slack about Mr Caine. I scanned the other faces for a hint of knowledge or disapproval of his behaviour, but they only paid attention to the food. It was easier to look the other way in big spaces, but the violence seething under Mr Caine's skin must have been unmissable within the confined walls of Myrtle Cottage. Still, Mrs Caine had never let on before she ran away. Had I looked the other way too?

Jackson appeared next to me.

'You all right?' I asked, offering him a glass of sweet tea.

His answer was lost under a storm of screams rising from the other side of Newhaven. Glasses and sandwiches dropped to the ground as Mr Caine and the other men bolted towards the main entrance.

'Stay here.' Wade Pruitt instructed us. Birdie and I exchanged a startled look before we both ran after the rest of the group, baskets forgotten on the grass.

A woman rattled the front gate, her silhouette blurry in the heat haze. She growled and screeched and frothed at the mouth like some rabid raccoon. So unbecoming of a woman, Daddy would say. As I got closer the screams morphed into a name.

'Jamie! Jamie!'

The woman stared at me and I froze – it was the woman who had been loitering in the woods this morning. The outline of the gun jammed in her jeans flashed in my mind. A few of the men had rifles in hand and the sight loosened the knot in my chest.

A shadow eclipsed my view. Daddy had stepped forward. Now he and the woman stood either side of the fence.

'Please leave. There ain't no Jamie here.'

'I know my sister and nephew are in here. I want to see them. You can't keep me away from them.'

'This is a safe haven for anybody who asks for shelter. You ain't welcome.'

'Please, they're my whole family.'

'She doesn't want to go with you.'

'Then bring her here so she can say that to my face.' The words dripped with a Yankee accent. Daddy's jaw tensed under his beard. A frisson of worry shimmied down my back along with sweat. I edged closer to them. I had to warn him.

'Daddy, she's —'

'Not now, Abigail.' Then to the woman: 'Please leave.'

'Is this your daughter?'

I slipped my hand in his.

'You took my family, how would you feel if I took yours?' Flecks of her saliva landed in his beard.

He stared at the woman. From behind him the clunk of guns' safety-off crackled in the air. I wanted to tell her to get out of here, but the words stuck to the roof of my mouth. His fingers tightened around mine until my knuckles hurt. The holster of his gun pressed against my waist. *God always finds a way to punish the wicked.* The idea froze the breath in my chest. God punishes the wicked, but Jackson got punished for no reason. Why did he deserve such hardship? He was just a kid. I wanted to tug my hand free, but it might bring the wrong kind of attention. *The obedient daughter respects her father.* I ground the pain between my teeth, waiting for the moment Daddy would be ready to release me.

36. Present day

Dark eyes on the birch trees' white bark observe me. They line up, the woods packed tight behind them. Somewhere at my back the church is crowded with the rest of Newhaven for Sunday service. The twins would be there too. The possibility I might be separated from them and baby Sarah escapes with a shuddering breath. Most people still blame the outside for the fire, but some . . . They've seen the rabbits and possums on the fence, the blood on my hands, my lack of tears at the memorial, my outburst at dinner. A shiver runs through me at what they would do if I told them the scraps I remember from the day of the fire – Mom's blood staining her dress, my hands too. I've given up the idea of handing them the blue letter – I ain't rockin' my boat when it's already sinking. The shade from the hanging tree is my only protection, its yawning branches dripping with webs of Spanish moss like the ghosts of a hundred hanged. Maybe that's how I'll end up, swinging from a branch rather than a fence.

I sit on a low branch, fingers picking at a chip of rough bark, the tips of my canvas shoes hovering just above the ground. My mind's unravelling, memories are returning. There's Summer. The outline of a face, a halo of dark hair, honey-colour eyes, little lines on either side of a mouth framing a smile. Then there's the woman I saw at the fence and the one from the hallway. She flits between evil incarnate

197

to a hallucination conjured up by stress and grief. My attention snags on a rustle in the undergrowth. Hand shielding my eyes, I scan the darkness between leaves and brambles. Nothin'.

'We all missed you at church.' Jackson leans against the branch. His lie draws a wan smile out of me.

A couple of ospreys hop along the edge of the woods, beaks pecking at the grass, hoping worms are hiding under the dry crust of the earth. They just keep going even though the ground is too dehydrated for anything to wiggle underneath. Won't be long before one of them realises they'll have more luck for food turning on each other.

'What are you lookin' for?'

'I'm lookin' for Summer.' The words escape without a second thought.

'Summer . . . Do you mean that podcast girl?'

My attention snaps back to him. 'You know her? You know where she is?'

'I think she's gone.'

'Why do you say that?'

'She hasn't bugged nobody in town with her questions for a while. Not since before the fire. Anita Jones was talking to Mrs Calhoun about it the other day, sayin' how she's glad that nuisance's over.'

Hope collapses in my chest. One person that might have had answers, and they've left town. I'll never know how she's connected to all this. But maybe her being gone is best for my sinking boat. Frustration frets under my skin and I just jab a nail into the tree bark until it hurts.

Jackson drops on the branch next to me. The branch groans but holds. His face is waiting for me, split with a wide grin. The sight curls the corners of my mouth, but my attention drifts to the church, where the congregation has spilled out and Tom stands talking to Pastor Abernathy. Jackson follows my gaze. His lips tense when he finds Tom at the end of it. A storm of emotions clouds his face.

'You should stay away from him.'

'What you talkin' about?'

'He's bad news, no better than your dad.'

The words jolt me. 'Daddy?'

'They're the same, Tom and your dad. They pretend to be all righteous an'all, and in the end it's just lies. They're both cruel, and only care about themselves.'

'You're wrong.'

'Don't you remember? You never trusted Tom before. You told me plenty at choir practice how he gave you and Birdie the creeps.'

'It ain't like that.' My fingers have found the end of my braid, rolling it around. 'Tom said things had changed between us before . . . He's been really good to me since the fire.'

'And you're buying that? Wow. You really don't remember nothin'.' He grabs me by the shoulders to steady my attention. The move feels like such an adult thing, at odds with his childish frame, but his grip is surprisingly strong. The branch sways under us, and my position feels precarious.

I shake my head, staring at the ground. All I've recovered from the weeks after the anniversary of Fleur and Pastor Munro's deaths are just a collection of snapshots. My memories are like trying to look at a whole room through a keyhole.

'They say the mind can sometimes block memories after an intense trauma,' I say.

'Who's they?'

'The cops.'

'I wish I could block my memories of this place.' Before I can ask what he means he continues, 'Anyway, Tom's a liar, the same way your dad was.'

'That's not true, my daddy –'

'Wake up, Abigail. Your dad wasn't a good person. You don't remember or don't wanna, but I do. Forget Tom. If you need someone I can look after you.'

'Jackson, you're just a kid.'

'We can leave this place. Ain't you worried they'll lock you up like they did Mrs Favreau?'

'Maybe they should. Maybe there's somethin' wrong with me.'

Jackson is still holding me. I try to shrug my shoulders free, remembering the blood on my hands, but his grip tightens as he pulls me into a hug. My stomach muscles clench to keep me from falling.

'Ain't nothin' wrong with you.' His next words are a hot breath in my ear. 'We could run away. This place's dangerous.'

His arms wind tighter around my shoulders, fingers pressing on my bones, chin digging into the curve of my neck. I wiggle a bit but can't feel comfortable. The air around us is choked with heat, driving sweat down my spine. Overhead, birds scream at us. The world shrinks with every breath.

'Get away from her.' Mr Caine's voice is as taut as the rest of him, and his warning whips the air above us. Jackson flinches against me and his embrace slackens. 'Did you hear me, boy? Get away from that girl. She's poison.'

'Dad, it's not what you think.' Jackson has let go of me. His shoulders drop. He seems so small suddenly.

'You shame me, boy. I told you and your sisters not to talk to that girl.'

Jackson's father swallows the space between us in short sharp strides. Jackson drops down and cowers with each step that brings his father closer. Mr Caine grabs him by his shirt collar. A button breaks as he yanks his son away from the tree. I grab on to the branch to stop myself from falling. The bark scrapes my palms. For a second, the dirty yellow of an old bruise appears on Jackson's collarbone. His face crumples under the fear. The scene tastes like a memory shrouded in the scent of animal sweat and trampled hay. Jackson and Mr Caine in the barn. The memory crumbles before I can fully grasp it.

They are quickly swallowed by the tide of people pouring out of church and towards Newhaven. No one else stops to speak to me. The eyes from the birch trees keep staring. I'm alone again with the truth Jackson has unleashed. Maybe I didn't know my own father. Uncertainty leaves me spinning inside my own body – Daddy, Tom, Summer, even Mr Caine. Eyes closed, I rub my temples, hoping to dislodge a memory or some kind of truth. *They're both cruel, and only care about themselves.* The words play in a loop, but the only images that rise from this soundtrack are of Daddy and me in the bathroom, me sitting on the edge of the tub while he tends to me with a damp cloth. The memory is odd, tainted by Jackson's spite because there's no love, only fear kicking through my body as I remember.

'You coming to breakfast?'

The question slices through the makeshift darkness and snaps my eyes open. Tom looks up at me, bright in the morning sun. The light sets fire to his blond curls.

'I ain't very hungry.'

'You can keep me company while I eat for two, then.'

He extends a hand and a smile. I reach, and he pulls me off the branch.

'Aren't you worried to be seen with me?'

'Nah. Anyway, I'm hankering for something sweet,' he adds.

There is an echo of recognition in the words, but I shake it off. Jackson doesn't know what he's talking about. He's just a kid angry at the whole world. Tom smiles at me. Summer's gone, whoever she was, but maybe the person I really need is still here.

FIRE AT NEWHAVEN – STILL NO REAL ANSWERS

By Marilynn Wasserman, Staff Reporter

It has been two weeks since the fire at Hunters Cottage, located on the grounds of Newhaven Plantation, which claimed the lives of Pastor John Heywood and his wife, Genevieve, and the Sheriff's Department and Fire Department are no closer to knowing what happened. Fire Marshal Wesley Dunlop has confirmed through preliminary findings that, even though accelerant was present at the scene, an accident cannot be ruled out at this stage. The presence of fuel can be explained by several kerosene lamps in the living room. Several candles were also found among the debris. Witnesses at the plantation have confirmed that the generator was malfunctioning that day due to the rainstorm. There is no evidence at this stage that the fire resulted from any criminal activity.

The Sheriff's Department still hasn't made any official statement about the cause of death of John Heywood and his wife. Autopsy results have not yet been released. However, a source in the Sheriff's Department has confirmed that they are keen to talk to a young woman, Summer Washington, who was in town carrying out research on the New America Baptist Church and the congregation at Newhaven Plantation. Miss Washington is the sole producer and host of the 'A Question of Faith' podcast. The police are keen to speak to her about her contacts with several members of the church. However, Carol-Ann Walt, Manager at the Sunny Inn Motel where Miss

Washington was a guest, confirmed that she checked out about four weeks ago. Furthermore, several witnesses have confirmed that she hasn't been seen in town since the fire. It's unclear at the moment if Summer Washington is a witness or a person of interest.

COMMENTS:

BlackStar
Click here if you want to learn how to make millions in crypto currency.

Anon_1978
Wouldn't surprise me if those religious freaks up at Newhaven did something to that girl. She was asking too many questions.

Girl_Interrupted
@BlackStar Reported for spam.

Sportsfanatic2000
Sounds like something for a Netflix true-crime special. I'm sure if they look into those people they'll find loads of f**ked up things.

37. Two weeks before the fire

Summer sunbathed on the pier, a bright red dot at the end of the wooden trail, the colour of her bikini matching her lips. Her foot tapped along to whatever music streamed out of the buds wedged in her ears. Something about good girls and hell. Corrupting filth, Daddy would call it. I swallowed hard and steadied myself. I hadn't been back since finding the locket, and now I'd come to see Summer, determined to establish the truth.

'What's up?' she said in a nonchalant drawl, taking the buds out. She didn't flinch when my shadow stretched over her.

'Why you wearin' lipstick here? Ain't no one around.'

'Do you always do things just to please others?'

'What does that mean?' I nodded towards the line of inked words on her stomach. She lifted her head from the planks to follow my gaze.

'Means dissolve and conjoin in Latin. It's about things breaking down and then being put back together to make something else. Reminds me where I come from.'

'Where's that?'

'A place where I got stabbed in the back by the people I trusted the most before they left me to rot in some shitty place, not so different from yours. Lots of rules and a high fence. People giving me shit every day. Anything else?'

Silence settled between us, a spokesperson confirming she wasn't interested in sharing any further details of her life.

'I heard you were in town yesterday, askin' some of the women from our congregation if they'd talk to you about their daily lives.'

'Yeah, podcast research, and none of them would.'

'Maybe they don't want to be made fun of.'

'If y'all live such wholesome lives in that place why wouldn't you want to talk to me about it. Or are you all hiding something?' Her voice dripped with condescension.

People wouldn't understand; they don't fear God or the devil, Daddy explained to me. Even though I'd had my doubts recently I wouldn't let no outsider criticise Newhaven. 'I reckon they don't want you to twist their words for your documentary. I mean, you're a stranger.'

'Podcast. You got me. Wanna talk to me so I can twist your words?' Summer smirked.

'I brought you somethin'. I guess I can let you question me too.' I smiled. I've got questions of my own I hope to find answers to, I thought.

Honey-coated fingers disappeared into our mouths, the sugar hitting our tongues. We had retreated from the sun and found shelter in the shaded, mildewed living room of the old shack.

'Can't believe you guys actually got beehives. This shit tastes so good. Way better than the store stuff.' Her fingers dived into the jar and broke a piece of honeycomb. Her mouth stretched into a smile and my mouth betrayed me by responding with one of its own. Even after everything. The body's weak, I reminded myself.

The afternoon light fell between the slats nailed to the window, the outside world creeping in, time edging towards me. I didn't have long. The light never liked to linger in this place, afraid to disturb the shadows and the darkness tainting the house. The idea she spent night after night alone in this house sent a shudder across my shoulders. A sliver of light caught the corner of Summer's book, and I licked my lips.

'You know, I really loved *Little Women*. They're all amazing, 'specially Jo, but I reckon my favourite's Beth.'

'Why doesn't that surprise me.' Her fingers disappeared into her mouth. She sucked the honey off them. 'Maybe I should just turn up at your place. Newhaven. See if anyone wants to talk to me on your own turf.'

'That's not a good idea. Daddy, he . . .' The incident with the woman at the gate was still a fresh scar on Newhaven's quiet life. Summer showing up now would be like a finger picking at the scab.

'What's he going to do? Preach me to death?'

Her carelessness sat heavy on my shoulders. I tried to shrug it off, but it clung to my skin. She sat opposite me, as straight as a match, and I had seen what Daddy did to matches after he'd lit a fire. My knuckles still radiated with phantom pain from when the woman had shown up at the gate. Disrespect, the one thing he hated most.

A piece of honeycomb lodged itself in the back of my throat. I swallowed hard and coughed. 'Do you have anythin' to drink?' I coughed again, beating a fist against my chest.

'Sure. Just a sec.'

As soon as she disappeared into the kitchen, I lunged for the book, pregnant with the familiar bulge, peeking out from Summer's bag. The pages fell open. My heart dropped. Instead of the locket, Summer's lighter stared back at me. I turned the book upside down and shook, frantically leafed through the pages. Still no necklace. Damn, my chance to put my mind at rest – to see whose pictures were inside – quickly withered with each passing second, the only real discovery a faded stamp on the title page which read PROPERTY OF BAY PINES JUVENILE FACILITY. Must have been some sort of library. I glanced at the gaping mouth of Summer's bag; the locket might've fallen in there.

'Whatcha doing?' Summer stared at me from the doorway, an eyebrow cocked with surprise or suspicion.

'I was thinkin' maybe I could borrow it.'

'I'd appreciate if you don't go snooping through my things.'

My cheeks burned hot with shame. 'I'm sorry.'

Her hand strangled the neck of a cola bottle. 'I don't like people touching my stuff. Out on the streets, you'd get the shit kicked out of you for something like this.'

'I . . . I won't do it again.'

'Good.' She tossed the bottle at me, but I was too scared to drink from it. 'Anyway, that's my favourite book. I had it for like, forever. It's very different from *Little Women* and loaded with pretty sinful and unsavoury . . . stuff.'

'Oh, all right.'

The idea of reading about shameful behaviours unsettled my stomach, but at the same time curiosity stirred in me, a desire to understand what made Jack Kerouac's *On the Road* so special to her. Special enough to steal it from a library.

'Tell you what, I'll let you borrow it. But first you'll have to do something for me.'

The way she said the words felt like a whole lotta trouble was coming.

38. Present day

I open the window, and the night climbs in. The forest stands one shade darker than the night. My fingers stroke the grooves in the windowsill, playing with the edge of a splinter. The shape of the rough cuts in the wood somehow soothe my breathing. Pastor Abernathy looked right at me this morning when he said God doesn't give more than we can handle and we should carry our load with humility. A few heads twitched, desperate to get a glance, but my seat on the last row and my scarf pulled low around my face shielded me from their scrutiny. God's really misjudged my threshold. Frustration builds in my chest. I pummel the ledge until my knuckles throb, awaking the old burns. They don't know what it's like to live with a mind that carries great gaping holes, that even after all this time I've recovered nothing more than a few terrifying images that point to a truth I don't want to acknowledge. I wipe my eyes, swallowing back the tears and a scream.

Maybe Tom's right. Today he surprised me with a picnic breakfast by the fountain after service, away from the congregation's increasing curiosity.

'Don't you think maybe it's a blessing not remembering? God's way of giving you a break during a horrible time?'

The thought stopped me chewing on my cornbread. I've been so intent on recovering my memories I've never considered.

'Instead of finding old memories, you could get busy

making new ones. I could help. Your first new memory could be you baking me a peach cobbler.' He winked, cheeks like a hamster full of cornbread and eggs. His eyes remind me so much of Daddy's — the same icy blue that seemed to look straight into your soul. A scene flashed in my head, Tom leaning on the doorframe in the kitchen winking at me. A shiver tumbled down my spine for no reason. I pushed the image back down by stuffing another cornbread piece into my mouth.

Mrs Favreau's message rests on my lap. Each key branded the paper, a letter at a time, each like a hammer nailing the words inside my chest with a sense of inevitability — *the devil's here*. The image of the woman at the end of the hallway bursts into my mind, the light frantic around her. The devil's here. Mom would know what to do. I don't allow myself to go there though, to think about her. It hurts too much and in those moments I just want what I can't have. She would tell me: look after your siblings, and live your life following the teachings of our Lord, and make new memories. Happy ones.

The note rips between my fingers, over and over until the old lady's warning is no more than shredded little squares in the palm of my hand. Suddenly her bad omen doesn't feel that scary. I toss them in the air, rough confetti to celebrate a new beginning. I watch them drop into the toilet bowl and they swirl around, unable to escape their fate, as I press the flush. No more.

From: Cameron McPherson
Date: Monday, September 12, 2022 at 4:05 PM
To: Jeb Abernathy
Subject: Re: Concerns – guidance needed

My dear Pastor Abernathy,

I wanted to give you more information about the potential solution I mentioned earlier that could solve your problems with Abigail.

After speaking with the rest of the Elders Council, I can share with you that we are building something new in Texas, a New Eden to create a congregation living according to God's laws. It will be completely self-sufficient and closed to the outside. It might be good to bring Abigail there if the situation worsens or if the police come back, so we can shelter her and help her find her way back to God. I don't think it's necessary to talk to her about this option at this stage. We don't want to confuse her.

Regarding the words you found carved on the windowsill in her room, I am very worried. You are correct that 'Solve et Coagula' is Latin. I did some research and I've found out that the expression is associated with the occult and ungodly practices. But my main concern is, where did she learn those words? Essentially, either the girl is speaking in tongues or she's been conspiring with people from the outside. God only knows what she might have been telling them. We need to protect the girl, but also protect Newhaven and the NABC. Under no circumstance should Abigail be allowed to leave Newhaven.

Under His guidance. Have a blessed day.

Pastor Cameron McPherson

39. Ten days before the fire

Summer's instructions were easy enough; the execution was trickier. Hanging outside of the window, my foot patted down until the gutter's metal brace caught under my toes. Slowly I used them like the rungs on a ladder.

I'd tossed around in bed after Daddy and Mom had gone to their room and the light had vanished from under their door. I counted to five hundred and then listened to the silence for another ten minutes before I dared get up and put Summer's plan into motion – the price to pay for being caught rummaging through her stuff.

Apprehension shimmied under my skin as my feet touched the grass. I'd never sneaked out at night before. Ever. The sin sat heavy on my shoulders, but I shrugged it off – if my parents could have secrets, then so could I.

Summer loitered at the edge of the woods, a shadow among others. The excitement buzzed in my bones. There was an old tear in the fence that hadn't been patched yet. Once inside the perimeter, I led the way, and she fell into step behind, tall grass swishing in our wake. We scurried around the dark shape of Newhaven to the back entrance. I felt a pinch of shame as I eased the back door handle slowly.

'Wait. This isn't locked?'

'Why would it be?'

'Mind-blowing.'

In the kitchen, I manoeuvred through the darkness, avoiding the edges of cabinets and any noisy dangers. We crept down the hallway, the only sound our breath loud in our ears and the soft clicks from her phone as she took photos. The Devotion and Outreach rooms burst into life under flashes. Her photographic enthusiasm tensed my shoulders. One look at me, and she switched to video mode. She opened a few of the study books, running her fingers along the ragged lines of removed pages. A loud creak sounded above us. We froze and tilted our heads towards the ceiling.

'Now what?' she whispered.

Now she was here, I strangely wasn't ready to let her go. Not just yet.

'Come with me.' I motioned, and she grabbed my hand. Electricity shot up my arm. We trekked back to the kitchen and a door cut in the corner of a wall. The hinges creaked as I pried it open.

'Old servants' stairs. Nobody uses them.'

We climbed in enclosed air thick with dust, neglect and old ghosts to the attic floor. She laced her fingers with mine, allowing me to lead her along the dark corridor to one of the rooms. Ignoring the cot bed and its mouldy mattress, we slumped on the floor facing each other.

'Well, that was a close one. I thought you said everybody goes to bed at the same time.'

'They do. We do. I don't know . . .'

'Nice digs you got here. This place is fucking huge. I wish I could have taken more photos and videos, especially all those books.'

In the darkness, she became mostly a disembodied voice, her silhouette blending in with the surrounding night. I should've got up and pulled back the curtains but I didn't want to move.

'Big enough to have a second set of stairs just for the servants.'

'You know they weren't though, right?'

I shifted on the floor. 'What do you mean?'

'They were no servants. They were slaves.'

'Oh.'

Suddenly I was glad of the darkness. I looked down at my hand, its palm still holding the warmth from her skin, while my cheeks held the heat of my ignorance.

'Maybe you should learn about the history of the place you call home,' she said, lighting a cigarette.

'You shouldn't smoke here.'

'Didn't you say this floor was empty?'

'Only Mrs Favreau.'

'That's the sick old lady, right?'

'Yes. Pastor Favreau's widow. He used to be our old pastor. He passed and Daddy took over. She's really old, and . . . not well.' I stopped at the edge of the truth.

'That reminds me, I found out more about what happened at the abandoned shack last time I was in town to get supplies,' she said, her attention lost inside her bag. The bottle she pulled out opened with a hiss. After taking a swallow, she handed it over.

I took a sip, the cola warm on my tongue. 'Who from?'

'Some guys I was hanging with.'

'Hangin'?'

'You know – oh, of course you don't,' she scoffed. 'Drinking with.'

I shaped the darkness in my mind into the guys she hung out with, sat together in the privacy of a booth with red leather seats. I wondered what else she might have done with them while hanging out. Lips moving against lips and soft moans, fingers skating down jaws and clammy skin, tasting sin like a peach – something messy and sticky. The images sent a fire through my veins.

'Turns out that guy, his wife didn't leave him. They found her body in the swamp a few weeks after he blew his brains out. He most likely killed her.'

The brutality of the outside world chilled me to the bone, a place so essentially broken, husbands killed their wives – Karen Elsher, the woman from the shack, and who knew how many others – most likely because of feminism.

Summer bathed in darkness. I wondered how she could stay in a place where such a tragedy had unfolded, but then again I lived in a place that had housed slaves. With each intake of breath, the ember of her cigarette glowed a bright orange and the shadows retreated to the edges of her face for a moment before shrouding her again, giving the darkness a heartbeat. She tapped her cigarette and a tower of ash crashed on the floor.

'This wouldn't happen here.'

'Only because women here submit to their husbands.'

'Because that's what God intended.'

'Really? Because I don't remember you submitting to Tom in that kitchen.'

'Because he ain't my husband.'

'What if he was?'

The idea of submitting to Tom as my husband made me want to heave. Daddy would never allow that. He knew how I felt about Tom.

'Ask yourself what kind of religion doesn't protect a woman from someone like Tom, even worse makes excuses for him.'

'The flesh is weak.'

'And how is it your responsibility if Tom's weak?'

I opened my mouth but found it empty of an answer. The stream of arguments had dried up in my mind, because in that moment my bones hummed with the truth – that day on the sofa, Daddy had chosen Tom's soul over my own.

On the other side of the darkness Summer took a long drag, her face ablaze with the fiery orange glow. She looked like one of the predators that stalked the swamp. I lunged for the bottle and gulped down too quickly, leaving my throat sore.

'Seriously, this place is so repressed I'm surprised no one here has lost the plot and gone on a killing spree.'

40. Nine days before the fire

Daddy stepped behind the lectern. He waited until silence was absolute, every sniffle and throat-clearing stifled, and Mr Garrett had given him the thumbs-up for the recording.

'Lemme tell you, they say evil's a beast with horns, but I say evil's a woman in a business suit. A woman who goes against nature and her natural role. Who nurtures a career instead of a family, who takes away jobs from men, deprives them of a chance to support or start a family, who likes to make men feel small. Her ambition grows like a cancer and distracts her from her responsibilities. 'Cause feminism is the snake in the garden of Eden. But we've made our true Eden in this place with the guidance of our Lord. A new haven. We're strong with His truth, but watch out, for flesh is weak and corrupts minds –'

The familiar scene pushed me back into last night's dream, after I had left Summer at the fence and snuck back into my room. In my dream, Daddy spoke similar words. They'd poured out of his mouth amid smouldering embers and ashes. Panicked, I had turned to the congregation, but rows of featureless faces confronted me, smooth like the pebbles you'd find on a shore.

'– we must not just put our trust, but our faith in the Lord. We have to look out for each other and protect the weak in our community. Society tries to corrupt the weakest flesh every time we set foot in Parkerville –'

I had tried to flee but I was bound to the bench, my legs

trapped by thick vines. At the lectern, Daddy's torso pulsated with an orange glow until he split like the bark of a tree, leaving a long gash of glowing embers across his chest. The smell of burning flesh threatened to overpower me. When the latent flames receded a familiar image appeared inside the rift of his chest. The pale glow of the TV screen beckoned me. I clawed at the vines until my fingers bled, until I was free. Hands on either side of the rift, I stepped through the opening in his chest and into a living room where Summer waited with a bottle of cola.

'But there're other evils, risin' in our society. Remember Leviticus 18:22, "Thou shalt not lie with mankind as with womankind: it is abomination." Abomination's rampant in our cities, they don't even hide anymore, walkin' in broad daylight, holdin' hands, desecratin' the sanctity of marriage, pervertin' young, impressionable minds. They're a cancer on morality, same as the slaughterhouses women visit to rid themselves of their responsibilities as mothers 'cause they can't close their legs.'

Fervent amens rose from the benches, emboldening him further.

'We can't stay idle 'cause they'll come for our children, you can already see it on the TV, and in their marches, wearin' rainbows or pink hats. But if they rally, so can we. Nothing's stronger than the faith in our Lord. Heed my call: tomorrow we'll protest at the slaughterhouse in Parkerville, and I invite y'all. No, I implore y'all to do the same. Rally and protest at whatever places sinners congregate in your city. Don't forget to film yourself and upload testimonies of you doin' His work.'

I should've knocked, but the door was wide open. Daddy's office lay in disarray. The mess, so out of place in this space, left me speechless. Every object had its place here, and order was an expectation Daddy had of everyone. He even expected the twins to put away their toys when they'd finished with them. All the drawers had been pulled out and gutted, most of their contents spilled over the desk top. A big velvet box I'd never seen before lay on top of a pile of papers, Daddy searching through it, his hands roaming around with a frantic energy.

Sensing he would not approve of being caught in a moment of agitation, I tiptoed back down the hallway before returning. I coughed a couple of times before pushing the door, and the scene inside his office had changed. He sat behind his desk shuffling paper, the box nowhere to be seen.

'Daddy, I was wondering . . .'

'Yes, darlin'?'

'Fleur's necklace, do you know where she got it from? I know her daddy gave it to her, but you know where he got it from?'

'Why you askin'?' His hands stopped, paper frozen in mid-air.

The words fell quick. 'I was just wonderin'. It was so pretty.'

After my failed attempt to find the locket at the old shack, I'd decided to find out how common a piece of jewellery it was. Mom had no idea when I checked with her.

Paper crackled as he crumpled it into a ball. It looked small in his hands, the way I felt small in his office.

'You should be ashamed. Envy and vanity are sins.'

I fiddled with the end of my braid, the familiar coarseness of split ends comforting. His reaction felt so extreme, so big for such a small ask. I must have caught him at a bad time. He had a whole congregation to look after, the pressure for maintaining its healthy spirituality resting on him, and I was talking to him about necklaces.

A corner of a blue envelope peeked from under a stack of paper, and I grasped the opportunity.

'Did we get another threatenin' letter? What's it say?'

He followed my gaze and snatched it from its hiding place before stuffing it in one of the open drawers.

'Never you mind, darlin'. Now, go and help your mother with dinner.'

41. Present day

In the Newhaven basement kitchen, my paring knife lifts skin from flesh. A strand of hair falls across my face and I blow it out of the way with a breath. The blade trembles as it fights with the peeled skin. I've over-estimated my skills and should've used a peeling knife. The peach slips between my fingers, the flesh squishy, juice staining my hand as the last bit of fuzzy skin falls into the bowl. The next set of instructions waits for me in Mom's neat handwriting. Next, she tells me, remove the pit and cut the flesh into wedges.

The sweet scent of peaches and cinnamon compete with the sharpness of lemon juice. All the ingredients for a new start, leaving the past and unanswered questions behind, lie out on the counter. They just need to be mixed together in the right amounts, and let heat and a little patience do the rest. Still the peach rests wobbly on the chopping board. My mind falters with a memory: Mom slicing peaches at the kitchen table. A younger version of me standing on a chair, hands deep in a bowl, blending butter with sugar and flour. The mixture oozing between my fingers.

'How are you doing here, Honey-bunny?'

Mom looked down on me, a smile on her face, her hair still Chicago-short. The room was bathed in a soft yellow glow, and I bathed in Mom's smile, discovering a new life together, trying it on like our new clothes, finding the personalities that matched this place. Newhaven quietness had been disorienting at first, but it had still been us girls together, figuring it out.

The memory swells in my throat, and I choke on it. I almost wish I could forget old memories too. I wipe my face with the back of my hand, smearing peach juice all over my cheek. The smell sharpens the images, ready to cut me deep. I redirect my attention to the peach. The knife hesitates as it rolls loose. Mom would've been able to do it, she could slice like no other, blade smoothly sinking into vegetables, chicken, beef, the occasional fish, with dexterity. Why couldn't I be more like her? The peach trembles again, and frustration gathers in my chest like a rainstorm.

'Something smells good here.'

Tom's presence fills the kitchen along with a sense of déjà vu. He approaches, blond hair damp with summer heat, cheeks red with exertion. His eyes shine with intent and my throat closes up. The feeling we've been here before rises, but it doesn't curdle into a memory. But it's all right, 'cause I ain't clamouring for the past anymore. I keep my eyes on Tom in front of me and let go of the feeling.

'I'm fixin' a peach cobbler.'

I turn my attention back to the peach and sink the blade into the orange flesh. Tom draws closer to my back, and it slows my breathing. The knife shakes in my hand. He smells like a day of hard labour, and the promise of a normal life. Maybe all the pain and the heartache will stop with him.

'I'm hankering for something sweet. Sweet like a peach.'

His hands on my waist and his breath on my ear startle me. The knife skids over the peach and sinks into my finger. I shriek. His words stir the earlier sense of déjà vu again, like I'm stuck in a familiar dark room, groping for the light switch. I scan his face as he cradles my hand, but I'm still in the dark.

'Oh, shh . . . shoot. Abigail, you're bleeding.'

My eyes follow his gaze to my index finger covered in blood. The red knocks the breath out of me. It ignites the swoosh of fire in my ears, echoes of screams. My whole body stiffens so hard it vibrates. Tom steers me to the sink. He runs my fingers under the faucet, where the water dilutes the blood into pink tendrils. They swirl down the drain until the water runs clear. Tension ebbs from me, and my body falters into Tom's chest. He wraps his arm around my shoulders, but it doesn't stop a shudder from tumbling down my spine.

Water gushes from the bathroom faucet. I rub my hands together over and over, following a manic rhythm, drops splashing everywhere. The Band-Aid falls into the basin to reveal the puffy red line of the cut. One day. The lull's lasted one day before the craziness whacked me over with another nightmare. The worse one yet. I stare at my hands and the Band-Aid Tom wrapped around the tip of my index finger yesterday. The images emerging from my nightmares have slowly been arranging themselves into an accusing finger, pointing at me. And this one has been the crowning nail. Why won't the devil quit me?

My hands haven't stopped shaking. They shook in my dream too. Red. Red dripping from them. The flames lick the blood on the floor, red disappearing under red. But that's not the worse part, only the gory prelude to this new main opus – Mom and Daddy's bodies sprawl on the floor. I look down and my hand seems so small, and the knife so big in it. There's never been a knife before. The blade shines red with blood. I can't see her, but I know she stands beside me.

42. One week before the fire

In Parkerville, our group crowded every inch of the sidewalk and hijacked the air with our impassioned truth. This place, with its white stucco façade and planters bloated with geraniums, was where women came to get rid of their precious legacy, a being they had a duty of care for, discarded because it didn't fit into their selfish lives. Mrs Calhoun thrust her placard up with fervour, always the same one with the picture of a life ended in all its dismembered gory details and the word 'Murderer' in a slash of red. Somehow her sign and the others felt wrong, almost grotesque, that day. I averted my eyes and focused on adding my voice to the others', shouting our slogans – this was my chance at redemption. I thrust my arms up with renewed faith, and the conviction I could make Daddy proud.

My eyes scanned the faces littered around the street, but Summer was nowhere to be seen. I didn't know how she'd react if she saw me here. On the opposite side of the road, a woman fidgeted, her bag squashed against her abdomen. Fear radiated off her in waves like heat from the sidewalk. If there's fear, they can be saved, Daddy would say; they felt it because they knew what they were doing was wrong. I could save her. I shouted along with the others, but the words tasted different than usual in my mouth. She looked up and her eyes brimmed with tears, and it hit me – my own words put the tears there.

'What's wrong with you people? Just leave her alone and let her through. It's hard enough on her as it is.'

It was Tania's friend. She had traded her flowery dress for a pair of jeans, t-shirt, and deep bags under eyes. The grief etched all over her face shocked me.

'Of course the lesbo's sticking up for the hoe who couldn't keep her legs closed.' The jab came from Tom. The truth somehow sounded seedy in his mouth. Tania's friend flinched before regaining her composure.

'Hey, genius, how do you think she got pregnant in the first place? One Sex Ed for that jackass.'

The comment earned a burst of giggles and a couple of woo-hoos from passers-by and melted Tom's hands into fists.

'Do you want me to go in with you?' she added to the young woman, who nodded quickly in response.

She was elbowing their way past when Tom shoved her hard. She hit the ground, while the other woman just bolted like a rabbit in a fox den and disappeared through the building's double doors. Without a second thought I kneeled down and slid a hand under the woman's elbow, helping her into a seated position.

'I'm sorry.' I wasn't sure why I apologised, but the responsibility swelled in my chest. Maybe I wanted to show her – I ain't like Tom.

'Are you? You're with them, aren't you?'

A flush ignited my cheeks, and my eyes dragged to the ground.

'I'm sorry about your friend too. You know, the accident. I mean, I'm sorry for your loss.'

When I dared look, the condolence had softened her face. Her braids were loose that day and falling freely over her shoulders. Neither of us moved, but I felt a wreath of people crowding around us.

My voice dropped. 'What did you mean that day when you shouted to my . . . to the man who was with me?'

'He was right next to us. He did somethin' to her somehow. He walked behind us at the traffic light and then it's just . . . just as if her legs gave out and she fell forward.'

You gotta stay sharp, darlin'. The words rung in my mind, wrapped in Daddy's voice. My heart went into free-fall. She had to be wrong. I opened my mouth, but before any words got out, an arm snaked around my waist and yanked me away. Tom's body felt clammy against mine. The intimacy of the embrace kicked the memories from the kitchen awake. All of them. A surge of adrenaline mixed with fear electrified my muscles.

'Don't touch me!'

It all happened in two terrifying shakes of a lamb's tail. For once my fist didn't use my thigh as a target, instead connecting with Tom's chin.

The well-rehearsed slogans died as all attention refocused on me, and Tom holding his jaw. My knuckles thrummed with pain. All eyes on me, judging me for what I'd done, without even asking why.

Silence had dominated the ride back home, stifling like the day's heat. Tom's dark glare had rearranged the air around like before a storm. It burned a hole in the back of my head. Still, not as bad as the pain radiating in my hand.

I dragged my body, heavy with all the day's events, up the stairs. Daddy and Mom were still at Newhaven, discussing the incident. They were all discussing it, but nobody bothered asking me nothing. The injustice of the situation stung my eyes. Especially when Daddy and Mom knew exactly what Tom had done to me.

I closed the door to my room. I didn't bother with the light before stepping out of my clothes, but I still couldn't escape. I slipped on my nightdress. How had my life changed so much within those short few weeks? Losing Daddy's trust, what Tom did to me, whatever secret my parents kept from me; my life used to be a series of immutable certainties, like the bald cypress trees in the swamp whose roots reach deep into the soil. Now I felt like a trailer park trapped in a tornado and dreaded the moment it would all come crashing down.

Daddy. I looked at him earlier, and the accusation from Tania's friend had played in a loop. *He did somethin' . . . just as if her legs gave out . . . gotta stay sharp, darlin'*. Those people lied all the time, I reminded myself. But my faith felt shaky.

The sheets rested lightly on my skin, more to hide my body than serve any other purpose in this heat. Summer surely slept on top of her sleeping bag, body exposed to the elements. A wetness spread across my lower belly, nightdress sticking to my skin. My arm brushed against a squelchy mass. Panic flung me out of bed. My hand smashed the switch. The violence of the exploding light forced me to blink a few times. My hand and nightdress were wet with a bright red stickiness, blood warm on my fingers. The goosebumps trailing down my spine told me I didn't miscalculate, I still had three weeks before my next period. I approached the bed with caution before flinging the sheet back. I recoiled, bile burning the back of my throat. The sight pinned me against the wall.

Nestled in the centre of the mattress a bunch of entrails gleamed menacingly under the light. An animal without a shape, without the identity of skin and the architecture of bones. The pulp of something that used to breathe, reduced to a bloody warning.

AUDIO FILE #12

Audio Quality: Good

[Voice A]:   Female

[Voice A]:   *(Coughing.)* This episode of 'A Question of
Faith' is part of our series dedicated to the
New America Baptist Church, a fast-growing
American unaffiliated Primitive Baptist church
with a number of congregations and com-
pounds around the southern part of the
country. Initially founded in Benton, Arkansas,
in 1980 by Pastor Jeremiah Spence, the church
is alleged to be a vicious hate group and
religious cult with an extremist ideology
rather than a … than a …

(Groaning noises.) Fuck it. Why am I doing
this anyway? It doesn't matter anymore. It's all
bullshit. None of this matters anymore. It's her.
It's all about her now. No need to keep up
pretences anymore.

43. Five days before the fire

I couldn't look at Mom's face. She sat at the kitchen table peeling potatoes, raw fingers curled around the knife. Another memory from Chicago returned, telling me the story of a woman who liked going out. A woman who'd go anywhere she pleased, a whole city sprawling at her feet, who didn't fear leaving her home. Images floated to the surface: Mom asking for help getting ready, living as part of a different community, a whole project of people, so much bigger than Newhaven, piling onto so many floors we practically lived among the clouds. A time before Daddy.

'Which one, Honey-bunny?' Mom had asked, holding out options from the packed clothes rail.

'The sparkly one, Mommy.'

Mom's clothes back then fitted like a second skin she shed all over the floor in the morning. After getting dressed she would sit in the kitchen, me cross-legged on the table. Body encased in sparkling blue, she'd examine her face in the mirror propped against the windowsill.

'Blush.' A tremor of excitement would shake Mom's voice as she held out her hand.

Little hands dived inside the toiletry bag with a shriek, fighting to retrieve the right one. The bag was a soft treasure chest filled with riches, shiny shells hiding powders of so many different colours, from shimmery copper to glittering pink or gold stardust. She put red finishing touches to puckered lips, before smacking them together. A loud bang on the front door, and her eyes shone in the yellow glow of the kitchen bulb.

'Be good, Honey-bunny. There's leftover pizza in the refrigerator,' she'd say as she rushed out of the door, wrapped in excitement and a flowery perfume. She'd leave but always be back by morning, smelling like someone else.

'You ever miss Chicago?'

Her body stiffened. 'No, I don't.'

'Don't you miss goin' out? You never leave this place. It must get borin' sometimes. I know I'm grounded but we should go to Parkerville together some time. Make a day of it. We could even take the twins.'

'I like it here. I have everything I need, why would I want to go anywhere else?'

The brutality of the last few weeks collided with Mom's opinion of Newhaven. What happened to me in the kitchen should've chipped at the veneer of this place, Tom forcing himself on me, touching me again in Parkerville, but she still acted content, peeling potatoes for Daddy's dinner. There wasn't enough potato peel in the whole of Newhaven to bury what had happened to me.

Suddenly it hit: the person responsible for all this misery was Tom, not me. In that moment, I hated Newhaven for making me the bad guy.

'Chicago ain't perfect, but Newhaven ain't either.'

The knife stopped, and she looked up from her task. 'You don't know what you're talking about. You were too young when we left. It isn't the place you've made up in your head.'

'I know Chicago ain't perfect, but this place's changed. We were happy there too. Just a different kind of happy. I remember. You went out all the time wherever you wanted. We had music, and dancing, we had . . . fries.' The truth burned my throat. She stood up, leaning over the table.

'Yes, you ate fries. You always ate, but I went days without proper food. And the loud music? That was to cover the shouts and so much worse.' Mom dropped back into her chair as if the words or memories had taken their toll. 'When John found us, found me, he reminded me what my true purpose was. I had forsaken my responsibility. I needed to give you a better, safer life.'

'That ain't true. You always were a good mom, even in Chicago.'

'You're the one that's been changing, Abigail, and not for the better.'

She resumed peeling potatoes, putting an end to the conversation and leaving me more confused than ever. I anchored myself to Summer's words – *you're the victim here*. All the talk about Parkerville and Chicago shaped into an idea, to show them all my devotion, while getting away from the confusion.

'Let's go away. Just for a little while. We can go spread the word in Chicago, I'm sure we can get Mrs Calhoun and Mrs Garrett to come along too. We could see our old neighbourhood, that pizza place we used to go to, and –'

'I can't leave . . .'

'Course you can. It'd just be for a few days. Don't you wanna see Chicago again?'

'You're almost eighteen, Abigail. You need to grow up.' Her body tensed with exasperation, the chair scraping back. 'Chicago's dangerous. We couldn't stay there any longer, especially after . . . And your dad . . .'

'Daddy wouldn't mind.'

'He would. John's a good man, he's provided us with a better life, given us the twins and Sarah, and he's keeping us safe.

But he has his limits, and we have to respect that. I owe him everything.'

'Is that why you always take his side instead of mine?'

'It's a small price to be paid after –'

'After what, Mom?'

'It's in the past.'

'What's in the past?'

'Nothing.'

'Nothing? That's convenient.'

'You don't understand.'

'How about thou shall not lie –'

'They were going to take you away from me!'

'What are you talking about?'

'Child Protection Services. They were going to take you away. We had to leave.'

'What?'

'They said I was an unfit mother, and neglectful. That the environment I raised you in was unsafe and unstable.'

She collapsed into the chair; the focus in her eyes blurred under a glaze of tears. I staggered back until I felt the comforting support of the kitchen counter. The air in the room felt thick like molasses. I swiped a glass from the counter. Water gushed from the faucet, filling it. I drank greedily, long gulps that hurt my throat.

The words didn't reconcile with the images I had. How she cared for the twins and baby Sarah now. When the twins had chicken pox, she slept on a chair in their room for four nights in a row. Even in Chicago, she gave up her food so I wouldn't go hungry. It was just us girls against the rest, and we managed. Her love shone down on me in the glow-in-the-dark stars she painstakingly put up in our closet so I could camp under a starry sky – summer stars, we called them. Those people knew nothing. My hand curled into a fist. What kind of government took kids away from a loving mom? Assholes, as Summer would call them, that's who.

'Don't you get it? If they find me, I'll go to jail.'

'But you're a good mom. I've seen you with the twins and Sarah. You stuck stars on the ceiling for me when I was little.'

The memory welled up in Mom's eyes and she quickly wiped a tear. The hugs Mom had smothered me in whenever she went to Parkerville, how frantic she was when she thought I had run off there, her refusal to leave Newhaven in all these years – they weren't a choice, but a necessity. The truth tainted every action with new meaning.

'Wash up before your dad gets home.'

'I'm almost eighteen. They can't take me away anymore.'

'I'll still go to jail. They could take the twins and Sarah.'

'Maybe they're not looking for you anymore.'

'Not another word. Please, just go wash up.'

How could she drop a revelation the size of Newhaven and refuse to discuss it? America was a big place, no way Child Protection Services could find us that easily if we avoided Chicago. She wasn't thinking straight, too much fear swarming in her head.

After locking the bathroom door, I climbed into the tub to think. All the little inconsistencies rattled in my head, feeding my confusion: Mom loving me so much that she became a fugitive, but not protecting me against Tom or Daddy; Newhaven judging me for what happened in Parkerville without even hearing my side of the story. The bloody entrails flashed in my mind, shaped like the gruesome images on our placards. They were meant as an anonymous warning, a block in my path telling me to turn around, but instead they had opened something in me. My fist pummelled my thigh, turning my frustration into a bruise I could press on to remind myself of this moment. Newhaven had always been a simple truth for me but now it had become something I didn't understand. Mom, Daddy. Even Mr Caine. All preaching one thing – the importance of family – and behaving the opposite, parents siding against their daughter, and a father hitting his son. For the first time, my faith brought me no comfort.

44. Present day

The church reverberates with silence, a shell waiting to be imbued with the ringing faith and devotion of its congregation. Daddy's passion really brought it to life every Sunday, he stamped his faith onto people, Pastor Abernathy's style is a lot more subdued, stoking the fire of their faith. My presence barely makes a dent in the emptiness. My lips move with fervour, silent words falling out of them. Head bowed and hands clasped tight, holding on to my faith and whatever sanity is left in me.

'Dear God in heaven, I come to you in the name of Jesus. I acknowledge to You that I'm a sinner, and I'm sorry for my sins and the life that I've lived; I need your forgiveness. Please protect me from evil, Father. Don't let it get hold of me. Please, God. Please make it stop. Amen.'

I shift my weight, knees protesting under bruises I can't remember getting. Fear creeps in my throat, but I swallow it back. I continue, the prayer slipping out through gritted teeth – a test from God I ain't failing. Heat competes with the silence in the church. It dampens every fold in my body. Everyone else is working or just going about their day while I desperately try to save my soul. My shoulders drop further and I almost lose balance. I've been keeping sleep at arm's length for the last few days, only allowing myself to snatch fistfuls of it here and there. My gaze latches on the cross above the stage. I think of closing my eyes and surrendering to darkness. What will I remember, which faces will appear in my mind or at the foot of my bed? Which voice will talk to me? My breath hikes up like that night in the hallway. The night she appeared inside Newhaven.

Words fall in a frenzy now, but salvation doesn't come. Images find their way through the cracks of my crumbling faith. Daddy, a horrified look on his face, saying forgive her, Lord, for she doesn't know what she's done, the screams of flames feeding in a frenzy, the woman from the hallway, the one from my dream standing in the doorway at Hunters Cottage, bloody rabbits and possums hung by their innards, the smell of rotting meat in the sun. The images chase me, but I don't want to remember no more.

I run out, stumble on the porch, panting, and almost collide with something soft.

'Hey, I was lookin' for you. You all right?' Jackson's eyes narrow at me.

'Fine. Do they need me to help with Mrs Favreau?'

He shoves his hands deep in his pockets, fabric bulging with his fists, shoulders up to his ears. 'No. I just . . . Can we talk?'

I motion to him, and we step back inside the shadow of the church. The heat is still as oppressive but at least the sun isn't beating down on us. I smile, but it doesn't ease whatever knots are stopping his words from coming out. He's always been such a quiet kid, but having witnessed Mr Caine's outburst, I guess he had to be. Daddy would've said our Lord is testing him. *That's some shit test!* I screw my eyes shut, fist light-tapping my thigh. She cannot be here, not in my head, not in the house of our Lord.

'C'mon, why did you want to see me?'

The request jolts him. ''Cause I wanted to say sorry.'

'For what?'

'For my dad. He was horrible to you.'

'It ain't your fault. He's pretty mean to you too. That happen a lot?'

His eyes have not once left the ground, where the tip of his shoe scuffs some imaginary mark on the carpet. I wonder how many other secrets hide in Newhaven, a place with so many closed doors, so many shadows even in the height of summer.

'Have you tried tellin' someone?'

'Your dad knew.'

'Daddy?'

'He knew. I asked him to speak to my dad. Know what he said?'

I shook my head.

'He said God made my father the way he is and that I should try harder to be a better son, and honour my father,' he scoffs. He stares at me, chin tilted up. 'I ain't sorry he's gone.'

My lips parted.

'Well, I ain't, OK?'

What Jackson says leaves me speechless. It doesn't align with my memories of Daddy, the man I remember saving me and Mom, but the stack I have is incomplete, still missing several weeks.

He snorts before continuing, 'You know what's funny? If Pastor Munro hadn't died, then your dad wouldn't have become the new pastor, and I might have ended up having a very different conversation. And before you say anything, no need to speak to Pastor Abernathy, he's too weak to do nothin'.'

My mind collects the names he's dropped and adds one of my own – Pastor Munro, Pastor Heywood, Pastor Abernathy, and initially Pastor Favreau: three out of the four dead, struck down by fate or something far more sinister, Mom and Fleur collateral damage, standing too close to great men. I wonder whether the other pastors got threatening letters. I always assumed it was only us.

Jackson's lips are moving again. 'You hear what I say? We'll never be safe here. We gotta go.'

'I can't go. My family's here – the twins and baby Sarah. Even if I wanted to, I got no money.'

'I've been putting some away whenever I can. I got close to five hundred bucks.'

'You've been stealin'?'

His foot changes target and hits the back of the bench in front of us. 'Donations are for the whole congregation, so I can use them too, you know.'

The sadness in his eyes tells me he can't handle any more rejection. The happy little boy he used to be vanished at the same time his mom did. One day Mrs Caine had gone on a protest at the 'Let's Go Burn Them' Center. She slipped into the bathroom at the Greyhound Station and never came out. Her absence has dug a hole in Jackson he hopes to fill with five hundred bucks, a bus ticket and the dream that he can somehow find her again.

Muffled work chatter drifts with the warm breeze.

'I'd better go. Promise you'll think about it?'

'Fine.'

One word, four letters is all it takes to split his face into a wide grin and send him running out into the blinding light. Silence reclaims the space. I lace my fingers together – forgive me, Father, for I have sinned . . .

The clock on the east wall tuts that I'm gonna be late with Mrs Favreau's lunch. And today's her favourite – cheesy grits with bacon. Below the clock, placards are propped against the wall, ready for the next protest. From the slogans slashed across the cardboard, it will take place at the Planned Parenthood. We call it devotion, they brand it hatred. I asked Daddy once, and he said it was a matter of perspective. You could look at the same thing and view it differently, depending on how close you stood to God. Those people stood too far away to see the devotion in the act. Like the rabbit/duck picture? I'd asked. He'd pulled me onto his lap. A soft rain had patted against the window, and the smell of warm biscuits drifted from the kitchen. That's right, darlin', just like the rabbit/duck picture. My brow knitted with confusion. What is it, darlin'? But which one are we, Daddy – the rabbit or the duck? The memory of his laugh that day accompanies me as I leave the church.

The present comes back full force when a hand pushes me back inside and pins me against the wall, my head slamming into the plaster. My breath cowers in my chest. A couple of the placards clatter to the ground. Mr Caine's face hovers inches from mine, tense with anger. His fingers grip the tops of my arms, dimpling the flesh under the sleeves. The pressure grinds my bones.

'I told you to stay away from my boy.'

'Let me go! I reckon –'

'Nobody asked for your damn opinion.' He slams my body back into the wall again, knocking the words out of me. Fear whips me into attention. 'I don't want filth like you corruptin' my son.' He says the word 'son' like you would say my table, my boat or my gun. 'Lemme tell you, your father was a good man but he was weak. He knew what you and your mother were, still he brought you back here where you don't belong. God punished him for his pride, cleansin' his house with fire. I don't want none of that perversion near my family and that includes Jackson. Understood?'

A blinding terror has wiped out my mind. I nod furiously. Without another word, he casts me aside before striding out of the church.

From: Jeb Abernathy
Date: Friday, September 16, 2022 at 10:27 AM
To: Cameron McPherson
Subject: Re: Concerns – guidance needed

Dear Pastor McPherson,

I pray this email finds you well.

I am afraid I have to inform you that the situation at Newhaven
has been escalating. I have been made aware that approximately
$500 is missing from our petty cash fund. I cannot think of
anybody who could do something like this other than Abigail. I'm
afraid to think what the money is for. She could be using it to pay
off someone for who knows what, or get to Parkerville, or worse.

I know you mentioned the possibility of Abigail moving to New
Eden. I was reticent at first, believing she is our responsibility, but
maybe she would be better in a new environment. We cannot
trust what she would say if she leaves the church, and New Eden
might have the tools to help her see the error of her ways. I owe it
to Pastor Heywood that his daughter is cared for and protected.

I'll await to hear from you and welcome your guidance.

Under His guidance. Have a blessed day.

Pastor Jeb Abernathy

45. Four days before the fire

Like every Sunday, the congregation quietened down. Like every Sunday, women covered their heads in respect. Like every Sunday, all eyes were trained on Daddy. Like every Sunday, he fed from their energy, their desire for salvation. But not everything was the same this Sunday. It didn't all align as it should, like an image through a glass of water. Tainted water.

Still, the air in church fizzled with electricity, and it all traced back to Daddy, slapping and rubbing his hands, his beard split with a wide grin. Even the mic on his lapel crackled with energy.

'I wanna try somethin' with y'all today. Rise to your feet. Even you watchin' online. Now husbands, take off your shoes.' A murmur of hesitation fretted through the crowd. 'Come on, y'all. You trust me, right?'

He led the way, taking his own shoes off. The other men followed, slipping out of their dress shoes, some new, some shining under the patina of age. People looked at each other, searching for someone who knew what was happening. I looked and wondered how many people here had run away from something, someone, or some government acronym. Toes to the heel, Mr Caine pulled off his shoes; my chest tightened at the memory of the barn.

'Now, ladies, put on your husband's shoes, and once you got them on, have a little walk around.'

Mom stumbled after a couple of steps in Daddy's five-sizes-too-big shoes. She wasn't the only one. Others tripped too, or walked slowly like calves on newfound legs. The experiment drew giggles from all corners of the room. Even he had a good chuckle. After a couple of minutes, the status quo got reinstated with the right pair of shoes returned to the correct feet.

'There's a very important lesson in this little experiment. Ladies, you struggled in your husband's shoes. Wouldn't you say that?' The question was met by a choir of agreement. 'That's the problem with society today, women tryin' to walk in their husband's shoes, takin' on tasks too big for them. Your husband's shoes ain't meant for you, nor are your husband's responsibilities. Here, we understand husbands' and wives' responsibilities are different. Husbands are meant to protect and provide for their family while their wives encourage them and look after that family. Under His guidance.'

The scarf felt tight around my head. I hooked a finger, pulling it away from my throat. I watched the stage, listening to a different voice – Summer's voice, whispering in my head, whispering a different story.

People trickled out of the old ballroom after breakfast. On the grand staircase, Melanie Le Roux sauntered next to Owen Nolan, now officially her fiancé with Daddy's blessing. I hurried past, eyes fixed on the steps. They didn't look like husband- and wife-to-be, more like father and daughter.

'I was swimmin' in your shoes. Couldn't have taken two steps without fallin' over.'

'That's fine. I'd have caught you.'

'What happens if you got feet bigger than your husband?' My question killed their banter. It slipped out without me knowing – Summer hijacking my mind again. The epiphany I had a few days ago that Tom was to blame for everything and not me had loosened a defiance in me I never knew existed. Melanie stared at me; she looked like a catfish out of a pond.

'You won't have that problem when we're married.' Tom walked past, a smug expression smeared all over his face. My punch hadn't knocked the arrogance out of him. My body hummed with the desire to hit him again, but too many people surrounded us. I slowed down my breathing.

'I ain't never marrying you. Ever.'

'That's not what your dad says.'

The words knocked me out cold. A couple of weeks ago this kind of snide remark would've felt like nothing more than lies, but now . . . Still I clung to the idea Daddy wouldn't do something this horrible – handing me a life sentence of misery.

'Of course, I can't have you questioning things, but you'll learn to make a good wife.'

'Not gonna happen.'

'Don't be so sure.'

'Never.'

'You'll never have to worry about walking in my shoes.'

Every answer grated on my patience. I snapped. My body folded over the banister, leaning so far out gravity might claim me. My voice ripped through the foyer, bouncing off the high ceiling.

'It was a stupid experiment, and I ain't never marrying you, even if you're the last man on earth.'

I rushed past all of them, knocking into elbows and hips along the way, leaving a forest of statues in my wake. His words clouded my judgement – *That's not what your dad says*. They fed doubts in my mind, eroded my faith. It was one thing for Daddy to blame me for Tom's reaction, but another to bind me to him until death do us part. The man from the old shack flashed in my mind, and the wife of his they found dead in the swamp. The heat outside smothered me, but I didn't slow down. I tripped and prayed for softness, but the sun had baked the ground into something hard. I got up and kept running.

46.

The front door banging shut jolted me, and I almost dropped my Bible. The comfort I had been looking for in the words of the Lord eluded me, my mind frazzled by Tom's threat. Footsteps boomed up the stairs, too heavy for Mom, followed by a sharp knock on the door. I flinched.

'Abigail, can you come down to my office.' The inflection in his voice didn't curve into a question. The hairs on my arms bristled. His tone had never sounded so flat. Its evenness unnerved me. I opened my mouth, but footsteps smacked the stairs again before a word got out.

I hovered at the open office door. A silence enveloped the house, telling me we were alone. The heat and worry dampened the back of my neck. I used to wonder if our Lord created heatwaves to remind us why we'd want to stay out of hell. Daddy's face looked as blank as the papers spread on his desk, no clues as to whether his betrayal was real. I didn't dare ask him about what Tom said. A lick of fear shivered down my spine.

'Close the door, will you.' It closed without a sound, sealing us in. 'Come here.'

Something crunched under my feet. I frowned, confused when I saw grains of uncooked rice littering the floor.

'I'm very disappointed, Abigail. At what happened at the protest, and your shameful outburst just now. You need to reflect and ask for our Lord's guidance and forgiveness.'

I shifted my weight from one leg to the other, waiting. He smiled, and for a moment my old daddy appeared in the warmth of that smile. The man who used to be so proud of me, who brushed the tears off my cheek with his thumb that day I fell down the front porch stairs, who listened to me recite the Young Women Pledge by heart, before clapping in approval.

'Now's time to kneel and pray, darlin'.'

I got down, flat hand ready to brush away the rice.

'Leave it there.' I looked up at him, the same benevolent smile pinned on his face. 'Just kneel. And pull up the hem of your dress.'

I stared at him, waiting for him to tell me where to kneel or to just laugh it off, telling me he was just joking like he did with Mom. His smile withered away, and so did all hope in my chest.

'I ain't repeating myself.'

My heart shrivelled with dread as I lowered into position, the weight of my body grinding the grains of rice into my knees. Shifting for a better position unleashed an onslaught of pain – the rice bit harder, and my teeth sank into the soft lining of my mouth.

'Luke 15:18 and 18:13. Out loud.'

'"I will arise and go to my father . . ."' Each verse wrung out of me, words ripped from my flesh. They blurred in my throat as gravity pulled at me, setting my knees ablaze.

While I was lost inside the pain, Daddy had left his desk for the sofa. Elbows resting on his lap, his lips hovered so close his breath and beard teased my skin. The close proximity jolted me. My knees burned and I ground the pain between my teeth.

'Hear my words, for I ain't repeating myself. Your inso-lence's gone far enough. I've allowed it till now, but no more. It stops here.'

I fixed on an imaginary point on the white wall opposite. I latched onto his words to distract myself from the stinging, but my mind kept slipping. The grains of rice burrowed deeper into my flesh, reigniting the burn. A violent pain shot up my thighs before it tore through the rest of my body. The room blurred under a wall of tears. Each swallowed, shud-dering sob ripped new pains inside. My whole body burned with it. Dying would hurt less.

'You'll behave like the obedient daughter you're expected to be. You'll behave like my daughter. I provide a good life for you and your mother, but if you disrespect me then you'll be responsible for whatever happens to her.'

My eyes widened at the words and their implication. I blinked and tears scalded my cheeks. They pooled at my chin before falling onto my fingers clenched into prayer. Still I fixed on the same point on the wall. My whole body throbbed with pain.

'What do you think will happen if I disown your mother, and kick her out? The twins and Sarah will stay with me, con-siderin' your mother's outlaw past. I know she told about Child Protection Services.'

His lips were so close now they brushed against my ear-lobe. His breath stank with sweet tea. Pain and the smell coiled around my throat, and my stomach lurched.

'That'll just break your mama's heart, before she's thrown in jail for kidnappin' and child endangerment. You don't wanna be responsible for that, do you darlin'?'

Tears and searing pain blurred everything apart from Daddy's voice – sharp enough to slice through it all.

'Remember, whatever happens it'll always be your words against mine. You really think anybody here will believe you?'

The rice cut deeper into my flesh, my knees ablaze with new pain. The intimacy of this threat trickled like ice down my spine before pooling in my stomach. He would do it. Mom would die if her kids were taken away from her.

'Do you understand?' The words whipped the air and jolted me into a nod. The rice ground further and snatched a whimper from my lips.

'Good. You can stand up now.'

Shifting my weight sent a shooting pain towards my pelvis. A drop of urine dampened my underwear. I winced before I faltered. Daddy caught me, slipping a hand under my elbow.

'Here. Lemme help.'

He lifted me and brushed the rice imbedded in the skin. The grains fell to the ground, leaving behind their shape in my flesh. Once finished he cupped my face and wiped the tears with his thumbs.

'Now, now. It's over. You're all right, darlin'. Let's get you to the bathroom and get you cleaned up.'

I followed him, too numb to say anything, my willpower left behind, discarded somewhere on the office floor among the rice. In the bathroom, he propped me on the edge of the tub, gently cleaned my face and dabbed a cold cloth and antiseptic over my burning knees. I didn't know what was more terrifying – the cruelty of his punishment or the tenderness of his care in the aftermath of his own cruelty.

47. Two days before the fire

A blackberry cobbler cooled on the counter. The pie was Daddy's favourite – as if it could be any other way. Nobody ever asked me what I wanted to eat. The thought of Daddy woke up the pain in my knees. Fear had replaced faith in my heart, hammering the dread inside with every beat. It drove all of my actions now and fuelled my motivation to be an obedient daughter.

I looked at Mom and all I saw was the woman who had made herself a criminal so she could keep her daughter. The way she fanned the pie, how she scrubbed the utensils and bowl, prepared Daddy's dinner, ironed his shirts, every gesture the proof of her love for me and how far she'd been willing to go to keep me safe. How close it got to being destroyed by my recklessness. After the office and the rice I wondered if he ever did anything similar to her; if her compliance was motivated by fear rather than solely by devotion. The shadow of his threat stalked her around the kitchen. A darkness I put there, and she didn't know nothing about it. Guilt lumped in my throat, and I swallowed it down.

Matthew rammed into the table, almost knocking over a glass. Sarah whined in her bassinet. The will to live escaped Mom in a long sigh that pulled her eyes shut.

'Want some help?'

She looked at me as if seeing me for the first time in a very long time.

'Could you take the twins? I don't know what's got into them today.'

I crouched in the path of Matthew and Elijah. 'Hey, guys. Wanna play hide and seek?'

'One, two, three . . .'

A flurry of giggles filled the makeshift darkness, and the patter of tiny feet padded up the stairs. My lips twitched into a smile – discretion wasn't the twins' forte.

'. . . fifty! Ready or not, here I come.'

I climbed upstairs slowly, coughing a couple of times for excitement to bubble in the boys' stomachs. On the landing I smirked at the door to the master bedroom slightly ajar. We'd played this game a hundred times, and they still hadn't found another place to hide.

'Now, where could they be hidin'?' The words dragged out, and a low rumble echoed deep inside the room. 'Could they be . . . ?'

I swung the door open further. The bedroom was bathed in alternating light and shadows, blades of light from the shutter stabbing through ribs of darkness. It always felt weird stepping into Mom and Daddy's room without them here. More muffled noise echoed from inside the wardrobe, and I suppressed a giggle. Mom was not going to be happy if they pulled down Daddy's shirts. He wouldn't care though. I crept towards the bed. My throat constricted at the quilt of floral geometric pattern – a wedding gift stitched by women from the congregation. Daddy hadn't said nothing about Tom's mention of wedding, and I wasn't gonna ask.

Flipping a quilt corner, I dived under the bed with a flourish. For a second, I expected to stare back at Summer, hiding with a smirk on her face, but the space only hid a lone army of dust bunnies. My heart dropped against my chest at the emptiness.

A new onslaught of giggles reminded me of my priorities.

'Now, where could they be? Where, where, where . . . ?'

The rest of the words were forgotten as a flash of green peeked from the top of the wardrobe. Eyes fixed on the shape, I threw the wardrobe doors open before climbing on the ledge.

'You find us, Abbay!'

The twins' shrieks drifted past as I stretched on my tiptoes towards the top. My fingers brushed one of the corners, but the box slid back. I strained, shoulder burning in its socket, sweat soaking the hair in the fold of my armpits. Hooking a fingernail, I scratched at the velvet. The box inched forwards until I lost balance and it fell with me.

The bottom of the box coated my fingers with a layer of sticky dust – the box from Daddy's office the day he had been frantically looking for something. The inside smelled like the condemned rooms at Newhaven. My gaze snagged on the curled corners of a stack of photographs. They weighed heavy in my hands. The faces staring back were those of strangers. A woman stood a step away from the other two, a willowy figure, arms crossed under her chest, holding her elbows. The ghost of a cigarette dangled from her fingers. The little girl held a man's hand – her daddy, I reckoned. He looked young, barely twenty. The roughness of the exposure blunted their features. The little girl's face tilted towards him instead of the camera. His hand rested on the woman's shoulder. Instead of eyes, shadows bruised the sockets on their faces. Especially the man. I felt him judging me. The sun and time had bleached the colours, leaving just shadows of previous lives lived, but it hadn't dulled the red of the woman's mouth, bold like a warning sign, just slightly smudged. I wondered who they were. Their clothes didn't reflect our dress code. The woman wore a sundress in faded yellow or white, the fabric draping a pregnant belly, bare shoulders red with the rawness of sunburn. The only scenery behind them was fields. The other photos depicted scenes from everyday family life. Happy scenes, but the expressions on their faces at odds with that. The last one was a wedding portrait, the woman's head thrown back in laughter, exposing her throat, the two of them looking no more than teenagers playing adults.

'Abbay . . .' Elijah tugged at my dress.

'Shush.'

I tucked the photographs back into the box, and their corners kicked loose a couple of misshapen pearls. I picked one up and saw it for what it was – a baby tooth, whose I had no idea. The twins hadn't lost theirs yet. At least there weren't adult ones. I dropped it back in next to a woman's watch, not Mom's. I reached for a small velvet pouch. A little bit of jiggling and a pair of hoop earrings slid into the palm of my hand.

My heart hitched in my throat in recognition. Images sharpened in my mind. The earrings had been wrapped in yellow tissue paper, I could still hear the rustling when Mom had opened the poorly wrapped present. *I love them, Honey-bunny! Thank you.*

'Can I see?'

I jerked upright, snatching my hand away from Elijah. He couldn't have them. Daddy never said no to them. I stared down at the twins, soft and round with happiness. They've never had anything to worry about, never suffered Daddy's rules or his punishment – the privilege of being born boys. I rubbed my knees. An impulse to lock them in the wardrobe and walk away flared inside. Have screams strip the innocence from their throats. They should learn like I did lately that sometimes when you cried in the darkness, nobody came. I needed company in my despair. Instead I lost myself in the gold lines of the earrings, followed the words looped on each one. They used to catch the light in our kitchen, it flared like shooting stars.

'Abigail.'

I shoved the earrings in my pocket as I straightened myself, twins still clinging to my skirt.

'Can you come down? Your father wants to speak to you.'

AUDIO FILE #13

Audio Quality: Moderate

[Voice A]:   Female
[Voice B]:   Female

[Voice A]:   So, what's the deal with that room in the basement and all the books with missing pages?
[Voice B]:   Wait, aren't you supposed to ask me if you can record me?
[Voice A]:   Shit, you're right.
[Voice B]:   S'okay. To record me. That room's called the Instruction Room, that's where we held classes.
[Voice A]:   What kind of classes?
[Voice B]:   Men and boys have Devotion classes every morning at 7am, and there's the Young Women classes.
[Voice A]:   OK, I'll bite, what's Devotion classes?
[Voice B]:   It teaches men about how to be leaders, spiritually and physically. How to use the teaching from the Holy Scriptures to become strong men, and moral leaders to rule their wife and family. It teaches how to spread the words of the Lord to those who need to be saved.

[Voice A]: *(Deep exhaling sound.)* So basically it brain-washes them into becoming dictators.

[Voice B]: You're being all judgemental again.

[Voice A]: Sorry, just trying to understand as it sounds completely crazy to me.

[Voice B]: How?

[Voice A]: Never mind. And the room with all the computers?

[Voice B]: That's where men do online outreach. They join online forums where lost men gather and they offer an alternative and how faith can help them live a fulfilling life. Men who have been robbed of a decent life 'cause of the trappings of modern society and the selfish-ness of feminist women. Men who found themselves involuntary celib –

[Voice A]: INCELS? ARE YOU TELLING ME YOUR CHURCH IS RECRUITING INCELS AND TELLING THEM THAT RULING OVER WOMEN IS THEIR GOD-GIVEN RIGHT?

[Voice B]: Hush your mouth. It ain't their fault –

[Voice A]: Your faith breeds dangerous men. Don't be surprised if they then turn around and abuse that power.

48. Present day

The words on the Bible page blur behind the images of my encounter with Mr Caine at the church yesterday. I ain't left my room since, apart from spending time with the twins. The knock on the door's just a formality. They always enter no matter the response, but tonight there's a change. Tom carries a tray in his hands and a smile on his face. Everyone else's given up on me – myself included – but he hasn't. He drops the tray on the bed next to the blue letter from Daddy's office. The mattress shifts under his weight as he sits. I don't know what to do with the letter now the cops ain't coming back and no one here trusts me, so for the time being it serves as a bookmark for my Bible. I slot the envelope into the middle of Genesis.

Tom's lips move. He's talking, but I've tuned him out. He offers me a smile which lights up his whole face. I respond with one of my own, but it doesn't stretch as far as his.

'You have no idea what I've just said.'

'Sorry. My mind's such a mess . . .'

Helplessness swells in my chest as tears swell in my eyes. I'm such a wimp, always on the verge of tears. They come more easily and better formed than my memories. I blink hard to keep them at bay. I shake my head. Once in motion I can't stop. My fist hits my thigh in frustration, the tray and its contents rattling on the bed.

'Hey, it's OK.'

He wipes a tear off my cheek with the pad of his thumb,

and my skin shudders with a memory of Daddy using the same gesture. We were in the bathroom, and he consoled me. From what I have no idea. Tom's hand lingers on my face, the palm of his hand a comforting warmth against my cheek.

'Not gonna lie, I'm a bit hurt I didn't make a lasting impression on you.'

He smiles again, and my teeth bite my lower lip to fight my own. The light flickers in the room. We both look around, waiting on the edge of another possible blackout. After a few seconds, the light's settling again but my heart ain't.

'I wish you could remember the last few weeks with me.'

The light shifts in his eyes, his fingers burn on my cheek. Deep down something wiggles in my stomach, pushing against the spongy walls, wanting to break free and rise to the surface. *Don't fucking believe him.* My muscles calcify into bones, bones into stones. It's her again. I bury her voice under the weight of the current moment and focus on Tom.

'But I have an idea about how I could help you remember.'

Pushing the tray aside, he edges closer to me. My breathing slows down, and the light flickers again. He leans in. His finger strokes my cheek. His lips brush back and forth against mine until they settle on my mouth. His mouth slackens into a soft kiss. My lips part and the tip of his tongue sweeps over my teeth. He cups my face as the kiss deepens. It picks up momentum, and his gentleness morphs into something else. His hand slides to the back of my neck, holding me firmly in place as his mouth turns hungrier and sloppy. A sense of danger hitches in my chest. His kiss bends me, pushes me back into the mattress before his full weight flattens me. I'm trapped. Her voice rides on my growing panic like one of the horsemen. *Fight. Fucking fight!*

I hit the side of his head, but nothing dents his

determination. He grows hard against my thigh and groans into my mouth. The voice in my head drives my hand, my fingers twist his ear until he breaks off his kiss.

'You bitch.'

Twisting my head sideways, my eyes land on the tray. I quickly pat the surface until my fingers curl on metal. He retreats, holding his hands out. I straighten myself, thrusting the fork in front of me.

'Get out. Get out of here.' I scream.

His assault has unleashed an onslaught of images and sensations – Tom in Newhaven's cavernous kitchen, him blocking the door, the unease of the encounter before the blinding fear as he takes what he wants, the pinch of his fingers. I remember it all.

'You attacked me. You attacked me in the kitchen. He was right. Jackson was right. You're a monster.'

My terror breaks his mouth into a smirk. 'You fucking tease. I'm being nice to you. I've listened and helped you search your dad's office. You could be grateful.'

'Get out. Get out. Get the fuck out!'

'Come on, don't be like that.'

'I'll tell them. I'll tell the cops about what you did.'

The way he looks at me kills any warmth in my body. His jaw and body tense, ready to hurt me. I scramble back until my back flattens against the headboard. I scream. The light throws a fit of its own. I'm terrified at the idea of being stuck in this room with him if the generator fails.

'Help. Help me, please. Tom, get out! Somebody –'

The door bursts open. Pastor Abernathy and Wade Pruitt's chests heave with laboured breaths. Mr Pruitt's fingers are laced around the grip of his gun, and my shoulders slacken with relief.

49. Present day

The commotion has drawn a few more people to the door, Mrs Calhoun included. Their numbers inflate my sense of safety, and my back eases off the headboard.

'Now then, what's happenin' here?' Pastor Abernathy asks.

Words pour out of me like people scrambling out of a burning building. The quicker they know, the quicker they can kick him out.

'He attacked me, Pastor. He said he wanted to help me remember, but he lied. He pushed himself on me. He said we were friends, but he lied 'cause he's dishonest and depraved. We can't . . . We need to call the sheriff —'

'Hold your horses, Abigail.'

A wave of whispers spreads at my words. Tom stands by the bed, a strange calmness running through his demeanour. Pastor Abernathy quietens down the onlookers before turning to him. He gauges his reaction to my accusations, but Tom doesn't waiver.

'Tom, what you gotta say for yourself?'

'Pastor, I don't want to speak badly, especially when I haven't been here for as long as some of you folks have been around.'

'Just speak the truth, son.'

'I'm afraid she's lying. I didn't attack her.'

'Pastor —'

Pastor Abernathy holds out his hand, cutting short any arguments I might have. All eyes are on me, waiting for what

I will do next. I swallow back the rest of my sentence and wait.

'Sorry, Tom, you were sayin', son,' Pastor Abernathy prompts.

'I've been helping Abigail. I've been feeling sorry for her after what happened with the fire. Losing your parents that way. Things like that mess you up. I didn't want to judge after the whole fence incident, you know.'

Pastor Abernathy nods, and more whispers travel through the group.

'I decided to do something nice, and bring her some food. She suggested for me to sit down, so, you know, we could talk. I did, wanting to be nice. But then she got all flirty and asked me if I could do her a favour.'

My mouth opens ready to protest, but one look from Pastor Abernathy shoots me down.

'She said she wanted me to post a letter for her.'

My head snaps in Tom's direction. He stares at me with condescension and a hint of disapproval. She stirs inside me, squirms about in the pit of my stomach like a snake. Her anger tightens my fingers around the fork. A quick glance around confirms that they believe him so far. He's confirming all their suspicions about me.

'I mean, I was happy to oblige. I wanted to make her happy. Help her in this difficult time. But something wasn't right about the letter. And then she started screaming. It's like the devil got into her.'

My eyes narrow at him but I still ain't seeing a point to this performance and all his lies. He pauses. His gaze sweeps through his audience, enthralled faces leaning in, eager to know the next instalment of his tale.

'It was the address. The letter was addressed to Newhaven.'

261

'Why would she send a letter here?' Pastor Abernathy asks. 'I didn't –'

'That's exactly what I thought, Pastor, so I opened it, and that's when she started screaming, when I wouldn't give it back. Anyway, I'll let you be the judge.'

Tom stares at me, the blue envelope now wedged between two fingers as he hands it over to Pastor Abernathy. My eyes flash to the bed where my Bible lies open. A few heads crane to read over his shoulder. The words drain all the colour from his face.

'What the heck is this, Abigail?'

'He's lyin'. The letter got nothing to do with it. I was actually going to give it to you. We got those letters in the mail at home. Hate mail. Daddy showed them to me. I went to Hunters Cottage and found that letter in his desk. Maybe whoever wrote it hated us so much they started the fire.'

'Really?' The question comes from Tom, a small smile hitched on the side of his face, laughing at a joke I ain't privy to. I feel dizzy, like he's been ahead of me the entire time.

'How can your dad have received this letter in the mail when it hasn't been franked?'

He holds the envelope in front of my face, the stamp unblemished by the ink of a US Postal Services franking machine. I stagger like when Daddy used to kick me in the back of the knee. How did I miss this in all the time I've had it? Bewilderment spreads under my skin. I read their interpretation in their parted lips and knitted brows. It confirms all of their suspicions, the ones who believe I got something to do with the fire, with the animal carcasses strung to the fence. Now they think I'm manufacturing an outside villain to hide my crimes. What would they do if they knew about the pieces I remember, about the blood, Mom's blood, about the knife in my hand? Would they coil them all together into a rope to hang me with?

'Abigail, why would you do that?' Pastor Abernathy speaks the words slowly.

I follow his gaze to my hand tightly clenched around the fork. My fingers loosen and the fork clatters on the floor. It echoes in my mind, like a stone dropped in a swamp, concentric circles spreading.

'What did you do, Abigail?' Pastor Abernathy asks when I fail to respond. The memories are rising now.

Pastor Abernathy's words fill the room, but I'm back at Hunters Cottage amid an overpowering metallic smell. There's a knife in my hand, both slick with blood. The blood isn't mine.   It's hers. Her life is all over my hands, wearing it like gloves.   Her blood, the knife slippery with it.   It clatters to the floor before Mom follows it, clutching her stomach, blood oozing between her fingers.

50. Two days before the fire

Dread pounded in my chest as I knocked on Daddy's office door.

'Abigail, come in and close the door behind you.'

'Hey, Daddy.' The greeting slipped out as I slipped into the chair on the other side of the desk. At least nothing crunched under my feet. My tongue rubbed against my front teeth. Nothing on his face hinted at the reason why I was here. My fingers reached for the stub of my braid, the hair brittle under my skin. His eyes flashed down to my hand, and the braid dropped back against my chest.

'Do you know why I've asked you here?' His hands lay flat on his desk, fingers pointed towards me. They seemed huge against the polished wood.

'I don't know. Mom just said you wanted to speak to me. Sorry.' I hated how my voice wobbled.

'That's all right. Just take a moment and think. Is there anythin' you wanna tell me?' His Southern drawl elongated the question and hiked the tension in my body. I balanced on the edge of the chair.

He leaned forward, elbows on the desk, chin propped on one hand. On the mantel the clock clicked at me in disapproval. I threw agitated looks around the room, but there was no way out to escape his question. Once in motion, my eyes couldn't find a place to rest. Everything in this space had a place, a purpose, an order – from the framed quotes lining the walls to the shelves carefully stacked with pristine books with virgin spines. And inside of all that neatness, me – a girl in an untidy state of confusion trapped on a chair, worry kicking under my skin. My gaze ran along the shelves again and I spotted it – the box of rice with its cheery blue and yellow colours, the smiling face of a housewife inside a drawn medallion, with her row of perfect white teeth. Fear stiffened my spine and memories of my earlier ordeal radiated in my knees. He could've forgotten to put it away after the last time, or had he brought it back for a specific purpose? I scoured my brain for an answer, any answer that would please him, but my mind was absolutely blank.

'Did you think I wouldn't find out?'

The tension in my bones vibrated under my flesh. I wished he would stop toying with me. This almost felt worse than kneeling on rice. The ghosts of all he could do to me lined up in my head. A helpless panic tickled my bladder. Inside my pocket, my fingers closed around the earrings. My eyes flicked from his face to the box on the shelf, still unsure what to say. The wrong words would hurt, but what was the cost of not giving an answer? Was it possible he already knew?

That morning I had sat on the edge of the old fountain after Young Women classes, porous stone rough on my skin. Newhaven's looming presence and humidity pressed on my back. Daddy had declared in front of everyone before morning prayers I wasn't to leave Jaspers Island until I had truly repented, and shown regret for my actions. No more Parkerville until further notice. He had shrunk my world to Newhaven and the honeycomb of land surrounding it. Doubt spread in my mind as fast as weeds around the fountain, finding its way through every crack. What if he'd never let me leave again? Not that I could argue with him. Not without heavy losses.

I sat in the company of the garden's old statues, with their crumbling noses or missing fingers. Gaze firmly on the ground, I avoided their hollow gaze and dulled features. They freaked me out. After we were told Lot's wife's story during Bible study, Mrs Calhoun had joked that the statues in the garden might be real people God had turned into pillars of salt because they had failed to be an obedient wife or daughter. Now I felt like one of them.

The idea pinched at my chest. I pulled at my braid until something stung my shin. Damn horseflies. My fingers brushed the air, swatting the invisible insect just before another one got me on the shoulder. The culprit rested inside the sag of my skirt – a tiny stone. I frowned at it before a new one smacked the top of my head.

'Faith.'

The voice caught my attention more than stones could. Summer loitered on the other side of the fence in her cut-off denims and workmen's boots, a smug confidence hitching at the corner of her lips. She stood dangerously close to Newhaven. Jumping off the fountain's ledge, I ran the distance between us. Switchgrass hissed in my wake.

'What you doin' here?'

'Apparently chucking stones to get your attention.'

'Sorry, what?' My words were for her but my eyes stalked Newhaven. Old houses had far too many windows and the glare of the sun didn't help.

'Never mind –' A long wail ate the rest of her sentence. 'Shit. What was that?'

I laughed at her confused expression. 'That's just the cows.'

'You got cows?'

'Yes. Chickens too.'

'Very Old MacDonald. Anyway,' she did that thing of elongating the word with the same carelessness you would stretch under the sun or linger too close to being discovered. I envied that. 'I had to check on you. Make sure you're good. I haven't seen you in a week.'

Her fingers weaved through the netting of the fence and knotted with mine. That close an aura of stale tobacco surrounded her as if marking her territory. A warmth spread through my chest at the knowledge that someone worried about me. In the distance Newhaven's windows gleamed down like a dozen glassy eyes.

'So, you good?'

'I've been busy.'

'There's something wrong?'

'No there ain't. Please, you gotta go.'

'Not until you tell me.'

'Please, they can't see you here. Patrol's gonna be here soon.'

'Then come to the old house.'

'I can't . . .' I turned around towards Newhaven, my insides knotting every which way.

'Sure, you can come see me.'

'Dammit, Summer, it ain't all about you!' I flinched. My stomach dropped, heavy with the fear someone had heard me.

She stared at me with mean eyes. 'Promise you'll come or I'll scream. I'll scream until this entire place shows up here.'

The words sent me into a panic. I nodded frantically, and she finally turned around.

'If you don't show, I'll come back here again and bring the house down, so if you don't want to get into trouble I suggest you show up,' she said over her shoulder as she walked into the darkness between the trees, her threat drifting in the air behind her.

The certainty nobody had seen us wilted under Daddy's scrutiny. Could he have been standing behind the glare of one of Newhaven's windows or did someone report the encounter to him?

'I understand you're worried 'cause pride is a sin, but I was glad to hear from Rebecca Calhoun that you apologised to her and the others who were at Newhaven and witnessed your outburst on the stairs after Sunday service.'

'I did.' The words breathed out of me.

I waited for him to say more, not trusting this was all. It felt like one of those misdirections in the old magic shows I watched in Chicago late on Saturday nights, when the assistant distracted the public so they wouldn't see the trick coming. The box of rice occupied most of my mind, the expectation that it would still enter the stage. He watched my gaze and smiled.

'That's all I wanted to say. I'm pleased you've started to behave again like the obedient daughter you ought to be.'

'I'm . . . glad you approve?'

'Good. What did you think this was about?' He didn't wait for an answer. 'Now, I've some work to finish before dinner.'

Without another word he redirected his attention to the book on his desk, casting me out of his mind before I had even left the room.

'One more thing, darlin'.'

My fingers clenched the door handle. I arranged my face in what I hoped would be a pleasing expression before turning.

'Yes, Daddy.'

'I'm sure your mama'll be real grateful for your change of behaviour.'

The wall guided me up the stairs. I didn't stop until I closed the door and lay in the bathtub – nobody ever came barging into the bathroom, and it was a much better place for privacy than my bedroom. In the comforting embrace of enamelled porcelain, the last stitch holding me together dissolved. I sobbed, a towel stuffed in my mouth muffling the noise. I hated him for having that power over me, the anticipation of what he could do enough to annihilate me, but I hated myself even more for being so pathetic and for giving him the power in the first place.

A devastating thought blitzed through my head – maybe there's no God. The idea crushed me, and I felt utterly alone. I swallowed back the rest of my tears. The salt tasted bitter; I was so full of tears, they corroded me, bristling the softness inside. My fist hit my thigh, punching the frustration out of my body. There was only so much someone could take. I would give anything for the satisfaction of seeing the same fear flash in Daddy's eyes.

AUDIO FILE #14

Audio Quality: Moderate

[Voice A]: Female
[Voice B]: Male
[Voice C]: Male

[Voice A]: Is it cool if I record you?
[Voice B]: Sure. Shoot!
            (*Laughter.*)
[Voice C]: Guess so.
[Voice A]: What do you think of the people living at
            Newhaven Plantation and the New America
            Baptist Church?
[Voice B]: From the moment they stay away from me,
            I ain't givin' a shit. I mean, they're Jesus-
            freaks obviously, but hey, man, to each
            their own.
            (*Background noises, muffled voices and music.*)
[Voice C]: Yeah, same. But they kind of freak me out, with
            their uniform and the girls with their braids and
            the same serious expression. It's creepy ... like
            that movie with the kids with the blond hair that
            all look the same and just kill everybody in
            town ...
[Voice B]: *Children of the Damned?*

[Voice C]: That's the one, thanks, bro.
(Background conversation and clinking noises, likely glasses.)

[Voice A]: You say they creep you out. Have you ever spoken to any of them? Or asked them questions about who they are and their community?

[Voice B]: They tried to convert me once. *(Gurgling sounds.)* Nothin' happened obviously 'cause I ain't interested.

[Voice A]: When did that happen, and what did they say to you?

[Voice B]: Last year. A couple of the younger guys from Newhaven Plantation were in town. They told me how that place gave them a purpose and made them feel useful and valued, and was that somethin' that's missin' from my life.

[Voice A]: And is it missing?

[Voice B]: I guess. I mean 'cause I don't make much as a trainee mechanic, I get to live in my folks' basement. They converted it into an apartment with a bathroom and my own entrance through the garage, but still.

[Voice A]: Were you tempted?

[Voice B]: Would be nice, I guess. I could get myself a wife and a home. You know, being appreciated and havin' someone waitin' on you, get a nice meal and stuff, but I ain't' givin' up my entire life for that. You know, night out with my bros, cold brewski and watchin' the game any given Sunday.

[Voice C]: Talkin' about drinks, are you gonna buy us a round? YOU OWE US!

[Voice A]: You said you were happy to answer questions.

[Voice C]: Nah, for scarin' that girl. My boy Zach here was pretty good. I call this dedication and commitment.

[Voice B]: I was pretty great. Brad Pitt ain't nothin' on me.
(Laughter.)

[Voice A]: Yeah, you did me a solid, but … didn't I pay you guys for this already?

[Voice B]: You sure did. Did you have to be so brutal though? I mean, insultin' my intelligence.

[Voice A]: I had to sell it.
(Laughter.)

[Voice B]: Still, it's worth buyin' us a round. Soothe my bruised ego. By the way, not that I ain't grateful, but why did you pay us to scare that girl just for you to tell us to beat it?

[Voice A]: *(Long exhale.)* I needed an in, didn't I?

51. The day before the fire

The woods blurred in greens and browns. Cypress and tupelo trees whipped past, trunks like sinews stretching towards the sky. Frogs and insects shouted how reckless my actions were, urged me to turn back, but I pressed on. I had no choice. My speed never dipped, heart thundering in my chest. I outran reason, sweating like a sinner in church. I didn't slow down as I jumped over the broken porch steps. Exertion burned in my chest. I burst into the living room, panting like a dog. The wooden floor was stripped bare of a sleeping bag, all traces of Summer gone – no bag, no clothes strewn all over the sofa, no empty wrappers. Nothing but the lingering odour of stale tobacco.

No Summer.

Relief should have washed over me. I should've run out of the shack and straight back to Newhaven. Instead the shock softened my legs and drove me to the ground, where the phantom scent of coconut lingered. She'd forced me to come, take stupid risks. Her absence tasted bitter. Abigail, so easily manipulated, everyone's little puppet to toy with. I'd risked so much coming here for nothin'.

My own stupidity weighed heavy. The energy that had coursed through my body while I sprinted seeped out. I didn't think I had any tears left after Daddy, after Tom, but the body was a resourceful entity. I dragged a finger down the grain of the wood, not even stopping at the bite of a splinter. I pushed harder, opening myself to the pain, the dirt mingling with blood below the skin.

'Faith?'

The old name yanked me away from my self-loathing. Summer filled the space in the doorway, hip cocked over low-slung shorts, the lace of a pink bra screaming against her skin. She was beautiful in a rebellious way, she was beautiful in just the fact that she was there. She almost didn't look real.

'I thought you'd gone.'

'No way. I just moved my stuff upstairs while I did some cleaning. I mean it's a shithole, but it's my shithole.' She dropped to the floor next to me, tossing her pack of cigarettes between us. 'Don't be so fucking dramatic,' she added, tapping my nose with her finger. She smirked, little lines around her mouth curved like parentheses holding her smile in. She mopped my tears using the corner of her own shirt, something bright pink and orange. Her smirk faded and her face turned hard again.

'I knew something was up. What has that crazy-ass step-father of yours done this time?'

A prick in my left side distracted me from her question. 'I got somethin' for you.'

'Oh yeah? Is it more of that sweet-ass honey?' She cocked an eyebrow while she slid a cigarette into the corner of her mouth. It faltered and missed the flame in her cupped hand. 'Where did you get those?' Her body slanted forward as if pulled in by the cheap jewellery, fingers hovering above the earrings nested in my palm.

'They're my mom's.'

'Faith, why did you get me those?'

'I found them a few days ago in an old box. It's to say thank you. And goodbye. I ain't gonna be able to come around as much, because things are real busy at Newhaven and my mom needs my help.'

A heavy silence grew between us. Her fingertip grazed the

looped H of 'Honey' with such gentleness her finger seemed to quiver. An urge to hug her overwhelmed me, but the small part of me that still wondered whether she had Fleur's necklace held me back.

'That's what my mom used to call me – "Honey-bunny".' I rubbed my tongue against my teeth. 'I reckon she won't miss them, and it's not like I can wear them.'

'She called you Honey-bunny?'

'I know it's silly, really. I used to have this gap in my front teeth, but it closed. It was a silly nickname anyway.'

I still didn't fully understand what compelled me to give the earrings to her. They were the only thing I owned, even if technically I stole them. They represented the last link to my life with Mom in Chicago. When Summer failed to take them, I looked up to see tears clinging to her lashes. They shocked me – tears were the last thing I ever expected to see on Summer.

'You don't have to wear them if you don't like them.'

'Are you kidding?' She sniffed. 'Love them,' she added, before snatching the hoops from my hand.

Her fingers worked the pins into the holes in her ears. She piled her hair on top of her head into a messy bun. 'How do I look?'

An electric shock ran through my veins. There was something alien and yet familiar at the sight of Mom's earrings dangling from her earlobes. It tugged at the root of something buried in the back of my mind, forgotten memories I struggled to unearth. Before I could dig them out, she pulled me into a tight hug, so tight she was the one now smothering me. The move, so out of character for Summer, shocked me. I froze. Until now I'd run against the great big wall she built around herself, and she'd just pulled me right through it.

52.

This more emotional version of Summer didn't stick around for long. Her embrace quickly loosened around my neck, like she remembered who she was. Her whole reaction to the earrings unsettled me, it felt so disproportionate. I suddenly wanted to get back to Newhaven.

'Damn hay fever.' She sniffed again. 'Listen, there's something I have to tell you —' She pressed on my knee; I flinched and bit my inner cheek. Her face scrunched into a deep frown. 'What's wrong?'

'Nothin'. I gotta go.'

'Don't you dare move.'

The harshness in her voice scared me into stillness. Her hand squeezed again, while her eyes fixed on my face. The sharp pain shooting up my thigh brought tears to my eyes. A whimper escaped through tight lips. Not waiting for an answer or another excuse, she pulled back my skirt. Her face narrowed with anger at my knees, marbled with bruises and red indents from the rice. Her jaw tensed so hard her shoulders trembled. Her whole demeanour scared me.

'What the fuck is this?'

I ransacked my brain for a plausible explanation, something that would stifle the storm darkening her eyes, but the words lagged in my head as Mom's face flashed in my mind.

'Did he do this? Answer me. He did this to you, didn't he?'

The tears came, and I hated myself for producing them

more easily than words. They seemed to be the answer to anything these days. I had to go back for Mom's sake.

Summer stared, anger seeping out of her in waves. It filled the room, oppressive like the heat outside.

She got up and ran into the kitchen and I glimpsed the moment to make my escape, but peals of shattered, breakable things stopped me. Summer's feelings raged in the derelict kitchen. She swung a piece of wood to the cupboards, housing piles of forgotten plates and glasses. A couple of scared palmetto bugs skittered across the counter.

'Fucking monster. And how could she let him do this to you? So pathetic.'

'Summer. Summer, please stop.' The violence of her emotions scared me. My skin rippled with a chill.

'Him and . . . and –' Summer swiped a glass on the counter. It exploded against the opposite wall. 'She's your mom! She's supposed to protect you.'

'I'm leaving.'

'Wait, what?'

'You don't understand nothin', 'cause you ain't got no family. Now quit it.'

I said the words the way I ripped the Band-Aids off the twins' grazed knees. I had to get out of there, and not look back. Her unhinged violence kicked a wild panic under my skin. I almost made it to the front door when a force yanked me back.

'You can't go.'

'Dammit, Summer, it ain't none of your business. We ain't even friends or anythin'.' She flinched. 'I was tryin' to convert you, but there's far too much sin inside of you.' I pulled away, but her fingers dug into the flesh of my arm. Fear jolted through my body. If I didn't make it home, he might take it out on Mom like he'd promised.

277

'Let me go or I'll scream. Some of the men are fellin' trees in the swamp. They'll come.'

I thrashed against her grip, but she was unrelenting and surprisingly strong. Darkness had taken over her eyes, and a chill ran down my spine. She'd been intimidating before with all her confidence and no-nonsense attitude, but for the first time she utterly scared me. The rusted blood on Fleur's locket flashed in my mind, and I struggled harder.

'Let me go, or I swear I'll scream. They'll find you. They got rifles, you know.' I swallowed hard. 'I'll tell them you touched me.'

Her fist hurtled towards my face at lightning speed and connected with the side of my face. The world wobbled, before tilting sharply. A lightness spread through my body.

Then nothing.

53.

This wasn't my bed. The mattress smelled like wet animal fur, and its grittiness itched on my cheek. The silence was all wrong too; no people, just frogs croaking in disapproval, only to be interrupted by the cries of an osprey. The air around smelled like muddy waters.

Propping myself on an elbow, I blinked away the dust in my eyes and a room appeared in snapshots, blackened walls and boarded-up windows allowing very little light in. There was pain behind my eyes and on the left side of my head. My fingers grazed the throbbing patch of scalp. I winced and images rushed back – Summer's fist hurtling towards me, the darkness in her eyes. Fear swelled in my throat. She pretended to be my friend, but she hurt me. She was no better than Daddy. My stomach flipped at the idea that I couldn't trust her.

Despite the heat, a chill spread through my back. The splintered headboard and the maroon stains on the mattress jolted me upright. She had put me in the bed of a dead man. A man who had killed his wife and shot himself on that very mattress. Evil lingered in here, the soot on the walls a reminder the room had burned hot like hell. My face had lain next to the crusted remnants of blood and brain. My body doubled over and I retched.

I had to get out of here. The door knob rattled furiously in my hand. The door didn't budge. I twisted the handle, leaned back, using my weight as a lever. Panic swelled in my chest, smothering my lungs, and my heart hitched in my throat. I pounded on the door. Tears stung my eyes; I just wanted to go home.

'Let me go. Please let me go,' I shouted, until breathless with desperation.

'Sorry, I can't let you out.' Summer's voice came from the other side. 'It's for your own good. You can't go back to people who hurt you.'

'You don't understand. Just open the door. I swear I won't say nothin'.'

'Not happening, sorry. Can't risk it.'

'My mom's gonna worry.'

'She should worry about what he does to you.'

'You know nothin'.'

'I'm not opening this door, so you can just forget it.'

A scream ripped out of me as frustration drove my foot into the door. My legs buckled under the weight of my own helplessness, and I slid to the ground. I corralled my body into my arms but I craved a different embrace. Mom would be devastated when I failed to show up for dinner – or had that already happened? My heart ached with the idea she might believe that I'd run away, that I'd abandoned her. My heart shrivelled at the idea of Daddy thinking I'd disobeyed him. My fist hit my thigh with frustration until the muscle throbbed.

'Why are you punishin' me? I ain't done nothin' to you.'

'It's not you. It's that place. Those people. They're danger-ous.' Her voice sounded closer than before, as if talking into the cracks in the wood.

'Why do you hate religion so much?'

A long sigh slid under the door. 'I don't have an issue with religion, but it shouldn't be something you're brainwashed into. Honestly? Religion helped me during a messed-up time in my life. That's what it should do – help. Not be a tool to control people or a leash to restrict them. Your stepdad? He's wielding it like a weapon of hate. That's not right.'

I wanted to tell her she was wrong. I wanted to say she didn't know what she was talking about. I wanted to say that Newhaven had helped so many people over the years, that I had seen women arriving from shelters, the skittish behaviour from fear living just under their skin, cowering at loud noises, the men depressed from being denied the right to be a provider, the unhealthy bodies, the restlessness or furious chewing of smokers mourning the loss of their habit, the ghost of nicotine clinging to their lungs and fingers.

But instead one memory reigned over all others. After she quit smoking, Mom used to chew her nails down to the quick, the ragged edges rimmed red. One day she'd emerged from Daddy's office, head down, red rimming her eyes instead of her fingers. Her nails had never slipped past her lips again. After my own experience I wondered what kind of ordeal she had endured in that room. Slumped on the dusty floor, my fist hammered my thigh.

Jackson and his dad, Tom's behaviour, Daddy and the rice. Newhaven embodied Daddy's favourite metaphor – the duck/rabbit drawing. Depending on where you focused your attention you saw a completely different picture. I felt my chest tightening. I dreaded that Daddy was just an illusion that I had always seen from the wrong angle, and had only now shifted my focus. The gathering scream I tried to stifle morphed into a wild cough.

'There's water by the bed, and I've left you something to sleep in. That dress of yours doesn't look like a comfortable option in this heat.'

On the other side of the door her footsteps echoed as she descended the stairs, before turning into muffled sounds somewhere below. I rushed to the window, trying to pry the planks off. The rusty nails stubbornly held on. Another memory tugged at my heart: watching Mom paint her toenails, feet on the windowsill, blood-red bottle at hand. Back arched, I pulled at a plank until my shoulders burned. *Does it look pretty, Honey-bunny?* She'd painted mine afterwards; we'd blown them dry. She kissed each toe as a test, her lips tickling my skin . . . Ten minutes later I gave up, freedom still taunting me through the gaps in the wood, my efforts earning me nothing more than chipped nails and a few splinters.

I greedily drained the water, rivulets running down my chin. I wiped my mouth with my arm before dropping the empty bottle next to a scrap of red fabric.

I stood in front of the standing mirror, its glass tarnished and stained with spots similar to the ones peppering the backs of Mrs Favreau's hands. I ran my fingers over the lightness of the fabric. Even with the dress on I felt naked. The girl in the mirror looked like an idea, someone who wore a dress like someone would a different name, what I could have been if I had grown up in Parkerville or Chicago. Stripped of the beige skin of my dress, the red strappy dress made me look like the rabbits lying on the kitchen counter, muscles and flesh shining under the yellow light, their fur hanging a couple of feet away from their bodies. A transition from being whole and alive to being chopped and sliced ready for stew.

I curled at the foot of the bed, wiping tears with my fingertips. I stared at the door until exhaustion claimed me, devastated that I had failed Mom and terrified about what might happen once Summer came back and opened the door.

From: Cameron McPherson
Date: Monday, September 19, 2022 at 9:15 AM
To: Jeb Abernathy
Subject: Re: Concerns – guidance needed

My dear Pastor Abernathy,

I have some wonderful news for you. The Lord and the Elders Council have answered our prayers. They have voted for Abigail to join us at New Eden where she will be able to start her healing process and reconnect with her faith.

Furthermore, one of our high-ranking congregants, Boyd Belmont, has recently suffered a loss and is looking to remarry. I believe Abigail would make a wonderful bride for him, and she will be able to reconnect with her true nature and place in the home, looking after Boyd Belmont's five children, all under ten.

I know you have been conflicted about what to do with Abigail, but I believe we can keep her safe and provide a fulfilling new life for her at New Eden.

Please let me know if we should start making travel arrangements for her.

Under His guidance. Have a blessed day.

Pastor Cameron McPherson

54. Present day

They drag me from the shadow and cast me out into the blinding daylight. Their hands fight over me. They pull me forwards, high-pitched voices leading me on, not giving me a choice. They expose me to the blistering heat, not letting me pause or wipe the sweat soaking my brow. Who am I kidding? Their will has always been so much stronger than mine. They won't let go so I just surrender.

'Abbay, come see the chickens,' Elijah says.

'Feed the chickens!' Matthew shrieks, shaking my hand in excitement.

The chicken coop in view, they let go of me to run freely, arms thrown out wide, fully embracing their innocence. Crouching beside them, I bathe in their joy. The chickens strut about, one behind the other, scratching and pecking at the dust. This feels normal, as if they're not orphans, as if they didn't lose their parents in the most traumatic way. As if everybody doesn't hate me here. I just want to forget about last night and Tom's betrayal. The twins grin at me for no reason; the urge to smother them in a hug prickles down my arms. A wisp of happiness flutters in my chest, but it doesn't soothe the sting.

'Grain, grain, grain,' they chant at me.

'Please, Abbay?' Elijah adds.

I smile, casting Tom out of my head. My fingers loosen, and the grain trickles into the twins' cupped hands. Inside the pen, they throw their grain into the air like petals at a wedding. They clap at the chickens pecking, before asking for more.

'Abbay,' Matthew says, his face all solemn, 'can Momma feed the chickens with us when she comes back?'

The answer jams in my throat as images flash in my head – random body parts covered in blood, unable to tell if they are all from the same person, my hand pulling a knife from Mom's body, the roar and crackle from the fire. A rusty, metallic smell makes me want to throw up until it is swallowed by the acrid smell of smoke. *What did you do, Abigail?*

'Don't be sad, Abbay.' Elijah's voice punches through the memories and dispels them.

I offer him a wry smile. 'See? I ain't sad.'

'Do you remember when I was scared of the chickens?' Matthew says.

I nod.

'But Momma took a chicken in her arm and she got me to pet it, and then I wasn't scared no more.'

'I remember,' I smile.

They both grin, offering little pearly teeth. Soon those will fall out, and Mom won't be here to put them in a keepsake box. Overwhelming love surges through my body, and I pull them both into a tight hug. The idea I could be a single mom tickles me. Girls everywhere, younger than me, take on those responsibilities. Jackson has $500 and a way out of here for us. The twins squirm inside my embrace, eager to get back to feeding the chickens. It would be so easy to wrap my life around theirs and start somewhere new together, before they send me away from my siblings.

'Get away from them boys!' Pastor Abernathy startles me and I loosen my arms from Elijah and Matthew. Oblivious to the warning they run towards the chickens, but Mrs Calhoun is already there, shepherding them into her arms.

'It's nothin',' I say, getting up. 'We're just feeding the chickens.'

'Of course, of course. But we reckon it's in everybody's best interests that we have someone with you when you're around the young'uns.'

'Excuse me?'

'We don't want them to tire you.'

'They ain't tiring me, they're my brothers.' I take a step towards Mrs Calhoun and the twins, but before I take another Pastor Abernathy bars the way.

'It's for the best, Abigail.'

'I don't need nobody supervising me when I'm around my brothers.' I cross my arms. 'I don't think I like your insinuations. Is this about Tom's lies?'

I sidestep him, but he grabs me.

'Let me go.' My voice hitches high. I try to wiggle out but his grasp is strong. His other hand clamps on my other arm. 'I already told you, he lied. I never gave him no letter to post.'

'Please calm down, Abigail. You're being hysterical.'

Mr Caine runs over from behind the barn, almost as if he's been waiting around the whole time to make his entrance. Behind Pastor Abernathy, Mrs Calhoun ushers the twins away, a bewildered expression in her eyes. They are the ones being all emotional over nothing – we're just feeding the damn chickens.

Mr Caine's arms close over me. They pin mine against my chest as he drags me away. *Fuck this shit.* She slips into my skin, the girl in my head – Summer. Back struggling against his chest, I kick and wriggle, but his grip is my own prison. As I fight his and Pastor Abernathy's hold, something rises from deep inside me, a raw energy shaped like a girl. *Come on, fight!*

Screams rip out of me as I thrash against them like some enraged possum. 'Don't touch me! You got no right. Just let me go.' My anger gives comfort to their insane logic.

'Help me take her back to her room,' Pastor Abernathy says.

Wade Pruitt has somehow joined them. Mr Caine's grip hardens, pressing my arms into my ribs. Pastor Abernathy and Wade Pruitt each snatch one of my ankles and swiftly lift me off the ground. *Show those assholes!* Molten rage burns through my veins, skin on fire, clothes drenched with sweat. My body convulses against their inflated sense of righteousness. My big toe catches on shirt buttons — somehow I've lost a shoe.

'Pastor, she's hysterical.'

'Pray to our Lord, he can help her find her way back to His truth. Drive the devil out of her.'

'Are you crazy? Just let me the fuck go!'

'You're right, Pastor Abernathy. She ain't right.'

Faces blur past as our demented procession enters Newhaven. My screams bounce off the stairwell and the high ceiling. Whispers about my breakdown hem our way. Tom stands back, a crooked smile creeping onto his face, eyes shining with glee. *Fight harder.* I kick my left leg and my heel catches Wade Pruitt in the ribs. His face twisting in pain stretches my mouth into a grimace. I want to hurt them. My muscles ache. My throat burns. I want to hurt them. Hurt them all.

They manage to get me to my room, or rather the place they've assigned to me on the top floor. There are no possessions here, it's all communal, nothing belongs to you, nothing to call your own, not even your mind. They throw me on the bed – a ragged doll collapsing in a heap, sweaty hair and clothes clinging in the wrong places.

Resentment mixed with rage propels me out of the bed and onto the closing door. My shoulder connects with the wood with a low thud. But the sound which really scares me is the click of the lock. I rattle the handle but the door doesn't budge. They've locked me in.

'It's for your own good, Abigail.' Pastor Abernathy's voice slips under the door.

'That ain't even my name. You can't do that. You can't! You got no right.'

My shouts compete with the sound of their receding footsteps. I pound on the door until my arms and legs grow tired. *Fucking useless.* Summer sinks back into the depths of my mind, her energy fizzling out. In her place, an acute loneliness bursts from my core.

Crumpled on the floor, I remember things I ain't sure happened now – snatches of conversation, afternoons spent toe-dipping in the swamp, even her coconut scent is a trick of my mind. I should just embrace the madness and give them what they want.

I think of the man living in the shack in the swamp, him and his wife. How he went mad and killed his wife before setting a fire and killing himself, almost burning the house down in the process. I can't help but wonder if it's what happened at Hunters Cottage – the devil drove one of us into setting a fire.

And by one of us – I mean me. I am the fire, I am the whispers carried by the wind that seeped into his mind. I am the heat at night that wouldn't let him rest until he killed his wife and burned his home. I am the flames that consumed Hunters Cottage. I am all that is bad. I've been foolish. There ain't no redemption away from here for me. Now I've done it again, I've driven them mad. Now the question is, what will they do to me?

55. Five hours before the fire

I sat cross-legged in the middle of the room. Earlier I'd flattened myself against the wall, ready to overpower Summer
as soon as she walked through the door. Until the silver of
the box-cutter flashed in my mind.

'Why you got this?' I'd said as I picked it up the night of
the lightning storm.

Her eyes had been focused on me, words at the threshold
of her mouth – waiting. Despite the heat it had felt cold and
heavy. My fingers found the safety tab. I pushed it up and the
triangle of blade appeared. Danger looked tiny. Mr Caine
used one to cut through feed bags for the chickens, grain
spilling out from the gash in the burlap.

'Protection. From guys like Zach,' she'd said, relieving me
of it.

Taking on a defenceless Summer would be hard, but Summer with a weapon? No chance in hell.

The click of the lock and instinct kicked in. I scrambled
away from the door. Summer walked in, plate in hand, the
dreaded box-cutter peeking out of her front pocket.

'You must be starving.'

Fat triangles of over-processed white bread oozed with
peanut butter and jelly. I hesitated to pick one up. My stomach growled with desire, and she sighed.

'I'm not trying to poison you. It's just food.'

The tinge of sadness in her voice surprised me. A strong
sweet smell hit me, and my mouth flooded with saliva. Maybe

just one bite. My teeth sank into the pillowy bread, and the mix of sweet and salt hit my tongue. I wolfed down the whole thing in three bites.

'Not as shit as you expected?'

'No.' The word pushed its way through the sludge of PB&J in my mouth. 'How long are you gonna keep me here?'

'As long as it takes for you to understand that place's toxic. Look what he's done to your knees,' she said as I pulled the red fabric of the dress over my bruises. I thought of Mom trapped at home with him, and me here with my own jailer. 'And there's something else we need to talk about . . .'

Summer fished a cigarette from her pack. Hunched over her cupped hand, she repeatedly pressed on her lighter. Frustration and a lack of flame distracted her. I swung hard. The plate crashed on the side of her head with a loud crack, from the porcelain or bones I couldn't say. I didn't stick around to find out. Adrenaline shot through me, and I bolted out. Images of Mom fuelled my escape. I tumbled down the stairs. The last step vanished, and my chin hit the ground. Ignoring the sharp pain in my jaw, I scrambled to my feet.

After the darkness of the house, sunlight bleached the outside into nothingness, the whiteness disorienting until the narrow strip of the boardwalk emerged. I was inhaling the muddy smell of the swamp when a weight slammed into my back. I hit the ground again, hard. Summer sat astride me, her pelvis pressing against my ribs, the scrap of fabric called a dress barely more than another layer of skin between us. I wriggled underneath, but it was hopeless. Panic swelled in my throat.

'Please, I don't wanna die. Please.' I didn't think before saying the words.

'Wait, what?'

'I don't wanna end up like Fleur.'

I landed punches on her shoulders and thighs, but they didn't have no effect on her. I'd never see Mom again, or the twins, or baby Sarah. I didn't want to die. Terror strangled me, and a wave of nausea rose inside me.

'Faith. Faith. Just calm the fuck down.'

It was hopeless. How did I ever think I would be able to escape? I swallowed back the tears and some of the bile souring my throat. Her legs pinned my arms to the ground. Her nicotine breath fell heavy on my face as the curtain of her curls shielded us from the light like Spanish moss. Drops of sweat fell on my cheek, and I breathed through my mouth. Death tasted salty.

'What do you mean, you don't want to end up like Fleur?'

'My friend Fleur. I think I found her necklace in your book. I'm sorry I looked. She never took it off. Please, I don't wanna die.'

'I know she didn't . . . Wait. You think I killed her?'

'I won't say nothin'. I promise.'

'I'm not going to hurt you.'

'Please just . . .'

'Listen. It's not what you think, I –'

'You got her necklace!'

'I found it at Newhaven!'

The revelation stopped my body bucking underneath hers and stunned me into silence. She found the necklace at Newhaven. Her eyes searched my face for a reaction to her bombshell, but my mind couldn't process the meaning of her words.

'Did you hear me?'

There was a big fat lump in my throat. I simply nodded.

'I went snooping in Newhaven. I knew about the opening

in the fence before you showed me, but I only managed to explore the church, and a couple of the houses. Easier to sneak undetected than the main plantation house. I didn't know one of them was yours. Found the necklace in a box. I just took it because of what I thought it might mean. I recognised it from when I interviewed her a while back as part of my podcast.'

She slid off my body, but the weight hadn't lifted off my chest. She pushed the hair off her face.

'Faith, the box was in your stepdad's office.'

I staggered up, the swamp swimming in front of my eyes, the heat pressing on the back of my neck, burning my scalp, a cacophony of croaking frogs filling my ears, and somewhere underneath Summer's voice asking if I was OK. The words careened in my head – *the box was in your stepdad's office.*

Daddy's velvet box. That wasn't possible. I stared at her, and I knew she wasn't lying. I bent over and threw up in the tall grass.

56.

The wilderness in the living room had receded – gone were the family of ferns and great clumps of earth, no flash of fur scurried at the corner of my eye. Summer had asserted her dominance over nature.

She'd convinced me to come back inside. She gave me some water to rinse out my mouth, but the bad taste clung on. Daddy had had Fleur's necklace. I shouldn't, but I believed her. I sat in a daze, my head feeling light and my body numb, my mind scarred with pieces of my life imbedded in me like shrapnel after she blew it all up.

'Here, drink this. It'll help with the shock.'

She thrust a bottle of Coke into my hands. The fizz and sugar hit my tongue, but not even that rush could wash away the mess of thoughts crowding my head. She'd said she wanted to keep me safe from Daddy, that was the reason she wouldn't let me leave after she saw my knees.

'What if it ain't what you think,' I said finally. 'He could have found it, maybe that's why he had it in the box?'

I didn't believe the words as soon as they left my mouth. A great big tiredness washed over me, pushing me to the ground until my head rested on her lap. She stroked my hair, and I tried not to think of Daddy and the massive hole in my heart, shaped like him.

'Why were you snoopin' around Newhaven?'

'Fleur. I was down in Florida for my podcast, spent time

with her congregation – much more welcoming than yours, by the way. She was a nice kid, so was her old man. After what happened to them, I had to find out. Took a while to get to Parkerville, chasing other leads first.'

'What were you planning to do with it?'

'Honestly? I don't know.'

'I can't believe Daddy . . .'

'Look what he did to you. Your knees. Whichever way you look at it, it's fucked up.' The air sizzled with the sound of a newly lit cigarette. 'It won't have been the start of it, either. Men like that start small before they escalate. Trust me.'

God always finds a way to punish the wicked. Daddy stood among the crowd at the crossing, ready to play God and deliver his judgement. Tania had disrespected him. The idea my punishment with the rice might not have been his most extreme retaliation chilled the blood in my veins.

I told Summer about Daddy, unspooled the tangled ball of his behaviour and our relationship over the last few weeks. I was grateful not to have to look at her. I talked about the playful kicks at the back of the knee, the lie about me coming to Parkerville, about the doubts, his words after Tania's accident, what Tania's friend said to me. I told her about the obedient daughter, how he often reminded the congregation how society corrupted women, how it made whores out of mothers and wives. She listened, never inter-rupting me.

Once I ran out of words, we stayed wrapped in a silence only disturbed by the crinkle of burning tobacco. With each sharp inhale, I imagined the ember of her cigarette pulsing with a glow so bright it might burst into flames. With a sharp flick, she chucked the smouldering stub into the fireplace. It hit the brick wall, firing an explosion of embers into the air.

'God, he's one vile asshole. And your mom married that guy out of her own free will.'

Her words pulled me out of the numbness. She hadn't. She married Daddy to keep Child Protection Services away. He had lured her with promises of safety, and in return she had provided him with the shackles to bind us to him. He had exerted that power when he forced me to kneel on the rice. He used threats of alerting CPS to keep Mom compliant, and used threats to Mom to keep me down too. An icicle of fear slid down my back – Mom still alone at Hunters Cottage with him.

I scrambled to my feet, before rushing up the stairs. I was wriggling the dress over my shoulders when Summer barged in. In that moment I couldn't care less about privacy.

'What time is it?' I asked, snatching my dress from the foot of the bed. It felt damp from sweat and mildew.

'I'm not sure, about two?'

'I need to know the exact time. Please.'

She huffed out of the room and stomped down the stairs. I finished getting ready in a hurry, putting a new plan into action. Mistakes existed so we could learn from them.

'OK, according to my phone it's 3:16pm, but there's no way you're going back, it's not safe. Faith?' she added when I failed to respond.

She moved deeper into the room. Holding my breath, I sneaked out from where I'd been hiding behind the door. I'd reached the threshold when a whining floorboard betrayed me. She spun around; her eyes widening at her mistake. Her gaze slid from my face to the lock. Betrayal and anger twisted her mouth. The sight tightened my stomach.

'I'm sorry. I gotta warn my mom.'

I slammed the door shut and locked it with one swift move, before running down the stairs and out of the shack. What did Jackson joke about when he ran away with a whole peach cobbler aged nine?

Better to ask for forgiveness than permission an'all.

Extract from Pastor Abernathy's sermon

'I have asked our Lord for guidance. Lemme know what should be done. I've prayed long and hard, and asked Pastor McPherson and the Elders Council at the New America Baptist Church for their advice. I'm afraid the devil has entered Newhaven again. He whispered his lies into the ears of our dear Elizabeth Favreau, until he corrupted her thoughts and seduced her to do his biddin'. And now we're on the cusp of losin' our darlin' Abigail. We have all witnessed it – her physical reaction at our Lord's words, nightmares and the screamin', the lyin', the incident at the fence, even her general apathy to her parents' deaths.

'Pastor McPherson has answered our call and provided me with wonderful news. A new compound is being built in Texas, a New Eden. He confirmed that they will take in our Abigail and help her heal and find her way back to God. A righteous man has also offered to marry her to provide her with purpose and duties to fulfil as a wife, and hopefully soon as a mother.

'A delegation from New Eden will arrive on Thursday to take Abigail to her new home and groom. Until then there's no need to mention this to her. We don't want to confuse her more than she is already. Soon she'll see this is for her own good.

'We owe this to our dear friend and leader, the late Pastor Heywood.'

57. Present day

My dress stinks. It's like a second skin I refuse to peel away. I smell like roadkill under the midday sun. Sitting cross-legged on the floor, I use what's left of one of my fingernails to work on the loose corner of wallpaper. I almost have it, but it slips away. I scratch a bit and lift it again. Yes. The paper tenses, and I pull. Like a thought it unravels and rips from the wall in one long strip, exposing the raw plaster underneath. In my eagerness it breaks before reaching the windowsill. It drops to the floor, joining the pile of its brothers. There ain't much to do here. The room's bare. My head's crammed with so many voices – Summer, Daddy, Mom. It's there underneath the fire what's happened to them, the origin of the blood, but I can't reach that deep and all that comes back are incomplete images, like torn bits of wallpaper.

A muffle of voices pulls me to my feet and to the window. A trickle of ant-size people bleeds out of Newhaven's entrance and onto the flaxen lawn before being swallowed by the dark mouth of the church. It isn't the right day for service, or is it? Time has become a mushed porridge where I can't distinguish one oat from another. About a day has passed since the twins were ripped from me, and they threw me here – I think. One figure trails at the back. He turns around, and it's like Daddy glancing up towards my window. He mouths words I cannot catch. I rub my eyes with the heels of my hands. But it turns out to be Tom and his crooked smile. My mind's playing tricks on me.

My gaze drifts towards the birches lurking behind the fence. Among their silhouettes, one of human form. All the ghosts are coming out to play today. Her face is all but a shadow; maybe she's coming for me. Women are weak, we've let the serpent in, we created the evil of feminism. Maybe the devil is a woman, and she's standing by the tree-line. Could I conjure her up inside Newhaven? Maybe I just need the right words, the ones I carved in the windowsill – *Solve et Coagula*. Her face is tilted up, wild hair barely contained by the red line of a scarf. Look at me, look at me. I'm right here. I'm ready. The window won't open; I bang on the glass when the click of the lock distracts me.

Tom closes the door behind him and leans back against it, his body an obstacle for me to overcome. Every muscle in my body stiffens at his presence. He doesn't fit in this space they've locked me in. When I look outside again the silhouette by the tree has vanished.

'Look at you. Don't you look like a right hot mess.' He leans forward and pretends to sniff the air. 'And smell like one too.'

'What do you want?'

Wrong question. He peels himself off the door; his steps slowly eat the space between us, pushing me back until the windowsill digs into my back.

'They won't help,' he says when he catches me glancing outside. 'They're all having a special meeting about what to do with you. Between your nightmares, screaming like a witch and freaking out the other night when we made out.'

'Quit lyin', we didn't make out.'

'And who could forget the fence incident. I wish I'd seen that. I thought I was clever, putting entrails in your bed – only fair after how you try to humiliate me – but it's child's play compared to whoever strung those suckers up.' He leans closer, smugness twisting the smirk on his face. 'Just between us, was it you? Come on, you can tell me.'

'What you doin' here?'

'I volunteered to stay behind and feed the animals.' His face slips open with a teeth-baring grin. Feeding the animals. The animal needs feeding. Like the fire that night fed on their bodies. He takes another step and another. Slowly I straighten my spine, but my legs feel light.

'I'm here to finish what we started.' His nail traces the line of my arm; on its way up it strays onto the curve of my breast. He chuckles when I swat his hand away. 'Don't pretend to be a prude,' he says, his fingers squeezing my nipple. He pinches hard and wakes her.

Summer's spirit rumbles in my throat, and flies out of me. *Fuck, no.* The glob of spit lands high on the side of his nose, sliding down his cheek. He wipes it away with the back of his hand. He smiles before my own cheek is set ablaze. The slap sends my head smashing against the side of the window. A ringing crescendos in my cranium.

'Must have been mad when I thought about marrying you. I admit I thought you would have been a nice challenge. It's no fun if there's no friction.' He smiles. 'Yes, you make me crazy. That's it. You've bewitched me with your filthy feminist mind.'

He looks at me, and Daddy flashes in his eyes. Even after his death he's not finished with me. Tom's hand rests on his belt buckle in a silent threat. Instead of Summer, fear rises in my throat, and I swallow back the bile.

'I'll tell. I'll tell them all. They'll all know what kind of man you are. That you ain't livin' according to the Lord's teaching.'

He grabs me by the throat. The rictus twisting his face freezes the blood in my veins. 'No one will believe you. You're just a crazy girl, spewing lies.'

301

'They'll see what you've done to me.' The words barely make it past the garrotte of his fingers.

'We all know you're a liar. I was off feeding the animals anyway. For all we know the devil did this to you, or you just did it to yourself.' The evenness of his tone tells me of the steadiness of his conviction.

There's no escape. He takes one last step forward. Closing my eyes, I brace for impact. His lips smother mine, his tongue buries my screams deep in my mouth. His hand slithers down to the fold between my legs. I hope he kills me once this is over. He owes me a kindness, and this could be it. If I'm dead, I could finally ask Mom what really happened that day. Why the fire didn't take me too. In the makeshift darkness, he's a weight crushing me – until suddenly he isn't.

My eyes snap open, and in the space where Tom should be, Jackson stands, holding the bedside lamp. It hovers high above his head, blood and matted hair clinging to a corner. His arm tenses ready to strike again. Tom is a mess on the floor. My pulse quickens at the sight.

'They're all busy inside the church so I reckoned it was the best time,' he says, dropping the lamp on the floor. 'Do you . . . do you reckon he's dead?'

My mind is too busy with the sight of blood and another body on the floor to answer his question. Another tragedy they will blame me for.

'C'mon, we gotta go,' Jackson says, grabbing my wrist. 'We ain't got much time.'

58. Four hours before the fire

Sweat dripped down my face, stinging my eyes. Undergrowth and low branches snagged on my dress, scratched my arms, but I didn't relent. I had to get to Mom. Get to the twins and baby Sarah. Get them to the old shack, then I could plead for Summer's forgiveness and hopefully the use of her car. It was 3:16pm. Daddy would be attending the weekly online church update. Hunters Cottage would be safe. Humidity and exertion calcified my muscles. I pushed on, flying over the old planks of the walkway.

I stumbled inside the kitchen, the screen door smacking the frame behind me, and crashed against the table. Mom looked ten years older, dark bruises stamped beneath her eyes. Guilt pinched my heart for what my disappearance had done. I flung myself at her, still frozen from the shock like one of the garden statues. The weight of my body jolted her. She fiercely embraced me, love and relief crushing my body.

'Praise the Lord. I knew you didn't run away.'

'Never. It's just us girls. I haven't forgotten, Mom.'

'Where were you? I was going out of my mind.'

'Ain't no time to explain right now. We gotta go before Daddy gets back.'

'I need to call your father. He and the others have been looking for you in Parkerville.' She stood up, letting go of me.

'Daddy's in Parkerville?'

'He thought you ran away because he wants you to marry Tom.'

The news softened my legs and I collapsed into the nearby chair. So what Tom said was true. 'He what?'

'You need direction, guidance. You're spinning out of control, Abigail. You need a husband to lead you. "Wives, submit to your husbands as to the Lord. For the husband is the head of the wife as Christ is the head of the church."'

Disbelief pinned me to the chair. He had brainwashed her. She'd kept me safe only to sell me out. My life had rested in the hands that used to give me the last fries when I was hungry, changed my diapers to keep me dry, stuck plastic stars on the ceiling so I wouldn't be scared at night. And instead of setting me free, Mom had given my hand to Daddy to give to Tom. Bile burned the back of my throat. I stared at her. The woman didn't deserve the title. A mother is supposed to fiercely protect her young, not willingly feed them to the nearest predator. How could this be the same woman who turned herself into a fugitive out of love for me? He had broken her down into so many pieces he was able to make her back into his own idea of a woman. But now was not the time. I swallowed back the anger.

'Listen. I reckon Daddy did something to Fleur and Pastor Munro. I reckon he's responsible for . . . what happened to them. We gotta go.'

'That's ridiculous. You're not making any sense.'

'Trust me. We gotta go.'

'Go where?'

'The old shack in the swamp past Marshall Point. I met this girl, she can explain everything. Then, I don't know. We could get a motel in Savannah for a couple of days.' Purpose gave my legs their strength back, and I stalked towards the hallway. 'Just pack the essentials.'

'I'm not going anywhere.'

'Mom, didn't you listen to everythin' I just said?'

'He's kept us safe so far, and he'll continue.'

'He's dangerous.'

'It's a small price to pay for our safety.'

'Really? What d'you call this?'

I lifted my skirt, my bruised knees the undeniable proof of his cruelty. Mom lowered her gaze.

'I'm sure . . . he had his reasons. It's up to a father to discipline the children. You just need to stay quiet and we'll be all right. It will all be all right.' She nodded.

'Discipline? You call that discipline? Really, Mom?' My voice hitched with frustration. 'How the hell can you defend him? We're family. We're blood. He ain't.'

My voice billowed in the space of the kitchen. Her head snapped back, her eyes hard but their green darkened with a shade of sadness.

'That's the problem right here, your attitude. Running off, scaring everybody, talking back. Every day, you remind me more and more of . . . myself when I was your age. This can't happen again.'

All the words I had for her burned under the fire raging through my body. I tasted their ashes in my mouth. I held their ghosts in the curl of my fists, strangling the meaning out of them. I'd left Summer behind, defended her against Summer's accusations, stood up for her. How could she fail to do the same for me?

'You can't see it now, but we're doing this for your own good.'

A veil of submission shrouded her eyes. Right there in front of me, the shape of my future stared back. I couldn't live the same life Mom had shrivelled into, an eternity of second-guessing my husband's every action, every word, never knowing what would set him off. And Daddy. I couldn't live in the shadow of a man who could have hurt Fleur.

'Just 'cause you've given up on your life, doesn't mean I gotta do the same.'

A slap stunned me and tightened my fists.

'Abigail, I'm . . .' Mom reached out with the same hand that had struck me seconds before, but I recoiled from the tainted peace offering. To think I risked coming back to save her.

'I hate you.'

'Don't you dare walk –'

I slammed the screen door shut before she could finish her threat. Whatever she had to say, she could just go to hell, even though hell seemed to have taken root outside. The air was packed with humidity, like breathing molasses, and dark-bellied clouds blanketed the sky. A nighttime darkness had chased away the day. I looked up as a couple of fat drops of rain crashed onto my forehead. Time stopped as I sucked the warm air in. When I exhaled the sky ripped open, unleashing a deluge. It lashed at me angrily. I started running.

AUDIO FILE #15

Audio Quality: Medium

[Voice A]:   Female
[Voice B]:   Female

[First part of the recording too damaged to recover.]

[Voice A]:   You? You know the Bible? *(Laughter.)*
[Voice B]:   'For there is nothing covered, that shall not be revealed; neither hid, that shall not be known. Therefore whatsoever ye have spoken in darkness shall be heard in the light; and that which ye have spoken in the ear in closets shall be proclaimed upon the housetops.'

Religion ebbs and flows but that particular verse stuck with me. It felt like God had written something just for me. How about that? *(Long exhaling breath.)* I like God best when he is at his most vengeful; after what happened to me that's when I felt the closest to him.

Anyway, after that I slept rough for a couple of years, until I met this pastor at a shelter. The old man spoke to me for hours the way you stroke a stray dog. All I had to do was listen in exchange for a free meal. That quote stuck with me, I even highlighted the passage in the Bible the pastor gave me. *(Soft laughter.)* The old man was pissed. 'You don't defile the word of God,' he said. In that case, God shouldn't have created the man who invented highlighters, I responded.

[Voice A]: What is it you like about that quote?

[Voice B]: Nothing can stay hidden forever, no matter how hard you try to hide it.

59. Three hours before the fire

Water dripped from my clothes onto the dusty floorboards in front of Summer, her head and looped earrings shaking in disappointment. Outside, sheets of rain battered against the old shack, water spilling in through broken windows, walls, finding its way through every crack and what remained of the roof. My boldness had all dripped out onto the floor too.

'How did you get out of the bedroom?'

'I got creative. Back so soon? Shouldn't you be home warning your precious mom?' She sneered through the curtain of cigarette smoke.

The mention of Mom triggered the onset of tears. My fist found that soft spot on my thigh, hit on the bruises weeks and months of frustration had created. I stared into her eyes, shining with that honey colour, and I envied their dryness.

'Shit. Sorry, it didn't mean to sound so harsh.'

Through the mayhem of emotions and the roar of the storm I was aware of her corralling me into her arms. I melted further into her, all edges gone, wrapping myself in her coconut and tobacco scent. Summer whom I had pushed away, Summer whom I had riled, Summer whom I ran away from, whom I hit with an actual plate . . . and yet, Summer who was still there for me, the way Mom should've been.

'I'm so sorry. I'm so sorry about runnin' away, and lockin' you up, and smashin' a plate on your head.'

'I was kind of impressed, to be honest.'

I snorted, a laugh sodden with tears. I shook my head against her chest. 'You were right. You were right all along.'

'What d'you mean?'

I shook my head again, overwhelmed with shame at my own naïve stupidity. Summer gently pushed me back. Her finger guided my chin until our eyes connected. Her gaze locked on mine and didn't let go.

'Tell me.'

'You were right about my mom. I went to her for help, and she sold me out. She fuckin' sold me out. She wouldn't leave him. She chose him.'

'"Fucking", eh?' Summer smirked. 'Sorry, but that word really isn't working in your mouth.'

I responded with a wan smile. 'Told my mom I hated her.'

'What did she do?'

'Slapped me.'

'Bitch.' Summer sprang up, letting go. 'She can't treat you that way. Makes me sick how they all treat you.'

I clawed at Summer's shorts, pulling her back to the ground so she could look me in the eye. She had to see my resolve.

'Forget my parents. Let's go.'

For once she was speechless. My lips stretched until the grin hurt my cheeks.

'I'm ready. Let's go somewhere . . . anywhere, like in your book, *On the Road*.'

Her face split into a grin. She'd always been beautiful in an unruly way, but now she was radiant. The sight sent my body lurching forward, and I hugged her again so tight I felt her heart beat in my chest. In that moment, I was embracing so much more than just Summer.

'Let's get out of here,' I said, my face still buried in her hair.

'Hold on. There's something I have to tell you first.'

'Later.'

'It's important.' She gently pushed me back, hands firmly resting on my shoulders. 'It's about why I'm here.'

Fleur's necklace flashed in my mind, along with Summer's confession about breaking in and roaming around Newhaven.

'I don't care. It can wait.'

Everything was different. Until now every time I'd had to leave the shack, I'd left with the knowledge that one day Summer would up and leave permanently, but now we would leave together. The rain drummed in a frenzied crescendo against the tiles that clung onto the roof and the shards of glass still remaining in the window frames. The roar dulled to a soft thud compared to the excitement drumming inside my body. We were about to embark on an adventure, and it carried the smoky edge of stale cigarettes.

Her hand cupped my cheek. An intensity shone in her eyes as if she was looking at me for the first time. My throat tightened.

'I don't know how –'

'Abigail!'

My name thundered inside the room and chilled the marrow of my bones. That voice didn't belong here.

Daddy loomed in the doorway, sodden, the hair plastered across his forehead and cheeks framing a look of disgust mixed with fury. His eyes darted back and forth from me to Summer, and his features bulged with horror.

'What are you doin' here?' he spoke slowly, the words stiff from the ice in his voice.

We scrambled to our feet. I gripped Summer's hand tightly, and she squeezed back. Whatever happened we were facing this moment together.

'Come here, Abigail.' Arm extended, he presented his hand. Did he really believe I would go to him willingly?

'Fuck off,' Summer said. 'You've done enough damage. She's coming with me.' She squeezed my hand again.

He paced back and forth, his anger swallowing the ground in long strides. 'How dare you speak to me like that. You . . . Her mother and I decide what's best for her.'

'What's best for her is to get the hell away from this place. I've seen what you've done to her.'

'You crawl back from whatever hole you came out of and leave us alone. I won't allow you to corrupt my daughter.'

'I ain't your daughter,' I screamed at him, but there was a tremble in my words. I was not the obedient daughter anymore. He stopped pacing and marched straight towards us.

'Enough, I won't be disrespected. You're comin' home. Now.'

We retreated deeper into the room until my heels bumped against the hearth. Summer side-stepped in front of me, arm slung across my chest, chin tilted up in defiance – a wall in the shape of a girl blocking his way. Slotted behind her, my hand rested low on her waist. My fingers brushed against the box-cutter in her pocket. The shape eased the fear knotted between my shoulder blades. In the low light, shadows danced on Daddy's face, drawing stern angles, his eyes shining within the carved pools of their sockets. My wet clothes clung to my skin and I shivered despite the heat.

'Get out of my way.'

'You don't care about her. You got your wife and kids, your precious family. Let me have her. You'll never see us ever again.'

But that's not in his nature. He might not care about me, but I belonged to him, and he held on to his belongings until he decided to discard them. Mom had tried to throw away a watch that didn't work anymore but didn't consult him first. He had sat at the kitchen table, peeling a boiled egg, as he watched Mom, elbow-deep in the trash looking for it. He had refused to let me help. Two weeks later he'd tossed the watch on the kitchen table and nonchalantly asked Mom to throw it away.

One final step swallowed the last sliver of space. Summer straightened, but she looked so slight compared to his bulky shape, a twig against the incoming storm. Rain battered the walls. Tucked behind her body, I snatched the knife protruding from her pocket. Daddy threw Summer aside, the way he would a bad idea. I fiddled with the safety tab, but my fingers shook too much. Daddy snatched the box-cutter before his hand shackled my wrist and twisted me into submission, my forearm close to breaking point. The bone thrummed with pain; my vision spotted with tears.

'Let me go. You're hurtin' me.'

'Enough now, you're comin' home.'

My shoes scraped against the floorboards as he yanked me across the living room. Despite the searing pain I struggled against him. The front door loomed at the end of the hallway. I dug my heels in – if he got me through it, I'd never see Summer again.

Summer leapt on his back, crushing his throat with the crook of her arm and hitting the side of his neck with her elbow.

'Let her go. You're not taking her again.'

His grip on my wrist faltered. I twisted away from him and joined her in the attack, kicking shins, pummelling his chest. She scratched his face and pulled at his beard.

'Get away from me, you whore.'

In one move he ripped Summer off him. In his fury, her body flew across the room and thudded against the wall before she collapsed in a dislocated heap on the ground.

'No!'

I rushed over to her motionless body. My heart pumped a helpless panic through my veins. Summer's head just lolled about when I shook her. I lifted it gently, my fingers wet against her hair. This couldn't be happening. I checked my finger, red with a coat of Summer's blood coming from somewhere at the back of her head. Bile pushed up my throat.

'Summer, answer me. C'mon, you gotta wake up. Please.'

I brushed a tangle of hair off her face, the blood staining her forehead.

'What did you do?' I hugged Summer, her skin warm with life, but her muscles floppy.

'She should never have come here.'

I barely registered the pain when Daddy's fingers knotted in my braid and he pulled me off Summer. Outside, the hiss of the thunderous rain swallowed my screams. The water numbed the pain, the outline of the old shack quickly disappearing in the deluge. My shoes slid in the mud as he dragged me into the swamp and back to Newhaven.

60. Present day

'We gotta hurry.'

Jackson leads us away from Newhaven, towards the boats. We're exposed out in the open, like the sun in its cloudless sky. The heat burns the back of my neck.

'When I heard about the meeting I reckoned this was our only chance. I snatched one of the boat keys. By the time they realise, we'll be in Parkerville boardin' the first bus to yonder.'

His grip is sweaty against my wrist. The friction of his fingers chafes my skin. He pulls me forward, and I stumble behind, pain building in my shoulder like a memory. *You whore, I should've expected this of you*, Daddy had said when he dragged me out of the old shack. My heels dug into the ground, my shoulders burning, my lips salty with tears. Memories clash in my mind – Daddy pulling me across the swamp, Daddy pulling me across the living room of our apartment in Chicago. Always pulling against my will. Memories blend and bend. *I know what's best for you.* Who said that? Daddy, with blood on his hands? A man with the sausage fingers and gold rings? So much blood. The fence bends around us. The walls of a living room loom around us too.

'Stop.' I jerk my arm away from him.

'Please, let's go. We don't have much time.' His voice hikes up with every plea. 'It's my chance, our chance. I ain't stayin' here no longer. Not with my dad.'

His shouts add to the others in my head. Behind him

seagulls shriek and hover, spying on our exchange. Waves lick the hulls of the boats. Predators lurk in those waters. The church's presence presses on my back, Jackson's open hand in front of me, and to the right, beyond the woods, the swamp, the old shack.

I bolt toward the woods through the rip in the fence, my body finding it without any prompts. A sharp prong scrapes against my cheek. The trees retreat to offer a path and I run deeper into the undergrowth. Jackson's and the seagulls' shouts chase after me but soon they fade away, replaced by the nonchalant croaks of bullfrogs. Branches snatch at my clothes, my hair, my hands swat them away. I've left Jackson behind, but the voices and the images have stuck with me. There's no outrunning ghosts. Their voices are in my head, their words stuffed in my mouth, their memories flashes behind my eyes. Up ahead, the woods grow darker, before shards of lights spear through the canopy of leaves.

Under my feet the baked earth morphs into soft, creaking wood. The boardwalk snakes between the trees and over the water, deeper and deeper into the heart of the swamp. Dizziness shimmies in my legs and I collapse at the end of the wooden walkway, panting. Water shows me an echo of my face floating on the surface, cheeks darkened with exertion, a scrape running across one of them. As my breathing slows, the screams of terror in my head bounce off the water – nightmares still around me. I need to keep running.

That's when I see it. The shack lurks at the end of the path, one side ravaged and disfigured by smoke and kudzu vines, broken windows like empty eye sockets. Even from a distance the place reeks of pain and abandonment; still it calls to me, tells me there's a part of me somewhere inside, as if I've left some answers in there. It pulls me to my feet and tugs me forward until I stand on firm ground again. He died in the upstairs bedroom, I slept where he shot himself, head on the same mattress, cheek against his blood.

'Why here?' The voice doesn't belong to the house but Jackson. He walks towards me, body slanted forward, his muscles tense, fingers shrivelled into fists. He looks like his father. His steps crescendo on the walkway. 'There's nothin' here. We gotta go.'

I don't answer him, just turn back towards the house.

'I ain't askin' again.'

His ultimatum hangs in the air, but all that's before me is the house.

The front door opens to darkness until a silhouette cuts out from it, and then there she is: the girl from the mirror, the girl living inside my head, outside the fence, in the hallway. Summer's back. An apple shines green in her hand, and a knife gleams silver in the other. She's the flame to the wick, and then the images burst into life – Summer holding another knife, the blood foaming at Mom's mouth, Daddy's shirt a sodden red, too many rips in the fabric to count. She advances towards me, red dripping from her long fingers. She's here. The fire shielded her, but now I see. She was there that day too.

She killed them.

Jackson's breath tickles my ear. I can taste his fear.

The devil's real. Now she stands in front of us, another knife in her hand, ready to finish the job.

Without another thought, I turn and run.

61. Two hours before the fire

I'd stopped resisting. There was no use. My only reason to fight lay lifeless on the dusty floor of the old shack. Daddy dragged me through the back door of Hunters Cottage, across the kitchen and down the hallway, leaving behind a trail of mud and water. Once he ran out of house, he threw me on the rug at Mom's feet.

The generator had given up too. Mom busied herself lighting candles before fiddling with the knob on one of the kerosene lamps, her gestures mechanical, her face a blank mask. The storm had pushed the day into an early darkness. My shoulder connected with the floor, but the pain didn't register. A spatter of raindrops darkened the hem of Mom's dress. I looked up at the woman now sitting on the sofa who wore my mother's face, a statue chiselled by Daddy's actions and words. The way she avoided looking me in the eyes pretty much spelled out who told Daddy where to find me.

'What did you do, Abigail?' Mom asked.

Rain lashed against the windows, accusing me too, but I didn't care. *What did I do? What did you do, Mom?* I didn't reply. I was done playing by their rules. Being a good daughter was meaningless. They didn't want to know, they just wanted my words so they could twist them out of shape, until they told the story they wanted to hear, the one that fitted their narrative.

Daddy stepped into my silence like we were at Sunday service. 'Thanks for the call. You were right, she was hiding in

that decrepit old shack past Marshall Point. I found her actin'
shamefully and without no decency.'

'I've failed,' Mom said. 'I tried, but there's no saving her.
What are we going to do?' She looked at him. Did she still
see her daughter or just an error to be rectified?

'Just let me go. Please. I'll disappear, you'll never hear from
me again. I won't be bringin' you shame, you'll be rid of me.'

I clung to her knees, and to the idea that maybe I could
reach whatever was left of the woman who once cared about
my real happiness, not some bogus version dictated to by
Daddy. She avoided my gaze and any attempts at a connection, her entire attention turned towards him.

'You ain't going anywhere. 'Specially not with that girl.'
His voice bellowed above the rain thrashing against the windows. He paced back and forth, propelled by some manic
energy. Summer's existence drew a deep line between his
brows – I had never seen him so unhinged. I had seen what
a calm and calculated Daddy could do; I had no idea what
this unrestrained version was capable of. Fear coated the
back of my throat, making it impossible to swallow.

'What girl?' Mom said.

The question seemed to hike up his restlessness, his strides
shortening, his hand repeatedly palming his beard. Frustration or something like it rumbled in his throat.

'It's her,' he snorted. 'She's here.'

'I don't understand. Who's here?'

'Summer.' The name detonated in the living room, and the
blast caught Mom in the chest. 'She was with Summer.'

Another short laugh, and he stopped abruptly, facing
Mom. Her jaw slackened with confusion; her lips parted but
she didn't say anything. My eyes darted from one to the other.
Listening to their conversation was like looking for the light

319

switch at night – I knew there was something there but I couldn't pinpoint it.

'Genevieve, did you hear me?'

The question jolted her. 'How is she here?'

'How should I know?'

'But they locked her up after what happened.'

A sense of dread settled under my skin. They talked like they knew her – more than just the podcast girl hanging around town. They knew her name and her past. Their tone, their words unnerved me. Who were these people, and how much had they been hiding from me? In that moment they felt more like strangers than Summer was.

'Well, looks like she's out now. Juvie ain't forever.'

The more I listened, the less they made sense. I propped myself on one arm, and a dull ache radiated in my shoulder. Fear ebbed, but still it fretted just below the skin, ready to kick at the first sign of danger.

'Summer's here.' Hearing Mom say the name opened something in the pit of my stomach. Like a hole waiting to be filled.

'She . . . How did she look?' She inched forward, craving his answer.

I wanted to scream at them, asking what they weren't telling me, but I was scared what might happen once he remembered my presence. Summer never mentioned knowing them. All she admitted to was snooping around Daddy's office.

'What else do you want me to tell you, Genevieve?' Daddy said, his face narrowing in exasperation. 'Your daughter's here. She's found us, or rather she's found her,' he added, gesturing to me.

Daughter. My mind emptied, their argument dulled into

static until all that remained was that one word – daughter. Your daughter's here. Summer. *Summer was Mom's daughter?* But they looked nothing alike. The two figures collided inside my head, the blast annihilating everything I knew about my life. In this new barren landscape one thought, one I hadn't considered until now, rose from the rubble.

Summer was my sister. I had a sister. It made no sense, and somehow it made complete sense – half-sister. Same mom, different dads. No wonder Daddy freaked out when he saw me with her. She had desperately been trying to tell me something before he showed up. Why didn't she try to tell me sooner if she knew?

One question rose above the pandemonium of question marks crowding my head. *How did I forget I had a sister?* The answer lay somewhere in the depths of Mom's silence. She never reminded me I had a sister, never included a sister on the rare occasions Chicago came up. That fight when Mom had spoken about sacrifices, decisions I couldn't understand – had Summer been the price of safe passage to a more comfortable life, the innocent sacrificed at the altar? The depth of my ignorance left me dizzy.

Just us girls. The words looped in my head as I climbed onto the sofa and nestled in the warmth Mom had left behind, wet clothes cold on my skin, as Daddy and Mom argued by the door. *Just us girls.* Crouched in the crook of the armrest, I slowly exorcised the lies that had tainted my mind and shrouded my sister for the majority of my life. Arms cradling my knees, I melted into the past before Newhaven, applying this new filter to all of my memories. Just us girls. It had been our motto, but not the 'you-and-me' I had thought. Isn't that right, Honey-bunny? Honey-bunny. Honey, Bunny. Summer, Faith. Over time my mind had straightened the inflection of the comma between the words into a bridging dash, erasing Summer from my memory.

After the move, my six-year-old self hadn't known what to call the voice that had used to soothe me, the hand that had brushed my tears or relinquished the last fries. My child's mind had shaped my memories around my new reality in Newhaven. Now a memory blazed through, vivid like a newly lit match – Summer balancing on a chair in the closet, sticking glow-in-the-dark stars to the ceiling.

This truth imbued my recent time with Summer with new meaning – Summer's eagerness at my remembering anything about Chicago, her reaction to the earrings, how she said her mom split when she was young. I squeezed my eyes shut, but it didn't stop the tears. They rolled down my cheeks, grieving for the sister I had lost and joyful at finally being reunited.

'Where is she? Where's Summer?' Mom's voice sliced through my thoughts.

'That ain't the priority right now, Genevieve.'

'Why did you leave her behind?' I asked, but neither of them replied, staring as if they'd forgotten I was there. ''Cause, that's what happened. You left my sister behind. Why? Was two girls too much work for you? That's why we left so suddenly.'

The suitcases packed by the front door, how Mom had ushered me, draped in the new brown coat – a gift from Daddy – for the surprise trip we were going on. My body suddenly flooded with the desperation I had felt back then. *Mommy, where's Summer?* Lost memories thundered back, red flashes against the darkness, of waking up in the night, crying for my lost sister – until time did its dirty work.

'You abandoned your own daughter. Why?'

The answer stood by the door. Something primal overtook me, darkening the edge of my vision, my fist furiously beating my thigh. It propelled me off the sofa. I lunged at him. My bones hummed with the want to break something.

'It was you. You took me away from her. Did her skin colour not work with your image of the perfect family?' I pummelled his chest, but none of my blows dented his demeanour. 'Why did you do this?'

'To save you,' Mom shouted back, her voice broken by a tremor of tears, wrenching her attention away from him. 'She was too far gone, but you . . . you were still so young. Things could be different for you in the right environment. I just had to get you away from Chicago.'

'You disgust me. You're such hypocrites.'

Tears clung to her lashes, but I couldn't decide if they were for the daughter she'd abandoned or shame for the crime she'd committed against motherhood. I didn't care either way.

'How is she? Summer –?'

'*How is she?*' Daddy's voice sliced through. 'When I found them, she was tryin' to convince Abigail to abandon her faith and run away from her family. That's how she's doin'. Everything she touches, she corrupts. You should have seen how she was dressed, embracing Abigail while half-naked.'

Horror filled Mom's face. But he was twisting everything. I'd been the one hugging Summer, and she didn't have to convince me of nothing. He was the one pushing me to run away, not Summer. Summer, who lay in the aftermath of his rage on the rotten planks of the old shack, hair matted with blood. On the other side of the back door, the swamp had never felt so wide.

'Ask him. Ask him what he did to Summer.'

Mom was silent. Daddy spoke, his voice low and threatening.

323

'You ain't goin' nowhere with that girl so you can forget about her. You're staying here where you belong. You'll be married to Tom, and you'll learn to submit to your husband. Time to pray for salvation.'

He loomed over me. In that moment, his idea of salvation sounded terrifying.

62. Present day

The memories flow through me like blood as I run from the shack, a stream of murky images and sounds that make my heart beat faster. I look at my hands and the blood on them has dried. Branches and undergrowth hold me back, but I don't slow down.

My lungs throb in my chest, the muscles in my legs ache, but I don't slow down.

The face of the girl in the mirror bleeds into my thoughts. She's real. Jackson saw her too. The devil's here. Her face flashes in my head, and I taste the blood. It chokes me up, replaces the oxygen in my lungs, but I don't slow down.

The bracken hisses around me. The boardwalk has given way to baked ground, but I don't slow down.

There's too much around. I need to slow down, but not here. I need to get to Hunters Cottage, see how memories fit into the space. Solve the jigsaw in my head. The forest shifts around me, and I don't slow down.

Not even when a tree moves in front of me.

63. One hour before the fire

Daddy loomed over me. I didn't know what he intended, but my knees throbbed with the memory of the last time he asked me to repent. Terror grabbed me by the throat, before reaching deep into my chest and spreading through every nerve.

'Kneel.'

The word bellowed out of him, but instead of bending me to his will, it snapped something inside. Chin tilted up, I stared at him and channelled my sister.

'No.'

'I won't allow for you to disrespect me no more. Now, I say kneel.'

'No.'

Fury twisted his face, nostrils flaring. I'd never seen him like this before, not when we fought at the dinner table the night of the lightning storm when I ran to the shack, not that day in his office with the rice. I planted my feet wide, anchoring myself in my defiance, ready to weather the storm of whatever he would unleash. His hand rose high ready to strike and my arm instinctively swung in front of me.

'I said, kneel.'

A blinding pain exploded in my shoulder, spreading to the bone in my arm. My throat was full of words, too many – in their stampede to get out, language reverted to a primal instinct. Screams ripped out of me. His hand had shackled my wrist and he twisted my arm so far back it folded my body.

Like an animal trying to escape a hunter's snare I inched forward but the slightest move brought a new wave of crumpling pain. My bone hummed on the threshold of breaking.

Mom had flattened herself against the opposite wall.

'Mom, help. Don't let him do this to me.'

My next plea disintegrated into a sob. My pain didn't dislodge Mom from where she'd retreated. He tightened the vice of his grip, increasing the agonising pressure. It brought my body closer to him. His breath fell on my ear and his chest rose against my back, wet shirt sticking to my dress. In one swift move, my foot came crashing down on his. The surprise snatched a howl out of him and loosened his grip. I stumbled forward, body delirious with the release from pain. The euphoria didn't last. He slapped me hard, sending my head flying and throwing me off balance. Before I could regain my composure he was back on me with renewed rage, twisting my arm behind my back once more. I yelped as I collapsed onto the ground, chin hitting the floor. I bucked under his weight, each move testing the limit of my shoulder, ablaze with pain.

'Get off me. Get off me!'

'Help me restrain your daughter. That's Summer making her act like this. Do you want her to end up like her sister when I can save her?'

Mom shuffled forward. My free arm swung around wildly, trying to hit him. Exhaustion washed over me, tears stinging my eyes, his weight smothering my breath.

'Mom . . . please.'

'Now, Genevieve, or are you surrendering another child to the devil?'

Mom kneeled down in front of me.

'Hold her.'

Mom restrained my free arm; her eyes refused to meet

mine. They held me down on the floor like an animal to be sacrificed. Hope seeped out of me; my body felt light. Perhaps I didn't have to stay there. I could just float away above Hunters Cottage, above the woods and the swamp, escape to the old shack, lie down next to Summer, and bury my face in my sister's hair. My mind drew the lines of the house, the front door I could step through and lock behind me. Another shooting pain up my arm tethered me back to the horror of the room. A sob choked me.

'Now repent, and agree to marry Tom in two weeks.'

'Mom, don't let me.'

'Answer me, Abigail.'

'That ain't my name.'

'Evil, I command thee to leave this body.'

The rug itched under my skin, saliva dribbled down my chin, mingling with my tears. Daddy leaned against me, his whole weight choking me, my shoulder raw with pain.

'By the power of our Lord —'

I twisted my head towards Mom.

'Mom, please . . . Mom, look at me.' There was a tremble in Mom's shoulder. 'Help me. Please . . .'

My last plea dissolved into a cry as he twisted my arm one inch further.

'Mommy!' The word cracked like a shotgun blast, whipping her face around. Our eyes locked, both shining with tears. 'Please don't let him do this. He hurt Summer. Don't let him hurt me too . . . Just us girls, Mom.'

The words burned my throat. The weight of his knee slid to the small of my back. Her grip loosened until her fingers left my wrist. But the hope fluttering in my chest didn't last. A cold dread washed over me as I watched Mom run out of the room.

64. Present day

Pain shoots up my tailbone as I hit the ground. Wade Pruitt blocks my path. Other figures detangled themselves from the trees in the background. A pair of hands plucks me from the ground and straightens me up.

'Where are Tom and Jackson? What've you done with them?' Wade Pruitt shakes me as if he can shed the answer from my body. I'm afraid if I open my mouth all that's going to fall out are incoherent screams. Faces surround me, wrapping me in their anger and contempt. Poor Jackson. I ran off, leaving him back there. With her. Lord knows what she's done to him.

'She ain't right in the head. Just look at her. Just look . . .' Their eyes bulge, wet with horror. The blood on my hands and the front of my dress screams at them. I forgot it was there. I was right, they'll blame me for this too.

'What've you done to Jackson, you bitch? Just answer.'

The slap stops the carousel of deaths in my head and leaves my cheek throbbing.

'I didn't do anything. He followed me. She . . . It's her, the girl in my head. She's real. She's the devil.' The ramble of words leaves me breathless. I can't tell them what I've done. The shame of abandoning Jackson with her swells in my throat.

'What's she done to my boy? What have you done to my boy?'

Mr Caine snatches me from Wade Pruitt's grip. He grabs

me by the shoulders, fingers digging into my collarbone, edging towards my throat. The skin on his neck is red and tight, a thick vein bulging underneath. His thumbs press inside the hollow at the base of my throat.

This is how I'm going to die – strangled by Jackson's dad. The air thins out in my lungs and dark spots bloom in my eyes.

'Ezra, not like this,' Pastor Abernathy says.

'She killed my boy. I know she did. Look at her.'

His hands spasm around my neck before they let go. Pastor Abernathy pats Mr Caine's shoulder, but Mr Caine swats it off in one sharp move. His body tenses under an animal wail, something primal fighting out of him. I want to tell him that if I've killed Jackson by leaving him behind, he's already killed him a hundred times, in every bruise and every broken bone, the slow death of his kindness and spirit. But I don't, worried that if I speak he will rip me to pieces with his bare teeth.

'Ezra, Ezra.'

Pastor Abernathy's voice lulls him until the tension in his whole body diminishes to just shoulder shakes. I've never seen Mr Caine cry or look defeated before. How can he feel so sad for a son he likes to hit?

'Let's find your boy first. Trust in our Lord to watch over Jackson. Under His guidance.'

'Under His guidance.' Mr Caine nods, but his voice has lost the fervent conviction it always had.

Pastor Abernathy dispatches five men to go with Mr Caine. The rest escort me back to Newhaven, Wade Pruitt and Mr Garrett flanking me while Pastor Abernathy leads the way. My mind has gone numb again, but rogue images flash in its darkness. Death attracting death. Blood attracting blood.

My hands dripping with someone else's life. Or are they Summer's hands? Mom's mouth, red foam at the corner. Daddy's shirt drenched with red. Fingers grabbing at the air. Something is rising and dragging up with it all the dregs from the deepest parts of my mind. Too much. The overload folds my body.

'Keep moving.' A hand shoves me forward and to the ground. Nobody helps me up, none of them slows down. Their Lord's mercy and infinite love doesn't extend to me anymore.

65. Forty-five minutes before the fire

Abandonment ran icy in my veins. I could only count on myself. *Fight.* I kicked my legs back, swung my free arm. Daddy somehow lost his balance. His hand let go, and I flopped on my back and wriggled from under him. He grabbed one of my wrists, and my teeth sank into his hand. I felt the bones beneath the skin, a rusty taste hit my tongue. His blood fuelled my resolve. His hands crashed on my throat, pushing the soft bones to breaking point. I gasped for oxygen, my vision spotting. I clawed at his hands, but they just squeezed harder.

'Get away from her.'

Mom edged into the room, one hand clutching a kitchen knife, knuckles white with determination. She thrust the blade in front of her like a talisman.

'What are you doin'?' Daddy's grip slackened.

'John, get away from my daughter.'

Her arm kept dipping as if it took more energy than she had to bear the weight of the knife. He slowly peeled himself off me but not quickly enough for Mom, who poked the blade in his direction.

'All right.' He held his hands out, backing up to a stand.

As soon as the weight lifted, I scrambled from under him and towards Mom's free hand, which was beckoning me. My shoulder still burned with pain. She stretched her arm in front of me, the same way Summer had at the old shack. After all these years, the woman who risked everything for me was back. My body slackened with relief. Fear and courage fought on Mom's face. She was still in there, the woman with the dark roots, flipping off the men who catcalled her. But the gratitude tasted sour in my mouth. She was the same mom who had abandoned her other daughter. Worse, acted like she never existed. Mom's lies had been perpetuated in me. Summer must've been heartbroken when I, her own sister, didn't recognise her.

On the other side of the rug, Daddy tucked his shirt before smoothing back his hair, reinstating the façade of righteousness. He reminded me of swamp water. Placid enough to forget the gator lurking beneath the surface.

'What now?'

'Go stand over there.'

He disregarded her instruction and stepped forward.

'Get back.' Mom's voice and the knife trembled.

'A knife? Really, Genevieve. What is it with you and knives in this family?'

'What does he mean?' I asked, but she stayed silent, her gaze fixed on him. 'What does he mean?' I repeated.

He loosely crossed his arms, his lack of concern angering me. He should experience the fear he inflicted. I dared him in my mind to come forward. It was us girls against him now.

'A knife's the very reason your mama decided it was too dangerous for you to stay in Chicago. It was why CPS came knockin' and sent your mother runnin'.' The words slid out of him like acid from a cracked battery.

'What does he mean?'

Her gaze flickered in my direction, and my stomach tightened.

'Put the knife down, Genevieve, or you'll never see your kids again.'

'Stop, please.'

'Ten years old, and your sister stabbed a man while she was supposed to be looking after you. That's the kind of girl you've been spendin' time with.' He smiled at the damage his revelation did. He read it in the wideness of my eyes, how it split my mouth open.

'Stop, John.'

'Have you hugged your children today, Genevieve? 'Cause you'll never see them again.'

The box-cutter flashed in my mind. Summer had stabbed a man, and I'd been there. Been there and couldn't remember, a tar pit where the memory should be. Time had dug so many holes, Summer and most of Chicago had disappeared into the honeycomb of my mind. Something squirmed in a dark alcove – the larva of a memory waking up.

I might have forgotten, but I knew Summer. Those hours spent together, my body had sought hers, a sun to orbit around, craving the inexplicable comfort I felt near her. Summer who always had my back, who gave me the power that night of the lightning storm, who stood up for me when I couldn't, who rescued me from Zach in that alleyway the first time we met in Parkerville.

'Why did she do it?'

Mom shrugged. 'All I know is I found you curled into a ball, hiding in the hallway closet crying, and I just knew I had to get you away from that place. I had to give you a chance at a better life. I couldn't save her but I could save you.'

'This ain't better, though.'

'Summer said he got handsy, but it's not a reason to stab someone.'

'She likes to cause destruction around her, that's why she did it. It's in her blood, Genevieve. You ain't even sure who her father is. Back then you were a promiscuous woman. Now give me the knife. This is your last chance to be a mother to your remainin' kids.'

'Don't listen to him. We can go to her, Mom. She's here. We can leave together with the twins –'

'Enough of this now.' His voice bellowed, reclaiming the space. 'You ain't taking my children anywhere. Give me the knife. Now.'

Not waiting for an answer he marched over to us, steady stride, open hand exuding the confidence that she would surrender the knife to him. Her fingers stiffened around the handle.

He locked his gaze onto her, and her wrist locked into position.

'Give me the knife.'

She held the knife closer, defying him for a second time. His face narrowed at the slight.

'I said, give me the damn knife.'

Without a pause he lunged, wrapping his hand around her fingers, crushing them against the handle. They tugged at it the way the twins would fight over their toy truck, but this tug-of-war was over something deadly. The fight brought them closer, neither willing to let go. Mom's face twisted in pain and sprung me into action. I grabbed his arm, but he wouldn't budge. I tried to find a way between the tangle of them, but there was no opening. Their struggle reached a frenzy, twisting them one way and another, the knife buried somewhere between them. I threw my weight in. Frustration growled in Daddy's throat, and a high shriek escaped Mom.

Suddenly she stopped. I backed away from their ominous silence and the knot of them. Daddy staggered back, legs softened under the shock. He stared at his hands and the blood. I turned towards Mom. My heart sank in my chest as she sank to the floor. The handle of the knife stuck out just under the ribs. Her mouth opened, but the screams poured out of mine.

66. Present day

They throw me in one of the empty rooms in the attic.

I sink to the floor by the cot bed, the ground furry with dust. Something catches my eye near one of the metal feet. The desiccated blueberry is a shrivelled ball of harsh ridges. Jackson always used to carry them in that damn handkerchief of his. With this token in my hand I allow one thought to rise to the surface, one I don't know how to process – I abandoned him. Ran away when I saw Summer and the knife. He needed someone to protect him, to run away with him. I've left him to die. They'll blame me for it too. And this is one thing they should blame me for.

All those shards of memories tell me that Summer is part of what happened during those weeks before the fire. She is the one who can pull back the curtain and reveal the mystery of the Oz I live in. How long have I known the devil? I shouldn't have run away, but seeing her, the blood ... I feel like somehow Summer and blood are intrinsically connected. The blood not only flowing through but around her too. Now, on the dusty floor, the old shack rises. I lie on its floor, Summer's heartbeat strong on my cheek.

When the lock clicks open, the sun has dipped low in the sky, stretching the shadows in the room. Dried blood has calcified on my dress. Sleep has come in fistfuls and with fragments of memories like Scrabble tiles, my conscious and unconscious mind trying to makes words or narrative out of everything that was lost in whatever fire had swept through my mind.

Mrs Calhoun and Pastor Abernathy fill the doorway. My guess is, with all that's happened, ain't nobody taking any chances being alone with me now. The only escape route is through that door, the main reason I'm sure they've locked me on this floor. Escaping through the window would allow gravity to do the job for them.

I wonder if they've found Tom yet.

Unconscious, Tom had weighed a ton. The gash on his scalp where the lamp had struck him bled a lot, filling the room with a metallic smell.

'Ain't no time for that,' Jackson said.

'Please, he can't wake up here, and they can't find him here either.'

Jackson gave up with a sigh. 'OK, but quick then. Where?'

'Mrs Favreau.'

Tom's head rested on my lap as I grabbed him under the armpits, blood soaking my hands and the front of my dress. Wrapping my nightdress around his head solved that problem. After Jackson hoisted him up by the legs, we lugged him out of the room and down the hallway.

'Why are we doing this?'

He doesn't understand. He can't. He never had to live under the expectations of the obedient daughter. I couldn't leave him on display in my room.

We dumped him in the tub in Mrs Favreau's bathroom. I wiped the blood on the front of my dress, but it was a pointless exercise.

I stared at Tom and the curtain of blood drawing down his face. Jackson grabbed my wrist and pulled me out of the door.

67. Thirty minutes before the fire

The knife resisted as I slowly pulled it out. I couldn't leave it there, the piece of metal he'd stuck inside of her. I pressed my palms over the wound, a makeshift Band-Aid to stop the flow. A failed attempt. Blood swelled between my fingers, warm and thick. The colour was repulsive, littering my arms with goosebumps. The impulse to run away twitched in my stomach, but I didn't move. I wasn't going nowhere.

A terrifying rusty smell spoiled the air, and a surge of fear mixed with nausea burned the back of my mouth.

'Mom? Mom, can you hear me? Mom!'

She opened her mouth but instead of words, blood speck-led her lips and her chin. Fear strangled me. If only Summer was here, she'd know what to do. Mom had stood up for me; she needed me now but I felt useless. My hands were losing their battle, failure soaking them red. I panicked, applied more pressure. A half groan, half gurgle rose from her in response.

'No, no, no . . . I'm sorry.'

Still I kept my hands firmly pressed down. The only stead-fast part of me, everything else shaking. Swallowing my fear, bile stuck in my throat, I turned towards the only person who could help.

'She needs help. You gotta get someone.'

From the other end of the room Daddy looked at me with horror on his face. 'What did you do, Abigail? What did you do?'

He didn't make sense; I hadn't done anything apart from pull out the knife. I couldn't leave it there, cold blade jammed in like that. Her lids fluttered, eyes unable to focus on anything.

'Mom, I'm here. Can you hear me?'

'Get away from her. How could you do this to your own mother?' Daddy wore an expression of disgust on his face, ill-suited to the role he'd played in the whole disaster. It had started with him.

'You stabbed her.' Under my hands, Mom's chest rose in shallow heaves.

'Don't try this with me. You got into the middle of us. Forgive her, Lord, for she doesn't know what she's done.'

'Please, Daddy, you gotta go to Newhaven and get Mrs Finch or Mr Abernathy. Call Parkerville for an ambulance, or a helicopter, or somethin'. Please.'

'And leave you alone with your mother so you can finish what you started? I don't think so.'

I couldn't abandon her, not right now. Last September when Mrs Calhoun had sliced her hand opening clams, Mrs Finch kept on telling her, apply pressure to the wound, make sure to apply pressure. I didn't know why, but Mrs Finch's tone made the command seem important.

A hiccup and Mom choked on her breath, sending my heart crashing against my ribs. Unconsciousness tried to claim her, sending her eyes rolling. Their whiteness terrified me – a white flag of surrender. Death crept across her face, chilling my bones. I ransacked my mind for something to say, words strong enough for her to hold on to.

'I'm sorry. I didn't mean any of the stuff I said to you. I was just mad. I love you, Mom. Do you hear me?'

Her gaze found its way back to me, away from the

darkness. She couldn't die, she was too young for that. She wasn't even forty yet.

'It's all right, Bunny.' The words drifted, barely a whisper. The hint of a smile flitted on her lips before pain twisted it into a grimace. 'Help me, will you?'

Together, we shuffled back until she half slumped against the wall. The effort snatched a long moan from Mom and a gasp from me.

'If you hadn't grabbed us, this would've never happened,' Daddy continued, still rooted to the same spot by the window. Just a couple of steps away from the outside, from getting help for my mom, for his wife. It all happened so fast. If I hadn't got in the middle of them, maybe, just maybe. Now I'd never know.

'John . . .' The name sucked the little remaining energy out of Mom.

'Mom, I didn't –'

'Bunny . . . What time. Tomorrow . . .'

Fear spread through my veins. Her mind was slipping away. Away, like the blood slipping through the slits between my fingers. Please, don't slip away. Stay. There were so many things she needed to know, like how I had lied when I said I loved her meatloaf, that I was the one who wrecked her favourite lipstick back in Chicago, or that I'd found the earrings, that I understood now why she kept them.

From the corner of my eye, I saw something move.

'I ain't losing all this because of you. I've sacrificed too much to become Pastor Heywood. I ain't givin' it all up.'

'Stay away from them, you sick bastard.'

My heart swelled with delirious joy at the all-too-familiar voice. Summer had claimed the space inside the doorway, defiant. Daddy glared at her. I had been so lost in my panic

I hadn't noticed he had been creeping towards me. His eyes flashed to the discarded knife in the space between us.

'Don't even think about it.' Summer scowled at him, leaning down and snatching the knife away.

He didn't say anything, but his answer was written in the tension in his jaw. Outside the wind had died down, rain sliding down the windows.

Mom's face was pale, her skin shallow and grey. I had to stay strong. Summer was there now. Kneeling down, my sister abandoned the knife and covered my hands with her own, putting pressure on the wound. We felt our mom's chest rise in shallow motions. The girls had found each other again.

'Mom, it's me. It's Summer. I'm here. I've missed you.' Summer stroked Mom's face, smearing blood on her cheek. She tried to smile but the breaks in her voice gave her away. 'It's me, Mom. It's Summer.' Tears muddy with mascara clung to the comma of her lashes, falling every time she blinked.

'Honey . . . Bunny.'

'That's right, Mom. Remember? Just us girls.' Grabbing the knife again with one hand, Summer slipped the other one under Mom's armpit, and I did the same. 'Come on, let's go.'

Mom leaned on us. The weight pulled at me, but I locked my shoulders in. Summer glared at Daddy, who blocked the door. We were getting out, even if we had to go through him. With Summer here, I felt we were invincible. But moving Mom in this state was almost impossible, and we faltered after a few steps. Tears and frustration strangled me. All three of us slumped on the floor. The knife clattered down next to us. Mom's hand crawled, inching towards our hands. We grabbed it at the same time. We exchanged a quick glance and a wry smile before leaning our foreheads against Mom's. For a brief moment all was right in our world. Just us.

'It's OK.' Mom's mouth stretched into a thin smile. A comforting gesture which choked me. 'You're OK. My girrrr . . .'

The word disintegrated, and Mom's eyes rolled over again.

'Mom? Mom, wake up. Wake up, Mommy, please.'

Her body tensed up under our hands. The sudden spasm jarred me, and my teeth sank into the lining of my mouth. A few more deep rasping sounds, and the tension left Mom's body. Everything was still. Too still. This couldn't be it. Not when my family had finally reunited.

68. Twenty minutes before the fire

The candles' flames flinched under my screams. The clouds outside added to the new darkness filling the room. Grief tightened my lungs, pulled at my skin and hair. I dissolved into another scream.

'You killed your mother. You killed your own mother. How could you? You'll spend the rest of your life in jail, if they don't give you a lethal injection.'

A grunt rose from Summer's throat. 'You bastard – *you* killed her. Don't try to frame my little sister for it.'

'She did it. Two sisters. Two killers. Who do you think they gonna believe?'

'You think they'll believe you?'

'I'm a man of God.'

'That's not all you are though.'

Every muscle in Daddy tensed. I waited for her to drop the revelation about Fleur's locket. Undo his smug confidence and façade with a few well-placed words, and expose his secret.

'Hardly the first time you've killed your wife, Pastor Heywood.'

The unexpected accusation whipped my head around. Another wife? Not the first time killing? No matter how many times I repeated the words they didn't make sense. I searched both their faces for a clue but found none. Summer and Daddy glared at each other, the Yankee and the Confederate on the brink of another civil war.

'I got no idea what you mean.'

'Really? That's pathetic. I know who you are.'

'I'm Pastor John Heywood –'

'Yeah . . . or is it Lee Elsher?'

The name folded Daddy like a punch in the gut. Even through my tears I saw it, finally, the thing that had never flashed in his eyes before, even when Matthew fell down the stairs – absolute fear.

'I knew it. I knew I was right,' Summer said.

The name tugged at me. A name Summer had mentioned before, but I couldn't remember when. I stared at my sister's face. My mind animated the scene from that first time at the shack. I had sat on the grass next to her, skin tight from the sun. The words had escaped amid a cloud of smoke. *Her name was Karen, Karen Elsher. They found her in bed, throat slit ear to ear . . . kids shot . . . never found him.* Daddy? The man who looked after me as I grew up. The same hands who tucked me and the twins into bed, the hands that cradled baby Sarah after she was born, those same hands had pulled the trigger on his own children as they slept in their beds.

'I have no idea what you're talking about.'

'But I know. I know what you did to your first wife and kids.'

'Did what? If you're so sure I did somethin' why aren't the cops here?'

Her eyes narrowed in anger. 'You know why.'

'They'll never believe you.'

'Not back then, but after what happened to Fleur and her dad? And Pastor Favreau? Now our mom? It's all piling up, Elsher.'

'Enough. My name is Pastor John Heywood.'

He glared at the knife on the floor, still sodden with blood.

345

What would he tell the congregation, that this outsider broke in and killed me and Mom before he had the chance to over-power her, killing her in self-defence?

She must have read his mind. She lunged at the knife. He snatched her wrist, her fist frozen in mid-air like some final judgement waiting to fall. The fight unfolded behind the cur-tain of my tears. She kicked his shins, her knee tried to find his groin, but he parried all of her moves. She went at him with a feral energy. The box-cutter that he'd taken from me slipped out of his pants pocket and clattered on the ground. I knew I should join my sister but I couldn't let go of Mom.

He punched Summer in the stomach, folding her body. She coughed away the pain, looking diminished under his shadow. Disoriented, she didn't fight back when he pinned her to the wall, squeezing her throat.

'It's all your fault,' he said, fingers digging into her soft flesh. 'Why couldn't you just stay gone?'

Summer's lips paled to a bluish hue. I couldn't let it hap-pen again. Darkness crept at the edge of my vision. The flames cowered on their wicks. Something burned its way out of some hidden depth. It seared through my veins and gathered in my throat like clouds in a storm. I'd felt like this before, a long time ago, when it was necessary.

My fist struck his back instead of my usual thigh. His hand spasmed around Summer's neck and let go. He wasn't going to take anybody else away. She was my family. My fist struck again. The knife sunk into his back over and over. It sunk into him when he fell to his knees. It sunk into him when he lay on the ground. It sunk into him after he stopped moving. I won't let him. It had happened before, it was happening again.

My hands.   Red.   So much red. My hands so

small.   The room flickered between the house and our apartment in Chicago. Daddy's body the same and different, stockier, hair shorter. The two united by the amount of blood they were losing.

I was a bad person. Good girls didn't do that. But I had to. I stopped him, and he won't wake up now.

My eyes fixed on the red dripping from my fingers, my mouth opened, and screams poured out. I threw them up in an endless stream. My fingers tensed, keeping away from each other, from feeling the blood coating them.

'It's OK. Just wait.'

The red glistened on my hands, too warm, too sticky. Gory images careened around my mind – the bloody fur of rabbits, the red foam at Mom's mouth, ospreys tearing the flesh of a woodpecker, the wounds in Daddy's back. The smell of death rose from my hands. So much red.

The air shifted next to me, Summer's voice in my ear. 'Here you go.'

She eased me out of my clothes, her movements slow and steeped in love. Next came the cleansing. Water drenched my hands, chasing the red away. The water washed away my screams too. She helped me step into a new dress.

'See, it's all right. You're OK.'

The water didn't wash away the images. Mom. She would be able to help. I crawled towards my mother. I left her once before, never again.

'Faith. Come on, we need to go before they find us.' Summer's voice only an echo, competing with all the memories and images which crowded my mind.

Something tugged at my body, pulling me away from Mom. Screams splintered the air, their jagged ends nails I used to claw at the hands restraining me.

The low thud of a weight hitting furniture, the clatter of objects falling.

'I need to get rid of the evidence, but I'll come back for you. I swear I'll come back.'

Mom's hand weighed heavy in mine. The same hand that wiped my tears that night, that stroked my back, that lifted me from the hallway closet. I placed Mom's hand to my cheek, but it wouldn't stay there.

A final shatter of glass before a whoosh of heat. I was lost in the maze of my memories. I couldn't find the exit. I just sank deeper and deeper.

AUDIO FILE #16

Audio Quality: Good

[Voice A]: Female
[Voice B]: Female
[Voice C]: Male

[Voice A]: Do you mind if I record this? It's notes and research for my podcast.

[Voice B]: Sure. What can I help you with?

[Voice A]: I'm looking for information on the death of the former pastor at Newhaven Plantation – Pastor Favreau. I've been checking the newspapers but they don't seem to have much.

[Voice B]: Mmmm ... Ferg might be able to help with that. FERG. HEY, FERGUSON! Can you come here for a sec?

[Voice C]: What can I do you for, darlin'?

[Voice B]: This young woman's lookin' for some information about the death of the previous pastor up at Newhaven Plantation, but there ain't much in the papers.

[Voice C]: Oh yessum, old Pastor Favreau. Messy story that was. They ain't sure if he tripped or he had one of them dizzy spells, but whatever, he ended up

349

at the bottom of that grand staircase with a broken neck. His wife was found next to his body. Hysterical, she was. Bless her heart. Rumour has it that maybe she pushed him. You see, my nephew's a paramedic. He's my great-nephew actually. He was on call and he reckoned she ain't all there.

[Voice A]: What do you mean?

[Voice C]: Like dementia or somethin'. Of course, folks over there think it's the devil in her head, makin' her sick.

[Voice A]: How do you know what happened if she's mentally impaired?

[Voice C]: The new pastor, he saw it all. Said the old man went down and fell head first. Imagine watchin' your husband die like that. The worst is that he – Pastor Favreau – apparently he was sup-posed to retire. He wanted to look after his wife. Even had a replacement lined up to take over the congregation, someone over in Florida, but can you believe, that man died in a break-in a few weeks after Pastor Favreau's accident. And his daughter got killed too. She was supposed to be away with her mother and siblings, but she wasn't feelin' well and stayed behind that day. Poor girl, only sixteen or somethin'. Breaks an old man's heart. Sorry, I digress. Mixin' it all up.

[Voice A]: Actually, Ferg, it's all making sense.

[Voice C]: Oh well, glad I could be of service, darlin'.

69. Present day

'Abigail, would you come with us, please?' Pastor Abernathy says.

I play along with the pretence I got a choice in this situation. The long stretch of hallway unfurls in front of us. The urge to bolt twitches in my stomach, but it's a long distance to cover between here and the main entrance and plenty of hands to stop me. Mrs Calhoun leads our small procession, Pastor Abernathy's strong presence at my back. I bide my time.

On the second-floor mezzanine we are stopped by a barrage of people made up of most of the community, with Mr Caine at its head. People who asked me to call them family, people who have eaten beside me, harvested the vegetable garden and orchard with me, people I have prayed with, united with against the evils that roamed outside, now united in hating a new evil – me. Ezra Caine stares at me with red-rimmed eyes that carry a black emptiness. They must've found Jackson dead, and I'm standing in front of his father, caked in blood. Doesn't really matter it isn't Jackson's but Tom's. My appearance fits the crime.

'Ezra, Ezra. I know you're hurtin', but y'all need to discuss this.' Pastor Abernathy side-steps next to me.

'All due respect, Pastor, the time for talkin' has come and gone. We've already decided what needs to be done to keep our . . . families safe.'

A wave of agreement whispers through the group behind him.

'Rebecca and you, Pastor, step aside, we don't want you to get hurt by accident.'

Anger tenses the muscles in his shoulders, all the way down his arm. His hand is cramped around something. He twitches and exposes the small rock he clutches. My eyes dart to the other people around him, all with their hands cradling rocks of various sizes. Mrs Calhoun detaches herself from my side and takes her place next to Ezra Caine. I almost expect to see her hand dive into her pocket to retrieve a stone.

Pastor Abernathy raises his empty hands. 'Ezra, let's not —'

Pain explodes in my collarbone. Pastor Abernathy jerks back. Ezra Caine stares, but striking me with a stone hasn't dampened the rage darkening his eyes. Another rock whistles past my ear, and I bolt, away from the exit and the angry mob. I hunch, running upstairs, my strides eating steps two at a time. Rocks chase me, some flying past, some striking my back, bruising my ribs, my spine. Each new pain reminds me I'm still alive, but each one narrows the distance between me and death. By the third floor, my entire back is one big expanse of pain ripping my muscles apart. My foot catches on the last step. My elbows hit the floor and a lightning of pain shoots through my arms. The threadbare carpet burns my palms. Their anger thunders up the stairs, catching up. Distorted faces leer over me. Everything I did has caught up with me, and I have to pay now.

Instead of the whistle of rocks, a long wail rips through the air, rising from the floor below. We all freeze. Another cry joins it, and another, and another. Screams so primal my skin bristles at the sound. Along with them rises an acrid and pungent smell. Most faces turn away from me. It's time to escape them, but I can't help but wonder what's happening.

She reaches the half-landing – all black dress and blue veins under paper-thin skin. Her mouth opens and out of its darkness comes another unintelligible wail.

'Mrs Favreau?'

My mind flashes to my escape with Jackson after we dumped an unconscious Tom in Mrs Favreau's bath tub. We'd scrambled through the door without looking back – or locking it.

'Your daddy's the devil. He took my Floyd. Where's Floyd?'

'Ezra was right. She's Satan's child,' Mrs Calhoun screams, pointing an accusing finger at me. She picks up one of the stones on the floor.

A breath shudders in my chest. Another waft of that almost overpowering smell, sharp like paint-thinner, but there's another smell buried under it. For a moment it comforts me, reminds me of when Mom used to smoke and would let me flick open her lighter and strike the wheel.

'My darlin' Floyd. This place's cursed. It belongs to the devil now.'

Hearing her speak after all these months of silence is unsettling, but no one else seems to care.

A crumpled photograph sticks out of Mrs Favreau's hand. Two faces, close together, eyes creased with the same happiness. Her eyes find me, even though she can't see. My body goes rigid with the realisation I know who did this to her, what happened to her, to her husband. *It's all a matter of perspective, darlin'* – her messages, the ramblings of a mad woman or the accusations of a grief-stricken widow? Daddy. Daddy was the architect of her pain and her husband's demise. The knowledge is intimate, but I got no idea where it comes from. More shouts rise from the floors below. Fear and unease thin out the group as some people rush past Mrs Favreau and down the stairs.

'Fire. Fire!'

On cue, a plume of smoke drifts from the lower floors, igniting hysteria among the rest of the group. I'm forgotten. The smell makes sense. The black colour of her dress has concealed how it's sodden. A small can of gasoline flashes red in her other hand. More people rush down the stairs, led by a new fear. Panic erupts but fresh shouts are swallowed by another cry from Mrs Favreau. She ain't done yet. The flick of the lighter turns people to stone. She drops it onto the trail of gasoline on the ground. The fire licks her skirt and snakes up her body. The front room at Hunters Cottage devoured by fire flashes in my mind, its walls scarred by flames. A powerful scream from her, and pandemonium erupts on the stairs. Mrs Favreau is going down, and she intends on taking the rest of Newhaven along.

The dryness of the place feeds the fire into a frenzy. I lean over the banister – floors below are already engulfed in flames. How many fires did she set before she got to us? Thick black smoke billowing upwards burns my throat with every breath.

A blinding terror kicks me into action. My body remembers the heat so intense it pulls at my skin and burns my lungs with each inhale. I run. The hallway fills with smoke and a dry cough roots deep in my chest. All around are screams, the sound of people shattering windows, of out-of-control flames. There's nowhere to go to escape the fire.

One of the old hotel door numbers glints faintly through the smoke. It beckons me, and I duck in. Even with the door closed the smoke snakes its way under and through every crack. The window stands proud, fresh air waiting for me on the other side. The latch catches and it takes three attempts to unlock it. Even then the window won't budge. Even with all my weight thrown onto it. Still nothing, the wood warped by years of humidity and poor maintenance. The breeze rustling the leaves outside taunts me. A coughing fit folds my body. I need oxygen, otherwise the smoke will kill me before the fire. Shoulder wedged under the sill, the effort reignites the pain in my back. I stop.

I rush back out and down the stairs. The smoke is so thick the hallway has disappeared. The air burns my throat. The blaze roars in my ears. I'm in hell. The flames bring back forgotten memories – the curtains in the front room two columns of flame, a blaze so intense it swallows my screams and burns off my tears. I collapse, desperately wanting my mom, but my survival instinct won't loosen its hold on me. On all fours, I pat the floor under my fingers, feeling rough edges.

Staggering back into the bedroom, the rock shatters the window after a couple of blows, and a welcome spill of air rushes in, which I gulp in great swallows. My elbow knocks the remaining shards of glass from the frame. Half hanging out, the sight of the drop makes my stomach tighten. Not a gutter in sight. The smoke in the room thickens, pushing fresh air away. My lungs itch from it, my throat raw from the constant coughing.

So gravity or smoke, I have to pick my own death. Keeping close to the floor I backtrack to the fireplace. It's waiting amid the dust and ancient ashes – one cigarette stub. It sparks a vivid memory of Summer sitting cross-legged, taking a long drag. She was here. With me. The memory comes back strong like the cough rocking my body. Curled up inside the hearth, I choose the smoke. Go to sleep and add my ashes to

355

those already here, holding a token from Summer. I'll be with Mom soon. It's all coming back to me. She's coming back to me, riding the flow of memories. I shouldn't have run away from her. If only my stupid, useless mind could have remembered earlier. The smoke settles heavy in my lungs like a blanket smothering me from the inside. It lulls me, and untethered, my mind roams the past. A voice reaches out to me. *Faith, Faith*, she calls. *Mom? I'll be with you soon, Mommy.* The voice rises over the roar of the fire, the tone urgent. It rises louder and louder, until it feels real.

'*Summer?*' Her name grates my throat. I salvage as much saliva as possible to swallow. 'Summer. I'm here.' Crawling to the door I pound on it. 'I'm here, Summer.' I drop the words in between coughs.

The door pushes against me. She's here, her face close to mine, the glint of tears in her eyes.

'I found you. I'm so sorry it took so long to get to you. There're people everywhere. Just trust me, OK?'

She offers me her hand like she's coaxing a frightened animal. I throw my arms around her.

'You found me.' Her arms tighten around my shoulders. The pain and the fire feel unimportant. The devil's here. No, she's more powerful than that. Whatever happens, my sister's here with me.

VOICE NOTE RECORDING

[Faith]:   I hope I'm doin' this right. Summer showed me how. I've forgotten so much over the years, over the last few weeks. Never again. I'm recordin' everythin' now, I guess this is my kind of diary. So, for my inaugural entry I've chosen the memory that started it all. She wasn't plannin' on ever tellin' me, but I forced her, so Summer, it's your words an'all I'm usin'.

Fat Travis sprawled on the sofa like a starfish. That's what we called him, because of his Jell-O belly and his sausage fingers. His legs were so far apart I could stand in the space in the middle, twirl around and not even touch his thighs. He watched TV in the living room, the fuzzy glow of the TV reaching you in the kitchen.

'Hey, midget.' You heard him from the living room. 'Grab me another beer, will yah.' You rolled your eyes even though nobody could see you. God, his voice is annoyin'. Why can't he go on home? Mom's not even here. 'Oh, and throw that away.'

I zoomed into the kitchen where you were peeling an apple at the table. The skin curled in one smooth ribbon under the knife. I grinned at you, and your heart swelled up like the first time you held me in your arms, the day you learned the weight

357

of responsibility. The day you made the oath and whispered it to the tiny baby I was: 'I got you, baby sister, forever and ever.'

Pulling the fridge door open, I reached on tiptoe for the pack of beers chilling on the top shelf. My fingers grazed the cans but they stayed out of my grasp. I huffed and I puffed.

'Can you help me?'

'Whatcha need, Bunny?'

'I need a beer for Fat Travis.'

'Can't he get it himself?' The knife ripped and the peeled ribbon broke before the end. You sighed; you liked when you could peel them in one go.

You snatched a can before slammin' the door closed; the fridge contents rattled in disapproval. While you took care of the beer, I chucked a cardboard box in the trash.

'Ouch!' I sucked on my fingertip. 'Somethin' stung me.'

'Let me see.'

Balancing on haunches, you checked my finger. A tiny red pinprick like a bull's eye for fleas crowned the tip. After blowing and kissing it better, you rummaged in the trash. What was inside the box tensed your shoulders up. Your face marooned with anger, the way it always did before you erupted – Summer Volcano, Mom called you sometimes.

You marched into the living room, muscles tight with the ache to make bruises. I called you wind-up monkey – wind and wind the key on its back, release it, and watch it go.

You planted yourself between Fat Travis and the TV before hurling the greasy box at his head. He swatted it away and a syringe rolled out onto the sofa.

'Don't bring your dirty syringes in this house, you fucking junkie. My little sister just stabbed her finger on it.'

'Fuck off, I'm watching.' Drugs slurred his speech.

'It's not your place. Just get lost.'

He snorted at you. 'You think I'm gonna take orders from a couple of midgets?'

Your fingers squeezed the beer can, tremors moving up your arm. Foam oozed from the dents. Out the corner of my eye, I braced for the incoming eruption. The can flew through the air in a perfect arc and hit him on the forehead. I had to give it to you – that was an awesome shot.

'You little shit.' He leapt up, his speed and reflexes surprisingly good for a man with a body shaped by years of fried food and bad decisions. He cornered you between the wall and the TV stand. He grabbed your throat, and the carpet disappeared from under your feet.

'You listen to me, you little shit, you just do as I say. No lip. Get it?'

You hissed and scratched like one of the feral cats that roamed the project. I pummelled his back but I was nothing more than a mild discomfort to him. I begged him to stop, but the thud of death drumming in your ears drowned my voice. He just didn't care.

'I said, is that understood?'

Your legs jerked, shedding the last crumbs of life holding on to you. Darkness smothered its way through every part of your body until the pressure around your throat vanished and you dropped to the ground.

'You leave my sister alone,' I screamed on a loop.

A sweet and metallic smell surrounded you, your vision too blurred to get a clear grasp on the room. Your gaze focused on me, crying and stabbing Fat Travis with the knife you'd left on the kitchen table.

He staggered, and his head hit the TV stand on the way down. He lay on the floor, his shirt mottled with punctures, his t-shirt disappearing under the red soaking it. My hands were soaked with it too – innocence shouldn't look so red.

My distress stabbed your heart. I sat on the floor, arms extended, keeping my hands as far from the rest of me as possible, holding them out towards you. You knew what had to be done. There never was any doubt that night. You followed the oath. You wiped my face with your t-shirt. You picked me up, and I wrapped my little arms tight around your neck. You winced but it didn't matter. Nothing mattered apart from me. In the bathroom you washed my crime off my skin, helped me out of the evidence I wore. Once cleaned up and dressed, you carried me to the hallway closet.

'Listen to me.' Your face was all serious, and I knew I had to listen carefully. I swallowed sobs back in and nodded. 'You stay in here. If anybody asks, I'm the one who stabbed Fat Travis. Do you understand?'

My gaze dragged to the floor. You knew what I was thinking – Mom always said we should never lie to each other, us girls stuck together.

'Look at me,' you said, hands on my shoulders. 'I know what Mom says, but this one time we can't tell her the truth. OK? It's really important, Faith.'

I nodded, and you smiled.

'OK. Stay with the stars.'

'Summer stars.'

'Summer stars.'

You closed the door and got on with it. I listened to you move on the other side. The sobs fought their way out again at the images. You cleaned the knife handle of any notions that I had anything to do with this. You wrapped your fingers on the clean canvas of the handle, wiped the blade on your shirt, gave them all the reasons to look no further. When the cops got here, your staging, your skin and where you came from would confirm all their suspicions about people like you.

You didn't care. They could think whatever the hell they liked. They could believe you were the worst kid in the world, they could believe you were the sum of all their biases and the girl who confirmed all their stereotypes. All that mattered was me, your little sister, and that I would be OK.

VOICE NOTE RECORDING

[Summer]: What are you doing? Are you recording me?

[Faith]: You reckon you're the only one that can interview people?

[Summer]: You wanna interview me? *(Laughter.)* Fine. Shoot!

[Faith]: All right. I've been wonderin' ... How did you find out that Da – I mean ... How did you find out he was Lee Elsher?

[Summer]: You go straight for the juicy stuff, don't you?

[Faith]: Summer ...

[Summer]: OK, fine. It all happened by accident really, not long after he started hanging around the apartment in Chicago. I found this photo in his wallet.

[Faith]: What were you ...? Summer. Were you stealin' from him?

[Summer]: You really wanted those heart-shaped plastic sunglasses from the bodega around the corner. You wouldn't shut up about them.

[Faith]: Wow. I reckon I remember those. They were red ones.

[Summer]: Yeah, you wouldn't take them off. Even slept with them. Anyway, as I said I found this photo. Looked like from a wedding or something.

There was a date and location on the back of it. For some reason it stuck with me. I tried to tell Mom but she wouldn't listen. She was always like that when she fell for a guy. So after I got out and finally landed on my feet, I thought it could help me track him down and find you and Mom. I headed down to the town and went to the archives to check the marriage register and found their certificate. After that it was a skip and a hop to finding out what happened, but after that the trail went cold.

[Faith]: What did you do then?

[Summer]: I tried to tell the local cops that Lee Elsher had turned up in Chicago, that he was hiding among some religious group, but they pretty much laughed in my face, especially after they had a look at my rap sheet. Pretty much made it clear I was on my own on that one. You can't imagine how terrifying it was to know you guys lived with him. I think it's one of the reasons I moved to the shack. You know? Be close.

[Faith]: Makes sense. Is that when you started the podcast?

[Summer]: That's when I started the podcast. If I visited enough of those churches we were bound to cross paths at some stage.

[Faith]: Gotta have faith.

[Summer]: Gotta have faith.

[Faith]: Hold on. I just realised your podcast title ...

[Summer]: *(Laughter.)* Took you long enough.

70. Present day

Buttery light falls onto the decking, painting everything gold, my skin included. Eyes closed, the ocean brine whips my face. Jacksonville hums behind me. My fingers probe the back of my neck, still not used to the absence of long strands of hair. My face tilts towards the sun as I enjoy freedom from the bondage of a braid, and the humid Florida heat.

'Bus leaves in ninety minutes.'

In the makeshift darkness, Summer's sticky skin rubs against mine. We stand shoulder to shoulder for a moment, a comfortable silence flowing between us. This part of the boardwalk is pretty deserted. She laces her fingers with mine and squeezes my hand with the same intensity as when we fled Newhaven. Crouching low, she tugged me along to the servant stairs, clouded with smoke but free of fire. We tumbled out of the burning building, coughing, lungs burning from air laden with heat. Hidden by the church, we waited until I spotted the twins, faces blackened by soot, crying on the lawn. Baby Sarah screamed in a Moses basket next to them. Scared but alive.

As much as I love my siblings they didn't belong with us. They didn't deserve a life on the run, of revolving identities and always looking behind. Walking away from them ripped my heart into pieces. Some of those pieces are still with Sarah and the twins. One day I'll find them, the way Summer's found me.

She dragged me away in the end. I sobbed as we picked

our way through the switchgrass down to the pier where the boats waited. She had stolen one of the keys while everybody was busy re-enacting the Old Testament by stoning me on the landing.

Even though it's too far, Jaspers Island is there hiding within the folds of the horizon. Poor Jackson. The idea he's still stuck there pinches my heart. Summer admitted to punching him out of the way when he came after her outside the shack, but she's adamant that she had nothing to do with the carcasses strung on the fence. Couldn't have been Tom, he confessed it wasn't him when he attacked me. I don't like to admit it, but I hope he didn't escape Mrs Favreau's fury.

My face splits with a yawn. I can't wait to finally be able to sleep through the night. My lids feel heavy. I have to thank Newhaven in a way; those stones they threw dislodged the memories from that day. Who knew what I needed was a good knock, or several, on the head? Snapshots slice my sleep – the screams, the blood, Mom's body, her eyes not fully closed, death leaving her unfocused, my hand driving the knife into Daddy's back, Summer knocking the side table on her way out, the flame licking the side of the sofa, feeding off the kerosene, eating the life on display, the throw pillows, family photos, the twins' smiles, the cuff from Daddy's pants. The heat of the fire, the roar of flames feasting on Mom and Daddy, the skin blackening and splitting. The smell, that gut-wrenching smell.

The memories of what happened in Chicago took longer. She helped me put the pieces back together. Reluctantly.

'I got something for you.'

Her voice opens my eyes. I quickly wipe the tears with my fingertips. The gift stores on this waterfront only sell the kind of junk she would snigger or roll her eyes at. Whatever the present is, it's wrapped in an old t-shirt of hers – the yellow vest she wore the time we met at the shack, back when I didn't remember who she was. Shame tugs inside my chest; I'll never forgive myself for forgetting her, but that inexplicable warmth I felt whenever I was near her – my body remembered her before my mind recognised her.

A smile lights up Summer's face. How did I not see it before – her father's skin stretched over our mother's bones. She joked that nobody ever believed we were sisters growing up. That titbit saddens me. I wonder if she'd've done it if she'd known, after everything, Mom would leave her behind. So many lives ruined to protect me.

One look at her and the certainty she would've still done the same flushes through my body. I haven't had the courage yet to ask her if she hates Mom for sacrificing her, for breaking her promise – just us girls.

I unfold the makeshift wrapping with care. A lump forms in my throat. Amid the fabric, the knife weighs heavy in my hand. The blade seems lacklustre, as if the steel has been dulled by the lives it took. She snatched it along with the box-cutter and my clothes that night at Hunters Cottage. Without the knife and the bloody dress, there was no clue to point at anything else beyond a fire.

It's up to me to decide its fate. It's been cleaned, but somewhere hidden under the handle there are microscopic traces of Mom. This knife is all we have left of her, but it's also tainted with him. We can't have her without him still clinging.

Our forearms rest on the rail. My tan will never be as dark as hers, but after a few days here I've been catching up, my skin no longer hiding from the world under a strict uniform. She's been teaching me I can wear whatever the fuck I want.

In an hour and a half we'll board the bus that will mark the real start of our great American adventure. Our next stop New Orleans for beignets at Café du Monde, and learning about music and life in smoky clubs, before losing ourselves in the Missouri plains. We'll stop in Tennessee and visit the graves of Karen Elsher and her kids, pay our respects, and live the lives John Heywood, or whatever his name was, stole from them. So many lives. I've wondered if the pictures I found that day I played hide and seek with the twins were of Karen and her kids. Fleur's locket rests against my chest, my fingers playing with the chain the way she used to. Ain't no leaving her behind. Just us girls an'all.

The first night after we escaped, we lay on a motel bed facing each other and Summer confessed that she'd initially believed Fleur was me. I mean, I get it, we're the same age, people told us all the time we looked like sisters, but the gap in her front teeth is what really had Summer fooled. It wasn't the first time she thought she'd found me. She saw variations of my features on other people's faces. She thought she'd come close many times, fooled by hope, desperation, and the tricks time played on her memory, before disappointment broke her down. In the end the truth was always the same – it wasn't me. No matter how many times she'd experienced it, the sucker punch never lessened. She clung to me that first night, my back nestled against her chest. 'Big poon, little poon', I used to call it when we were kids. I couldn't say 'spoon' apparently. She's the custodian of so many of my lost childhood memories.

A boat races by the pier as the knife hits the water too fast to make a sound; it instantly disappears under the white crests of the wake. Burial at sea. Summer kisses my cheek, and the smell of nicotine lingers on her breath. We still have the best of Mom with us. She lingers in our blood. She is in me and Summer. It's a fact. Science. Mom. Me. Summer. Just us girls. Our stories are etched in our bones, written under our skin. Our cells will carry her inside of us wherever we go. Like Summer carried us when we left her behind, our blood in her veins calling out, pushing her to look for us once she got out of juvie. She said she only did it so she could tell Mom to her face to go fuck herself, but I know different.

'Come on, let me buy you a beer. It's about time you tried.'

'Ain't I too young?'

'No worries, I know a guy at the bar near the motel.' She smirks.

I smile. Of course she does. She moves first. Under Her guidance.

TRAGEDY STRIKES AGAIN AT NEWHAVEN PLANTATION

By Marilynn Wasserman, Staff Reporter

Only a few weeks after a fire claimed the lives of Pastor John Heywood and his wife, Genevieve, Newhaven Plantation on Jaspers Island has been rocked by yet another tragedy when a blaze ravaged the main plantation house.

Fire Marshal Wesley Dunlop confirmed that eight people died in the fire, and a further nineteen suffered injuries, mainly from smoke inhalation and jumping from the second-floor balcony to escape the flames. None of the children residing at Newhaven were among the victims. Several witnesses stated that the fire was started by Elizabeth Favreau, late wife to the former congregation pastor, Floyd Favreau, who passed away nine months ago after an alleged accidental fall. Marshal Dunlop said the investigation hasn't yet been able to corroborate witness statements. Still missing are seventeen-year-old Abigail Heywood, and fourteen-year-old Jackson Caine.

After the fire, Samantha Crawford from Lynchburg, Virginia, was reunited with her sister, Jamie Baez, and nephew, Tommy Baez. Miss Crawford had been staying at the Sunny Inn Motel in Parkerville while trying to reconnect with her sister after she left Miss Crawford's home, where she had been staying after leaving her husband. Miss Crawford claimed that the New America Baptist Church brainwashed her sister and preyed on her when she was at her most vulnerable. *Parkerville*

369

Gazette reached out to New America Baptist Church officials at their headquarters, but they declined to comment.

A separate investigation has been opened after the lifeless body of Harry Vance was discovered in the tub of one of the bathrooms of the plantation house. Vance has an outstanding warrant in the state of Maryland for an assault on his neighbour, Selina DeLuca, after she turned down repeated requests for a date. Vance had been living in Newhaven for the last eight months under the assumed name of Tom Vermont. County Coroner Nia Kordell confirmed that Vance was killed by a deep cut across his throat, most likely made by a sharp edged blade such as a box-cutter. No murder weapon has been recovered at the scene. At this stage of the investigation the police have no leads or suspects.

Acknowledgements

I cannot believe I got to do this again. Book two has been such a strange beast. My debut unfolded on my own terms, but for the first time I had to create on a deadline. No more luxury of taking three weeks to mull over a scene or going through ten drafts before letting anyone see it. I wouldn't have succeeded in completing this book without the help and guidance of my editor, Clio Cornish. Thank you for stirring me in the right direction, while allowing me my creative freedom and necessary 'mourning period' before I killed any of my darlings.

To my agent, Juliet Mushens, thank you for making all of this possible, for being my biggest (most stylish) cheerleader. To quote the words of Emily Henry, '. . . on the writers' end, she was something like Miss Honey, the sweet teacher from Matilda, mashed together with a sexy witch'. This is absolutely you.

It takes a village to publish a book. Thank you to the team at Penguin Michael Joseph – Emma, Sriya, Jen, Nick, Eugenie and Lauren – and the Mushens Entertainment team – Liza, Kiya, Rachel and Catriona. Thank you to the writing community: all the booksellers, reviewers, bloggers and librarians for being champions of books. A special thanks to fellow authors for being so supportive – people have been so generous with their time, advice and support. And not forgetting my critique partner Philippa, who read an early draft of this book and helped me shape my first steps. Thank you to my family for their support and all the ways they have been championing my books.

Once again, thank you to the readers, whether you read the hardback, paperback or eBook, or listened to the audiobook, and whether you got your copy from the main retailers, indie bookshops or your local library. Thank you for picking up this book, and I hope you enjoy it.

Finally, if you have been affected by the issues raised, especially the depiction of physical and psychological domestic abuse, Refuge is an intersectional and inclusive organization helping women and children victims of domestic violence, www.refuge.org.uk.